Early Praise

MW01067418

"The colorful character of Fin Button comes resplendently alive in the pages of *Fiddler's Green*. Peterson has done his research well and found the human heartbeat at the center of both history and legend. He finds beauty at the root of sorrow in his stories—and that alone makes them worth reading."

—Douglas Kaine McKelvey, author of
The Angel Knew Papa and the Dog

"The best of Peterson's work in *The Fiddler's Gun* is matched and tripled in his action-packed sequel, *Fiddler's Green*. He proved himself an able writer of a worthy tale in *Gun*, but as I read *Green*, I felt like I was witness to the magical moment of a certifiable author being born. There were passages that took my breath away and brought tears to my eyes. Stunning prose, unforgettable characters, a rip-roaring page-turner of an adventure that I couldn't put down. I thoroughly enjoyed this book! Now, tell us another story, Mr. Peterson."

—Jason Gray, singer-songwriter,
Everything Sad is Coming Untrue

"*Fiddler's Green* is the sort of story that sated all my desires as a reader. I wanted adventure, and the fiery Fin Button and her intrepid crew whisked me away on an impossible quest. I wanted keenly described, colorful lands full of adventure, and this tale sails into foreign ports and castles, follows knights and pirates from dungeon to high sea battle. Most of all, I wanted the sort of story that would sail me deep into the regions of the soul, and this tale took me right there, filling my heart with the haunting music of the Fiddler's Green. I was invited into a beauty that offered a glimpse of redemption, and a step down the road that will take me home. Keen in insight and imagination, redemptive, and epic in scope, *Fiddler's Green* is a book to be savored."

—Sarah Clarkson, author of
Read for the Heart

A.S. Peterson has written an exciting adventure, but it is so much more than that. The characters will get inside you, and you will live, ache, die, and find freedom with them as you enter their stories. *Fiddler's Green* is raw and real, a very human tale, and nothing short of transformational.

—Travis Prinzi, author of
Harry Potter & Imagination

"Mercy, honor, trust, dignity, reclamation: these words are not typically associated with pirate folklore. In Peterson's astounding sequel to *The Fiddler's Gun* however, the author manages to save the best for last. *Fiddler's Green* is just as replete with action and adventure as it is with love and reclamation. When I finished reading, two things happened: I cried, and I zealously wished for a sequel."

—Eric Peters, singer-songwriter,
Chrome

"There's more to this story than meets the eye. Sure, there's peril, piracy, heartache, and humor, yet enveloped within the expected is the unexpected. Fin is not always who I want her to be—instead, she is who she is. She wrestles with goodness and redemption—and they wrestle back. I love characters who reach out, grab my arm, and pull me into their lives, forcing me to look them in the eye, to bear their burdens and joys. Peterson is right up there with my favorite authors who write truthfully, and who know how to take the hurt and "turn it to beauty.""

—Jenni Simmons, editor,
Art House America blog

Also by A.S. Peterson

———————

Fin's Revolution Book One:
The Fiddler's Gun

and

The Fiddler's Gun: Letters

Fiddler's Green

FIN'S REVOLUTION: BOOK TWO

A. S. PETERSON

RABBIT ROOM
— PRESS —
NASHVILLE, TENNESSEE

FIDDLER'S GREEN
© 2010 by A. S. Peterson

All rights reserved. No portion of this book may be reproduced, stored in a
retrieval system, eaten, or transmitted in any form or by any means—elec-
tronic, mechanical, photocopy, abductatory, recording, scanning, mind
meld, or other—except for brief quotations in critical reviews, ships' logs,
or articles, without the prior written permission of the publisher.

Published in Nashville, Tennessee
by long-eared carrot-eaters in the productive employ of:

Rabbit Room Press
940 Davidson Drive
Nashville, Tennessee 37205
info@rabbitroom.com

Cover artwork by Evie Coates
Edited by Kate Etue

Library of Congress Control Number: 2010915236

ISBN/EAN 978-0-9826214-1-7
ISBN 0-9826214-1-7
Printed in the United States of America

Second Edition
2013

For the Rabbit Room community—
without whom this book would not exist.

"And shadow itself may resolve into beauty."

—Annie Dillard
Pilgrim at Tinker Creek

Sunken on a dark sea,
mates long gone;
adrift in the drink,
an' dreamin' o' th' dawn;
but yonder lies a place
where the dark's never been;
sail me clear tomorrow
to the Fiddler's Green.

—Seaman's Shanty, 18th Century

PART I

THE CROSSING

CHAPTER ONE

As soon as Fin Button stepped out of the captain's cabin, Topper was up to his old tricks. He stuck out his considerable chin, snapped his heels together, and tugged his shirt down over his belly. With a devilish smirk on his face he called, "Captain on deck!" and the crew perked and turned. They each stopped their work, shouted "Captain on deck" in acknowledgement, and saluted. Topper thumped himself on the paunch and grinned over his mischief.

Fin wished she had something to throw at him. Something hard. Something heavy. Something that would leave a mark. In the week since the *Rattlesnake* had sailed from Ebenezer, Topper had learned that announcing her arrival on deck was a painful mistake if he was within punching distance. But this time he'd kept well out of reach as he made his announcement. Fin looked around hoping to find a mallet or a hefty block pulley but, fortunately for Topper, the crew kept a clean deck and Fin had to settle for throwing a narrow-eyed glare. She put enough effort into it to make it count, and Topper recoiled just as if he'd been physically struck. When Fin took a threatening step in his direction, he scurried through a hatch and out of sight.

Ridiculous, Fin thought. The charade had been amusing for a while, but now that Creache was gone, the men seemed to lend it real credit.

They'd even voted on it. Voted her to the office of captain. Fin was certain Topper had put them up to it. *Ridiculous.*

She hauled herself aloft and stood on the main yardarm with her arms curled around the mast. The horizon was clear. No cloud. No sail. To the west, North Carolina's Outer Banks huddled low and wide. Topper had steered them here—said he knew of a place to hide away for a while, a place the British didn't know of and wouldn't come snooping. Fin surely didn't know what to do or where to go—and that was exactly why the notion of electing her captain was so unthinkable. She was already wanted for piracy, mutiny, and murder. Living up to the title of captain was more burden than she cared to shoulder.

Below her the helmsman called out a course change and heaved the wheel around. The *Rattlesnake* groaned and tilted as they eased westward and slipped into the waiting arms of the Outer Banks. Fin kept her eyes to the south, straining them toward the horizon for any glimpse of British ships that might have followed. None appeared and soon they were safely tucked away amid the sheltering isles of the Carolina coast.

But Fin's eyes returned again and again to the south, where far off in a Georgia woodland, beyond any threat of British pursuit, there sat a tiny farmhouse on a green field. And upon its porch, she imagined, Peter LaMee waited, patient and still. She closed her eyes. and in an instant, her perch atop the mast seemed to change; she was in her bell tower again. She was a little red-haired girl, sitting crossed-legged and staring into the distance, toward some faraway place beyond the walls of the Ebenezer orphanage. Then the vision receded as if she were being pulled high into the air above the little town, and at the very last she saw the white swan atop the chapel's steeple seem to come alive; it twisted and fluttered on its pike, trying in vain to break free of its anchor and fly. The vision faded away and Fin opened her eyes.

The *Rattlesnake* slipped into a cove where a scatter of shanty rooftops peeked over the oat-whiskered dunes. Below her, Topper called out for anchor and the rhythmic footfalls of the crew answered. Fin climbed down as men untied the ship's skiffs and lowered them to the water. They lumbered at their work; there was little talk and no singing. With Tan gone, the ship's company seemed a lesser thing than it had once been, as if he'd somehow bound them together and without him they were subject to a gradual unraveling.

And Jack had been as good as gone too, lying abed unconscious since they left Ebenezer. A musketshot had severed his leg mid-shin and the stump was swollen and gray. Dark purple lines ran up his calf to his knee and he shook, day and night, with a sickness. Topper wouldn't say it, but Fin could read his eyes and they told her he saw death in Jack's fever. Fin wouldn't believe that. Too many had died already.

Knut, at least, was himself and he tended Jack without complaint.

On the shore a man hobbled over the dunes and waved. He dragged a pitiful boat down to the water and rowed it out to the *Rattlesnake* while Fin fetched Topper and Armand Defain to help her with Jack. Topper mumbled that it was going to take a lot more than the three of them to manhandle Jack Wagon off the boat, and in the end he was right—it took eight. They had to use the capstan to lower him down to the rowboat like a side of fresh beef. Topper set a watch to keep the ship and gave leave for the rest to go ashore. A handful of the crew climbed aboard the rowboat with Jack while the rest boarded the *Rattlesnake*'s skiffs and followed.

On the beach, their host scrambled out of his boat and greeted them. He was long unwashed if the flies attending him were any indication, and he stank of brine and waste. As he approached them, he threw both arms in the air and lifted a rotten-toothed smile.

"Flanders Topper! Hoo-he! Come 'round to snuffle me boots," he croaked at them. Fin stepped back a pace and wrinkled her nose in disgust.

"By heaven, Hank, you still not bathed?" Topper waved a hand in front of his face and squinted his eyes as they began to tear up.

"Never!" cried Hank and threw his arms in the air.

"Fin Button, meet Hank Dooley. Not bathed now in," he scratched his temple and rolled his eyes in thought, "what is it now, Hank? Sixteen years?"

"Seventeen!"

Topper leaned toward Fin and cupped one hand to the side of his mouth. "Hank swore off bathing when his wife refused to be driven off by lesser means. She stood him nearly a year before she run for sweeter air."

"Hoo-ee, glad to be rid o' that woman!"

"Hank reckoned he best keep it up, just in the unlikely case she changed her mind and took it in her head to move back in. He ain't risked a bathing in seventeen years and, well, you can smell him for yourself." Topper motioned for her to have a closer sniff. Instead, Fin stepped back a pace.

"Smart lass," said Topper. "Hank, this here's Captain Fin Button. I reckon you heard of her."

"Hoo hoo," said Hank, "Give them British a fit ain't ye?" Fin shrugged and smiled at him. In spite of Hank's vile aroma, Fin found him somehow likable.

"Well, come on up, ye old dogs," said Hank. "Won't be no British 'round here to bother ye. Have a sit. Got some geese cooking what I just killed this morning."

They followed Hank over the dunes toward the ragged clutter of houses pitched in the sand, making sure to keep upwind of him as they went. The makeshift village was constructed of the remains of old boats and ships, and nowhere was there a square joint or a straight line. The entire affair was curving this way and bending that. "Dooley's Retreat" they called it. Fearing that even his forswearing of couth may not keep his wife away, Hank had likewise shunned all civilization and landed himself among the sand and gulls and geese. In the years since, smugglers, pirates, and anyone in want of a place to be unfound for a time had learned Hank's hospitality was second to none—if one could abide the odor.

They ducked inside one of the shanty structures, and the smell of a roasting goose filled the air. Knut and seven others carried Jack inside and settled him on a pallet by the fire. He moaned and tossed in his fevered sleep and Knut sat next to him and flinched a bit each time Jack muttered a sound. The other men bustled about and found themselves corners to claim and fall asleep into. Fin did the same and, hungry as she was, she was fast asleep before the goose finished its roasting.

They spent a week in Hank's company and though the crew was cheerful and content in their leisure, Fin was lonely for Tan's company, and for home. Her nights were fitful and long. She awoke often in the dark, startled by the solidity of the ground. Without the ocean to rock her, she felt out of place and set apart from the life that the sea was calling her to. But answering that call meant giving away her claim to any place of earth. Some men could sail the ocean and never really give themselves to it. But others, real sailors, men of salt and timber—they were different. Fin could spot it in a man almost instantly. It wasn't the leathery skin and deep-lined face; it wasn't the sun-bleached hair or the smell of rum and salted meat. It wasn't the calloused hands and curse-ready tongue. It was something inside, something elemental and rooted deep in the marrow. Such men belonged to the wind and built no landward home. Their foundations were of wave and storm, running fluid and deep, deeper than any mine or grave. Any true man of the sea could tell you when he gave himself over to it. It's the moment when men are divided one from another, sailors of a season on one hand and true men of wind and wave on the other. It's when one man looks toward home and the other comforts himself in knowing his home is his berth.

Giving oneself like that means being cast away, set adrift on the world and beholden to nothing—no man, no country, no law but the sea. But the trade of it, the joy of it, is that home is what a man carries with him; when he pours his blood into a ship and cherishes her and knows her like a lover, his home carries him far and safe across all oceans and vasty deeps. Topper was such a man; his joy was the spray off the bow and the breeze on his sunburnt pate. Jack was certainly, as Tan had been, and Armand also, though joy wasn't often in him as a virtue. Fin suspected that Armand was a man not only given to the sea, but lost to it, adrift in monstrous waters. As she lay awake, aware of the unmovable certainty of the world beneath her, Fin felt her own call to that weathered citizenship. She'd felt it for a long time. She'd longed to give herself to the deeps the first day she stood in the tops of the *Rattlesnake* and saw the ocean poured out before her. It was this that frightened her when she thought of Peter. Her heart and soul wanted only two things in the world: Peter and the sea. The anchor and the unknown. The knowledge that she might one day have to choose between them chilled her and she longed for the numbness of sleep.

Fin had hoped that undisturbed rest would aid the healing of Jack's leg but after a week at Dooley's Retreat it looked no different—which was both good and bad depending on how she thought about it. Jack tossed in his sleep and rivers of sweat collected on his brow and ran down his face. His fever held him tight and Fin whispered awkward prayers over him. Praying wasn't something she'd ever quite got comfortable with, and trying it out now seemed pointless given her lack of practice, but she could think of little else to do for Jack in his condition.

On the morning of their eighth day ashore, Hank waddled around the fire on his haunches, stoking it back to life and sending great whooshes of foul-smelling wind into any nostril haplessly perched in his wake. All about the hovel, men coughed and snorted themselves awake. Hank chuckled in merriment and placed a fresh catch of fish on the spit for breakfast.

Fin was just stretching the sleep from her limbs when a yelp from outside the hovel startled her. The room quickly emptied, and Fin stepped out behind the rest. The *Rattlesnake* stood offshore at anchor, but it had found company in the night. A tall warship waited alongside and a line of boats was visible between the ship and shore, each filled with blue-coated soldiers of the revolution. Before Fin could take in the entire scene, a group of twenty soldiers crested the dunes. Some of the crew turned and ran. Others darted back into the shanty to look for weapons. Still others balled up their fists and proclaimed that they'd not be arrested without a sizeable fight. Fin backpedalled and looked for an escape route. Then Topper flew past her and ran right into the midst of the oncoming soldiers. Fin was impressed with his bravery until she realized he was laughing. She looked closer and saw that, not only did all the soldiers still have their muskets shouldered, but she even recognized two of them: Ned Smithers and Fred Martin. Topper slapped Fred on the back welcomed him to Dooley's Retreat as Fin sighed and relaxed.

"Let's go inside, Topper. We need you to have a good listen and keep your calm." Fred motioned to the door. Before they could take a step toward it, Hank, who was standing near the hovel and pondering the new arrivals, bent down, picked up a handful of seashells, and began lobbing them at the soldiers.

"Git back, I ain't going without a fight!" he wailed. "I ain't going, I ain't!"

One of the soldiers unslung his weapon, but Ned ordered him at ease.

"Just cause I'm dressed fancy don't mean I'm draggin' you off to your wife, Hank. But by the blue, if you hit me with one of them shells, I'll drag her back here and scrub you clean to boot." Ned took off his hat and grinned at Hank.

"Gah! Why you dressed like a gov'ner!" said Hank. He dropped his handful of shells and scratched himself.

"War's on," shrugged Ned.

"Hoo-he!" Hank smiled, farted, and danced as he welcomed the marines to his house. Several of them threw up their hands in disgust or plugged their noses as he neared them. They cast sidelong glances at Ned, wondering if he hadn't gone quite insane.

Ned chuckled. "Shall we?" He motioned to the door.

Fin, Armand, and Topper followed them inside and asked for privacy. The rest of the crew obliged with shrugs and grunts, and Fred ordered a guard posted at the door. All the formality and secrecy made Fin uneasy. The look on Armand's face told her that he felt it too.

"What's all this about, Fred?" Topper asked as he took the spit from the fire and pulled off a blackened strip of fish.

"Where's Jack? We need to talk to him too," said Fred. He looked toward the door as if he expected Jack to walk through it.

"Jack's hurt," said Fin. "He's been in a fever since we left Savannah."

"Fever or not, he needs to hear me out."

"He lost his leg." Fin paused as Fred and Ned raised their eyes at each other. "Hasn't been himself for nearly a week. He needs a doctor." Topper nodded and grunted agreement as he chewed on his fish.

"Well, I'll lay it out then, and keep your head. I'm your friend, Topper. Jack's too, and that ain't changed."

Topper spit a fish bone into the fire and cleared his throat. "Out with it, the both of you."

"We need to take you in," said Fred. Armand's eyes flicked toward the door.

"What the hell's that mean, 'take us in'?" asked Topper, chuckling.

"We've got orders to arrest you and your crew."

Armand bounced to his feet and daggers twirled in his fingers. Topper erupted in laughter as he reached for another strip of fish. Fin found herself somewhere between the two reactions. Part of her wanted to run, far and fast. Another part told her that this was surely a joke; after all, these very men had saved them from the British only days before.

"Sit down, Defain," said Topper. "The day Fred Martin arrests me will be the—"

"This ain't a joke, Topper," said Ned.

Fin jumped to her feet.

"Calm down!" urged Fred. "I said to keep your heads."

Topper protested and Armand took a step nearer the door. His eyes darted about like an animal's.

"*Listen* to me already!"

Topper settled himself and tried to reassure Fin and Armand with a look. Fin stayed tense and ready to run but she sat back down. Armand dropped his daggers an inch or two, no more.

"What's this all about, Fred?" said Topper.

"After we pulled your necks out of that scrap with the British Navy, we were bound to report the affair. Me and Ned vouched for you and our captain took us at our word or he'd not have let you go. But it seems someone else got wind of the affair, and listening to the lowly swears of me and Smithers ain't about to sway them. So they sent us out to find you and bring you in.

"But listen, Topper, hanging ain't what they want. Word is they want to deal with you or, more to the truth of it, with Fin. They want to talk to her. I don't begin to fathom their reasons, but believe me, mate, if I thought they wanted to stretch your neck I'd never have led them here."

"You led them right to us?" Fin said, her voice raised in anger.

"Aye, and mind your manner, Captain Button, I don't run my friends up the gallows. We heard you ran north out of Savannah and when we hadn't seen you anywhere else, we reckoned you'd head here to lay aground with Hank till the English got calmed down. But by my own right ear, if I smelt an ill wind I'd have run 'em all over the Banks and never give you up to any man, especially a stuffy officer." Fred chuckled nervously.

"So you just expect us to give ourselves over and be arrested?" Fin asked.

"Well now, if you'll come quiet and all, then I believe the captain could be urged to let you sail back to Charleston with the *Constellation* as escort."

Fin looked at Topper for counsel.

"You're the captain," he said as he chewed on a fish. A fine bit of help he was. The entire 'captain' nonsense was now totally out of hand. Everyone was looking at her, waiting for a decision.

"I'm not going anywhere," she said. From near the door she heard Armand grunt his approval. Fred shook his head in exasperation.

"You heard the captain," Topper said with a grin.

Outside the shack, Hank howled. The door burst open and an officer entered, followed by two marines with guns. The officer was a stiff, thin man that kept his hands clasped behind his back and his head precisely upright and forward. When he looked from side to side, he swiveled at the waist instead of turning his head. Through Hank's howling they heard soldiers outside cocking muskets and ordering men to stand fast.

"Captain, I—" started Fred in protest.

The captain swiveled toward Fred and frowned. "I've heard enough, Sergeant. I gave you the opportunity you asked for and you failed. Now we do it my way. Seize them."

Armand lunged, knives drawn, but the marine at the door was already bringing his musket stock down. In a swift stroke, the stock connected with Armand's skull and he fell to the ground in silence.

Fred yelled and waved his hands in the air. "Stop, stop!" he shouted. Fin had no intention of following that advice. She was on her feet, fists up. Several more marines filed into the shack and surrounded them. Once more, the captain voiced his order to seize them. The first man to step forward garnered a black eye from Fin for his trouble. As another man threw his arms around her from behind, Fin was comforted by the thought that she hadn't gone without some measure of fight.

Topper and the rest put up little protest. They were ferried out to the captain's ship with their hands tied and their questions ignored. Topper sat across from Fred, cursing him for a traitor.

"Couldn't listen, could you?" asked Fred. "Tried to make a friendly go of it—and I had to do no end of convincing the captain to get that! Fine lot of good it was. You should be weaselin' me the apology, Topper, not t'other way around." Topper's eyebrows shot up in disbelief and he opened his mouth to see what would come out. "Clam up, Topper!" spouted Fred. "Quiet your trap and listen wise. When the captain sees you, keep your tongue and you'll be glad of it. There's a fair deal to strike for one with an open ear."

"I make no deals with devils."

Fred spat on the deck between his feet and turned to consider Fin. He stared at her hard and long, as if he were gauging a cloudbank that might be worth the trouble to sail around rather than through. When he turned back to Topper, he leaned in close and waited for him to meet his eyes.

"For my soul's sake I hope your lassie captain's got a cooler head and wiser ears, Topper. I've no keen to see your neck stretched on my account." The way Fred talked about her as if she wasn't there rankled Fin's sense of place in the world. Though she spent plenty of time reminding herself that her station as captain was ridiculous, being reminded of it by someone else brought her down to earth hard enough to smart.

The small boat slipped alongside the ship and a soldier untied Fin's hands so she could climb aboard. Any thought of flight was out of mind. There was nowhere to go outside of an easy musket shot to the back or a long swim before drowning.

Once on deck, the captain instructed his men to see them to the brig, and when Fin didn't move of her own account, a soldier prodded her in the back with his musket. She stumbled forward a step and turned around to shoot a glare back at him. He raised his musket stock, daring her to protest further.

"At ease, Corporal," ordered the captain. He considered his next words carefully and exchanged a look with Fred Martin that clearly relived some past disagreement. "Perhaps our guests have been imposed upon enough." The soldier lowered his musket and bowed in deference.

"I apologize that we must accommodate you and your crew in the brig, Captain Button. But your stay will not be long. You have questions, no doubt. And I have answers that I will be happy to afford. All things in good time. In the present case, I think lunch shall be as good a time as can be made." He bowed and motioned his hand to the nearest hatch. "If you please, Captain."

Fin's first inclination was that he was mocking her. His manner, however, was consistent and his crew unamused. She warily bowed in return and proceeded toward the hatch.

"And Captain Button, I trust you will report to me any inhospitable service you receive when next we speak, yes?" Without a waver of his smile, he cast his eye on the armed men in Fin's escort.

Fin smiled at the nearest marine. "I guarantee it."

CHAPTER TWO

A S EXPECTED OF A ship's brig, it was smelly, dark, and devoid of convenience; and although Fin was determined to remain indignant, she found herself comforted by the suggestion that she was a sort of guest. Certainly this small comfort had nothing to do with the fact that the captain had addressed her as an equal and seemed to mean it. And certainly it had nothing to do with the fact that she had missed breakfast and expected to dine with said captain for lunch. Certainly not.

Armand roused himself soon after they'd been deposited in their "quarters" and said little. Being back in a dark brig didn't seem to surprise him at all. He acted as if the world had simply returned to its natural state. Topper was equally silent (no doubt contemplating the coming meal), while Knut was content to hum a shanty and herd rats around the room in delight. The mood was odd to Fin. Normally she'd expect curses, plans for escape, or lamentations of bad luck to issue from one and all. But the situation, the attitude of the captain, and Fred's cautionary words were working in strange ways upon them. Each of them—Topper, Armand, and Fin—felt a quiet sense of uncertainty that made them uneasy. Certainty of imprisonment, certainty of death, certainty of abuse—these produced definite results, and actions. The feeling they had now, however, produced apprehension and hesitation. Fin didn't care for it.

The ship had not raised sail and there had been no sign of the rest of the crew. The only members that seemed to have been "invited" aboard were the four of them. There had been no word of the fates of the other thirty men ashore, or those on watch aboard the *Rattlesnake*. Now that the captain had his quarry, why was he not underway to turn them over to the powers of prosecution? Fin couldn't account for it. And so silence prevailed upon them until at last the bolt was thrown and the luncheon was joined.

A single unarmed marine escorted them across the deck to the officers' galley, and a quick glance across the horizon confirmed that they were yet at anchor and the *Rattlesnake* still at rest alongside. In the distance, a thin line of smoke rose from Hank's hovel but there was no indication of the whereabouts of the rest of the crew.

Once in the galley, they were greeted by the smell of fine cooking, the likes of which Fin hadn't enjoyed since she left Bartimaeus's kitchen. A thickly larded ham was the order of the day. It sat in the center of the table and commanded the attention of all the finery about it. China, silver goblets, and bowls of sundry greens and tubers all gathered in formation about the kingly cut of meat and awaited their call to duty. At the head of the table stood their host and captor, dressed in his finest blues and watching patiently as they filed into the room and gathered around the feast.

"Thank you, Corporal. That will be all," said the captain. "Set guard outside the galley and see that no unwelcome ears attend us." Their marine escort clicked his heels and bowed in acknowledgement, then excused himself and slipped the door shut behind him. The captain, while genteel enough in word and hospitality, betrayed a measure of unease in his wrinkled brow. His manner suggested that he hid something and struggled to keep it hidden. "I'm honored that you would join me."

He didn't look at Fin when he spoke, and she suspected that the captain didn't believe his own words. From the corner of her eye, Fin saw Topper's nostrils quivering in delight at the smell of the meal, and before she could answer the invitation, a rumbling yowl echoed from the depth of Topper's belly. Topper leapt into the nearest seat with a moan of pleasure. Fin, Armand, and Knut took their seats—Knut readily, Armand and Fin with suspicion.

"I'm afraid we have yet to be properly introduced," said the captain. "I am Nicholas Bettany. The *Constellation* is my ship and her marines are in my command." He bowed and looked at Fin expectantly.

Fin looked at Topper, hoping he would return the greeting and introduce himself, but he had eyes only for the ham. A look toward Armand fared her no better. He smiled at her and nodded his head, urging her to answer. Fin stood up, feeling awkward, and introduced herself as a captain for the first time.

"Captain Fin Button, of the *Rattlesnake*. I hesitate to call it a pleasure."

Captain Bettany grimaced. "A hesitation that I hope may be reconsidered, Captain Button. Please, sit."

As she sat down, Captain Bettany plucked a fork and knife from the table and circled the room to stand next to Fin. Armand tensed and his eyes followed the knife.

"Please allow me," said Captain Bettany as he trimmed a hearty slice of ham from the hock and offered it to Fin. Fin nodded and he placed it on her plate then proceeded to cut a serving for each of the others before allowing himself a moderate piece and returning to his seat. Topper finished his helping almost before it hit the plate and made short work of what beans and potatoes he could help himself to. The rest of the company ate in a peculiar silence.

"Business on an empty stomach is the toil of thieves and beggars. Wouldn't you agree, Captain Button?" He raised his tankard and smiled.

"It's often the toil of sailors as well," said Fin.

"Too true, but not today."

Topper grunted a happy reply as he chewed and the company ate in silence, watching one another with suspicious eyes.

"I'll have you tell us why we are here," said Armand; his words were almost a threat.

Captain Bettany set his fork before him and squared it against the angle of the table's edge. When he was satisfied with the placement of his tableware, he spoke plainly. "I have little patience for the criminal and less for the mutineer. Were I here of my own accord it would be to harvest your necks for the noose and the good of modern civility." Topper coughed and choked on his ham. "Against my better judgment, however, I am here on behalf of the Congress to convey to you a proposition. One that, personally, I find repugnant."

He appraised Fin in silence as if weighing how much information he ought to afford her. "What do you know of the war?" he asked, directing the question not to Fin but to the entire room. The question may have been rhetorical, but Topper attempted a blubbering answer before the captain cut him off. "The war is lost. We have met defeat upon defeat, and in a year's time the revolution will be little more than a brief insurgency in the annals of the empire unless help is persuaded to our cause. For some time now Benjamin Franklin has been at the royal court in Paris entreating for our defense. Until now, no offer has come his way.

"The Countess Caroline de Graff, however, has lately been abducted." The captain looked around the room. He searched them for a reaction but saw none. "While en route to Jerusalem on pilgrimage, the countess's ship was assailed by pirates of the Barbary Coast. She was taken. The pasha of Tripoli now holds her in ransom and vows her head shall top a Moorish spike before the year is ended. The countess," he met Fin's eyes, "is the niece of the king." Fin didn't see what the affairs of the French nobility had to do with her. "And King Louis is sorely intent upon paying whatever ransom he must to attain her safety. This, Captain, is where you may be of service. If the king drains the royal treasury for love of his niece, then no finance shall be left to aid our waning war. If, however, his dear niece should be returned in good health, ransom unpaid, and more, returned by an American, well then, the aid of France shall be ours and the British will trouble us no longer." The captain stopped, satisfied that all had been explained.

"You want us to do *what* exactly?" asked Fin.

Captain Bettany sighed in exasperation. "What little navy we have is needed here, Captain. And any naval ship sailing east is sure to find harassment from the Royal Navy. You have quite the reputation in these waters. A reputation that may quickly come to a bad end if your situation is not changed." He slipped a hand into his waistcoat and produced a page of *The Gazette*. Printed clearly thereon were Fin's face, name, and bounty. "This, Captain Button, could conveniently disappear." Fin was breathless. Her heart pounded in her chest. Armand leaned forward to study the paper carefully. The captain worked his next words around in his mouth before managing to get them out. "As could the crimes of all your crew, should your service to the Congress end in success."

Armand's eyes narrowed and he looked up at the captain. "Full pardons? For all crimes?"

"Full pardons. For all crimes," the captain said with distaste.

Armand shook his head. "You think we can make the crossing and breach the Mediterranean when you cannot? The 'Snake is the most wanted ship in the Atlantic. It is madness."

"Your fair captain affords that opportunity." He motioned to Fin. "Her name and deeds are known up and down the colonies and word of her capture would spread like balefire. If you agree, then we will allow you safe travel to Charleston where you may refit and crew your ship as you desire. Upon embarking for Europe, however, we will give chase and return with news of your deaths at sea and the sinking of your ship. We will send word ahead of you, of course, to announce your demise to the far side of the Atlantic, where you may arrive in your own ease and in your own time, untroubled. The English, sirs, are not your difficulty. Your trouble will be with the Barbary pirates. They are far more beastly than any you have known in this sea. They enslave all they capture and sell them to the mines of Araby. Their ships are light, quick, and deadly. They do not tack by sail alone but by the oar and the arm of the slave. They slip upon you in the night and slit your lines before you wake. Gaining their capitol and winning the retreat with your prize will be no easy task, I assure you. But you will risk it or else hang upon the gallows within the week."

"It's a fool's errand, *cherie*," said Armand in a harsh whisper. Captain Bettany pretended to ignore him and clenched his jaw while he waited for Fin to answer.

"Why does the king need *us*? Surely the French navy could do a better job of it," said Fin. Armand turned his narrowed eyes on the captain.

"King Louis has no wish to ignite a war or incur an increase to what monies he already pays to ensure his merchants some measure of safety from the pirates. The pasha of Tripoli holds the entire world in ransom. Any country wishing to breach Gibraltar's pass and sail the Mediterranean must pay an annual duty to ensure their ships are not plundered and sunk. For ages the world has found it far simpler to pay this duty than fight a war with an enemy that bides no rules of engagement.

"While there are still occasional acts of piracy, such as that which has befallen the countess, the waters are, in large part, safe passage for a country that pays the devil's due. Should the French openly attack Tripoli, French trade in the Mediterranean would take years to recover, and the annual duty would increase dramatically. I assure you, Captain Button, neither the French, the English, nor even we Americans will dare to lift a finger against the pirates of the Coast; the cost is too great. You, on the other hand, *are* a pirate. And what risk is there in a squabble amongst thieves?"

Fin looked around the room but Topper and Armand were no help. That the decision should fall to her was preposterous. "Is it certain that if we succeed the French will come to our aid?" she asked.

"It is not. In fact, the situation is so uncertain that I am of the opinion that more good is to be had of your hanging than of your help. Know then, that should you refuse this opportunity, I will delight in having you locked away in the brig where you will not see the light of the sun until the day you wear the hangman's noose."

"Some choice," said Fin.

"The waters of the Barbarie are red with blood," said Armand. "To trespass against the pasha of the Coast is a costly game."

"What's to stop us from agreeing to your proposal and then simply disappearing? We're pirates after all. Being hard to find is one of our specialties."

"You will be found again. And understand that presently the Congress views you as an ally. While you may technically be a criminal, it is well known that you prey upon the English. Are you so foolish that you think you could long evade capture if you were hounded by the Continentals as well?" Fin hadn't thought of that. "And think on this. If you do not make the attempt, then the revolution will certainly fail, and the English will be thicker in these waters than you can imagine. Every port will be a danger to you. You will be cast out of your own country and chased to the ends of the earth."

As his words faded in Fin's ears, the room closed in around her. In her mind she imagined herself, grown old and weathered and living from island to island, scraping out a life in an underworld of thieves and miscreants. She saw herself sitting at a table, gnawing on a crust of bread and flinching each time the door swung open, fearing that the British had finally boxed her in. She saw a soldier with an eye patch and a jagged scar across his face. He stalked her with his lidless eye and opened his mouth in hideous laughter as he tightened a noose around her neck. She saw fires sweeping across a field of green while insects and animals fled before the scourge. The fire consumed the field and turned its fury upon the home beside it, a home she knew from her dreams. A man sat in the shade of the eaves and rocked in a wooden chair. His face was covered in shadow. The blaze engulfed the house, and the man stood and spread his arms wide to welcome his fiery death. Then, in a flash of light, she was back in the galley. Captain Bettany stood across the table and looked down on her expectantly.

"We'll do it," she said, "on one condition."

"A condition?" The captain raised his eyebrows in disbelief. "Surely you're not serious."

"We need a doctor. My first mate is badly wounded and will soon die if he doesn't get help. If you want us to do this, we're going to need him. The *Rattlesnake* will not sail without Jack Wagon."

Topper dropped a clean hambone onto his plate and said, "Here, here!"

"Grant that, Captain," said Fin, "and you will have your countess. Your war will be won." *And I can go home.*

CHAPTER THREE

THE LANTERN SWINGING FROM the overhead timber wasn't bright enough to light the entire cabin; the space was too big for it. As the *Rattlesnake* yawed gently back and forth, the light swept shadows from corner to corner, never shedding illumination on any one thing for more than moments. Fin felt small in the room. It was the captain's cabin, her cabin ever since the mutiny against Creache, and still she felt too small to fill it. She had been comfortable when she'd berthed with the crew. Their company and conversation had been dear to her. She missed the closeness of Tan's friendship, of Knut always sleeping nearby or dallying in his madness, of Topper complaining about food, of a dozen other murmuring voices humming her to sleep like a lullaby. But here in her "place of honor," the captain's quarters, she felt the quietness. It was lonely.

The fiddle case on the table in front of her had been repaired, its splintered lid fashioned back into shape by a man named Tillum, one of the prisoners of the *Justice* who had proven himself an able ship's carpenter. She thumbed the latches open and propped the lid. A shadow threw itself across the contents, and the lantern light would not swing far enough to expose them. Fin's hands found their way by memory. They lifted the delicate violin by the neck and body and brought it out of the case. She held it close to her face. Scents of oil and wood filled her head. She plucked the strings, and their long-untuned voices whispered back in the half-light. The cleft of her neck welcomed its old companion. She took up the bow and drew a halting note into the air. The instrument was painfully out of tune. She turned a peg and plucked a string then adjusted the peg some more. For several minutes she alternately plucked and adjusted. First a note was too high, then too low, then too high again. She'd done this a hundred times; it should have come to her naturally, but she couldn't seem to find the right notes. Frustration flushed her face red and she took a deep breath. She slowed down and tried to remember how she'd been taught. Bartimaeus's face came to her, smiling and creased. She saw his brittle, old fingers dance across the fingerboard as he played. The memory calmed her frustration somewhat and fueled her determination to get the instrument in tune. She tried again. Too high. Too high. Just right? No, too low. Too high. Her anger rose again. She gritted her teeth and had to stop herself from flinging the violin across the room. She put it back in its case and cursed. Then she let her fingers remember Betsy. She lifted it out of the shadows and, as she had done with the violin, held it close to her face. Gunpowder: acrid, sweet. She loved the scent of it. She tightened down the thumbscrew on the flint and locked back the hammer. Then, squeezing the trigger, she gently set the hammer back down with her thumb. The old blunderbuss still worked like a faithful friend. And it would need to work a while longer yet. Bartimaeus's face came to her again. No smile this time, rather, a grimace of pain, maybe fear. *Terrible things*, he whispered, and Fin shuddered. She placed Betsy back in her cradle and shut the lid.

Captain Bettany hadn't agreed to her condition. He did, however, agree to convey her terms to his superiors in Charleston. He dismissed them, and Fred Martin piloted them in a rowboat back to the *Rattlesnake*, where they found the rest of the crew waiting. Despite Fred's multiple attempts at conversation along the way, Topper refused to acknowledge him and they suffered the brief boat ride in silence. Armand clearly had words for Fin, but it seemed he had yet to find the proper time or place to let them be heard, so he too was silent. The crew greeted them with questions but Fin put them off, saying only that they were to sail immediately for Charleston to refit and recrew. They were underway in an hour and expected to arrive in Charleston before noon the following day.

Unable to sleep in the oppressive silence of her quarters or to busy herself with music, Fin descended to the ship's surgery to check on Jack.

His fever still had hold of him. His face glittered with sweat in the dim light, and his trembling shook the bed. She wetted a cloth and wiped his face. Jack flinched away from her but didn't wake. The bed coverings were soaked with sweat and through the urine smell of his fever she noted the faint reek of rot. She plucked the lantern from the wall and shone it upon the wound. The bandages tied around his calf were also soaked through, but with blood, not sweat. What troubled her most, however, was the sickly color of the skin running up his leg past his giant knee. His breeches had been cut off around the thigh and the visible skin had turned a horrible yellow and was shot through with dark black and green. The stench came from his leg. He needed that doctor, and soon.

As she reached to hang the lantern back on its hook, she nearly tripped over something. She looked down to find Knut asleep on the deck at the foot of the bed. She was glad she hadn't woken him. For Knut's sake, if no other, she prayed Jack could be mended. Jack was the bulwark that often kept Knut safe from the cruelty of the crew. Fin also tried to protect him, but she didn't command the same authority that Jack did. Knut wasn't the only one that had need of him, though; she'd committed to a course of action that she'd scarcely begun to consider the complexity of, and she needed Jack's help to see her through it.

She placed the lantern back on its hook and climbed the ladder to the main deck. The night was clear, and a steady wind eased their way. The men on watch were quiet and didn't disturb her. She made her way up to the poop deck and leaned over the edge of the rail to watch their wake curl and seethe behind them.

"It is a great risk, *cherie*." Armand's voice. He was sitting in the crook of the railing, one knee up, his eyes raised to her.

"That bothers you?"

He didn't answer right away and Fin didn't care. Fin wasn't even sure why he was still with them. He had promised her his help, but only so far as his own revenge would take him, and he seemed to have gained that with the death of Creache. He had no reason to remain, unless the temptation of a full pardon was one he indulged. He didn't strike Fin as the sort of man that cared for pardon, though. He was the sort that would rather be hidden away and chased after.

"Why did you want Creache dead?" she asked.

Armand raised his misshapen hand into the moonlight and spread his fingers. There were only small stumps where the ring finger and little finger had been. He curled what was left of his hand into a fist and withdrew it without speaking.

"Why did he do it?" asked Fin.

"Because something was taken from him," he answered, now looking at her. "Something he did not wish to part with. Something he would do anything to get back."

"Bart's gold?"

"It is no matter, *cherie*. We do what we must to take back what is lost." He stood and bent close to her. "Whatever you have lost must be precious to you. You gamble our souls to regain it."

Fin opened her mouth but had no answer she was willing to admit.

"To contend upon the Barbary Coast, I tell you that we must match them in barbaric deed and cut without mercy. Else I fear you have doomed us, *cherie*. And this thing we intend, this rescue, this countess, it will see the end of our days."

"I didn't ask you to come. You're welcome to leave when we reach Charleston."

"Indeed, or I would not be here," he replied with a grin. "But I will go with you. You are not the only one who has lost. We all must seek an end."

"What is that supposed to mean?" asked Fin, but he was already walking away and she had no desire to follow. She didn't trust him. And yet she acted as if she did. She'd accepted his help in the dark of the *Justice*'s hold, he'd helped them escape to Ebenezer, and he'd even played a part in saving Knut's life and ending Creache's. She couldn't account for him. The man was twisted and evil, but he continually found ways to make himself useful—and there was no denying that a man of his nature had his uses. Though she was loath to admit it, the promise of his assistance was a comfort, especially since Jack wasn't around.

When the sun came up, the familiar sight of Charleston's wharves greeted them. The wind had made quick work of the night's travel, and by noon they were at anchor along the pier and ready to disembark. Fin sent orders through Topper to convene the crew in the galley for instructions before being permitted ashore. In short order, the men had all assembled. She entered the crew's mess and Topper banged on the table. "Captain on deck!" he shouted. Fin glared at him.

"Before you go ashore, you need to know why we're here. The Congress has asked for our help." Eyebrows variously raised or lowered dependent upon the owner's surprise or skepticism. "They've offered each of us a full pardon for all crimes and offenses if we're successful." This information wasn't received happily. The men were wise enough to know that such a reward carried a heavy price. Fin calmly removed a parchment from her coat and placed it on the table. Topper set a pen and inkwell beside it. "I can't tell you anything more. But any man wishing to come must sign his name here." Fin made no mention of the possibility that her terms may not be met and they all might yet be hung. "Whether you sign or whether you go, I ask you to keep the matter to yourselves. I'd rather loose tongues didn't entertain English ears."

Topper signed his name first and then Armand. A line formed and nearly all of the men aboard signed their names. Fin was reminded of the day they signed the round-robin. That signing had made them criminals, and this one may yet deem them otherwise.

When the room had emptied, Topper read over the parchment and counted the names. "Twenty-eight," he said. "That's all but seven. Fair number."

The door to the mess swung open and Captain Bettany stepped inside with an escort of marines. Without waiting to be recognized or greeted, the captain spoke. "I will meet with my contact within the hour to discuss your terms. Until I return, you, Captain Button," he sneered as he said the word *captain*, "will be in the company of my men and will not leave this ship." Fin, though far from happy about his rudeness, had no argument to offer. Captain Bettany turned and left.

"I'll be glad when we're rid of that bugger," grumbled Topper.

"I'll be fine here 'til he gets back," said Fin, waving her hand at Topper and Armand.

"We'll spread the word that the 'Snake's hiring crew. And I'll make arrangements for supplies."

"Thanks, Topper. Don't know what I'd do without your help, you know that?"

"Ain't nothin', Fin. I just hope we make it back to see that pardon. I had enough of the pirating."

"Make sure you don't let on about the pardon in town. We'll be overrun if word gets out."

"Aye, Captain," he said with a wink and then left.

Armand appraised the soldiers left to guard her. "I should stay, *cherie*. This captain is not a man I trust."

Fin disagreed; it was Armand she didn't trust. "I'm fine. Go with Topper."

Armand bowed slightly and dismissed himself, leaving her alone with the marines. Almost alone. She'd forgotten Knut, as usual. He was sitting quietly in a corner trying to look inconspicuous, and succeeding.

"What do you think of all this, Knut?" she asked. Knut started and looked around to confirm that she was speaking to him and not some other Knut in the room.

"'Bout what, Fin?"

"Nevermind."

"'Bout the other ocean? I been there. Long time ago. Been to lots of places."

"The Mediterranean?" Fin ought not to have been surprised. After all, it was on a passage from Africa that Knut had been made the way he was, made simple by Creache's wrath, beaten until his mind had been shattered.

"Aye, why we goin' there, Fin?"

"We have to help somebody, Knut. Then we can come home for good." Knut seemed to like that explanation and his face brightened. She ought to put him off the boat here in Charleston rather than drag him with her into danger, but she was too selfish to let him go. He was one of the few things that made her life tolerable. He didn't expect or demand anything from her. She was no captain in Knut's eyes, and no criminal. She was merely herself, merely his friend. He grinned and picked at his ear and she smiled.

Fin sat down at the table and looked over the parchment, counting the names and reading each one under her breath. Twenty-eight people willing to follow her on an impossible mission half a world away. She hoped they hadn't signed their own death warrants. She folded the parchment up and tucked it inside her vest.

"Knut, would you go to my cabin and get a piece of paper?" she asked. He nodded and left the room. She would write to Peter. Their time together in Ebenezer had been so brief that she had no time for explanations. He deserved to know what was going on, and he deserved to know that when this was over she'd be back. Back home. Back to stay.

Knut returned with the paper and laid it on the table. He sat down in his corner to watch Fin write. Had anyone else sat and stared at her like that she'd have been self-conscious or insulted, but it was Knut's strange way and she was accustomed to it.

In the letter, she told Peter all about Creache and the *Justice*, about Bartimaeus's map and her unlikely captaincy. She pleaded with him to give her apologies to the sisters for the way they and the children had been treated, and she promised enough money to repair the chapel floor twice over when she returned. She wrote of how she'd missed him and how she longed to see again the home they'd built. Finally she told him of their plans across the Atlantic and her hope of pardon and peace upon return. As she wrote, she found that she continually assured him that she'd be back and that she dreamed of coming home, but she only half-believed it. She had more to say but the paper hadn't the space to hold it. She thought of asking Knut to fetch her another sheet of paper but he was napping in the corner and she chose not to wake him. There would be time enough for writing later, she thought, and she tucked the unfinished letter into her pocket.

Just as he had promised, Captain Bettany returned within the hour and was accompanied by a small man, no taller than Fin, with tiny spectacles and fair skin. Upon his back was slung a patched sack filled to bursting with what must have been, by the strain exhibited on the man's face, something very heavy. Captain Bettany directed him to unburden himself, and he dropped the sack to the deck. Several books tumbled out and the man muttered under his breath while he bent over and tucked them back into the bag then retied it.

"Well?" she said.

The Captain motioned toward the small man. "This is Dr. Lucas Thigham."

Dr. Thigham fidgeted with something in his pocket and pulled out a handkerchief to scrub his spectacles clean. When he was satisfied that they could be seen through once more, he worked them back onto his face and extended a quivering hand toward Fin.

"A pleasure, Captain," he stammered.

Fin shook his hand, nodded, and tried to offer a smile.

"I trust this satisfies your condition?" asked Captain Bettany.

"Dr. Thigham, one of my crew needs your help as soon as possible." Fin didn't have a clue how to discover whether a doctor was worth his salt or not, but she'd find out soon enough.

"C–certainly. Show me to him and I'll see what can be done." The doctor's eyes flitted all about the room as he spoke, never meeting Fin's. He had his hands back in his pockets now and was bouncing on the balls of his feet like a nervous child.

"A few details, Captain, and I'll be on my way." Captain Bettany drew a wallet of papers from his coat and placed one upon the table in front of him. "This is a letter of acquisition. The Congress will fund the fitting of your ship and resupply of rations. Simply show the document to any merchant here in Charleston and the matter will be taken care of." He withdrew another document from the wallet and placed it on the table. "This is a likeness of the countess and a collection of personal information that you must use to ensure you procure the correct person." Fin wrinkled her brow in confusion. "One never knows what treachery may present itself. Be wary." Then he withdrew the final paper and placed it on the table. "These are your delivery instructions. Should you succeed, you will sail to Le Havre-de-Grâce. Do not attempt to return to France's southern coast. The pasha's fleet will be upon you. You must make for Gibraltar with all haste. Once through the strait, you will be safe. The pasha's fleet is too small to contend with the Atlantic and you will easily be lost to him. To Le Havre. Do you understand?"

"Le Havre," replied Fin.

"Inside this envelope are your instructions upon reaching Le Havre. They will lead you to your contact who will direct you in the delivery of the countess. Follow these directions precisely. To do otherwise is to forfeit your success." He looked at her, studying her face for any doubt or question.

"And our pardons?" Fin asked. She handed Captain Bettany the parchment listing the names of her crewmen. He studied it and then tucked it into his coat.

"They will be delivered to Le Havre where you will receive them upon the success of your mission. A messenger will depart for England tonight with word of your deaths at sea. In a month's time you will be dead to the world, Captain. Use your anonymity wisely."

"Then are we finished?" asked Fin.

"Once you have filled out your crew, send me their names as well. My ship will wait off-shore for your departure. Once you are underway, we will give chase and harry you with cannon then return to Charleston with news of your sinking." He paused and considered her, almost as if he felt he were required to, and added, "Good luck, Captain. I shall pray for your success."

Without any further formality, he left.

Beside her, Lucas Thigham squirmed in his shoes. "The patient, Captain?"

"Follow me."

Fin led him out of the cabin and down to the surgery. She couldn't imagine where they had dug the man up. When she conjured the image of a doctor in her mind, what she saw was very nearly the opposite of Lucas Thigham. He wasn't tall, confident, well-dressed, in control, or even very clean. She'd always thought of doctors as members of the upper class, something Dr. Thigham didn't appear to belong to. Hard as she tried, she couldn't think of a single place where the nervous little man would look at home, or even mildly comfortable. He looked out of joint with everything about him, and seemed painfully aware of his own peculiarity.

As they approached Jack's bed, the rotten smell of his leg was the first thing to greet them. Sweat-soaked blankets were strewn about, and Jack had torn his shirt open in his fever. His chest, neck, and face all glistened with sweat, and tremors wracked his sleep.

"Oh, dear," said the doctor, whether in terror of the task before him or in genuine concern, Fin wasn't sure. He stooped over Jack and felt his sweaty forehead, neck, and chest then scrubbed his hand on his coat to dry it.

"Oh, dear. Oh, dear. Oh, dear," he repeated to himself under his breath. He examined the leg and sniffed of it cautiously. "Oh, dear."

Knut slunk in the door behind Fin and deposited the doctor's hulking bag on the ground by the bed. The doctor ignored Knut and squatted next to his bag. He plundered around in it, first taking out a large book and scowling at it in disappointment then drawing out a long metal saw to consider for a bit then producing a small box filled with something that rattled when he shook it. He fretted over the box and listened to its rattling closely before replacing it into the bag and digging around a bit more. He continued to inspect the contents of his bag for several minutes more, producing all sorts of strange curios: a bottle of beans, a strange pair of spectacles with what appeared to be a spyglass attached where each lens would normally be, a stuffed marmot, a great many books, even a human skull that was, for some reason, painted blue. At last he pulled a pair of scissors from his bag of endless oddity and exclaimed, "Goodness!"

Dr. Thigham returned to Jack's bandaged leg and began cutting the dressings away. Jack jerked and moaned in his fevered sleep. With each moan and jerk, Thigham glanced fearfully around the room as if he were scouting out an escape route should the affair turn to his disadvantage. When he'd finished, he carefully pulled the bloody dressings away from the wound. Fin had seen men killed and maimed but she'd never had to stand in peace and look upon the scarlet ruin a body could endure. Her stomach rolled over and she nearly vomited, but her curiosity quickly took over and she found herself fascinated with the doctor's work. The stump wasn't clean and neatly severed, as she'd imagined it would be. Instead, it was ragged. Flesh hung in clumps and splinters of bone jutted out at angles. Instead of being red and bloody, the leg had soured into a mottled, pus-ridden milk of grey-green and black. The smell was almost unbearable.

"Oh, dear. Oh, dear." Dr. Thigham scratched his pate in apprehension. "This man will die, I'm afraid," he said and stared at his feet.

The blood drained from Fin's face.

"What?" she yelled.

The doctor took off his spectacles and fidgeted with them.

"What do you mean, 'he's going to die'? Isn't that what you're here to fix?"

Thigham shook his head back and forth and stared at his feet. "No, no, no. I can't. He's too far. A wonder he's not dead already."

"But he isn't. He isn't dead. He's alive and you'd best keep him that way." Fin stepped forward and jabbed at the man's shoulder with her finger. "I tell you what. I don't know who you are, or what kind of doctor you claim to be, but mind me, Mr. Thigham. If Jack dies, I will have you keel-hauled, flogged, and thrown overboard."

With each word she said, Lucas Thigham looked increasingly distressed and staggered backward. "Oh, dear. Please, Captain. His leg has soured—perhaps if I had been here a week ago. But now—" he trailed off and resumed his *oh, dears.*

"Until he's well and back to himself, you don't leave this room! You eat here. You sleep here. You live here. You understand me, Doctor?"

Lucas Thigham didn't answer. He stared at his feet and fiddled with his spectacles. Fin jabbed him in the shoulder again.

"Hey!" she shouted. "You hear?"

He pushed up his spectacles and kicked his heel. "The leg will have to be cut again. Hot water. And fresh dressings and . . . and someone to hold him down."

"Knut, get whatever he needs."

While Knut loped out of the surgery, Fin considered the problem of restraining Jack. One did not simply "hold down" three hundred pounds of Jack Wagon. She crossed the room to a stowage locker and retrieved a hank of rope. She passed one end under the bed and fed it up between the frame and bulkhead, then pulled it over top of the bed and settled it across Jack's chest. She pulled it tight and tied it off, securing Jack's upper body to the bed. Then she did the same with two more ropes across his middle and thighs. It was crude, but it was the only way she could manage to restrain Jack's size by herself; the rest of the crew were already ashore and she didn't want to waste time by sending Knut after them. The doctor ignored her labors and offered no help while he rummaged through his bag and muttered under his breath.

Knut returned with a kettle of steaming water from the galley and a handful of old towels and underbreeches to use for dressings. As soon as Knut set the kettle down beside the bed, Dr. Thigham tossed a bone saw, a scalpel, and an assortment of other instruments into the water. When he was satisfied with the contents of his bag and the kettle, he turned to Fin.

"I'm sure he'll pass out from the pain after moments, but until then he may be most unpleasant." Then, without waiting for acknowledgement, he snatched a scalpel from the bowl and placed it just above Jack's knee.

"Oh, dear," said Lucas Thigham.

He began cutting and Jack came alive like an angry bull. Fin had assumed that the ropes alone would do the job. She was mistaken. Jack howled every sort of curse ever formed and jerked against his restraints hard enough that the bed frame was in danger of snapping in half. Fin leapt on top of him and yelled to Knut for help. As she tried her best to wrestle Jack to the bed, the doctor yelled, "Oh, dear! Oh my!" loud enough to be heard even over Jack's screaming. The doctor dropped the scalpel into the kettle and took up his bonesaw. Fin couldn't see the work but she could hear it, and she didn't think Jack was overreacting one bit. Each time the saw ran forward, a wet, crunchy zip induced spasms of pain in Jack, and still he didn't pass out. His eyes bulged angry and white from their sockets, and his face twisted and convulsed. The skin under his beard turned first white then red then deep purple. Fin was terrified to see tears streaming from Jack's wide-open eyes. She hadn't thought Jack capable of tears—yet here they were. The doctor's arm sped to its work and the blade continued its zipping. Jack gave up his cursing and a wordless, harrowing wail came out of his mouth, a sound scarcely human. Then at last Jack fell back to the pillow and went silent. Fin heard a dull thump as something hit the floor. It was a piece of Jack. She stared at the amputated, partial-limb in horror. Five minutes ago it had been part of someone. It had been kicking around, alive. Now it was twelve inches of dead meat and bone lying on the floor. Dr. Thigham had sweated through his clothing and looked like he'd been dunked in the ocean. He continued to work over the leg, pulling skin down and stitching it together over the stump with a needle and thread.

Carefully, Fin climbed off of Jack's chest. Her head spun and she stumbled. She caught herself on Knut's shoulder then staggered toward the door and let herself out into the fresh air. All she could think was that after going through that hell, Jack deserved to live. No one should have to endure that and still die. She leaned against the bulkhead and slid down to the deck.

A few minutes later, Dr. Thigham emerged. His clothes were stained dark red from neck to foot. Had he not been small and bespectacled, he'd have looked like the devil himself.

"It is done. But he will almost certainly die. The sour leg has poisoned him. He should be dead already."

But he wasn't dead already. Fin clung to that. He had already lived through more than most men could endure. Surely he could endure a little more.

"Thank you, Doctor."

Chapter Four

T HE MORNING AFTER JACK'S surgery was full of business. By noon, a long line of wagons waited along the pier filled with everything from salted pork to cannonball. Taking on supplies for an Atlantic crossing was a more serious undertaking than their usual method of garnering sparse supplies from port to port. While in the middle of the ocean there would be no quick stop into Nassau for flour, meat, or grog, and once they arrived in Europe no merchant was likely to be impressed by an order from the Continental Congress. So Topper ensured that each hold and every nook and corner on the ship was stuffed with staple rations, spare rigging, raw timber, hopeless chickens, baking supplies, gunpowder and anything else he suspected they might have want of.

Armand took charge of hiring new crew and set up a small desk on the pier next to the gangplank where he interviewed all comers and judged whether or not they were in possession of the proper mettle. Most were not. Fin instructed him to make certain that any man hired was well advised of the dangerous nature of their work and Armand saw to it that what men they took on were the sort likely to be a benefit under fire. None were told about the mission, of course, that would have to wait until they were underway, but the reputation of the *Rattlesnake* was well known and no sailor was surprised to hear they expected to see battle.

Fin made good on her threat that Lucas Thigham would not leave Jack's bedside until he was healed. She placed Knut in charge of making sure the doctor heeded her order. The two made quite a pair. They sat nervously on opposite sides of the surgery and stared at one another, each wondering whether the other might suddenly pounce.

"Oh dear," Fin said when she entered the room and discovered their peculiar association. The doctor's eyes flashed; he knew she was mocking him. Fin walked to the bed and checked on Jack. His fever hadn't broken but he seemed less fitful. The dressings on his leg were clean and no bleeding was apparent. Thigham seemed to be tending him well. As she left she reminded Knut to notify her immediately if Jack woke or if the doctor tried to leave. He nodded without taking his eyes off of Thigham.

By dinner the ship had been loaded, the holds were packed to the last inch and the filling out of the crew was nearly complete. Armand and Fin stood on the wharf as the last of the wagons rolled away empty. The *Rattlesnake* groaned and sat low in the water, heavy in her belly. As the sun set, lamplighters roamed the streets goading streetlamps to life and the crew traipsed across the plank by twos and threes to seek entertainment ashore. The old crew waved at Fin as they passed but the new hands stiffened and snapped their hands up in salute.

"We've sixty good men, *cherie*," said Armand. "Few of them green and none of them soft. With luck we shall have another ten, perhaps twenty, tomorrow and sail with a full company."

A new hand, no more than a boy, younger even than Fin, jogged off the ship and halted meekly before her to salute before running to catch up with his shipmates.

"What opinion do they have of the ship's captain?" asked Fin.

"They ask, 'Does the captain dye her hair with English blood?' One said to me, 'The captain rides a cannon into battle and commands the creatures of the deep against the British.'" Armand threw his head back in laughter. It was the first time Fin had seen him do so in genuine humor. "And another, 'Her ship will never founder because her hair is a flame that chases water back into the sea.' Armand slapped her on the back as she rolled her eyes. "Tales are the bastard children of bored sailors and ale, *cherie*."

"Will they listen to me, Armand?" The sailors she'd commanded until now, those that gave her the position of captain by election, did so because they knew her and had shared her experience. But these new men didn't know her. How would they respond when a wiry redhead from a Georgia backwater ordered them to fight for their lives?

"You are bigger than yourself, *cherie*. They do not see *you*. They see their own hopes, their own fears. What men fear, they respect. What they hope for, they heed. You must be scarce on the deck. You must be distant to them."

Fin remembered her first encounters with Tiberius Creache. She only saw him by glimpses as he came or went. Her imagination crafted him and he fed the image with his absence. He was never mad as some claimed, in fact he'd been chillingly sane, but he never disputed the rumor of his dementia; it worked in his favor. Fin would have to do the same. She would have to let the tales men told be thought true, let them see her little if at all, and let her word be carried out by those close to her. She needed Jack.

"Turn a man's mind to your will and he is yours. You are his master, he your slave. Your tales will serve you well, *cherie*. And they will make you immortal. But you must believe them. If you do not, then who else can? You must know yourself to be the monster they see, and then you will be powerful." Armand was standing too close to her. His chest brushed against her shoulder and his head was bent to a subtle angle so that his words fell gently into her ear, almost a whisper. A quiver ran up her neck. But he was right. She could use the situation to her advantage. Use it to get back home. Just like Armand had used the dogs of the *Justice*'s bilge. He controlled them utterly; they groveled before him and did his will with slavish obedience. She was sickened by the thought, but inspired by the possibility.

"Thank you, Armand."

He dismissed himself and she retreated to her quarters deep in thought.

THE FOLLOWING MORNING, AS Armand continued his inquisition of prospective crewmen, Topper huddled over a navigational chart in the captain's quarters. He was trying to convince Fin that they were not about to get themselves lost at sea. Fin had certainly never attempted a crossing of the Atlantic before, and while Topper had sailed his fair share, he'd never had any use for learning how to navigate one.

"Have you asked Armand?" said Fin.

"How hard can it be? East by nor-east. We sail right between the Azores and Madeira, through Gibraltar, along the coast to Tripoli and then we're good as gold. Home by Christmas." Fin had an inkling it might be more complicated.

"And what if we're off course? I'd rather not put in at the North Pole for directions. I'll ask Armand."

"Bah, we'll be fine. Don't need no help from a Frenchman to find our way to Europe." Topper turned the map to a new angle to study it.

Fin shook her head and glared at him as the door creaked open and Armand stuck his head in.

"Armand. Speak of the devil." Fin said.

". . . and the frenchman appears," grumbled Topper.

"We could use your advice," said Fin.

Armand's face was troubled as he stepped into the room and shut the door behind him. "There is something that we must discuss, *cherie.*"

Fin ignored him. "Despite Topper's obvious knack for nautical charts, his skill at navigation doesn't inspire me with anything but reasonable doubt. You have any experience that could help? Who better to lead us to Europe than a European?"

Armand frowned. "I am not from Europe. I am from New Orleans."

Topper grunted. "Wonderful."

"But I can help you. I have plotted many crossings." He stepped to the table where Topper was studying the map. Armand shook his head, picked up the map and turned it right side up.

"I knew that," said Topper.

Armand didn't answer him. "*Cherie,* there is a matter you should know of."

Topper sat down and leaned back in his chair as Fin turned her attention from the map to Armand.

"Our company is filled. Yet there is a man here for work. He is old, as I am, and I do not trust his manner. I would not offer him berth or wage. But the decision is yours." Armand returned to the door.

"If we're full and he's worthless then I don't see—"

Armand opened the door and a man shuffled in. He wore a dirty, patched cap and his entire dress was unkempt and unclean. The stench of rum and human filth entered the room with him. His beard was a tangled mess of red and grey framing a mouth turned up in an empty smile. Fin saw instantly why Armand didn't trust him; he had the eyes of a beggar, a man who will tell any lie to earn his next meal. She wrinkled her nose in disgust—and yet, he was oddly familiar. Fin felt like she knew him but couldn't remember from where or when. She tried to imagine him younger and beardless. She was certain she'd seen him before. He meekly pulled off his hat, revealing a lousy mess of matted grey hair. He stood before her with his head down.

Armand closed the door and explained, "He says his name is Phineas Button."

Fin staggered back a step. The room went eerily silent. She froze and stared at the familiar stranger in front of her. He was squalid and disgusting. Questions shot through her mind but they died on her tongue, unspoken. *My father? How? Why?* She wanted to smile. She wanted to laugh. She wanted to cry, to scream, to run. *He can't be. Not this wretched thing.* Yet the truth was written in the lines of his face. He raised his eyes to look at her and she was horrified. His eyes told her the only reason he'd come was because he thought he might gain something for himself: a meal, a wage, a bed—but not a daughter. *She* wasn't the reason he was here. She was only his means. His eyes darted around the room, only making contact with hers for the briefest instant before shifting away. His look was that of a man whose pride has been parted from him, whose conscience has long gone mute. She hated him and he had yet to speak a word.

"You're not my father." She meant it as a statement but it came out like a plea. She knew the truth, knew it as surely as she knew her own face in a mirror, but she resisted it. *Not him. Oh God, not him.* She felt the truth pulling at her, dragging her forward, but she fought it, raged against it.

The man wrung his cap in his hands and looked toward her, but not at her. "I come looking for work," he said meekly and paused before adding, "Ma'am."

"Armand, get him out of my sight." Fin spat the words from her mouth. "Get him off my ship!"

The man dropped to his knees in front of her. "I can work. I got nowhere to go. Phinea—" When he said her name his eyes beheld her for a moment, but he couldn't hold them still and they scattered away.

"Get him *out!*" Fin yelled. The sound of her name on his lips enraged her. *Please, not him!* He had no right to speak her name. He didn't know her. He'd never known her. She wanted him gone. Thoughts spun in her head: questions, accusations, a million things to say.

Armand grabbed the man under the arm and tried to pull him to his feet, but he shrugged off the attempt and remained knelt on the floor in front of her as if she expected him to do so and he'd done it a hundred times before.

"I don't want nothing. I got nowhere else."

Every word out of his mouth sounded like a lie. Fin was about to drag him out of the room herself when Armand saved her from it and muscled the man through the door without pity.

Fin paced the room with her hands on her head feeling like her skull might explode. She wanted him gone, but if she let him go she'd never have answers to her questions. She wanted to go to him, to touch him, strike him, tear him apart, embrace him—she didn't know which. She grabbed the edge of the table and flung it across the room, sending maps and papers fluttering to the floor.

"Easy, lass," said Topper.

"That man is *not* my father!" she cried. "He *is not!*"

Topper approached her carefully and tried to put his arms around her. She wasn't about to indulge consoling. She didn't need consolation because she didn't know the man. He was an impostor. She shoved Topper away.

"Course he's not, Fin. Any fool can see that."

Fin took a deep breath and pushed her hair back from her face. "Topper?" She struggled to hold back tears. She refused to let herself cry. "I don't want to see that man. I don't ever want to see him."

Topper nodded and left, closing the door behind him.

As soon as she was alone she lost her fight against the crying. The harder she tried to stop the more stubbornly the tears fell. She pounded her fist into the bulkhead again and again, sobbing harder with each strike until her hand went numb in a clutch of bloody knucklebones.

Chapter Five

THE *RATTLESNAKE* EMBARKED WITH the tide in late afternoon. As the ship slipped its moorings, Fin stepped out onto the quarterdeck to observe their departure. The deck was crowded with men, more than she'd ever seen aboard. Under Creache's reign, the *Rattlesnake* had been kept far undermanned to increase profits and decrease the likelihood of successful mutiny—the latter of which Creache had sorely miscalculated. Now a full crew ran the ship. Eighty souls, all told, and at the moment all eighty were at the rails or in the tops to wave farewell to South Carolina. They looked across the cityscape with smiles, etching it into memory to hold against the day of their return.

Fin was relieved that her presence on deck was overshadowed by the moment of departure. What looks she drew from the crew were either friendly, from those who had known her in the past weeks and months, or awestruck, from those who knew her only by tale and reputation. The reaction she cared for was the one she aimed to squash, and the one she loathed was the one that circumstance dictated she embrace. She couldn't rule a ship when the common tar was friendly with the captain. She had to distance herself from men she formerly worked among and fought with. The course she plotted for herself wound ahead of her, twisted and dark, yet she was fixed to it and had no intention of veering.

As the port shrunk into the distance, Captain Bettany's plan sprung into motion. His warship approached from the south and announced itself with a volley of cannonfire. The *Rattlesnake* was well out of range; they were in no danger, but to anyone observing from the shore such details would be impossible to gauge.

Fin had purposely kept this part of the plan secret from the crew, her reasons twofold. First, they could risk no sailor letting on about the affair in a local tavern or over pillow talk during his last night ashore. Their mission depended on freedom from English chase, and if people suspected they were anything other than captured or dead, the way ahead would be needlessly and further complicated.

Her second reason was less objective. She intended to use the mock battle to her advantage with the new crew. An early victory was sure to be well received.

A second volley of cannonfire boomed from the long nines of the pursuing ship.

"Beat to arms!" she shouted across the deck. Topper ran to the bell and swung the clapper as he bellowed orders. He and Armand were the only men aboard who knew what was actually happening; she'd included them in her act. The crack of cannons and the ringing of the quarterdeck bell dashed the bittersweet farewell of the crew.

"Cannon, Mr. DeFain," said Fin. "Full shot and away on my mark." He *aye-ayed* and dropped down the hatchway to the gun deck. Fin met Topper at the wheel and in mock seriousness consulted with him over their course of action. Topper pleaded loudly with Fin to take in sail and surrender.

"We can't match the guns of a man-'o-war, Cap'n. And we'll not outrun her!" he cried.

Fin pulled Betsy from her belt and pressed the barrel into Topper's chest.

"Surrender is a coward's tactic, Mr. Topper," she said. All hands on deck watched her. It was suddenly silent except for the flapping of slack sails.

"The '*Snake* will outrun her or she will taste our cannon." Fin turned away from Topper and waved Betsy around the deck wildly.

"What are you boys waiting for?" she shouted. "Loose the foresail, batten the hatches, run up the colors of war! We've a wind to catch and little time to catch her! Up, up, and to the east we go, else we'll neck a noose by nightfall and swing the gallows' howe!" Fin pointed Betsy high in the air and fired. The shot cracked across the deck like a whip and men threw themselves to work. Then, as if to reinforce her orders, a third volley of cannon erupted from the warship behind them.

Fin winked at Topper and tucked Betsy back into her belt. Topper's face was white; she hadn't told him Betsy would be loaded. He turned to the wheel and spun it hard to starboard, turning them away from the wind. The mainsails thumped full and the Rattlesnake lurched into a run. With each fall of the prow, spray flew up like a geyser.

Fin smiled. She felt like she was home.

As he said he would, Captain Bettany gave chase until dusk then turned back, sailing to Charleston with news of their deaths. When the crew saw the chase was won, they sounded three cheers for Captain Button and broke into song. Fin enjoyed the victory from her cabin and did not make an appearance to gloat over her success. The less she was seen, the better. Let their imaginations go to work.

"Did they swallow it?" Fin asked.

Armand poured them each a shot of rum. Topper sipped his glass and winked. "Hah! Did they ever. Even heard a few of 'em let on that there'd been no wind till you gave the order for it to blow." He laughed so hard he nearly choked on his drink.

"A fine sham, *cherie*," said Armand. "And a fine beginning to a long and lonesome crossing."

"How long, do you think?"

Armand had charted them a course, more or less east by northeast but well out of common merchant routes—or so he said. Fin had little choice but to trust him. She certainly couldn't let the crew find out she didn't know how to chart a course.

"Six weeks," said Armand, "five perhaps, if the wind favors us. Five weeks of straight sail and boredom."

Fin had lived long at sea, but never outside of a day's sail to land, and never without a quick purpose or destination. A crossing was foreign to her. Five weeks with nothing to look for or forward to but empty sea. It was unnerving. She thought she'd seen and learned all the sailor's life had to offer but this was new.

As Fin crawled into her hammock for the night, her thoughts strayed back to Phineas Button. It seemed impossible that the man who had given her life had sought her out. As a child she'd drawn images in her mind of who her parents might have been, what they might have looked like. And though she never dared to imagine that her father was wealthy or high-born or handsome, she'd neither envisioned a man drunken and vagrant. *Why him? Oh God, why him?* But he'd sought her out—and she'd cast him away. And now, having abandoned him as surely as he had her, Fin was lost in a sea of questions with no map to chart a course by.

IN THE FOLLOWING DAYS, the crew gradually fell into routine, and by the start of the second week the men could run the ship in their sleep. Three full watches manned all posts day and night, and the excitement of their departure turned to boredom. Between watches and meals the men played dice, sang songs, told stories, fished, and made up games to keep their minds busy.

There seemed to be no ill will among the crew, a good sign according to Armand, but Fin worried that men could only be kept so close for so long before they began to turn against one another. As yet, the only problem of any mention had been from the cook, Pelton Quinn, "Pelly" as he was called, owing to the combination of Pelly and Quinn sounding like *pelican*. He was as thin as a tent pole, a trait Fin wasn't convinced was a good sign in a cook. When she asked Armand why he'd hired him, his logic was that a skinny cook clearly wasn't a good one, therefore the men were likely to eat less and their rations were more likely to hold out. Fin countered that if they ate less they'd be hungrier and more likely to ransack the rations in revolt, but Armand waved her worry aside. So when Pelly had come to her one evening enraged that a gang of insolent rats had been pilfering his kitchen stores, Fin was less than surprised, suspecting that the accused rats were more likely hungry sailors. Rats on board a ship, however, are no small matter, so traps were set, Pelly was calmed, and once again all was peaceful for the *Rattlesnake* and her captain.

Since leaving Charleston, Fin had been mulling over what to rename the ship—not permanently, but for the duration of their sojourn in the Mediterranean. It would not do to advertise to the world that they were, in truth, not as sunken and drowned as reports would have people believe. Her first inclination was to rename her the *Liberty*, but after a few days' consideration she decided against it.

She considered a plethora of others, *Flame of the West*, *The Serpent*, *Georgia*, and *Ebenezer* among them, but she finally settled on a name from a story Tan had told her.

She commissioned the change of name, and Topper set the crew to work. They hung over the rail in rope slings and painted away the *Rattlesnake*'s old identity. Then, in white letters on a green field, they painted her a new one: *Fiddler's Green*.

"It's good," said Topper when the work was done. Fin agreed.

UPON THEIR TENTH DAY at sea, Knut slunk into her doorway and announced that Jack's fever had broken. Fin went to him immediately and found Dr. Thigham sitting next to the bed hunched over a thick, leather-bound book full of macabre illustrations of the human body.

"How is he?" she asked.

Jack lay sleeping. His skin had a healthier luster, and for the first time since his surgery, he looked like he was actually resting.

"He is, ah, not dead yet," said the doctor.

"And just what is *that* supposed to mean?" Fin asked. Jack looked better than he had since taking the wound, and the best the doctor could offer was that he wasn't dead yet. Thigham should have been beaming and anxious to take credit for his work.

The doctor turned a page in his book and pushed his spectacles up on his nose. "It means that the man has not yet died, a condition that I'm sure will not last."

"All right, Thigham," Fin said. She'd had enough of the little man's oddity. "Explain to me what exactly is wrong with you."

He looked up from his book and gave her a confused stare.

"What kind of doctor expects his patient to die?"

"I'm sorry, Captain, but I base the prognosis on my experience—which tells me, I'm afraid, that your man will almost certainly not live out the day."

"That's what you said two days ago."

He screwed up his eyes in recollection. "So I did. He should be dead already you know. That's why it's so difficult to find work for a doctor. After all, who wants someone around to announce that people are going to die?" He shrugged at her and resumed his reading.

"Have you ever had a patient that lived?" asked Fin, not entirely sure she wanted to know the answer.

"Indeed not. A pity."

Fin's mouth dropped open.

"Are you sure you're a doctor?"

Thigham jerked his head up, aghast. "Really, Captain! Should I ask if you are actually a captain? Should I question your ability to chart us a course or command men in battle? Should I question your training, experience, and qualification simply because you do not *look* like a captain?" Fin winced. If he only knew how little his line of reason bolstered her confidence in him. "I thought not. And I'll kindly ask you not to question a man of my significant education and understanding on the nature of his profession!" The doctor suddenly became aware of his tone. He blushed deep red and seemed to shrink three inches into his clothes in embarrassment.

Before Fin could formulate a reaction, the hatch banged open and two sailors bumbled through the door with a third man slung between them. The man they carried was groaning in pain and cursing each time he was bumped too hard or jostled too rudely.

"Barker fell out the riggers. Says his leg is broke," said one of the men. Barker howled in pain as they set him down on a cot next to Dr. Thigham.

"Get off me! Get 'im off!" growled Barker, slapping at the men that brought him in.

Thigham reluctantly placed his book aside and stooped over in front of Barker to roll his pants leg up. The leg was bent where it shouldn't be and cocked out at an odd angle between the shin and knee.

"Oh, dear," said Thigham. "He will surely die."

"What did he just say?" asked Barker. When no one answered right away he became alarmed and widened his eyes in worry. "Did he just say—"

"You're not going to die," Fin assured him. She closed her eyes and shook her head.

"Oh, dear," repeated Thigham and jerked the man's leg straight to set the fracture. Barker screamed and leaned forward, intent on throttling Lucas Thigham into unconsciousness. He was dutifully held back by the two men who had brought him in.

"What the blooming cripes is wrong with you!" he yelled at Thigham.

The doctor ignored him and went about splinting the leg and muttering, "Oh, dear. Oh my."

As the doctor tended his dying patient, Fin turned back to Jack. She ran her palm down his face; it no longer burned with fever. His huge barrel-like chest rose and fell in regular breaths, and he slept untroubled. His leg was wrapped in clean dressings and there was no sign of blood staining the cloth. She leaned over and kissed his forehead then whispered in his ear.

"You're going to be fine, Jack. No matter what Thigham says."

Knut was waiting in the corner, patiently watching everyone around him. Fin assured him that Jack was going to be fine and reminded him to alert her the moment he was awake. As she returned to her cabin, she called for Topper to hunt down Tillum, the ship's carpenter, and send him to her quarters.

After a few minutes, Tillum knocked on her door and she called him in. "Tillum reporting, Captain," he said from the doorway. He stood in a preposterous stance of attention, his heels together and his chest pushed out as if he expected to lift himself from the floor and float by the sheer power of his exertion. He stared wide-eyed at the back wall of the room and did not look at Fin.

"Relax, Tillum."

"Aye, Captain." He didn't.

"You were on the *Justice* with us, weren't you, Tillum?"

"Aye, Captain!"

"Why were you in prison?"

Tillum's face lit up. "Stealin', Captain."

It was odd that he seemed proud of the fact, and odder still that simple stealing would land a man in an English prison hulk. Fin dug a little deeper. "What did you steal?"

"The gov'ner hired me to build him a house outside Richmond. I done it, and done it well. But the gov'ner was a damn Tory, so's I built a secret door or two and came back a month later. I sneaked in and got my taxes back. Decided I might as well get some other folks' taxes back while I was there. Didn't leave much. I'd do it again."

"I like you, Tillum."

"Thank you, Captain!" Tillum thrust his chest an inch closer to the ceiling.

A week prior, none of the men from the *Justice* would have taken her position so seriously. And yet, here this one stood as if he were in the audience of a general. Did they really believe the stories they told, even when they knew better?

"You mended my violin case didn't you, Tillum?" Fin pointed to it sitting on the floor next to her hammock. He jerked a quick glance at it and then resumed his examination of the back wall.

"Aye, Captain."

"Then I've got another job for you. Jack Wagon needs a leg." She paused and waited for him to answer.

Tillum wrinkled up his face in thought, screwing it one way then another.

"Never made a leg before," he said at length. "Made a foot once," he added. His face lit up with pride.

"Well then, I've sent for the right man. Get started right away, Tillum. Feel free to visit Jack in the surgery for measurements and let me know if there's anything you need."

"Aye, Captain." He nodded but didn't move.

"Dismissed," Fin said with an exasperated shake of her head. As he turned to leave she added, "And Tillum, ignore anything Dr. Thigham says. Let me know if he gives you trouble."

Chapter Six

After two weeks of fair weather the third began with thick clouds and turned to rain and a blustery wind that blew one minute north and the next south, never settling long on where it came from or went. The world became a colorless drizzle. The sun was no more than a lightening in the grey as it wheeled overhead. The limit of the world seemed a stone's throw from the ship in any direction; everything beyond was swallowed by fog. The sound of the sails whipping full or slack upon the inconstant wind echoed back to them out of the mist like a ghostly omen, and the crew avoided the deck. They busied themselves in the dim, cool holds. The weather sapped their spirits and many spent the hours between meals or watches in fitful attempts to sleep away the drear. The watch stood their duty in silence, squinting into the wispy grey hoping to catch a glimpse of its end.

In the midst of this mid-Atlantic gloom came Topper and Armand with ill tidings of the crew. Fin was sitting in her cabin wrapped in a woolen blanket, trying to keep the cold away as she looked over a scattering of sea charts that Armand had been teaching her to read.

Topper shambled into the cabin, shaking his head and grumbling under his breath. "We've a thief aboard," he said.

Fin had spent time enough as a sailor to know that thievery while underway was a rare thing. Only a fool stole from the men he slept with when he had nowhere else to go and nowhere to hide what was stolen. A thief on a ship was doomed to discovery.

"You sure?" said Fin.

Topper scratched his belly and shrugged. "Few days ago one of the men come to me sayin' his blanket was gone missing. So I mustered the crew and turned out the berth looking for it. We didn't find it, but then it turned up during the next watch in a corner somewhere's else. So's I figured it was just misplaced." He pulled up a stool and sat down at the table across from Fin. Armand crossed his arms and leaned against the wall in the corner.

"Then yesterday, one of 'em come to me saying his lucky corn cob what his missy give him was up and disappeared. Who in the bright blue steals a corn cob, I ask?" He shook his head in wonderment. "So I tell him he must have tuck it away and let it slip his mind. Come this morning, it still ain't turned up and the poor devil is mad to find his buggerin' corn cob, so I line 'em up in the berth and have 'em all search their havin's while Armand and me are looking for this accursed cob. Turns out that when they all go to searching that about ten more of 'em find out they got stuff missing. Nothing big, mind ye. But little stuff—a trinket, lady's hanky, a looking glass . . . a corn cob. And we can't find no trace of it. It don't make sense."

Fin agreed. "Did you ask Thigham?"

"The doctor?"

"Don't know I'd call him a doctor, but he's got a bag of strange stuff he holds on to. I wouldn't trust him far."

"Hadn't thought of that. I'll shake him down good."

Armand stepped forward and bent over the table so he could speak softly and be heard. "You must warn them, *cherie*." He was nearly whispering. "You must show them anger and let them see that you will give them justice. If you do not, they will turn on each other to find it for themselves. The crossing is long. Tempers are short. You must be swift and hard if you are to keep them tamed."

His voice made her shiver. She hated it when he whispered. But she heard wisdom in his advice. If the thief was not found, then the crew would find one. Whether he was the right man or not, they would blame someone and turn on him.

"What do you suggest?" she asked.

Armand's lips curled up, almost imperceptibly. Fin didn't notice.

TOPPER SOUNDED THE WHISTLE and all hands slunk to the main deck for muster. The weather hadn't changed. The ship floated through a cloud, going nowhere. The crew muttered and complained. They huddled together and crossed their arms, tucked their hands away, shivered in the wet drizzle of the half-rain.

Fin stepped out of her cabin.

"Captain on deck!" shouted Topper.

She was dressed for the part. The lockers in the captain's cabin were full of Creache's old clothes and she'd chosen a long, blue frock. Fin thought it looked rather captainish. Tan's rapier hung at her waist and Betsy was tucked into her belt where it could be easily seen. Her hair was pulled back and tied. She looked fearsome. She felt ridiculous.

"Thank you, Mr. Topper," she said. Topper bowed smartly and stepped down to join the crew. She walked to the rail of the quarterdeck and looked down on her eighty men. None of them looked pleased to be outside in the rain, but none were foolish enough to speak of it. They stared at her in silence.

"We've a rat aboard the *Green*." Fin glared at them. "A ship despises a rat. I won't tolerate thievery on my ship, gentlemen. The man in question will present himself at my door before noon tomorrow. He will confess. He will return what he has taken, and he will receive a week's half-rations for his crime." Most of the crew nodded in agreement and a few called out for the culprit to disclose himself immediately. Men scowled at one another with narrow-eyed mistrust.

"Should the thief choose to remain a rat, he's welcome to it. But he'll be caught and when he is, he'll receive thirty strokes of the cat's lash." Several men whooped approval. Fin spotted Knut across the deck. At the mention of the lash, he flustered and rocked back and forth, shaking his head. The sight sickened Fin but she wasn't finished.

"Mark this too, if any seaman takes my authority in his own hand, he'll feel the lash, same as the rat." She looked around to see that her point was taken. Silence and wide eyes told her it was. Knut slunk out of sight behind the foremast.

"That's all, Mr. Topper. Set the watch." Fin turned on her heel and marched back into her cabin. As soon as the door was closed, she leaned against the wall and let out a long breath of relief.

THE FOLLOWING DAY, THE crew was silent and thoughtful. They tiptoed across the deck and looked repeatedly toward the captain's cabin. Whenever a man had cause to pass near it, he shrunk under the watch of his crewmates' suspicious eyes and hurried on past. Fin, Armand, and Topper waited patiently inside. They ate without speaking. They studied maps and sea charts, and read quietly to themselves until noon came and went, and no knock had rattled the cabin door.

"I guess I wasn't scary enough," Fin muttered.

"Then you must be hard, *cherie*. When the man is discovered, you must show him no mercy. Make of him an example."

"Aye, Fin. He's right. And you know I'd tell you if he wasn't," said Topper.

"You don't seriously expect me to flog a man?"

"You must, *cherie*," urged Armand, "or you will lose the crew. Your word will mean nothing."

"And what of it? I'm no more a captain than any of them. Why should my word carry any weight?"

"Their yoke is easy now, they have nothing to gain by losing your favor. But the time will come when you will order them to bleed. And what then, *cherie*? What will stop them when they turn on you? What will stay their mutiny when they take your ship and cast you aside?" Armand leaned closer. "Fear. They must fear you, *cherie*. They must believe that you are monstrous."

Topper frowned and looked at Armand with narrowed eyes.

"I'm not like you, Armand."

Armand held silent and considered her. Fin sensed he was judging her, wondering how hard he could push her, how far.

Before Armand could answer, Topper spoke up. "Pains me to say it but I think he's right, Fin. If you don't follow through, they'll turn on you."

Fin clenched her jaw. "I will not flog a man," she said. "Leave me alone. Get out."

Topper huffed but obeyed and left. Armand lingered. His slitted eyes searched her face. He pushed the limit of her order. Before she could tell him to leave a second time or accuse him of defiance, he smiled and walked out.

She knew the sting of the flogger's lash and wore its scars. It was a horrific thing, and she could not bring herself to visit the same torment on another human being. It was unthinkable. She would threaten the man perhaps, carry through with the pretense of a flogging until the last moment then offer a reprise. Then no one could say she hadn't followed through. They would see her mercy and approve. She could not flog a man. She would not. The man would be caught or not, and she would deal with the situation when it presented itself.

She put the issue out of her mind and busied herself with other things. She retrieved the papers Captain Bettany had given her and sat down. On the first page an etching of a woman's head and shoulders was framed in an embellished oval, below which was written: "The Countess Caroline de Graff." Fin had expected a French countess to be a ravishing beauty but was amused to discover that the woman in the etching was rather ordinary. Not ugly, simply ordinary. Had her hair not been done up into something that looked like a jewel-studded log, she'd have looked right at home on a farm or even at the orphanage. Until Fin looked at her, she hadn't realized that she expected to dislike the woman, but seeing her ordinary face she thought she might like her instead.

Fin put the picture aside and looked at the second paper. It was written in a neat, properly tilted script and detailed the countess's life. She was born in 1757, only two years younger than Fin. For some reason that made Fin smile. She had assumed the woman would be old. She read further that her favorite food was *foie gras*, her favorite pastime was riding horses, and she spoke three languages fluently: French, English, and Arabic. She had a scar on her left cheek (the etching was a profile of her right side, to hide the scar, no doubt) from a childhood riding accident. The last tidbit of information was that she was married to Count Martin de Graff, a man ten years her senior. Fin wrinkled up her nose and felt some relief that at least some part of the woman was ridiculously French.

The last document was short and simple. It said she was to return the countess to the city of Le Havre-de-Grâce and contact a Mr. Terrason at "Le Bureau du Maire." Armand had translated the French and scribbled "Office of the Mayor" at the bottom of the page.

Fin laid the instructions on the table and picked up the etching again. She stared at it, committing the woman's features to memory. It was odd that, try as she might, she couldn't stop herself from considering her a woman. She was two years younger than Fin, and Fin scarcely considered herself a woman. The countess was just a girl. Two years ago Fin had been clueless about the world, stumbling through it, barely managing to keep herself alive (still the case, she had to admit). This girl was the prisoner of barbarians in a foreign land. Fin couldn't imagine the horror she must be living through.

As she folded the papers and put them away, Fin felt that somehow she had made a connection with the Countess Caroline de Graff, as if some ethereal strand had tied them together across the world and Fin was tugging on it, each heft of the line drawing them closer to an inevitable union. She had a mission now, a real one, not an errand to run for a Congress she'd never seen. Rather, a person in need of help—a person who seemed ordinary enough to be real and worthy of rescue. No longer was this madness just a means to finding her way home to Peter, it was a means that mattered.

CHAPTER SEVEN

THE OPPRESSIVE FOG AND rain continued for days, but at last the wind settled on the east and drove them steadily. Each morning, Topper stomped his way to the quarterdeck and craned his neck back to appraise the grey sky. He'd spit on his finger and hold it into the wind and proclaim, "We'll be out of this soup before you can slap me and call me bald!" Had anyone ventured to slap him or call him bald, however, they'd have done so without any interruption by the fulfillment of his prediction. But at least the wind had settled on a direction, and though they couldn't see where they were going, they were moving east, ever east.

Fin had grown fond of Pelly's cooking despite Armand's hope of the cook's poor taste and she'd given him a standing order to deliver a breakfast of two eggs and a plate of griddle cakes each morning before the first watch. The ship had not exactly been a bastion of fine dining in the past, so the simple pleasure of a good breakfast each morning raised Fin's spirits and helped keep the gloomy weather from soaking in.

The first time Pelly had served her his delectable griddlecakes, Fin, who was no stranger to the ways of the kitchen, had been fairly baffled. In all her time apprenticed to Bartimaeus she'd never learned any way at all to cook griddlecakes without milk. When she questioned Pelly on how he managed it, he let on that he'd smuggled a sow aboard and kept her in the hold for special recipes where a little milk might be of use. The chickens needed someone to keep them company anyway, he explained. Fin didn't care for griddlecakes the following morning, but eventually she admitted that she missed them and didn't care if they were made with milk of the pig-squeezed variety or not.

The smell of cakes and eggs woke her up, and as she languished in her hammock, Fin followed the sound of Pelly's footsteps as he clomped his way out of the galley, up the companionway, across the deck, and stopped outside her door. Her mouth watered for a taste of what her nose had already been enjoying, and she climbed out of the warm hammock to start the day. After two knocks on the door, Pelly entered and set her food on the table.

"Morning," she groaned.

Pelly grunted an unimpressive reply and turned to leave, muttering complaints about rats in the stores as he went. He let the door bang closed behind him.

"Good to see you too, Pelly," she said as she drowned her breakfast in cane syrup. She took a bite and listened as Topper arrived on the quarterdeck and proclaimed once more that the end of the ill weather was nigh. A volley of groans and shouts for him to "clam up" followed, and Fin imagined the eyes of twenty sailors rolling in unison. She chuckled to herself as she devoured her second griddlecake and savored it in delight. It was nice to be the captain, she mused. At least for now. Less so at times, naturally, but at breakfast it seemed a good thing.

She listened to the business of the ship go on through the walls of her cabin and enjoyed the pleasure of having nothing to do and no one to require her attention. She ate her food in lazy delight until she heard a rumble deep in the ship, a sound like a boulder rolling around in the hold. She stopped mid-chew to listen closer. She could just make out a bit of shouting too. Then she distinctly heard a hatchway bang open and the sound of footsteps running across the deck. In burst Knut, breathless and panting.

"Jack . . ." was all he managed. He bent over with his hands on his bony knees and tried to catch his breath.

Fin dropped her fork and jumped up. "What is it, Knut? Is Jack awake?"

"Dr. Thigham . . . he's gonna hurt him . . ." said Knut between breaths. Fin didn't like the sound of it. If Thigham had done something to hurt Jack then she was going to have him taken care of once and for all.

She rushed out of the cabin and flew down the ladder. There was a gaggle of crewmen crowding the hatchway into the surgery. Fin ordered them to move aside so she could get through, but no one heard her over the squabble at the door and the ruckus inside. She wriggled her way between the men and got into the room with no more than a few accidental elbows to the head.

When she saw what was going on, she realized what Knut was trying to say. No one was going to hurt Jack. Jack was awake and was every inch himself. But he was dead set on visiting hurt upon the doctor. Thigham cowered at the far end of the room with a chair held out in front of him like a man trying to fend off a wild animal. Jack was on the floor, struggling to stand up. He grabbed a stanchion for support and hauled himself upright. Then, balancing on his good leg, he hopped around to face Thigham. The doctor's face was white with terror. Jack let out a roar and hopped his way across the room. Normally, the sight of Jack howling mad and roaring would have been terrible to behold, but the roaring and the hopping didn't go together quite as well as the usual roaring and charging. Fin burst into laughter, and Jack halted his hop to turn and see who had dared to laugh.

Fin clapped her hands over her mouth to stop the laughter and tried to straighten her face. She failed miserably and burst into laughter again as Jack stared at her.

"Where's my leg, Button?"

Thigham, not sharp on his timing, took the opportunity to explain. "Sir, your leg was—"

He didn't get far. Jack hopped back around to face him and snarled, "*Where's my leg?*" as if the doctor might produce it out of his pocket and reattach it. When the leg wasn't produced, Jack resumed hopping. Just as Thigham was within reach, the doctor yelped and leapt past him. He ran to the opposite corner of the room and cowered. Jack tried to spin around to catch the little man as he scurried past but lost his balance, flailed, and fell to the deck with a thunderous crash.

To the great misfortune of the crew peeking in at the doorway, they erupted into laughter. As Jack pulled himself back to his feet—foot—he scowled at the men in the doorway and the laughing abruptly ceased. Those men who were smarter than the rest took the opportunity to go about their business and clear out of the doorway. A rumbling sound, familiar to Fin, started in the depths of Jack's mountainous chest and worked its way into a curse as he hop-charged the door and bowled ten men into a heap.

"Jack, let me explain," cried Fin, but he was beyond listening to reason. He pulled himself up from the deck again and looked as if he was about to kick the man in front of him until he realized that kicking didn't work so well with one leg. He flailed his stump back and forth and resumed his cry of "WHERE'S MY LEG?!"

"Jack!" Fin shouted.

He started another wild hop-charge in her direction. Fin crossed her arms and raised a defiant eyebrow then side-stepped and tripped him. Jack crashed to the deck amid an irate spew of curses. The rest of the crew scattered out of his way while he got upright and hopped at Fin again. Once more she stepped aside, nonchalantly stuck her foot out, and sent him tumbling back to the deck.

Fin bent over him and said calmly, "We can do this all day, you know. Or you can gather your wits and be happy to see me."

Jack emitted a growl as he got up and charged her again. Out went her foot and Jack stopped at the last moment. He glared around the surgery. The crew was standing back as far as they could, staring in rapt silence at the wakened giant. Fin smiled to herself. Few of them had ever met Jack and they were being treated to a marvelous first impression.

Jack pointed to one of the men. "You there, hand me that oar," he growled. The man's eyes widened in fear and he looked to Fin to see if she might tell him otherwise.

"Do what he says," she ordered.

The man plucked an oar from the bulkhead and cautiously approached Jack. As soon as the man was within his reach, Jack snatched the oar from him and turned it handle-down to use as a crutch. The man scurried back to his place.

"What are you lot looking at?" bellowed Jack at the crew.

Fin ordered them back to work and motioned Jack toward the captain's cabin. He snorted and limped his way up the ladder, violently shrugging off all of Fin's attempts to assist him.

Topper stood next to the door and grinned. "Good to see you up, Jack."

Jack grunted and shuffled into Fin's quarters. He settled himself into a chair and propped his oar against the table.

"You don't remember?" asked Fin. She sat down and Topper filed in after.

Jack scratched his beard with one hand and tested the feeling of his shortened leg with the other. "Remember what? Misplacing my leg? No, I'd say that plain slipped my mind!" He patted his other limbs down and checked his extremities as a man would after discovering he'd lost his purse to a pickpocket. "Ain't nothing else missing, is there?"

"Just the leg," said Fin. "You should be thanking the doctor instead of trying to kill him. He saved your life."

"And just what did he save it from?" asked Jack.

"You lost the leg to an English musket ball but we didn't have a doctor to tend it. By the time we met Thigham, the leg was soured and you were nearly dead of fever. Thigham had to cut the leg again, but he seems to have saved the rest of you."

"So it was English that took the leg, eh?" Jack cocked one eyebrow into the air.

"One of Creache's lot," said Topper.

"And where's Creache?" asked Jack

"Dead." Fin and Topper said it in unison.

"Good riddance. Thought that damned beady-eyed doctor was one of Creache's cronies having sport." Jack relaxed and then started laughing, slowly at first, then building into a great belly laugh.

"You shoulda seen the look on that one's face when I woke up and found him pokin' around where my leg ought to been!" He threw his head back and laughed so hard he lost his breath and threw himself into a coughing fit to get it back. It didn't take much imagination for Fin to know exactly how the doctor must have reacted.

Jack remembered everything up until he and his leg had parted ways but recalled nothing else up to the moment he had opened his eyes to find Dr. Thigham examining him. Fin related their current situation and he listened quietly, grunting now and again. She couldn't read enough of his face to tell if he was pleased or angry about the deal she'd made with Captain Bettany. When she finished her explanations they sat in an awkward silence until Jack proclaimed his judgment. "Bugger" was the sum of his opinion.

"No hurry, Jack. But the ship needs its first mate when you're up to it. Topper's filled in fine but he hasn't quite the knack of it like you do," said Fin.

"Aye, too much scowling about for my taste. Never been the sort to scowl," said Topper.

Fin sat upright in her chair in excitement. "Oh! Topper, go find Tillum and see if he's got the leg ready."

"The leg?" asked Jack.

"Told the ship's carpenter to make you a new one. Ought to be done by now," she explained.

"Don't suppose you saved the old one, eh?" asked Jack.

Fin hadn't really thought about it. What exactly did a doctor do with part of a leg after amputating it? She imagined Thigham tucking it away into that bag of his and shuddered.

"Don't seem right not to keep it is all I'm sayin'." Jack shrugged.

The breakfast that Jack's waking had interrupted sat on the table growing cold. Fin pushed her plate across the table and Jack tore into it like a man starved—which, of course, he was. Fin stuck her head out the door and hollered for Pelly to cook her up another breakfast. By the time she made her way back to the table, Jack was licking the plate clean of syrup and managing to get most of it in his beard. When Pelly finally arrived with Fin's replacement eggs and cakes, she gave them to Jack as well.

While Jack finished his second breakfast of the morning, Tillum presented himself in the doorway. He thrust his chest out impossibly far and held what Fin assumed to be the leg tucked under his arm.

"Tillum reporting, Cap'n!"

"That the leg?" Fin asked.

"Aye, Cap'n!" He marched in and placed his creation on the table. It was a thick trunk of oak, hollowed at the top end, hinged at a knee that looked to be made out of a modified pulley block, and carved into a rather convincing foot at the bottom. "See I bowled out the top bit here so's you can put your, uh, well, the stump in it and cinch this belt up 'round your shoulder to hold her tight. Carved her out of a fine block of oak, and while she's a mite heavy, I reckon you're a heavy one yourself so's maybe it'll be about right. The knee here," he rapped on it with his knuckles, "she'll bend just like your old one, and I rigged her up with an arresting block here so's she can't bend back the wrong way, that might get folks to looking at yer funny, eh?" He chuckled but Jack didn't seem amused. "All you got to do is give her a little kick and that leg'll bend and swing just like one the Lord made. So then the foot there, right proud of that I am, that oak's hard like a stone and bugger all to carve, but I fit her to your boot and she's a match, sir." Tillum's grin was as wide as his whole face and he repeatedly pointed out the workings of the leg to make sure everyone saw and understood the quality of his craftsmanship.

"You expect me to wear that bloody thing?" balked Jack.

Tillum's face sagged.

"Come on, Jack! Try it on!" Fin said. She jumped up, snatched the leg off the table and knelt in front of Jack, offering him the open end of the leg.

"So much as smirk and I'll beat you with it," Jack warned. He scooted forward and settled his stump into its place. It fit snugly and covered his thigh up to just a few inches south of the hip.

"Stand up so's we can strap her on," said Tillum excitedly.

Jack stood and leaned on the table, not trusting the leg to hold his bulk. Cautiously, he shifted his weight onto the wooden leg, wincing each time it shifted in a way that the appendage wasn't happy with. Fin and Tillum threaded the leather strap around his shoulder and back down to the backside of the leg and buckled it tight. Jack tested it, rocking back and forth, shifting his weight around, trying to find a comfortable set. As Fin and Tillum backed up to get a look at him, he ventured a small step forward and had to catch the table to keep from falling. He shot a warning look at Fin to make sure she hadn't dared to laugh. She managed not to, but only just. He kicked the leg back and forth and the lower part flapped like a merchant's shingle and creaked loudly.

"If I don't oil this bugger up they'll hear me coming a mile yonder," he complained.

"When has anyone not heard you coming?" said Fin. "I think it looks quite impressive. Good job, Tillum."

Tillum beamed. "Aye, Cap'n. Thank ye."

Jack attempted another step. He kicked the leg out and set it down. Then he let go of the table and with a grimace shifted all his weight onto the new leg. He lurched forward and blew out a long breath of relief as he put out his hand and leaned on the bulkhead. Had he been bald, naked, and two feet tall he'd have looked exactly like a child taking his first steps in the world.

Fin gave in and laughed.

Jack shot her a stony look. "Your day's a comin', Button." He took another step and pinwheeled his arms to keep his balance.

"You'd have to catch me first," Fin pointed out.

By noon, Jack had nearly mastered his new leg and was making rounds of the deck, growling at anyone who looked at him with too much curiosity. His gait was a pronounced swagger, first kicking the oaken leg out to let it flop to the deck with a loud creak, then throwing his weight on it and bringing his hulking body forward. *Creeaaak. CLOMP! Creeeaaak. CLOMP!* He was certainly going to stand out in a crowd. But then, Jack Wagon had always stood out.

Chapter Eight

THE RETURN OF JACK Wagon wasn't an enjoyable event for the crew. Those few that knew him before his unlegging noted a distinct new level of irascibility, and for those who had never known him at all, lessons were quickly learned of the barking giant and his run of the ship. No slackery escaped his gaze and no slinking buttock long evaded his boot. His ability to kick while standing on a mechanical wooden leg was a rare feat of determination that Jack had set himself to at the first opportunity. After a week, he had mastered it entirely. He discovered, however, that the creaky hinge of his new knee was a shirker's best friend. The *creeaakk-clomp* that heralded his coming chased off any determined sluggard long before he could be effectively motivated. This prompted Jack to procure a bladder of teak oil which he slung from his shoulder and carried with him wherever he went so he could quiet his *creak* at a moment's pause. Managing his *clomp*, however, was a livelier challenge, much to the relief of the crew.

After a few days of Jack's motivation Fin appreciated a clear new vision of how clean, tight, and orderly a ship could run under the proper observance. Topper hadn't done a poor job exactly, but Jack's talent for forced motivation was a thing few other men could achieve. Topper resumed his jovial old habits of dickering food from the galley and snoozing in unwatched corners as oft as he could get away with it; he seemed happy that the world had returned to an even keel.

At Fin's insistence, Jack presented himself to Dr. Thigham to offer an apology. But Jack first had to make solemn assurances to him that he didn't intend to visit any more violence upon the poor man. After some convincing, the doctor emerged from his stowage locker to be apologized to, though even after the apology the doctor still seemed ready to flee as if the whole affair were a ruse meant only to draw him into the open. After all his predictions that Jack was going to die, he deserved some grief, so Fin did nothing to calm his fears and was instead content to keep him terrified for her own amusement. She did permit him out of his infirmary at last, though, keeping good on her promise that he would not see the sun until Jack was mended. When he first peeked out onto the deck, he darted back into the hold like a scared rat to let his eyes adjust before daring again the long unseen light; he was nearly as blind as a mole and it would be hours before he could re-enter the world above.

Suspicions of the thief aboard died down briefly while Jack's ascendancy took hold, but after a week the matter re-emerged and haunted the conversation of the men. Little things were found missing: curios, trinkets, keepsakes. Not often, perhaps once a day, someone would complain of a misplaced item, and just as often it would later be found. Suspicion has a way of tainting even the most innocent situations, and soon anything not in immediate sight was suspect of having been stolen, even if it had simply been misplaced or borrowed in good faith.

Jack stewed over the issue and was determined to uncover the scoundrel at fault. Fin told him of her threat to the men and the consequences the man would win and Jack agreed. "He'll wear the mark of the lash," he said.

Fin had not changed in her conviction that shredding a man's flesh was sickening to her. She knew Jack and Armand were right; she knew that a real captain would follow through on his sentence, but she wasn't a real captain.

When at last the weather showed signs of lifting, Jack *creak-clomped* into the cabin and slammed the door shut behind him.

"We got the bugger," he said. "Found him in the lower starboard hold sleeping behind the beans. Made himself a little hooch to live in. Stacked the sacks up like bricks. Had him a bag full of all what's gone missing and didn't even try to explain hisself."

Armand opened the door and slunk in. "Who was it?"

A jagged stone sunk in the pit of Fin's stomach.

"Don't matter who it is. He's a thief. Was Sam Catcher what rooted him out. I ain't been down to see for myself yet."

"So what now?" Fin asked.

Armand approached her like a stalking cat. "You must do as you said, *cherie*. You must deliver him the lash. If you withhold it, then you will lose the crew. You must act." He was almost whispering again.

"We got to sound captain's mast," said Jack. "He's right, Button. It's a dirty thing but it's the way of it."

Armand locked his eyes onto her like an animal sensing the weakness of its prey.

"Do it," she answered and Armand smiled. "Muster the crew in an hour."

"It is the only way, *cherie*."

Fin wasn't so sure. Armand wouldn't be happy about what she was going to do, but he would have to live with it. He wanted her to be a monster. But she knew that despite what he said, it wasn't the only way. She would do it *her* way, like she always had.

The next hour stretched out until Fin thought it would never end. She despised having to put herself on the stage and play a part, and she hated being the focus of attention among a crew of eighty. But there was no way around it. She pulled on one of Creache's old frock coats and dressed to look official. Brass buttons. Tasseled epaulets. Stiff collar. All lies. She wore Tan's rapier and kept Betsy at her waist to look fearsome. Another lie. She pulled her hair back to look neat and proper. Yet another lie. She stood in front of the mirror and wondered how she'd come to this point. She tried to console herself with memories of Peter, hopes of homecoming, and the desire to once again live a simple life. She reminded herself that she only had to endure such things a while longer.

Her hands trembled as she pulled open the gear locker in the corner of the room. Inside it were the tools of a captain: an astrolabe, dividers, sea charts and star charts, an old oar, a tricorne hat, two spyglasses (one broken, one new), and a bandolier of shot and powder. Her hands moved across the items, touching each briefly, as if noting its position and angle, until at last she stopped at the instrument she'd come for: the cat-o'-nine-tails. She took it. Its tethers were stained dark with blood at the ends. Small bits of glass, rock, bone, and metal were twisted and tied into the end of each strap. Her shoulder blades twitched in memory of the pain she'd borne to protect Knut from this same tool of authority. With a shudder, she realized that the blood staining it was her own. A wave of abhorrence washed through her and she involuntarily dropped the lash to the ground. She was close to tears and cursed herself in a whisper. The last thing she wanted was to appear on deck looking weak, like a crying girl. She ground her teeth together and picked it up. She didn't need to fear the weapon. She wasn't going to use it. She would show mercy. She was not a monster.

When the hour had finally gone, Jack found her sitting in the dark considering the lash on the table before her.

"It's time, Button." His voiced betrayed worry, and not for the man about to receive sentence.

Fin stood, straightened her coat, and checked her appearance in the mirror.

"He's strapped to the mast, all you have to do is . . ." He dropped his eyes and didn't finish.

Fin plucked the lash from the table and nodded. She knew what she had to do and was ready to get it over with. Jack turned and left as she walked to the door. Outside, the sounds of the crew jeering the thief and cursing him were cut off by Jack's reappearance on deck.

"Captain on deck," shouted Jack with a stomp of his foot. The world was quiet. Even the wind and the waves seemed to hush. Tied to the mast was a skinny whelp of a man. His back was shirtless and toward her, his arms were drawn high and bound to the mast. He didn't move. He simply hung where he was placed and awaited his torment. His head lolled beside the mast and he didn't look up. He didn't speak, tremble, or even seem to breathe.

Fin could scarcely stomach it. The lash in her hand felt like it was growing heavier by the moment. With every step, it seemed to double in weight. A few more steps and she feared she might drop it and look like a fool.

"Thievery has no place aboard the *Fiddler's Green*," she said. She tried to sound authoritative but failed to convince even herself. "This ship, this crew, and your safe return all depend upon your trust in the man beside you. Thievery betrays that trust and will not be tolerated."

Several men hooted in approval and were eyed into silence by Jack.

"Does the thief wish to say anything before his sentence is carried out?" If he could offer a convincing retraction of his ways it would certainly work to her favor. But the man didn't move or speak.

"He ain't said a word, Captain," explained Jack.

Fin inched forward and called out to the man, determined to have words out of him. "Speak up, sailor!" Wasn't he scared? But for the shallow rise and fall of his chest she'd have thought him dead.

"Captain's talkin'!" growled Jack. "Answer your better, dog!"

On the other side of the mast, Armand stooped down to look the man in the face. He spoke in the harsh whisper that Fin hated. "Speak to your captain and she may withhold the lash," he said, grinning and malevolent. The man raised his head briefly, as if in consideration, but dropped it again without speaking. Fin walked around the mast so she could look him in the eye. He hung his head and held his silence. She addressed him in a calm whisper that the crew watching couldn't hear.

"Speak, sailor. I don't want to do this any more than you want it done."

When he still didn't answer, Armand turned to her. "Do it, *cherie*! You must keep your word. You must do it!" Armand sickened her; he was enjoying it. He was looking forward to seeing the man in pain.

"Why won't you speak?" she asked him.

"*Answer your captain!*" hissed Armand and with gleeful cruelty he grabbed the hair at the back of the man's head and jerked it downward, forcing his face up to Fin. The man's eyes stared up, eerily familiar, then shifted down, away from her. It was Phineas Button.

Fin recoiled. She studied his face hoping to find that the features had changed, that they no longer mirrored her own, but their answer was the same: the man was her father. Part of her wanted to bend down and touch him, wanted to reach out and confirm their kinship with an embrace. But he hung before her in apathy. Lice wriggled across his scalp. He stank. He coughed once and spat, but didn't speak. He wouldn't even look at her. Fin wrinkled her nose in disgust. A fountain of revulsion welled within her. The hate she'd felt when she first saw him returned. *Oh God, why him?* A spasm of vertigo wracked her. Fin staggered against the impossibility she was confronted with. It was impossible that he was here on the *Fiddler's Green* when Armand had put him ashore. It was impossible—impossible that this man who'd made her and abandoned her had found his way through the world to hang before her in judgment. Yet there he hung, matted hair, liar's eyes, and a thief's indifference.

Somewhere outside her small sphere of focus she heard the wicked cackle of Armand. "You must do it, *cherie*!" But his words compelled no action. They didn't have to. The raw anger inside her lightened the weight of the lash and her arm held it high and ready. Her actions didn't seem her own. She no longer controlled her own limbs, hatred did. The appearance of the pitiful man before her kindled something terrible in her heart, and she burned with it.

Armand urged her again and she watched as the lash fell. Some weak thing deep inside Fin's mind cried out and recoiled in horror but it was overwhelmed by the greater part of herself that was livid with rage. The scourge carved a cruel gouge across the flesh that had given her life. Rivers of blood ran across his back, the same blood that flowed through her veins. Fin trembled with satisfaction. Again, and again, and again, her arm wielded torment. Blood flew. Flesh hung from the lash. The ribbons on Phineas Button's back grew longer, deeper, wider. The only sound she could pick out of the air was that of Armand's laughter. But where were the screams, the howls of agony, the pleadings for mercy? There were none. Phineas Button bore the lash in silence, denying her his admission of pain. Again and again the lash flew out, again and again reaping its scarlet harvest. Blood spattered her face; it ran like tears. She tasted it in her mouth like vinegar. She wanted to hear him scream.

Not him. Oh God, not him! He is not a part of me.

Jack grabbed at her. She dodged him and delivered another stroke, spitting a curse at Jack for trying to stop her and another at the bloodied carnage of a man hanging from the mainmast.

"Enough!" shouted Jack. He wrenched the lash from her hand. Fin spun on him and tried to snatch it back. Until Phineas Button screamed for mercy, she wasn't finished. She couldn't explain her anger and couldn't rationalize her actions but she convinced herself that she needed him to admit agony. But even as the thought formed in her mind, she knew that she was lying to herself; she didn't need it, she *wanted* it. She wanted him to cry out, to scream, to hurt. She advanced on Jack trying to get the lash from him. He put out a hand and shoved her backward. The push knocked Fin off her feet and she tumbled against the rail.

Her anger turned on Jack, and she drew Betsy as she jumped to her feet. Jack's eyes narrowed into a warning. The crew watched in bewildered silence. She saw Knut crouched at the rail near the forecastle with his head held between his hands. His mouth was pulled open and his eyes were squeezed shut. He was wailing softly. Then, like a frightened animal coaxed out of its hollow, Fin became herself again. She lowered the gun to her side and looked on the horror she'd worked. Phineas Button hung before her, his body torn, his blood spreading across the deck. Fin shouted for the doctor and walked off the quarterdeck.

In her quarters she froze in front of the mirror. She was covered in nearly as much blood as the man who had bled it. Her hair was caked with it. Her eyes gleamed eerie white out of a sea of red. Tears came. They washed down her face in white rivulets. Hilde's voice: *What have you done?!* Fin wrestled herself out of Creache's coat and hurled it across the room.

Sobbing, she poured water into the basin and tried to scrub herself clean. Soon the water was as red as blood. She threw it out and filled the basin again. She had to change the water twice more before she recognized her face in the mirror. When she turned around and collapsed into a chair at the table, Jack was standing in the doorway.

"What in all bloody hell was that?"

"I don't know," she answered.

"Well I doubt there'll be any more thieving!"

"Leave me alone."

Jack opened his mouth to speak but thought better of it. As he shut the door behind him, Fin got up and dropped the shade on the porthole then blew out the lamp. The darkness was complete.

THE NEXT MORNING, Dr. Thigham reported to Fin's quarters at her summoning. He shuffled inside with timid glances around the room and wrung his hands.

Fin sat in the shadows of the cabin scrubbing her hands with a stiff brush. She could no longer tell if they were bloodstained or merely red from her own scouring, but she didn't stop. When Dr. Thigham cleared his throat to announce himself she spoke without looking up. "I want him brought here, Doctor."

"He musn't be moved, Captain. If he is moved so soon, he will surely—"

"Enough, Thigham! Move him into my quarters and I'll tend him."

"But, Captain—" He bounced back and forth on his feet and wrung his hands furiously.

"That's all, Doctor. If I need anything else, I'll be sure to ask."

Thigham fidgeted a moment longer then shuffled out the door to comply.

Minutes later, Topper and a group of sailors carried Phineas Button through the door and arranged him gently on the cot in the corner of the cabin. He was unconscious, and they laid him on his chest with his head turned to face the room. Bandages covered his back and both arms to the elbows. In spots, blood soaked through the dressings where the wounds had been disturbed during his transport. Fin ordered everyone out of the room and told Topper to have fresh dressings brought.

When the dressings arrived she dismissed Topper, then pulled a chair from the table and sat next to the cot. She was thankful that he was unconscious. She had no idea what she might say to him if he were awake. Fin bent over him and touched his face lightly. High cheekbones, pointed and upturned nose, even freckles. Their likeness was clear. Grey had long since chased most of the red from his hair, but traces of it remained.

Fin unwrapped his bloodied dressings and tossed them in a pile near the door. His flesh was thatched and gouged and thinly scabbed over. She dabbed at the bleeding areas with a clean sponge and then rewrapped him in fresh, white dressings.

When she finished, she lifted his head and turned his face to the wall. His face made her uncomfortable and she couldn't stand the thought that he might open his eyes and see her.

During the night she lay awake, deviled by the memory of what she'd done. She recalled Armand, recalled how he'd enjoyed it, how he'd urged her to it. He'd known the man was her father and still he'd pressed her. Jack knew nothing of the man, but Armand—Armand should have warned her.

She sent for him the next morning and he swaggered in wearing his filthy grin. He was proud of himself—or proud of her. She didn't know which she would despise him for more.

"Why didn't you stop me?" she asked as he sat down.

"Do you think I could have, *cherie?*"

"Stop calling me that."

He leaned closer to her and lowered his voice. "Do you believe that anything could have stopped you?" Fin turned her head away and ground her teeth. "Now your power over men is absolute. They will die for you. You have become their fear. You should thank me, *cherie*. You will need their help before the end. The blood of a man you hate is a petty price to pay for such a thing."

"Even if that man is my own father?"

"*Especially* if he is your father." His grin was gone. His voice was low, steady, and certain. "What does it matter? It is done."

"I won't be like you, Armand. I will not become a monster."

His response was barely audible. "Ah, but you already are, *cherie*. You already are."

"Don't call me that." Her voice barely managed a reply at all. The words escaped her like a leper's groan.

He bowed his head in assent. "As you wish, *mon Capitaine*."

"Get out."

How did he always manage to make sense? He was right, wasn't he? She'd only done what was necessary. Nothing more. The crew would think her weak had she not. Armand always made sense. But she always felt uneasy when she listened to him. Fin couldn't see the end of the road he was steering her down, but she began to fear that no map could lead her back.

CHAPTER NINE

THE FOLLOWING DAYS WERE marked by fortunate weather. The sun returned and a strong wind with it. If the wind held, they could reach Gibraltar in just over a week. With the capture of the thief and the return of the crew's belongings, tension eased on the ship and spirits lifted. That was well because battle loomed. Gibraltar meant the end of the Atlantic and the beginning of the Barbary threat.

During the weeks since the ship had embarked, the subject of what awaited them at the end of the crossing had been kept a mystery. The crew rumored all sorts of speculation on why they were paid so well to cross the Atlantic with nothing to trade or sell. Some said they were bound for Africa to take on slaves. Others scoffed at that and whispered that one of the crew was a spy to be delivered to London to assassinate the king and end the war. Others muttered that Captain Button was to lead the French against England and take the throne for herself.

Fin had strictly instructed the few who knew the truth to keep silent. The truth would be more terrible to the men than any rumor they contrived among themselves. Stories of the Barbary pirates and their wickedness ran thicker in the blood of sailors than any barroom talk of her alleged exploits.

With the lightening of the crew's mood and the boon of fair weather as omens, Fin called a meeting with Jack, Armand, and Topper to lay plans.

"Don't suppose any of you've been to Tripoli?" Fin asked as they sat at the table considering a map of the Mediterranean. Each of the men shook his head. "Well, I certainly haven't. I don't see why we shouldn't just make port as a merchant, secure the countess, and be gone as quick as we come."

Jack scratched at his beard. "The Barbarie don't suffer their women to show their faces, far less to captain a ship. We best hide you or disguise you, Button," he said.

"You thought I was a boy for months and I wasn't even trying to fool you," said Fin.

Jack grunted.

Armand pursed his lips and kneaded his half-hand. "What you suggest will suffice, but we must prepare for the complication of simplicity. It is my experience that things are never simple."

Fin nodded. "But none of us have been to the city. We can't very well guess where the countess is. And until we know that, we can't make plans to retrieve her."

Jack grunted again then spoke. "What we do know is that we're like to have all hell on our heels leaving port. And *that* we can plan for." Jack straightened up in his chair and thumped Topper on the back. "Topper and me will drill the crew. We'll be ready as can be on the cannons and battle stations. When we get to Tripoli, the crew will stay aboard and be ready to make way in a hurry when the time comes. I'll see that they know what to expect and what to do."

Topper nodded in agreement. "Aye. We'll have her standing by when you come running. Though, we best hold that action till the wind and tide favor us." Jack voiced a guttural agreement.

Armand straightened his back and leaned forward. He drew his lips tight. Fin and Jack raised their brows and waited for him to voice the thoughts he kept.

"What is it, Armand?" As little as Fin liked his advice, his experience was valuable. "Out with it. If you've something to say, then say it."

His thin lips parted and let out a breath that whistled across his teeth. His voice followed it, flowing out of him like a poisonous wisp.

"We chase the wind, *cherie*." Fin bristled at his tone and his name for her. The sly, lecherous grin that usually accompanied him was gone.

A cool pallor on his face and a barely discernable quaver in his voice convinced her that his declaration was one of honest dread. "What we endeavor is a lunatic dream. To walk in the black man's land and take from him the prize of his house? Sheep in the slaughterhouse, *cherie*. Men will die. And the dead will be the fortunate. These moors are slavers. Their ancestors have despoiled the world for a thousand generations. Nations cower before them. No man can win this prize. We will find no pardon in this, only death."

"You've heard one too many sailor's tales," said Fin. "We fought the British navy and lived to tell of it. Why should we be afraid of a rabble of pirates?"

Armand's face knurled into an angry glare. "You know nothing, girl! You begin to believe your own shadow."

"Mind your manner, Defain," said Jack. He backed it up with a faint growl. "I'm with Fin on this. I've heard plenty of dire tell about these pirates but can't see how half of it is true. If you know something more than a drunkard's tale then let's out with it. Otherwise, clam up and keep your ill wind to yourself."

Armand spat. "Would it sway you then to know that Tiberius Creache himself was wizened by his scars on the Barbary and never sailed it again in his life? He was as cunning and cruel a man as any to sail the west but he feared the Coast and would not trespass it."

The group sat in silent consideration. Fin knew Armand was somehow associated with Creache. It was why he was here to begin with, why he had agreed to help her. Revenge. But his revenge was satisfied.

"How do you know what Creache was afraid of?" said Fin.

Armand pushed away from the table. He stood up and paced the room. He held his half-hand in his whole one and kneaded the cloven flesh like a man trying to wake up a limb gone to sleep and needles.

"How does a man know his brother fears the dark?" he whispered. His words hung in the air and drew out questions. "Tiberius and I were children, together in the world as far back as my mind can paint the picture." He turned to look at Fin and saw the trouble on her face. "No, not brothers by blood. A brotherhood of necessity. He taught me to speak his English and I showed him how to pick a gentleman's pocket, how to relieve a lady of her jewels, how to slip a knife between a man's ribs so that he dies without crying out. The first blood he spilt was with my blessing and instruction. Gamins we were, scavenging the filth of the rich in the alleyways and tenements of New Orleans. When our faces grew too familiar to pass freely in the city, we went to sea and learned the life of the pirate. We were like kings in those days. We followed each of us our own passions but always we came together again.

"He spent a season in the Mediterranean, and when he returned he was covered in a shadow. Something horrid and black fed upon him and grew while my brother dwindled. It was the long arm of the Barbarie. He grappled with them both on land and sea, and what he saw haunted him. Think you, what manner of thing haunts a man such as he? He never spoke of it, not even to me. But he learned from them ways of cruelty and war that served him, served us, well. Never would he sail the Coast again. He shunned it. No profit and no prize could draw him to it.

"You ask me how I know? I know because I knew my brother's heart. A heart so black and terrible as his feared nothing short of hellfire and the devil's very teeth. Yet he feared these Barbarie and so, then, shall I."

Fin and Jack passed a worried look between them. Fin was glad to finally hear answers out of Armand, but his revelation presented more questions than it satisfied.

"If that's true then why were you so eager to see Creache dead?"

Armand returned to kneading his half-hand. "There was another. A third." Armand stopped pacing and fixed his slitted eyes on Fin. Gooseflesh rose on her skin. Fin was suddenly uncomfortable and shifted in her seat. "He betrayed us. Bart Gann. Your Bartimaeus."

Fin's mouth dropped open and Jack's bushy eyebrows crawled halfway up his forehead.

"He was the best of us. The mediator, the peacemaker. He was wretched as any pirate of the main, but he had a nature about him that was different, gentle." Armand shrugged. "The whores loved him for it.

"When I learned he'd disappeared with our gold, I wasn't even surprised. It was like him somehow. Thought it was clever, in fact. But Tiberius didn't take it so well. He was enraged. Lunatic. Got it in his mind that I had helped him, that I was in on it, and then—" he lowered his head and stretched out the remaining fingers of his hand. "The darkness of the Barbarie. He took my flesh. He chained me to the mast and ordered me to tell him where Bart had gone. I told him the truth, that I did not know, and he took his boots to me. I told him lies to make him stop, but he saw them through and laid his knives upon me. And he cut. And he did not stop his cutting. Do you know the inescapability of such torment? A man's mind is not made for it; it must twist and bend to survive it." As he spoke he unbuttoned his shirt and removed it. His torso was a waxy thatch of scars.

"He made of my body a ruin and when he had done his work upon me, he spat on my head and abandoned me to the justice of King George. I prayed for death. I cursed his name and Bart's every night in my prayers, and years on end their curses I sang until at last the dream of vengeance came to warm me. And you, *cherie*, you are my salvation. So I will follow you, even unto the Barbary Coast. But I tell you plainly that I go in fear. Heed me, *cherie*, you must be sly, sly as the fox, else we are lost."

WHEN THE SUN CAME up the next morning, Topper rang the bell and ordered the crew to battle stations. To Jack's displeasure and no one's surprise, the drill was disastrous. Some men slept through it. Some ran amok on deck wondering where they ought to get to. Most meandered to their stations with eyes rolled up and muttered foolishness on their tongues.

When Jack saw how sadly the drill was progressing, he tried to charge the nearest sluggard but lost his footing when his leg came clean off. He cursed Fin's ears red as he hop-crawled across the deck to retrieve his mechanical leg then hurled it at the poor sailor hard enough that he might have killed him had his aim been true.

When he'd got his leg back on and was upright once more, Jack was red with anger, and his entire body was aquiver. A thick purple vein bulged out on his forehead and throbbed under his skin like a drum. "What in the flaming blue hell was that?" shouted Jack. The crew gathered around him on the main deck and Jack *creak*-stomped through the crowd, pointing his finger and jabbing his chin out at each of them. "Do a one of you filthy greens know the call to battle stations? Beat to arms? Any heard of it?"

A timid hand rose among the crew. Jack's eyes widened and he pushed his way through the crowd to see whom it might belong to. When he'd come close enough, his eyes traced their way down the offending arm and found that it was connected to the body of Lucas Thigham. The doctor trembled and blinked madly behind his spectacles.

A roar sputtered around in the back of Jack's throat. The crew, who had learned to associate this sound with the onset of considerable unpleasantry, slowly moved back to create a small circle around Jack and the doctor.

"You know the drill, do you?" said Jack through clenched teeth.

The doctor spoke as if he was in a great hurry to get his words out him. "The call, 'beat to arms', is given upon the suspicion of any perceived danger to the ship or crew. Gunners to the gun deck, hands to the armory for issuance of weaponry and then to battle stations as assigned by the first mate or captain. I have read a great deal about such things as they are related by Lord Dunsinger in his exhaustive work on the life of the nautical man entitled *The Life of the Nautical Man: An Exhaustive Work*."

"And what did your book say about where the ship's surgeon ought to find himself when he hears the call, eh?" As Jack spoke, the doctor began to back away but Jack seized his coat and drew him up onto his toes.

Dr. Thigham opened and closed his mouth in puzzlement as he considered this new question. "I . . . I . . . the ship's surgeon? I fear Lord Dunsinger had little to say upon the matter." Jack began to growl again. The doctor blinked hugely behind his spectacles. "I should venture to think that the surgeon's place ought to be in the surgery."

Jack eased the doctor back to the ground, released his coat, and smiled briefly. Then he stooped over and bellowed in Thigham's face so loudly that the fragile doctor's eyes fluttered in fear and he nearly swooned. "THEN WHY IN THE DEVIL'S LIVER ARE YOU ON DECK AND NOT IN THE SURGERY?" Jack grabbed the doctor by the shoulder, spun him around to face the nearest hatch, and kicked him smartly in the rear with his real leg. The doctor cried out and ran for the surgery as fast as his spindly legs would take him.

The rest of the crew split like birds from a gunshot and made for their respective stations with rare determination. The rest of the day was filled with the ringing of bells, the pounding of feet, and the thunder of Jack's displeasure.

As captain, Fin was free of the commotion. She retreated to her quarters to let Jack, Armand, and Topper deal with the drilling of the crew. Armand's tale about Bartimaeus and Creache was still heavy in her mind. She couldn't reconcile her memories of Bartimaeus with the tales she'd heard from Creache and Armand. Had it all been a lie? And if so, which part was the lie: the pirate or the cook?

Phineas Button let out a faint groan and shifted in his sleep. Fin stood over him and considered the lines of his face. She saw her eyes, her nose, even a hitch in the shoulders that she recognized as her own. The brow, though, was strange to her; so, too, the jawline. She imagined that those were features her mother had given her and her heart leapt.

"Why didn't you want me?" she whispered.

His bandages were bled through. She lifted his arm and unraveled them, taking care to ease them apart when they stuck. She put the rags aside and dressed them with new linens then laid the dressed limb back upon the bed. The rest of his bandages needed changing as well, but she would have to send for more. When she walked toward the door, he spoke.

"She wanted to keep you."

Fin stopped and closed her eyes, gritted her teeth. She didn't turn to face him. His voice was brittle and slurred, drink-ruined.

"Prayed for you when she thought I didn't hear." His voice struggled through the sounds of the ship to find her, and the sound of it, even broken, wracked, and fragile, made her chest swell with questions and emotions, years of anger and hope.

"Daughter," he said. But it was an empty croak. Like a thing rehearsed, something of mere fact but no real account. She wanted to throw her hands over her ears and rip the word out of her mind. She wanted to un-hear it. But she couldn't and it felt like a searing iron in her skull. The word opened up an abyss inside of her and she cowered away from it, terrified of its unseen depths. She wanted to scream. She wanted to run. Worst of all, she wanted to turn to Phineas Button—she wanted to go to him, she wanted him to put his arms around her so she could know how it felt to be wanted, to be home.

"Daughter," he croaked again. The dark chasm in her heart widened and yawned and she shrank from it.

Fin smashed the door open and fled. She retreated up the main mast into the tops and cried for a long time where the wind could hide her sobs.

CHAPTER TEN

THE ISLAND OF MADEIRA lay a week's fair weather west of Gibraltar. For the *Fiddler's Green* it would be the only stop of the crossing. When the ship slipped into the port city of Funchal with its glistening limestone edifices and green hills, the crew was hungry for it. Not only had they been shut up and driven nearly sea-mad by six weeks underway, but each and every sailor aboard knew the name Madeira and held it precious. Madeira was the isle of wine—the best in the world.

But Armand reminded Fin that where sailors and wine run free, tongues are set loose. A loose tongue could arouse suspicion. So to the dissatisfaction of the crew, she would give no leave to go ashore. The risk was too great. The *Fiddler's Green* was in port for one reason only: to send a man into the city to learn what he could of the waters ahead.

Topper alone walked down the plank and onto the crowded quay, and Fin put her captaincy into exercise in order to calm a rowdy crew. When she emerged from her quarters to answer the angry calls from the deck, she was fully prepared. She'd tied her hair back and rolled it up under a white-rimmed hat. To cover her canvas pants and filthy, once-blue shirt, she wore a long coat stitched with lace and fastened with tarnished brass buttons. The coat and hat were Creache's; she felt monstrous and small within his clothes, and they smelled of him. Tan's rapier hung at her side, and the final piece of the costume was Betsy. She tucked the blunderbuss into the front of her belt and let it go before her, prominent and threatening.

"Give leave or we'll take it!" shouted an angry sailor from the forecastle. An eruption of cheers answered him.

Fin put her hands behind her back and issued an order. "Withdraw the plank, Mr. Wagon."

Jack aye-ayed. He pulled the plank away from the pier and dropped it to the deck alongside the rail. None of the crew protested outright but a smatter of grumbling made its rounds.

Fin drew in a deep breath and tried to speak loudly enough to be heard but calmly enough to sound confident and in control. "We've no time to grant leave ashore. We are needed at our destination and haven't time to spare either for your leisure or mine."

"And what's Topper got leave for?" shouted a young sailor. Fin didn't even know his name.

"His business is mine and not yours. He will be done with it before nightfall. We sail on the morning tide."

This declaration was not taken well. Men stamped their feet and riled each other up with protests and indignation. Fin expected just such behavior. Armand and Jack had warned her.

"I will remind you that every hand knew this crossing would have its peculiars. Every man agreed to abide them." The deck quieted. "In reward for your agreement, I have instructed Mr. Topper not to return until he has procured for us three barrels of Madeira wine."

The grumbling ceased. Several men's eyes widened. One whooped. A smatter of cheering began and washed across the deck. In sharp contrast to the mood only moments before, the deck erupted in chaotic declarations of Captain Button's vast and terrible virtue then coalesced into a raucous pageant of singing and dancing. The wine hadn't even arrived yet.

Fin tried to raise her voice above the din to regain the attention of the crew but it was pointless. She deferred to Jack. He stomped his good leg thrice upon the deck and loosed an elephantine roar that brought the whole affair to an abrupt stop.

"Thank you, Mr. Wagon," said Fin and then addressed the crew. "You have leave to take your leisure and your wine until daybreak. But understand that no man is permitted to go ashore and anyone who attempts to do so will be put off the ship without pay or compensation."

Fin didn't know what else to say and was anxious to get out of Creache's clothes. She nodded at Jack to let him know she was satisfied. As she retreated, he put the crew at ease.

Once in her cabin, Fin removed the coat and hat and opened the corner locker to put them away. The scourge hung on its nail, accusatory and blood-crusted, an affront to her conscience. She hung the coat and hat to hide it then removed Betsy from her belt and placed it back in its case. She laid Tan's rapier across the table.

Across the room, Phineas Button lay awake. He coughed and wheezed and cast dispassionate glances in her direction. Though Fin despised him, hated him even, wanted him gone, she still had the undeniable urge to keep him close. She had questions and wanted to demand explanations. Soon he'd be fit enough to care for himself and he'd be gone again.

Fin dragged her chair to the bedside. She looked at him. He met her eyes but only briefly. When she sat down, he erupted into a spasm of coughing. Fin watched coldly as he shook and wheezed. He curled his fingers into an arthritic fist and raised it to cover his mouth and wipe away the spume on his lips. When he eased himself back onto his pillow, he turned his eyes to the wall. His breath rattled as he drew it. It came out of him like the rasp of iron on a whetstone. His matted beard twisted across his face, hiding the deep hollows of his cheeks behind a tangle of reddened roots. His eyes were sunken and underslung with great bags gone purplish brown with age. He was a miserable and wretched sight.

"Where is my mother?" Fin's question was empty of hope, uttered without the expectation of an answer.

He didn't look at her. He worked his mouth around, sending his beard into a fit of twitches and shudders. Spittle hung from his mustache.

"The smallpox," he said. He shifted and almost met her eyes before he turned back to the wall. He nodded softly to himself, periodically grunting as if agreeing to a silent argument in his mind.

"Tell me her name."

He continued nodding to himself, the movements of his head becoming sharper, more insistent. He cleared his throat and spoke. "Matilda-Mae."

The sound of her mother's name washed over Fin, it rang in her ears like a musical note. Silently, she formed the name on her lips as if she might taste it. The knowledge of the name itself suggested a form to her, a face, a color, a scent. She could never know what her mother looked like, but the name painted a picture in her mind that she could believe in. She imagined a woman, tall and square-shouldered with a graceful neck and hair that tumbled down in wheat-colored ropes. If she tried to imagine her too specifically the image fell apart, but she caught glimpses, impressions: a smile on thin lips, a forehead creased with worry, slender hands, calloused but elegant. Fin even caught an ephemeral wisp of laughter, a raspy sound, mingled with notes of sadness. She said the name aloud. "Matilda-Mae Button." It was sweet on her tongue and Fin chased after the phantoms it conjured in her mind.

Phineas Button lifted a gnarled hand and gestured in the air. His fingers moved up and down in a counting motion. "Lucy first. Then Bella." He raised his hand as he said the names and nodded his head, jerking his chin sharply down to his chest. "'Tilda was third, 'Tilda-Mae." He waved his hand in front of him like a man trying to clear a stench from the air. "All of them."

"Who?" said Fin.

"Gone. Lucy, Bella, Isannah, Ellen-Mae . . ." He broke into another fit of coughing. Fin raised her hand and leaned forward as if to comfort him somehow but hesitated, refused.

"Who are Lucy, Bella, and Ellen-Mae? Are they my sisters? Where have they gone?"

"The smallpox," he said through his coughing.

Fin leaned further forward and took hold of his shoulders. She shook him until he looked at her. "Are they dead? Tell me."

"All gone to the pox."

She wouldn't let him turn away, but his eyes wouldn't settle. They glanced at hers only moments before jumping to the right, to the left, always shifting.

Fin's lips stiffened. She was afraid she might begin to sob. She gritted her teeth and shook him until she could speak. "Why are you here? Why?" A dark, abyssal emptiness widened inside of her and the word 'daughter' billowed out of it. His eyes darted, circled her face, considered everything in her periphery but wouldn't consider her. He forced his head to the side and lay limp in her arms until she released him.

Fin rose and crossed the room to Betsy's case. She placed it on the table and unlatched it. Phineas Button followed her movements with his eyes.

"I have one more question for you." Fin's heart hammered in her chest; she felt the beating of it in her ears. "Sister Carmaline—at the orphanage—she told me why you left me there." Fin held the question on her lips. She rolled it across her tongue, tasting it—cold, bitter, like the tang of metal. When she was certain she wanted to spew it, certain she could abide its answer, she gave it life and breathed it out. "If I had been a boy, would you have kept me?"

The question hung between them like a tendril of lightning, capable of both illumination and destruction. Fin lifted the case open and laid her hands on Betsy's cool barrel. She traced its lines with her fingers, caressed it. Phineas Button shrank into the linens of the bed and clutched his hands to his chest. He cleared his throat but did not speak. Instead he held his eyes upon her at last and answered with a single decisive nod of affirmation.

Fin's blood cooled. If he had lied to her, if he'd made excuses, she might have killed him. The truth, however, was his pardon and his damnation both. She raised the fiddle and bow out of the case, closed the lid, and went to the door.

Before she walked out, she turned to him. His eyes were wild again, scattered around the room, fixing on everything but her. She didn't wait for him to see her. She no longer cared.

"Then I am an orphan still," she said.

Fin left the captain's cabin and went to the crew. Bartimaeus had taught her long ago what to do with grief.

Turn it to beauty.

CHAPTER ELEVEN

FIN DESCENDED ONTO THE quarterdeck, fiddle in hand. The crew parted before her and their carousing ground to a halt. Mutters and warnings of "captain on deck," passed among them as the eyes of men twice her age and some three times her size followed her steps. A voice whispered that she no longer had it within her to make the fiddle sing. The voice was Creache's; it was Hilde's; it was Armand's. It was Phineas Button's. In response, she called on her sacred memories of Bartimaeus and replayed them again and again in her mind.

Turn it beautiful.

His words came faintly at first, but they came again and again, always softly, always with the insistence of an elder commanding wisdom.

Turn it all to beauty.

She walked to the rail. When she turned and sat upon it, she heard a sailor in the crowd murmur that she might play them a tune. She hoped he was right. She needed the voices to be wrong.

Fin raised the instrument to the cleft of her neck and closed her eyes. She emptied her mind and let herself be carried back to her earliest memory, the first pain she ever knew: the knowledge that her parents didn't want her. The despair of rejection coursed through her. It fathered a knot of questions that bound her, enveloped her. Waves of uncertainty and frailty shook her to the bones. Her body quivered with anger and hopelessness. She reeled on the edge of a precipice. She wanted to scream or to throw her fists but she held it inside; she struggled to control it. She fought to subjugate her pain, but it grew. It welled up; it filled her mind. When she could hold it no more, exhausted by defiance and wearied by years of pretending not to care, Bartimaeus's words surrounded her.

Got to turn it beautiful.

She dropped her defenses. She let weakness fill her. She accepted it. And the abyss yawned. She tottered over the edge and fell. The forces at war within her raced down her arms and set something extraordinary in motion; they became melody and harmony: rapturous, golden. Her fingers coaxed the long-silent fiddle to life. They danced across the strings without hesitation, molding beauty out of the miraculous combination of wood, vibration, and emotion. The music was so bright she felt she could *see* it. The poisonous voices were outsung. Notes raged out of her in a torrent. She had such music within her that her bones ached with it, the air around her trembled with it, her veins bled it. The men around fell still and silent. Some slipped to the deck and sat enraptured like children before a travelling bard.

The pain of abandonment ran its course and Bartimaeus flooded her mind. His rescuing of her, his face as he called Betsy back to life after so many years of silence, his smile as the rope snapped his neck. Every creaky laugh, every fatherly admonishment, every smile between them erupted from the fiddle in a billowing crescendo of grief and love. Broken strands of hair hung from the bow in locks, dancing, sweeping from side to side, driven by the ethereal shape of the song. The music evolved. It became Peter's: gentle, quiet, and steady, like the flow of rivers or the crystalline gaze of mountains. The rhythm of his hammer and the cadence of his voice ordered her notes into their places and sent them winding forth, out into the morning air.

The crew gathered around her in awe as the song grew. One man, a sea-hardened old salt, stretched out a darkened arm and touched her upon the ankle. He withdrew his hand and placed it to his lips. Light shimmered across his face. It was as if he had just remembered the most precious thing in his life and could see it before him.

The song continued to build and change and fill the air. More strands of the bow's hair frayed until they swirled, thick and wild. Fin didn't notice; she was deep inside the song, insulated from everything around her. She was running through an endless green field toward familiar voices. They called out a strange name as if it were her own. Her clothes were clean, her body strong, her lungs full of lilac air. Tan gave her music now. She fashioned it out of his friendship, out of the pain of his death. The gaping wound in his chest became a blossom of flowers sanguine as a sun in its last decline. Creache, too, came into the song. He fed it with cruelty and hatred, and it exploded in an effulgence of sound as he dwindled into silence.

When the people of her past had come and gone, the music became less specific. It throbbed and pulsed, channeled by elemental forces of fear, love, hope, and sadness. The bow stabbed and flitted across the strings in a violent whorl of creation; its hairs tore and split until it seemed the last strands would sever in a scrape of dissonance. Those who saw the last fragile remnants held their breath against the breaking. The music rippled across the ship like a spirit, like a thing alive and eldritch and pregnant with mystery. The song held. More than held, it deepened. It groaned. It resounded in the hollows of those who heard. Then it softened into tones long, slow, and patient and reminded men of the faintest stars trembling dimly in defiance of a ravening dark. At the last, when the golden hairs of the bow had given all the sound they knew, the music fled in a whisper. Fin was both emptied and filled, and the song sighed away on the wind.

She lowered the fiddle and opened her eyes. The crew was ringed around her like a halo. They didn't move or speak but remained still, many with their heads canted to one side, straining to hear the last dwindling notes as they fled. She took hold of the moment and cherished it with them, with her crew. Fin noted their faces, each one, men who had come to follow her. No matter what their reasons at the beginning, they were here now and they were hers. They would fight for her, and some would die for her. She picked out the round meaty face of a boy and committed it to her memory. She noted another, middle-aged with deep lines in his face, his skin burnt dark by the sun. And yet another, old enough to be her grandfather, his deep grey eyes reflecting memories of a hundred crossings and a thousand ports. She found Jack, all somber and swarth, standing at the mast, rapt as all the rest. Then she saw Knut leaning against the rail opposite her and picking at something in his ear. Seeing him made her smile, and she recalled her first days aboard the *Rattlesnake*. She'd been almost carefree then; Knut still was. The sight of him picking at his ears and nose made her laugh. At her cue, the crew joined her in mirth, and as they returned to their merrymaking, she heard Topper on the pier calling out for the plank.

With him was a wagoneer and his cargo of three black casks of Madeira wine. Fin ordered the men to bring them aboard, and as they hurried to oblige she retreated into her quarters to restring her bow.

She returned to the deck, and as the bung was tapped and the wine began to flow, she took joy in music again and played for the merriment of the crew until mid-afternoon. When she retired to her quarters, Phineas Button was gone. Fin felt herself lighten. The emptiness of the bed where he'd lain was a relief and the cabin seemed altogether brighter in his absence. Whether he had gone below to join the crew or had gone ashore to seek a fairer berth, she didn't care. He knew nothing of her mission and in all likelihood would only seek the bottom of a rum bottle and his own misery. Good riddance.

She placed the fiddle back into its case with a smile, snapped the lid shut, and stowed it under the bed. Someone knocked at the door.

"Come."

Jack crammed his head in.

"Topper's got news of the Coast."

Fin nodded and he entered followed by Topper and Armand. Topper's face didn't seem troubled. That was good news. But the front of his shirt was powdered with some kind of white dust. He noted Fin studying him and attempted to swat the powder off his shirt.

"What on earth have you got into, Topper?"

His eyes rolled up and he moaned. "Pastries. Oh, they were this big"—he made a circle with his hands, one that Fin had to admit indicated a respectable pastry—"and covered in cane sugar and molasses and stuffed with something that was soft and creamy and smelt like heaven. Fin you got to try—"

"Did you find the pastries while you were buying the wine or while you were sniffing the locals for news of the Coast?" said Jack.

"A tavern ain't the only place a man can find some news, you know. In fact I plied the baker's daughter for the better part of the morning and discovered all manner of useful information."

"Oh you did, did you?" Jack didn't look convinced.

"What did you find out?" asked Fin.

"Learnt you can get a tasty commission transporting Madeira wine, and we talked quite a bit about selling some of them fine pastries back in Charleston. Not sure they'll keep, but I offered to take a crate along with us to find out. 'Fraid the baker wasn't so pliable as his daughter, though. He threatened to toss me in his oven if I didn't leave off." Topper frowned and then discovered a bit of molasses gummed on one finger. He stuck the finger in his mouth and sucked on it.

"About the Coast, Topper," said Jack with a stomp of his wooden foot.

Topper removed his finger from his mouth and hid it behind his back. "Oh, right! The Coast. Well, seems that any English, Dutch, or French ship that gets within a hundred miles of the Coast has a good chance of falling to pirates. But the Spaniards, I hear, have paid their duty to the pasha within the month, so their ships got fair sailing as far west as Joppa."

"And you heard all this from the baker's daughter, eh?" said Armand.

"I did, in fact. But I also heard it from the butcher, a fancy German strudel maker, an Italian pie man, and a monger of the finest melons I ever saw."

"Not a whit of it does us good," said Jack.

Fin disagreed. "It does us all the good in the world, Jack. If the Spaniards have safe passage, then all we need is a Spanish flag."

Jack was about to say something but he raised his brow and snapped his mouth shut. Armand nodded and Topper went back to sucking on his finger.

THE FORGERY AND FRAUDULENT hoist of a nation's flag was an offense notably despised by maritime powers, and as such, a Spanish merchant's ensign was not something easily bought without following the proper procedures and providing all the necessary paperwork. Fin had no paperwork at all and no intent to go anywhere near proper procedure. She sent Topper once more ashore, this time with a shopping list, a full coin purse, and a warning not to spend it on pastries.

When Topper returned at dusk with a bolt of fresh bleached woolen cloth and a measure each of red and yellow dye, Fin found a use at last for her years of forced stitchwork and textile instruction under Sister

Hilde. She retreated to her cabin and spent the night dying the cloth and stitching together a passable ensign.

She emerged the next morning with her fingers raw from needle pricks and stained purple by dye. It took her the greater part of the night to finish her work, but in the end she was pleased with it. Five horizontal stripes: two red, three yellow. It was plain, simple, and most importantly, indistinguishable from an official Spanish merchant's ensign.

Jack called the crew to muster and gave them a brief inspection to ensure all were present. Phineas Button was among them. Fin was surprised he'd remained aboard. He didn't look at her, didn't even bother to pick his eyes up from the deck. Fin expected to feel disgust when she looked at him but she didn't. She didn't feel much of anything. He was just another hand, sorry though he may be. She gave the order to throw off lines and get underway. The *Fiddler's Green* followed the tide out and chased down the sea toward Gibraltar.

As they drew closer to the strait, they sighted more and more ships. The entire flow of commerce into and out of the Mediterranean funneled down to the narrow channel separating Europe from northern Africa. At a mere three leagues wide, even the smallest blockade of the strait could bring Mediterranean trade to a standstill. West of Gibraltar lay the Atlantic, the sailing route of the world, but pass through it and the waters for a thousand miles became the prowl of Barbary pirates. It was a gateway to a world ancient and mysterious, a world that stretched back through history, past the age of Charlemagne, past the Caesars, past even Rome and Christ himself, a world of civilizations that had raised pyramids and worshipped dark gods and now spoke only in timeless whispers etched in the crumble of ruins.

When they entered the throat of the strait on the fifth morning underway, fog settled thick and low and constricted the air. Fin kept the helm with Topper while Jack paced the deck like a caged animal. A young sailor named Billy Wright perched on the bowsprit with a lantern held aloft in the mist. The wind was steady and easterly but they couldn't use it; the trade fleets of the dozens of nations converging on the waters of the passage rendered the fog perilous. If the ship outran its lights and bells, it wouldn't see an approaching ship or the jagged rocks of the strait before it was too late. As Jack paced by the mast each time, he struck the bell to warn away any ship hidden in the grey space around them. The peal slapped across the waves and died in the fog like a song muffled in a closet.

Though Fin couldn't see it, she felt the closeness of land around her. From beyond the grey veil she could sense the oppressive weight of two great continents crowding down to the sea, each to kneel and contemplate the nearness of an ancient earthen brother.

Occasionally, other bells answered Jack's toll, and ghost-like, amid otherworldly creaks and gentle splashes, another ship would coalesce out of the fog. The crews would stare across the colorless water to appraise each other in silence before dissolving again into nothingness.

At mid-morning a faint darkness approached from the port side. It grew and towered above them. Young men on deck made the sign of the cross and muttered prayers. The Rock of Gibraltar loomed. It penetrated the dim-lit grey air and rose, dark and immovable, jutting through the fog. The great promontory stabbed out of the gloom like a wedge driven into the heavens. It dominated the sky, the sea, everything around it. The mount was a signpost struck into the air to warn all passers that they were at a point of transition. A point that divided one sea from another, divided the land of the Arab and Moor from the land of the Anglo-Sax. They were now sailors in a stranger's sea.

The rock slipped behind them, into the west, and Fin ordered the Spanish ensign hoisted while the fog could conceal their treachery.

"A week's sail to Tripoli," said Jack. "A week to make ready."

THE SEA WIDENED BEYOND the strait. It lay in a calm blue sheet, unlike the chopping grey of the Atlantic. They sighted ships night and day, sometimes four and five at a time, but each they saw was content to keep to itself. No one came near and most made course changes to keep their distance.

On Armand's advice, Fin doubled the third watch. The crew grumbled over the change, but they abided it. They knew as well as she did that their biggest threat came at night when pirates could slip upon them unseen.

Four days east of Gibraltar, a sailor of the watch spotted a pillar of smoke on the southern horizon. The crew gathered at the starboard rail and stared at it in silence. A thin black finger snaked up from the sea some leagues distant. Fin stepped up beside Jack and shaded her eyes as she looked at it.

"What do you think it is?"

Jack chewed his bottom lip a while before answering.

"Could be whalers. Could be a signal fire. Could be near about anything."

"The Barbarie," said Armand. Fin cut her eyes over at him as he sidled up to the rail beside her. Jack didn't speak up to disagree.

"Could be anything," said Fin in protest. "All the same, we'd best double the drills."

Jack nodded. "Aye."

Fin took in a deep breath and whistled it out. "Tomorrow I'll talk to the crew. I'll tell them where we're bound and what we mean to do."

Chapter Twelve

FIN RAN HER HAND across the railing, feeling its texture: pitted, worn, scarred, but solid. She lifted her hand and inspected her fingers for dirt. They were clean. Jack considered her inspection from beneath his furrowed and bristly eyebrows. Nearby, a young crewman named Roberts gulped and held his breath. He'd finished his task of scouring the rail and polishing the port side brass and wrung a soiled rag in his hands as he awaited Fin's judgment.

Fin dropped her hand without speaking and moved forward along the rail to a freshly polished brass cleat. She scarcely believed it was the same cleat she'd used a hundred times herself, so high was the polish. She frowned at it and heard another distinct gulp from Roberts.

She rubbed the cleat with her thumb and asked, "How long did it take you to polish this, Roberts?"

Roberts popped his eyes wide at the question and scratched his head. "Can't have took terrible long, Captain. You want I should polish it again?"

"I want that you should teach Mister Simmons how to polish proper. He started the starboard brass at the same time yet it isn't half done, nor done half so well."

Mister Roberts stamped one foot on the deck and slapped himself in the chest. "Aye, Captain! I can teach him good. You want I should kick him some? I got good boots for kickin'. I'll show him how to do. I'll show him to rub it 'round in tiny circles and spit on what needs spat, and I'll knuckle him up and kick him wise if I got to. Just 'tween me and you, Captain, I think I seen Mr. Simmons sitting down a bit ago to take him a break when wasn't no one looking and—"

"Quiet up, Roberts. Keep your boots to yourself and do like the captain says!" said Jack. Roberts smacked his mouth shut and trotted across the deck in search of Simmons.

"The 'Snake's fitter than I ever seen her. The men are sharp." Jack shifted his eyes briefly toward the starboard. "Except maybe that Simmons."

Fin nodded. "It's a wonder we ever ran her with so few of us."

"No wonder about it. Was hard work and good seamanship. Twenty men, together as one, men that know each other's minds. Men like that can run circles round a green crew of a hundred."

"This isn't a green crew anymore."

Jack snorted. "I'll allow they're a sharp bunch and quick learners. Reckon if I put my mind to it, I'd be proud of them, but they're far yet from salted."

Fin continued her inspection. It was ridiculous that she should be inspecting work she ought to be doing herself, but as Armand said, it was her duty to put on the mask. The men expected their captain to be hard. She inspected the decks, the hold, the standing rigging, the sails, the galley, the guns, the surgery, even the bilge. If she meant them to be loyal on their part she had to be officious in hers.

In the surgery, Fin discovered Lucas Thigham blinking wildly behind his spectacles and squirming in his clothes as he stood for his inspection. She opened one of the storage lockers on the bulkhead and Thigham darted across the room. He hastily rearranged the ordering of a stack of books then ran back to his place and wiped his face. Fin shot a look at Jack and smirked in wonderment.

Inside the locker, Dr. Thigham's surgical instruments were arrayed neatly, hung by pegs and hooks and each shined to mirrorlike perfection. Even his bone saw was polished and shined. It twinkled a sharp-toothed smile, and Fin winced at the memory of its work on Jack's leg.

When she closed the locker, Dr. Thigham squeaked in alarm and dove to the floor where he plucked a speck of lint from the deck. He leapt up and hid it behind his back. Fin looked over at Jack again. He wasn't amused. Fin was.

Fin sauntered across the room with her hands clasped behind her. She stopped in front of a sea chest tucked into the corner and opened it. The chest was packed with all manner of medicinal oddity. The lid was fashioned into a brace for dozens of colored vials filled with various potions, tinctures, and syrups, and the hollow of the chest itself was packed with rolls of bandages, arcane books, and an extensive collection of dried herbs.

"By hell," said Jack.

The cause of Jack's curse was a human skull sitting atop it all. It was painted blue and looked up at them with an empty-eyed stare and a toothy grin. Jack reached down and snatched the skull out of the chest. From across the room, Lucas Thigham yelped and ran to its rescue.

"Out it goes, Thigham!" yelled Jack. "I don't abide the dead to keep berth! Bad luck. Bad as there is." Jack had hold of the skull by the brainpan and was shaking it in the air as he decried it. "Over the rail it goes, and you with it if I wasn't a Christian."

Thigham was in a terrible state. The little man went strawberry red and leapt into the air trying to grab the skull as Jack kept it just out of his reach.

"Give that to me. That's mine."

"Oh, no I won't, you leg-thieving little cretin!"

The doctor managed to alter the rhythm of his jumping enough to catch Jack off guard and get a solid handhold on the skull. A brief tug-of-war between the two ended with Dr. Thigham clinging to the skull in desperation as he dangled a foot off the floor. He kicked his feet and looked like a man running in midair, going nowhere.

Fin broke into a fit of laughter. Her outburst caused Jack and the doctor to cease their struggling and turn their attention her way. After a moment's reflection, Jack realized how preposterous the squabble was. He lowered the doctor to the floor and released the skull. Then Jack, too, erupted in wails of laughter. The two of them carried on for some time while the doctor first hugged the skull to his bosom then fetched a rag to polish it off before gently replacing it into the sea chest.

Before she left the surgery, Fin wiped her eyes and cautioned the doctor to keep the chest secured and the skull inside so that the crew wouldn't see it. Fin didn't believe it was bad luck as Jack claimed, but she did believe that a human skull on board could ignite the sort of self-induced luck that superstitious sailors thought it would.

After the inspection, Jack mustered the crew. They gathered and leaned on the rails. They hung in the ropes and straddled the yards, all crowding around to hear their captain's address. As she stepped out of her quarters and scanned the deck, she saw uncertainty on their faces. Or was it fear? She'd asked much of them to sail so far and with no knowledge of their destination. They'd trusted her and now they knew that trust was due to be tested. They knew that the end of the voyage was near. They knew it by the frequent battle drills and the inspection and the simple fact that the ship was framed in by the Mediterranean, only days away from any port upon its shore. They knew that whatever purpose had sent them the thousands of miles across the Atlantic, it was now at hand.

"We are two days' sail from Tripoli."

Some of their faces remained blank and expectant. But others widened their eyes, a few scratched their chins in dire consideration, some balked outright.

"Tripoli is a nest of Barbary pirates!" someone cried.

"Aye. That's why we're here. You were all told that this wouldn't be an ordinary crossing, and each of you agreed to sail though you didn't know our destination or aim." Fin paused, half expecting she'd have to calm a riot. But the men were silent. They were hungry for the truth.

"The Revolution has need of us, and need of secrecy. Our destination is Tripoli. You're wondering why we fly a Spanish ensign. The Spanish have safe passage upon the Barbary Coast. Remember that when we reach port: you are sailors of a Spanish merchantman. If questioned, you will say that we set forth from Valencia a week prior to trade in Tripoli. Our true aim is the rescue of a woman held captive by the pasha."

Once again, Fin expected an uproar, but none came. To her surprise, they seemed to embrace the mission. She saw it in their eyes. They trusted her. They rested in the strength they believed her to have. Where they'd come by that belief, Fin could only guess. But it was there. She saw it. She watched one man nudge the sailor next to him, grit his teeth, and pound a fist into his open palm. Their drills had made them confident, the long crossing had made them anxious, and their captain had made them bold. They were ready for action. Fin related the rest of the plan, such as it was, and fell silent. The crew was somber, every brow wrinkled in thought.

"That is our aim, gentlemen. Will you have it?"

The oldest of the crew were the first to assent with nods and affirmative grunts, and the younger men followed until Fin could spot no dissenter.

"Then go and make yourselves ready."

Fin threw a glance at Jack to let him know she was done. His voice roared and the men split to their duties. For the rest of the day, Jack drilled the crew, and instead of keeping out of sight as she usually did, Fin stayed among them. She walked the decks in silence. She kept a hard eye, and the crew ducked from her stare and raised their hands in salute when she passed.

When night fell and Fin retired to her cabin, she collapsed into bed. She was exhausted from the effort of holding herself tense and stern, of wearing the mask and playing the part. But tired as she was, sleep eluded her. Her mind was filled with the madness of what her life had become. The road her life had taken, from orphan to ship's captain, seemed unbelievable. She traced each small step, one to another, amazed at how each one had brought her further from home, further from Peter, and nearer to this stranger's sea. She was adrift, caught in an uncharted current that took her wherever it willed while she clung to the gunwales of her life and tried to hold on. But she also felt that the nature of that journey was changing. She was no longer just holding on for survival. She was at the helm. For the first time, she could steer herself where she wanted to go. She could direct her course and find her own way in the wind. The thought troubling her mind was that she didn't know where she wanted to go anymore. Did she want to go home, to Peter, or was it the freedom of the sea she wanted? As she lay awake, she saw many roads stretching out before her. Some wound and circled and intersected with others or ended abruptly having reached, it seemed, no destination at all. Others ran straight and true toward points unknown. She imagined herself walking forward and many of the roads faded away; they flickered and vanished. And with each step, others appeared making new intersections and dashing toward the horizon like unfurling ribbons. But as she moved forward, one road alone stood out. It was sharp, crisp, and wide, and it led into the heart of a distant storm. A storm named Tripoli.

As if in answer to her thoughts, thunder sent a shudder rolling through the ship. The first pattering of rain dappled the deck as Fin escaped into sleep. She drifted away and it grew to a roar.

Chapter Thirteen

FIN TIED HER HAIR back and crammed Creache's hat down onto her head, glad she didn't have to wear any more of his clothing. For once, she had no need to play the captain's part. But she couldn't just be herself either—she had to be a boy again. At least that didn't require her to act. Passing for a boy wasn't something she had to put much effort into. All she had to do was tie back her hair, dress in loose clothing, stand back, and watch. She hoped their plan worked as well as Armand said it would.

Most of the crew was gathered at the starboard rail watching the Barbary Coast roll by as they approached Tripoli. Jack was on the quarterdeck and dressed better than Fin had ever seen him. In his coat, he managed to look positively distinguished, though Fin wondered where the tailor had found the acre of wool that went into making it. The coat was ornamented with brass buttons that Jack continually inspected and thumbed clean. It even looked as though he'd combed his beard. When he saw Fin approach, he tugged at his lapels and wrenched his shoulders around nervously.

Fin sidled up next to him and stuffed her hands into her pockets. "Right nice tent you got there, Jack. Room in there for me?"

Jack ground his teeth. "I'll bury you in it if you like, Button." He pulled down on the cuff of his coat sleeve and twisted his shoulders around again. "Where's Armand?"

Fin shrugged. "Practicing his Spanish, I hope."

Jack grunted and tugged on his lapels. "I don't like it, Button. Don't trust that one."

"It'll be fine, Jack. Just stick to the plan." Fin walked to the helm to stand next to Topper as the ship swung south into the harbor.

Tripoli jutted out of the rock-strewn coast like an exposure of bone. Its alabaster walls and minarets gleamed in the sun and stretched around the half-moon bay in a barbarous, white grin. Broad, squat buildings hunched around the waterfront while behind them, looking over their shoulders, brazen domes, lance-like spires, and crystal white towers mounted up and shimmered in the heat.

The bay itself squirmed with trade. Small ships fitted with gaff-rigged sails scuttled across the water driven by oars splayed from their sides like insectine legs. The *Fiddler's Green* dwarfed most of them. She stood out like a beetle among ants and they parted before her as she passed. Dark sailors hung at the ropes of the small ships and considered them in silence. At the forecastle, Knut waved to each ship they passed, but his greetings went unanswered.

"Got a bad feelin', I do," said Topper.

Fin ignored him.

Ahead of them, a skiff pushed away from the wharf. Four men heaved at its oars while another stood in the bow with one hand held in the air. He was dressed in a white robe that hung to his feet and had a black scarf wrapped around his neck. A tiny, wine-colored cap sat atop his head and a tassel dangled against his ear. As his boat drew nearer, he began to wave.

"Dockmaster?" asked Fin.

"Suppose so," said Topper.

Armand slipped up beside them. "Follow him," he said.

Topper raised a hand in answer and turned the wheel toward the small boat. The robed man shouted at his oarsmen and flailed at them with a crop until they had their boat turned back toward the wharf.

The crew brought the sails in, and Jack cautioned everyone to keep their eyes sharp. To either side of the ship, smaller vessels drew in alongside and followed. The sailors on their decks were dark haired and swarthy with loose, billowy pantaloons and long beards. Few wore shirts. Some wrapped their heads in thick turbans; others wore the same style of tasseled cap as the dockmaster. There was nowhere among them a smile. They whispered to one another and stared at Fin and her crew like children do at strange animals in traveling shows. Here and there the sun glinted off of the wide, curved blade of a scimitar.

The ship approached the wharf and the dockmaster shouted in his native tongue as he motioned them to their berth. Topper complied and guided the *Fiddler's Green* to rest.

The dockmaster clambered out of his dinghy, swatting at his underlings when they offered help, and paced the wharf until Jack extended a plank for him. The man hobbled onto the deck of the *Fiddler's Green* and spoke emphatically in a strange tongue.

Armand stepped forward and spread his arms in welcome. "*Somos de España.*"

The dockmaster motioned at the merchant's ensign flying from the mizzen. He shrugged and wrinkled his face as if he had been insulted. "*¿Vosotros venid a mí ciudad sin saber hablar mi idioma?*"

Armand put his hands together and bowed his head. "*Perdónanos. Nuestro intérprete ha muerto de enfermedad y nuestro capitán habla sólo Inglés.*"

"*¿Un inglés?*" The dockmaster sneered and spat on the deck. "*¿Dónde está vuestro capitán?*"

Armand stepped back without lifting his eyes from the deck and swept out one hand to indicate Jack. "*Nuestro capitán está aquí.*"

Jack stepped forward.

The dockmaster studied him briefly then spoke in English. "Only a cur comes to the door to bark. A man speaks in the tongue of his master."

Jack bowed. "We ask forgiveness. Our translator has gone to God."

The dockmaster nodded to himself several times then pulled a kerchief from the folds of his robe and blew his nose into it. "Then he is in better company." He tucked his kerchief back into his robe and continued. "The pasha welcomes the Spanish so long as they bear the proper documents. You are under contract, no doubt?"

Jack grunted in affirmation. "Aye, contracted by Laurencio Escriba-Fuente of Valencia."

The dockmaster nodded, "For what cargo?"

"Salt and linen," Jack answered and handed over the sealed trade contract. The dockmaster snapped the seal and studied it. When he was satisfied, he handed it back to Jack.

"You have three days. Do not linger."

The dockmaster pulled a ledger from his robes. He announced fees for docking and scrawled down the ship's name once paid. He departed without thanks or salutation.

"That went as smooth as can be expected," said Jack.

THE ACTIVITY OF THE waterfront was much like that of any other port city: busy, full of merchants and workmen coming and going, shouting and singing. But where the predominant colors of waterfronts Fin had known were brown hues of filth and disrepair, the chief shades of Tripoli were of white and ochre and here and there fiery reds standing out like violent accents. The buildings shone white as if the sun had burned away their color. Where their mud façades had chipped and worn away near the corners and foundations, darker stone peeked out and radiated cracks like thin fingers.

In a courtyard nearby, an auctioneer mounted a platform lined with men and women. Each had a metal collar fastened about the neck, and a chain ran from collar to collar linking them together. Another chain linked the shackles at their wrists. Their heads hung forward, weary and resigned. The auctioneer pushed a skinny young woman out to the edge of the platform, and in the crowd, hands went up. The auctioneer pointed and cried out as each new hand rose, but the young woman kept her head bowed and wrapped her arms around her bosom.

To the east rose the pasha's keep, visible to Fin above the waterfront storehouses and smaller buildings. It was a castle in the oldest and most stalwart sense. An edifice of stone erected high and foreboding with the singular purpose of defense. Atop the battlements and outer baileys, guards paced the walls and peered from tall arrow-slits.

"Well, we won't find a way in from here," said Fin. She called Topper and gave him a handful of coins. "Bring us back some of those robes and caps everyone's wearing. We'd better fit in."

Jack grunted. "The rest of you can do all the seein' you like. I best stick here." He kicked his wooden leg out and stomped it on the deck. "This thing'll do naught but slow you down and draw eyes."

As Topper trotted across the plank, Fin said "Just clothes, Topper. Pastries can wait."

Topper grimaced and shook his head. "I don't like this place, Cap'n. Doubt there's a pastry to be found. And even if there was, I got no hanker to taste the devil's honey." His face drooped and he ambled off down the street.

Topper returned an hour later with a bundle under his arm and handed it to Fin. Inside were tasseled caps, black sashes, and white robes. Fin tossed a set to Armand and ducked into her cabin. She retrieved Betsy, loaded her, and slipped the gun into her belt. Then she pulled on the robe and tied the sash at her waist, trying her best to arrange it the same way she'd seen the men ashore wearing them. Once satisfied, she donned the cap and left the cabin.

Armand was dressed and waiting for her. Jack had an amused smirk on his face now that he wasn't the only one dressed up.

"We'll be back directly," Fin assured him.

"Keep your wits and don't do nothing foolish," said Jack.

Fin waved his cautions aside. "We'll be fine. We're just having a look."

Fin and Armand crossed the plank and stepped onto the wharf. Though she felt conspicuous in her costume, she was swept into the river of people on the waterfront without garnering a concerned glance from anyone. In the chaos of the street, Fin lost sight of the fortress. She stopped to look around to see which street led in the right direction, but as soon as she slowed, men pushed her to the side to rush past. She was bumped first one way then shoved another. In moments she had lost her bearing completely. She wasn't even sure which side of the street faced the sea. Then Armand was in front of her. He grabbed her arm, pointed down a side street, and pulled her toward it.

"Do you know where you're going?" she asked Armand.

"This way, I believe," he said and continued on. They passed through a market filled with strange fruits, and goats, and something Fin had never seen before: a tall four-legged animal with shaggy brown fur and a massive hump on its back. A camel, Armand called it. As Fin passed the animal, it stuck out its teeth and bellowed at her.

A group of women passed with veils across their faces so that only their dark-lined eyes were visible. They picked through the fruits and meats of the market and never spoke. Children clung to their robes.

When Fin and Armand emerged from the market they turned east and beheld the fortress. It rose up some forty feet above the street. The battlements were split at intervals by arrow-slits, each darkened by the shadowy hint of a gunman at his post. The gate was open and watched over by a dozen guards, some in the street before the gate and more atop it, peering through the windows of the barbican.

Armand pulled her to the side and they huddled behind a wagon. They watched as men arrived at the gatehouse on business. The guards stopped each man or group that approached. Though neither Fin nor Armand could understand what was said, it was clear that everyone entering the keep was questioned. If the questions were answered agreeably, the men were searched. The guards opened each man's bags and satchels and flung open wagons. Some men approached with camels, and the guards shouted at the men until they forced their beasts to their knees so the guards could inspect the bundles tied to their humped backs.

Often a group of merchants approached with multiple beasts or wagons filled with goods bound either for the stores of the keep or for the pasha's personal treasury, possibly bribes or offerings from lesser lords. Whatever their purpose, Armand gleaned from these large deliveries a weakness in the guard. If the guards searched a single man or a small group, they were thorough and studious. But when faced with large deliveries, they were irritated by the time required to search each wagon or beast and further irritated when the queue of men behind gathered up in wait. As a result, whenever a large delivery fell under inspection, the search was half-hearted, cursory.

"You see," said Armand, "they look once at each wagon and not again. A man could slip into one after it is searched and enter without notice."

Fin and Armand remained, watching the gate for the rest of the afternoon, noting each entrant and how he was treated and what the guards searched and what they did not. When they made their way back to the ship at dusk, Fin was confident that Armand was right.

"THEN WHAT?" ASKED JACK. He raised an expectant eyebrow.

Fin and Armand glanced sideways at one another.

"Then we steal into the keep and find the girl," said Armand.

Jack paced the cabin. His leg clanked and creaked and he shook his head back and forth. "And that's the easy bit, I take it? This sounds like a good idea to you, Button?"

"And why wouldn't it?" said Fin.

Armand placed his hand on Fin's shoulder to quiet her and spoke to Jack. "There is foot traffic in the keep. We can move about as well as any other. We will find the countess, dress her as we are, and slip out like any other merchant."

Fin shrugged Armand's hand away.

Jack harrumphed. "You think this countess will be unguarded? You think no one will see she's missing?"

Fin snapped back at him in irritation. "You haven't even been off the ship, Jack. We have. We've been there. We've seen the keep and Armand's right. We sneak in, we get the countess, we sneak out. That's all there is to it. If you've got a better plan then spit it out!" Fin knew immediately that she'd overstepped her bounds.

A deep rattle filled Jack's chest. His brow came down and put his eyes into shadow. "Mind the size o' your britches, Button. Your little captain game is about gone an inch beyond my liking. You want to give your speeches and play your part to the crew then you go right ahead, but you best not take that tone with me, sailor. This ain't no barroom tussle we're plotting here. This is grown-folks' business."

"What choice do we have, Jack? Either come up with a better plan or we do it like Armand says."

Armand smiled faintly and crossed his arms. The rattle in Jack's chest grew into a rumble. He stepped up to Armand and towered over him. "We ain't thought this through, Button. And I don't trust this one."

"Well, I do," said Fin.

Armand's smile deepened and he inched closer to Jack. He had a knife in his hand and he raked his thumb along the blade. "Like the captain said, Jack, either offer up a better plan, or we do it my way."

Jack's lip curled up and he ground his teeth. Each man leaned toward the other, and wound himself tight.

"Enough!" shouted Fin. "Armand's right. Just follow the plan and have the ship ready."

Jack quieted altogether and slowly turned from Armand and looked at Fin. His fists were balled up and the vein on his forehead stood out, throbbing and purple. Fin gulped and took a step backward. Without another word, Jack pushed Armand out of the way and stomped out of the cabin.

THE NEXT DAY, FIN and Armand once again dressed in robes and tasseled hats. Armand carried a second robe in the folds of his own and Fin concealed an extra hat folded in her sash.

They approached the portcullis and waited. A steady stream of men approached, were questioned, and searched. Most came alone or in small groups. Few brought more than what they carried in their arms. When merchants with larger loads did approach, they came when the guards were unbusied by other visitors and Armand judged it too dangerous to attempt their entry. They waited, and hoped for an opportunity when the gate was crowded and the guards were overworked. Twice, Armand felt they had lingered too long and were in danger of suspicion so they sauntered back down the street to meander through the market for a while.

When they left the *Fiddler's Green*, Jack hadn't said a word. He ignored them and went about preparing the ship for sea. He'd given Knut a bell and sent him aloft with orders to set it ringing as soon as he saw Fin and Armand coming back with the countess. Fin imagined Knut perched all morning on the mainmast with the bell in one hand and the clapper in the other, his eyes peeled wide and aimed down the street. She hoped he didn't fall asleep waiting for them.

Armand nudged her. "Opportunity, *cherie.*"

A caravan of four wagons and several camels clogged the gate, and a long line of single merchants crowded behind it. The guards were in an uproar trying to maintain order.

Armand fell into the line at the rear and Fin followed. Her stomach fluttered wildly. As the bulk of the guards searched the caravan and questioned its drivers, another group motioned the smaller merchants to the side. The line diverted to the left of the gate, and Fin held close to Armand as he stepped to the right and poised himself behind a wagon filled with bolts of cloth. A guard climbed onto the wagon and prodded at its contents with a scimitar. He shouted something at Armand and moved on to the next wagon. Armand took Fin by the arm and urged her into the wagon then quickly leapt in behind her. They arranged themselves beneath a canvas and waited. Fin could barely breathe. Her heart kicked in her chest like a fretful animal and the oppressive heat made the air thick and difficult to breathe. Armand clamped his hands down upon her and held her firmly in his grip.

Fin told herself that once the wagon was in motion, they'd be safe. But when the wagon lurched forward, she found the opposite was the case; they had passed the point of no return. Fin broke into a shiver. Jack was right. This was madness.

Armand's arms tightened around her. "Take ease, *cherie*. We are within."

"How long should we wait?" she whispered. Armand kept silent.

The wagon moved along in fits and jerks. Around them Fin heard footsteps and voices. Once, someone beside the wagon ran the blade of a scimitar down the length of it, letting it clatter across its boards. Fin wanted to fling the canvas away and run but Armand held her fast. Then the voices around were gone and the only sound was the creaking of the wagon's wheels and the sharp bray of animals.

"Now, *cherie*!" Armand pulled the canvas away and pushed her from the wagon.

They were in the mouth of a tunnel. Like a black throat, it descended into the depths of the keep. Armand slipped out behind her and the wagon jerked to a stop. The driver turned and stared at them in contemplation. Then he began to yell. His cries echoed off the walls of the tunnel and ended in an abrupt gasp as Armand silenced him with a knife.

Armand swore and rushed to the head of the tunnel. He pressed his body to the wall and peered around the corner into the courtyard. He snapped his head back and swore again. Atop the wall a guard stepped from behind a stone battlement and peered down at the wagon driver lying dead on the ground. The guard pointed and shouted then ran off. A moment later an alarm bell pealed through the keep.

Men were coming—a lot of men. Armand said something but it was lost in the echo of rushing feet and clattering buckles. The noise rattled through air and bounced off the flat stone of the keep. Sound seemed to come from every direction at once. A lone guard charged around the corner. The scimitar in his hand gleamed like a silvery crescent moon. He saw Fin and ran toward her with his blade high. Unseen, Armand spilled from a shadow. His arm struck out and he opened the man's throat with a knife. The man groaned and continued running until he disappeared into the blackness of the tunnel, leaving a trail of blood to mark his way.

"We must run!" shouted Armand.

Chapter Fourteen

They ran out of the tunnel and dashed across the open space, stopping at the corner of a building along the edge of the courtyard. Guards swarmed through the keep in chaos. The alarm had stirred them up, but they had yet to notice Fin and Armand.

Fin jerked Betsy from her robe and primed the pan. *Why didn't I listen to Jack?* She should have been afraid, terrified even, but the only thing she felt was anger. When the gun was ready to fire, she nodded at Armand. He split his lips and grinned, a malevolent sight.

"We must be quick, *cherie*. Do not hesitate. Do not stop." His hideous grin fell flat and he twirled the knife in his half-hand. "And do not let them take you alive."

They stepped around the corner. A group of armed men had gathered before the gatehouse. They raised their blades and rushed forward. Fin and Armand charged. When she was within feet of the guards, Fin raised Betsy and fired. The blunderbuss coughed out a fury of smoke and peppershot that sprayed the entire group in front of her. The foremost guards crumpled to the ground, and those behind tripped and stumbled over them. Betsy's shot left a billow of smoke that bellied out and drifted lazily across the courtyard. Fin angled her run to put the cloud between her and the rest of the guard. She bounded onto a stack of crates and leapt onto a stair leading up the wall to the battlement.

Armand panted behind her and kept at her heels, urging her onward. "Fly, girl!"

Fin reached the top of the battlement and ran toward the gate. In the courtyard below, the guards recovered. A man in a tasseled cap pointed up at Fin and shouted orders. Guards raced up the stairs behind her.

When Fin reached the eastern corner of the keep, she flew out into the flat of the bailey and skidded to a halt. Guards were coming toward her down the battlement of the north wall. There was nowhere else to run. She climbed atop the stone parapet and the rooftops of Tripoli spread out below her.

"Armand!" He leaned against the wall and panted. "Armand, we have to jump." Fin bent down and reached for him. Armand waved her off.

"I cannot, *cherie*." He flipped one of his knives around and caught it by the blade. "Save me, and then save yourself." He held the handle of his knife toward her, urging her to take it. When she hesitated, he raised his chin and drew a finger across his neck. He thrust the knife toward her again. "Do it!"

Fin shook her head. "I won't. Come on!" The guards were nearly upon them. A musket shot whistled past her ear. Armand raised his arm and offered his knife again. She grabbed him and pulled him atop the wall.

Another musket ball struck the stone at her feet and raised a puff of powdered rock.

"Ready?" Fin said. Armand clearly wasn't, but he nodded anyway.

Fin jumped. The span wasn't great, and the rooftop of the adjoining building was lower than the top of the wall. Her knees buckled when she landed. She rolled with the impact and came up on her feet. Armand wasn't with her. He was still atop the keep. "Armand! Jump!"

He looked down at the gulf between them, raised one hand to her, and smiled. "*Au revoir, cherie!*"

"Armand!"

He turned his back to her and looked down at the guards gathering around him in the bailey. A musket shot pierced his shoulder. Then, with knives at his fingertips, he leapt upon the men below. In the brief second between his leap and his passing from her sight, Fin saw his lips curled upward. She gathered one last appraisal of Armand's wicked smile. There was no valor in it, no bravery, no sacrificial calm; there was nothing but the promise of a bloodletting. The hairs of her neck stood on end and she felt relief that she'd never more have to endure the corrupt joy of that smile. Then, beyond the parapet, in the distance, a face appeared in the highest window of the keep. It was an oval of ivory white skin that stood out like a beacon against the grey stone. Locks of yellow hair tumbled down around it. The countess. Her eyes met Fin's, and for the smallest instant, Fin felt she knew her, or that they knew each other.

A musket shot punched into the rooftop near Fin's feet. She turned from the countess and fled. She lit across the rooftops, leaping from building to building, ever lower, ever closer to the waterfront. The streets below were in chaos as dozens of guards poured through the crowds with their eyes up to the sky, looking for her.

Fin spotted the masts of the *Fiddler's Green* and cut a direct course across the rooftops. She glimpsed Knut on the mainmast. He was shifting from side to side and craning his neck to get a look at the source of the musket fire. Fin stopped and crouched down, out of the sight of people in the streets below. She fished Betsy out of her robe, reloaded her, then raised the gun into the air and fired. The shot crackled through the air and Knut froze. Fin waved her arms. When Knut spotted her, he slunk around the mast to hide on the other side and peeked out from behind it. Fin snatched off her tasseled cap and shook her hair out.

"Knut!" she shouted. "It's me!"

Knut hesitated a moment more then pointed at her and shouted down toward the deck. When he looked up again, he waved and smiled. Now she had to buy Jack time to get the ship moving.

The gunshot had done more than get Knut's attention. It had also given her away to every guard around. She peeked over the edge of the roof at the street below where a dozen men were running toward the building; she pulled her head back and waited, tucking her hair under her cap again. The men below banged on the door and cried out until someone inside answered. Fin waited for them to enter the building then slipped over the edge of the rooftop and dropped into the street.

She stepped into the crowd in hopes of fading into it, but a raised voice from the rooftop behind her caused everyone in the street to stop and look up. One of the guards on the roof was pointing down at her, and amid the swarms of bronze-skinned and black faces, there was no doubt of who the intruder was. The guard spat out words and gesticulated madly. A man beside Fin grabbed her. She twisted her arm loose and tried to run, but she was enmeshed in a tangle of arms and hands. They grabbed her clothes, her hair, her arms and legs. They hit and scratched at her. People pressed in around her and seemed to suck all the air out of her lungs. The heat of their nearness threatened to suffocate her. At first she only twisted and turned, but soon panic pushed her into the mindset of a fight. A jerk became a drawback for a punch; a twist: an opportunity to strike. She lashed out with elbows and knees and even bit into an arm when it presented itself. Her pocket of space within the crowd began to widen. When she saw a gap, she exploited it. A small sliver of light opened among the limbs of the crowd, not enough to run through, but enough to suggest a weakness. Fin twisted violently to free herself then stretched one arm out to the light and lurched toward it. As quickly as it had appeared, it vanished again. But it didn't matter. That it had been there at all meant that the crowd was thinner in that direction. Fin's elbows flew wild. She shuffled her feet forward, an inch, a foot, a full stride. Then she was loose. Air rushed into her lungs, cool, and full of sea-scent. She ran.

She pushed men aside and flung women to the ground if they crossed her path. Behind her, the sound of the mob clamored and swelled with the threat of violence. Her fight had left her turned around with no clear idea of the way to the ship. She scanned the air over the rooftops, hoping to spot a mast, but saw nothing. When she reached a cross street, she turned and knew immediately that she'd gone the wrong way. Even as she was turning left, she saw the sun reflecting off the water of the harbor to the right but she couldn't afford to correct her course. If she slowed for even a second, the crowd would be upon her. She'd have to circle back around.

She darted left again at the next corner and found herself in an alleyway so narrow that two men couldn't walk through it abreast. Good, she thought, that'll slow the crowd.

When she turned left out of the alley she'd come full circle and ran right up against the tail end of the mob that was chasing her. Men had their fists in the air as they surged forward. They raised themselves up on their toes, stretching their necks out to see the subject of all the commotion in front of them. Fin smiled to herself as she plunged into them and pressed forward. The men behind her raced out of the alleyway and closed upon the rear end of their own horde like a serpent engorged on its own tail.

Fin squeezed through the throngs of people until she reached the intersection. To the right, the road to the harbor was open and clear. She slipped out of the chaos and walked calmly, trying not to draw attention. The noise faded behind her as she reached the waterfront.

Jack had the *Fiddler's Green* loose of its moorings and was at the rail with one hand up to his eyes, looking down the street for her return. Fin waved and hurried aboard.

"Where's Armand?" said Jack.

Fin ignored him. She shouted for the plank to be drawn and sails to be set. The *Fiddler's Green* stirred into motion. As they pulled away from the quayside, the mob burst around the corner and rushed the ship. Several men leapt from the pier and rolled onto the deck. Jack had prepared the crew well. They fell on the boarders with knives and swords and pushed them overboard into the harbor.

When the ship was too far from the pier to be threatened by the crowd, Fin breathed a sigh of relief. But as they gathered speed, the entire harbor turned against them. Small single-masted ships crowded with Barbary sailors took shots at them with their cannons and muskets. Their cannons threw chain shot. It scattered across the decks and tore through the rigging, leaving ropes tattered and limp. Musketshot popped against the gunwales and crackled through the air. The crew stooped each time a shot rang out. They'd gone from the lazy boredom of a hot afternoon to the driven quarry of a hungry fleet in the space of seconds. It unnerved them.

"Set the foresail!" ordered Fin.

A sailor next to her hauled himself into the rigging to comply and was unheaded by chain shot. His body crashed through the ropes and dropped to the deck in front of Fin.

Fin didn't spare time to mourn or pause in shock. She stepped over the body and shouted her order again. "Set the foresail!"

The crew around her was motionless in consideration of their unflinching captain and the dead boy at her feet. Fin felt her anger rising, but before she could speak, the crew acted. Fearless now, they scampered up the lines. They held to their work. The sails rustled out and unfurled, high and tight.

The ship gathered speed and Fin ran to the helm to stand beside

Topper. Cannon fire came from every direction. It sounded like the first drops of a monstrous summer rain on the roof of the orphanage. A mist of gunsmoke rose around them. The Barbary ships were like the mob that chased her, not knowing the aim or reason for the pursuit, but hungry and wanton and ready to stir themselves for the sake of violence.

A ship ahead of them tried to tack alongside. Its crew lined the rails with grappling hooks in hand.

Fin pointed. "Topper!"

"I see 'em."

Topper rolled the wheel, and the *Fiddler's Green* dug her bow into the side of the ship. Hooks flew. Topper heaved the wheel over again and the *Fiddler's Green* briefly mounted the smaller vessel amidships before driving it in twain with her keel. The men who had thrown their hooks hauled themselves aboard and charged, but the ready crew fought back the boarders and cast them into the sea.

Dozens of ships swarmed around and in front of them. Jack raged across the deck, directing each man to his line, swearing, spitting, stomping his wooden leg like a gavel. The sails were nearly all flown. The ship rose high in the water, climbing the waves and hammering them down. Barbary pirates arrayed their ships before them like a man-wrought island of timber and iron.

"What you think, Fin?" said Topper.

"Clear us a path." said Fin. She ran to the quarterdeck rail and shouted, "Take cover!"

The crew dropped out of the ropes and knelt at the rails. They packed their muskets and drew swords.

"Jack, help me hold her true," said Topper. "She'll buckle wild when we hit."

Topper moved to one side and Jack stepped to the wheel. They each took it in both hands. They spread their feet and readied themselves. The first small ship in their path slid easy along the sheer line and passed behind without incident. Then it got bumpy. Topper drove down anything in their path. Some ships hauled to the side and peppered them with chain shot as they passed. Some sent boarders across.

Fin and the crew held the deck. The air sizzled and popped around them. A steady surge of boarders clambered over the rails. They grappled and cut, bled and died. Fin skewered a pirate as he attacked one of her crewmen. When the crewman turned to thank her, a cannonball blasted him into the sea. Fin scarcely noticed; another boarder had already replaced him. The deck was a battlefield. The maddened pirates didn't slacken their fire even to spare their own; their guns killed boarder and crew alike. More and more men leapt aboard amid the unceasing cannon and musket fire.

The *Fiddler's Green* shuddered and lurched as it rode ships down or drove them aside, but Topper and Jack steered them true. The ship's speed was such that they barreled through the clog like a juggernaut plowing a furrow of wrack and destruction. When they gained fair sea at last, a flotsam miles long seethed in their wake.

CHAPTER FIFTEEN

FIN WISHED THE SAILOR lying on deck would pass out. The thick of his thigh was a ruined mangle of flesh and bone and the shredded canvas of his pants. She couldn't tell what had hit him. A cannon ball, a musket shot, shrapnel? Maybe even a stray grappler's hook. Whatever the cause, the result was bloody. Jack wrapped a belt around the man's leg and cinched it tight. The belt stopped most of the blood flow, but it did little for the sailor's comfort. Though he didn't scream or speak, he kept his teeth clenched so tight that Fin worried he'd shatter them. Every few seconds his eyes went from jammed shut to stretched fully open and rolled up white. And he trembled. Fin's stomach rolled over and made her look away.

"Get him to Thigham."

"Aye, Captain." Three sailors swept forward and muscled their crewmate into their arms. He slammed his eyes shut, went rigid, and moaned as they carried him away.

Fin and Jack exchanged a troubled look. Jack opened his mouth to speak, but Fin pushed past him, following the sailors as they carried the wounded man below.

"Where's Defain?" Jack called after her.

His question begged more than a location. Fin broke her stride and stopped, turning her head as if to speak, but she couldn't think of an answer worth giving. Before Jack could ask again, she descended into Lucas Thigham's surgery.

The room was filled with a chorus of sobs, cries, and groans. Puddles of blood had collected and red boot prints were stamped and smeared across the deck. Thigham was bent over a wounded sailor. He drew one hand high into the air, and the needle between his fingers threw off a pinprick of the lantern's light. He was stitching the man closed. His bone saw lay bloody at hand. Fin spotted a tub at the head of the doctor's table filled with a wreck of limbs that, like Jack's leg, had been cut away.

A thin, wavering voice called out from the far corner of the surgery. "Captain?" A young sailor sat on the floor leaning against the bulkhead, and he beckoned her.

"Captain?" he said again.

Fin remembered his face. It was Roberts, who had been so eager to please during the inspection only days before. His head was wrapped in a dirty bandage. He was young—younger than herself even. When she played for the crew in Madeira, he'd sat at her feet and smiled up at her like a child. Here he sat at her feet again, smiling in the aftermath of a different music—a chorus of cannon, a melody of violence. The music of the gun.

"I'm no captain," she said to him.

"Captain, you done it." His smile was so big, so innocent. How could he be smiling? "We goin' home now, Captain? Now that you done it?"

Fin covered her mouth with her hand. Her eyes stung with tears but she couldn't let him see. She mastered herself and knelt beside the young man. He had a blanket pulled up over him, and except for the bandage around his head, he seemed uninjured. He extended one hand toward her and muttered about how she'd "done it."

Fin took his hand in hers and held it firmly. "No, sailor. It's not done. We've still got work to do." She expected his smile to wane. She expected anger or distress or frustration. But, impossibly, his smile grew. His eyes brightened.

"Send me out, Captain. Send me out and I'll go. I can work and fight and I'll do 'til it's done and home we go. I'll do and do 'til doing's done."

Fin nearly lost her composure again and had to look away. How could she ask more of him? How could she have asked anything at all? And here he was smiling, like Bartimaeus at the gallows.

The sailor pulled her close.

"Captain, help me get my boots on so's I can go with you. So's I can help. I can't find my boots, Captain."

Fin looked down at the man's feet as he pulled his blanket aside. But there was nothing to see. Both of his legs were gone below the knee.

Fin let out a cry. She jerked upright and pinwheeled backward, catching herself against the bulkhead.

"I can do good, Captain. Just help me find my boots. I can do good, you'll see."

Tears rushed up and she ran from the room. As she left, the last thing she saw was Lucas Thigham half-turned toward her in the light of his flickering lantern. His hair was matted, his eyes stony, deadened. The bone saw in his hand was sticky and blackened with gore. Like a figure out of nightmare, his shadow danced on the wall, poised and eager to cleave.

"Sometimes the wound must be cut to save the man," Thigham cried out. He sounded like a man pleading for mercy. The sailor on the table bucked at his restraints. His eyes were shot wide and white and full of the knowledge that the doctor's saw was hungry and soon to eat.

"Cut the wound to save the man!" Thigham cried again as Fin fled to her cabin. She wondered who he was trying to convince.

The door to her cabin stood open. She wanted to retreat into solitude and cry, but Jack sat at the table with his arms crossed into a barricade before him. His eyes were on her the moment Fin entered and she couldn't hide from them. The tears on her face didn't soften Jack's resolve. They didn't even dent it.

"Sit."

It was an order. Jack hadn't spoken to her in that severe and expectant tone since before the signing of the robin. Since she'd been named captain he'd obliged, deferred, and held his tongue. But no more.

Fin sat.

She bore a seemingly endless endurance of Jack's stare that put her in mind of days long-passed when she sat before Sister Hilde awaiting judgment.

"Where's Defain?"

"He's gone."

"Gone how?"

Fin chewed her bottom lip and didn't answer.

Jack shifted in his chair and asked again. "Gone how?"

"It went bad, Jack. We had to run and—"

"And what?"

"—and he couldn't keep up!"

"So you left him?"

Fin pulled her head up and straight. "He left *me*. Not the other way around. He turned back and wouldn't come. He left me."

Jack settled in his chair and twisted his brow into a knot over his eyes.

"What about the countess?"

"We barely even got through the gate."

Jack grunted. A sound that Fin translated as a lack of surprise.

"So we got a dozen men dead and half the ship blowed apart for nothing."

"How bad is it?"

Jack shrugged. "The mizzen's splintered and unlike to fly sail again. Something's sprung below and the water's coming in steady. The boys'll be sore of the bilge before we find a port for repairs. Half the sails got holes torn through. Most o' the rigging's got shot up." Jack let out a long breath. He uncrossed his arms and pressed his fingers against his forehead. "She's ragged and broke. We're lucky she's yet afloat."

Fin and Jack sat in silence a while before Jack spoke again.

"Best pray we don't come afoul o' pirates before we find safe harborage. We'll not sail free of another fight."

Again, they were silent. They each huddled into their chairs, unmoving, waiting for the other to speak. Fin was tired and numb.

"What do you aim we should do now?" Jack asked.

Fin raised her head and looked at him. Her face was reddened and wet. She wiped at her eyes but they wouldn't clear.

"I don't know, Jack!" If she'd had the strength, she'd have yelled it. "I've never known. Why are you even asking me? They might call me 'captain' out there," she pointed at the door, "but you know better." She jabbed her finger at him. "You know better!"

"Aye, I do." Jack straightened and gathered himself up. He put his great hands on his knees and leaned toward Fin. "I do, and I said so, and you wouldn't hear it."

His words stung her. Fin opened her mouth to defend herself but held her tongue because nothing she could say would absolve her.

"Armand's gone and good riddance! Never naught but poison in the water was that one." Jack stabbed a sausage-sized finger at her. "And you know it, Button."

Jack stood and stomped his mechanical leg on the ground to reseat the stump of his leg. He muttered to himself and tried to pace the room but the exertion and inconvenience of kicking his leg around made him give it up. He stopped and propped himself on the table with one arm.

"We need to make for Sicily. What we'll do when we get there is beyond me. That letter from your Congress won't do us no good there and we got nothing in the hold to trade." Jack ran his hands through his hair and blew air out his nose. Then he snorted. Fin looked up, wondering what was wrong with him. His head was down and his massive ox-like shoulders were shuddering. Fin thought he was crying. But when Jack finally lifted his head, she saw he had mirth in his face. A thunderous laughter pealed out of him and he shook with it.

When he saw the question in her eyes he reined himself in and took two deep breaths to calm himself. "Armand was our navigator. Ain't that something?" Several more bolts of laughter sparked out of him, and he brought one hand down on his mechanical knee. "Our navigator! And you lost him!"

Fin didn't see the humor. "We'll pick up a new one in Sicily."

"Oh, we will, will we? And how will we ever find Sicily without one?" Jack's laughter faded away and he became stark and serious. "This ain't our coast, Button. Back home any man can reckon north and south and spot the seaboard by landmark, but here's a stranger sea. I don't know it. Topper don't know it. Sicily's somewhere to the north but without someone to scry, and math, and plot the course we'll as sure sail past it in the night as ground ourselves on a shoal."

"So what do we do?"

Jack collapsed back into his chair and bent over to cradle his head between his hands. "I'll have the boys bring in sail so's we don't go blind into the broadside of an island. In the morning, I reckon we aim us north and hope for the best." Jack looked up at Fin. "Maybe things'll look some clearer come tomorrow."

Fin nodded and stared at the floor but as Jack left the cabin, she stopped him. "I'm sorry, Jack."

Jack didn't answer. The door closed behind him with a merciless rattle.

IT WAS LATE, BUT Fin had no notion of whether it was high midnight or near-dawn. Sleep eluded her. As she lay in her bed, she could feel the ship's lack of momentum. The Mediterranean swept the *Fiddler's Green* from side to side, and without forward motion for stability, the world seemed to bobble and wash aimlessly. Without Armand to navigate, there was no telling where they'd end up. *Good riddance*, Jack had said. And although Fin felt the same, she also felt a new rope of guilt tied up inside her. She was glad to be free of his whispering and yet, the torment she'd abandoned him to was unthinkable. He'd even asked her to kill him. He'd asked it as a mercy and she withheld it. She couldn't do it. She hoped he'd died quickly.

The knot of guilt winding its way through her was redoubled and multiplied by each of the sailors killed and each one cut in the surgery. They'd come here to mount a rescue of one person and she'd already lost thirteen others. No more, Fin told herself. No more.

Cut the wound to save the man.

She wouldn't let anyone else suffer or die while she was trying to be someone she wasn't.

Fin gave up trying to sleep. The fiddle case lay beneath the bed waiting for her. She knelt down and drew it out. She needed music to stretch and unwind her, to pull her straight and true.

Out, into the cool night she went, case in hand. Under the moonless sky, the sea was a dark expanse more felt than seen. The deck was unusually quiet, but she didn't mind. She didn't want sailors crowding around her as she played. She wanted to be alone under the stars and let the music lead her. She crossed the quarterdeck and paused at the helm. It was unmanned; she should scold someone but secretly she was thankful. She didn't want to speak and would certainly have been spoken to had the watch's helmsman been at his post.

She went to the poop deck and set the case next to the transom rail. Her foot struck something soft. She stared down and waited for her eyes to gather in enough light to see. In the darkness she made out the faint definition of a form. A sailor was lying against the rail, asleep on his watch. Normally, Fin would have prodded him awake and berated him, but she let him sleep. After the day's bloody wreck, he deserved a respite—they all did.

Fin sat down and folded her legs. The deck was wet and she bristled as the seat of her pants soaked through. She put one hand to the deck and frowned. Just her luck, she'd found quite a puddle. It wasn't until she wiped her hand on her shirt that she wondered at how warm the water was. An icy finger tickled the back of her mind. She stretched her hand into the darkness and delicately touched the sailor sleeping at the rail. He didn't move, so she prodded his shoulder. Still, he didn't move. She took him by both arms and shook him. She touched his face. The skin was warm but—her eyes finally gathered enough light to form a clear picture, and what she saw made her cry out. The man's throat was cut. Blood pooled around him and glistened in the starlight.

Surely they hadn't left him here when they collected the wounded and dead. She knew they hadn't. She'd walked the entire deck herself, etching each dead or wounded sailor's face into her mind. Someone had killed this man, and very recently. She sped lightly across the deck. The helm was still unmanned, but the third watch helmsman was a big man, much bigger than the dead sailor. She tiptoed to the starboard rail. There were two vessels tied alongside, small ships, gaff-rigged with black sails, and oars. Barbary pirates.

Fin ran to the quarterdeck bell and rang it. "To arms, to arms!" she yelled out. She tried to sound like Jack, full of authority and menace, but what came out sounded like a mockery. "Jack!" she cried. "Topper!"

As she rang the bell, the deck exploded with life. There were Barbary pirates everywhere. Until she sounded the alarm, they'd been quiet, moving slowly in the darkness. Now they cast off their stealth and sped to their work. They gathered blades and ran toward her. Jack clanked out of a hatch with a lantern held high. Light spilled across the deck. The crew of the watch lay prone, arranged like cargo, tied and gagged. Some looked unconscious or dead, but most struggled against their bonds and chewed at their gags. A group of pirates stood along the rail passing captured crewmen down into the slave holds of their ships. The *Fiddler's Green*'s rigging swung free in the air. It had all been cut, and the ropes hung like dead vines swaying in the wind.

A pirate raced up the ladder. Fin met him with a kick and sent him back down. He crashed into the men below him and they tumbled into a heap.

"Jack!" she called again. He was on the deck amidships. He hung the lantern and hop-charged into three pirates. Two went down under his fists. The third swung a scimitar and knocked Jack's mechanical leg loose. It skidded across the deck and clanked against the rail. Jack collapsed and another pirate clubbed him in the head.

The rest of the crew emerged from below. They erupted out of the lower decks armed and enfuried. But the pirates were ready for them. Muskets sputtered out sharp blue flashes of light. The crew broke under the gunfire and the pirates rushed. Men scattered across the ship in chaotic chase.

As Fin watched in horror, a man hauled himself onto the poop deck beside her. She drew back her fist but he was no pirate—yet neither was he one of the crew. It was Phineas Button. He wrapped his arms around her. Fin struggled to break free but he gripped her like a vice and dragged her aft. She kicked and screamed and demanded to be let loose. The crew was dying; she couldn't fail them again; they needed her help. She'd die trying. But he wouldn't ease his grip. He dragged her kicking, biting, and howling toward the rail. At the forecastle, fire bloomed and raced up the lines into the sails. The flames illumined horrors on deck. Men tied like animals. Men cut and hacked and hurled into the sea. Her men. Running. Pleading. Dying. Firelight danced in the rigging. Burning embers drifted down into the madness like an accursed rain.

"Let me go!" Fin shouted. But Phineas pulled her relentlessly onward. And then with a shove, she was falling. She struck the water and it knocked the wind from her lungs. Seawater rushed down her throat. Then there were hands on her again, pulling her upward. Her face broke the surface and she gulped in mouthfuls of air. Phineas Button was with her, his arm under her chin. He clung to one of the ship's cut lines and held them afloat. Fin stopped fighting. She hung limp in his grip and looked up at the shadows in the orange smoke as they shuddered and flitted over the deck. The fire spread. It engulfed the ship. Muffled screams and shouts echoed distant and otherworldly through the hull.

The two pirate ships slipped from behind the *Fiddler's Green* and slid quietly into the night.

As her ship burned, Fin hung from Phineas Button's arm, helpless. The blaze crackled and wailed. A black column of smoke twisted upward like a pillar of hell. In flashes and infernal hues, the cloud whirled and spouted and stabbed at the heavens. Then, amid the groaning of the immolation, the flames breached the powder magazine and detonated it. A blinding luminance billowed skyward. In a thundering instant, the ship was unmade, shivered to flinders. A rain of flotsam spattered into the sea and darkness followed.

When the phantoms of the explosion's brilliance cleared from her sight, the night was eerily quiet. The blast had thrown them across the water. Phineas Button lost his grip on her, and she slipped away. His strength was gone. He bobbed up and down, struggling to keep his head above the water, but there were only moments left to him. He would go down as surely as the wreck of the ship.

Fin reached out and took him. She wrapped her arm around his chest and began to swim. Without any idea where to or what for, she swam. And when she came to the end of her strength, she too flailed and dipped and struggled, straining upward toward the precious air. The muscles of her legs burned out and she slipped beneath the surface, holding her final breath long and dear. Images of Peter flickered in her mind and she wished she could apologize to him. In a last act of hope, or stubbornness, or defiance, she reached heavenward with her hand, raised it to the watching stars as if to wave farewell. And her hand came against wood. A hard corner in the formless deep struck her. She seized upon it, pulled herself toward it. She broke the surface and gulped in the night air. The fiddle case bobbed lively in the water and she clung to it. The night wind sighed and licked at her face. She pulled Phineas close and held him.

WHEN THE SUN ROSE, Fin was thankful. The world opened up beneath it, released her from the close walls of the night. But her thanks only extended into mid-morning. The sun was a tyrant's eye, wide and bright, trained on the intruder in its realm, searing her with an unrelenting glare. She dipped her face into the water for relief. Salt stung her lips where they had begun to split.

Phineas faded in and out of consciousness. The wounds on his back had yet to fully heal, and though he never complained, Fin knew the salt burned and prickled at them. She found a length of rope in the flotsam and lashed him atop a drifting timber. With another length she tethered him to the fiddle case so she could rest and not worry that she'd lose him.

Why had he saved her? Why had she saved him? Why did she care at all? At times she came close to cutting him loose to drift alone, but even as she allowed such thoughts to sweep her along, she found that in the midst of the reverie she would pull him close to stroke his face or spoon water across his sun-ravaged skin.

At times, he woke. When he did, he coughed and sputtered and looked around. But his eyes wouldn't linger on her. And he never spoke. Even when she tried to ask him how he felt or what he thought of their situation, he maintained his silence.

At night, the sky collapsed in upon them. The earth and sea became as small as the reach of an arm. And because sleep was nearly impossible, the night was a waking nightmare. Fear crept into them. How long could a person live afloat? How long could she thirst and not slake? How long could her belly complain before her body surrendered? No matter how long she could hold against such things, her father would fail far more quickly. And in that consideration, she finally began to think of him with that word: *father*. At first she cursed herself when her mind allowed him the title. But slowly, she gave way and accepted it. Whatever he was—however wretched, however empty or hollow—he had given her life. And more, no matter what his reason, he had sought her out. Surely that endeavor had earned him the title if nothing more.

When the sun rose again, Fin saw that he didn't intend to live through the day. He had resigned himself to his end. Fin saw it in the way he lay. He no longer attempted to comfort himself or shield himself from the sun's battery. He was a man jealous for the grave. And yet, at times, he'd rouse and pull upon the rope between them as if to reassure himself that they were fast together. Then he'd relent once more and lay exposed like an offering.

For the first day, Fin kept a vigilant watch for passing ships. But by the second, she had accepted the reality that even if she did spot a sail, it was false hope. A ship would have to come directly upon them or they would never be seen at all. Without the hope of rescue to order her mind, she fell into delusion. At times she saw Hilde standing over her; her nose waggled and quivered and she thrust a bony finger at Fin in accusation. Once she thought she saw Peter nearby, just over the next wave. He was struggling to keep his head above the water. Each time the waves parted between them she cried out but he didn't hear her. His head slipped under and when the waves parted again he was gone. Fin called to him for hours in her delirium. She even saw the sea itself change. It became a green field that stretched to the horizon in every direction. The wind blew across the grass and it undulated and rippled. Far in the distance Fin thought she saw a house, small and humble on the plain. She tried to swim toward it but the distance was too great, and even in her visions she despaired.

What Fin didn't know and couldn't have seen from her waterline view, was that the *Fiddler's Green* had accomplished one last act in the service of her captain. She'd left a trail. The flotsam of the wreck, though dispersed by great ocean currents and invisible to Fin, stretched out in a line for miles. Broken timbers, barrels, remnants of sail, shattered furniture, sea chests of the dead, and the dead themselves splayed in the water, a road of refuse extending to the horizon. It was this watery road that the *Esprit de la Mer* came across and turned to follow.

When Fin heard sailor's voices calling out, she shook her head and ordered them away. She damned them as visions and phantoms. But the voices wouldn't be driven. And soon they had forms and faces to accompany them.

A stranger's arms pulled her from the sea. The arms lifted her gently and cradled her head against harm. She saw Phineas Button borne along beside her. His jaw was slack, his body limp and dangling. She was carried out of the sun's assault and laid upon a soft surface and beneath light that didn't burn. Water. Cool water. It dripped through her lips and ignited life upon her tongue. A wave of luxuriance spread through her body. More drops rained into her and she buckled and shuddered with the goodness of it. Water, so simple, so pure. It flowed down and wound into her and created her anew.

When her mind and vision resolved, her surroundings took on definition. A ship. A cabin. A porthole on the wall. A beautiful face looking down. Bright eyes, set deep. It was a man's face. Not a young man, but neither an old one. His beard was light and short. It framed his smile and didn't obscure it.

The man spoke: "My name is Jeannot Botolph, and in the name of God, I have drawn you from the sea."

PART II

DAYS OF REMEMBRANCE

CHAPTER SIXTEEN

THE CREW OF THE *Esprit de la Mer* propped themselves against the rail and scanned the water in silence. The somber atmosphere reminded Jeannot of a funeral rite. Their heads were bowed, their faces dour and unreadable, their silence among them like an expectation. As the ship crept northward, sightings of debris came at longer and longer intervals. Each time a scattering of timber and refuse washed past, the men shuffled toward it and murmured over what they saw. At first, such sights were frequent and eventful, sometimes offering a chance to pull a floating sailor's trunk from the sea, a gift from the dead; other times they came upon the remnants of men torn to pieces by the explosion and they crossed themselves and whispered. Only once had they pulled survivors aboard.

"*Il n'y a plus rien à trouver, mon Capitaine.*"

The crewmen standing nearby turned to listen.

"In English, Remy." Jeannot spoke sternly but leavened his tone with a smile. English was the language of the Knights, and Remy knew it, but the men were lazy. Jeannot didn't blame them. To speak in one's own language eased the mind. The knights of the other *langues* might allow their crews to fall out of discipline while at sea, but not Jeannot. Discipline kept their minds sharp.

"There is nothing left to find, Captain."

"So you said yesterday. And yet we've drawn two from the water."

Remy frowned and pulled at his ear. The men nearby turned away, resolute and sighing.

"The girl is sea-mad, Captain, and the man is nearly dead. It will be a miracle to find another."

Jeannot smiled. "That is why we look, Remy." He reached out and patted his First Officer's shoulder. "That is why we look."

Remy pulled at his ear again and shook his head.

"Call me at once if our miracle appears. We search until nightfall. Then set us a course for the City."

This seemed to satisfy Remy. He left his ear alone and moved to the rail to join the rest of the crew in their search.

Jeannot ducked his head and descended through the companionway. The ship's surgery was uncrowded and clean, a state he was thankful for. His knighthood was scarcely a decade old, four of those years as captain of the *Esprit de la Mer*, and he'd seen the surgery blood-spattered and filled with the dead too often. Not so now; the room was put to the service of recovery rather than death, and for once, he felt at ease when he entered it.

The man they'd drawn from the water lay on a cot against the bulkhead, shirtless, with his back exposed. His skin was a thatch of half-healed stripes. The flesh was swollen and oozing.

"Will he live?" asked Jeannot.

Pierre-Jean knelt beside him and placed his hand on the man's face. "He burns. And—" he swept one hand through the air above the man's back. "Slavers. The man has been treated as an animal." Pierre-Jean made a spitting sound. "But the sea has cleansed his wounds. He will live, I think, *oui*." Pierre-Jean stood and wiped his brow. "You've found no more?"

Jeannot shook his head. "We will continue searching as long as the sun permits." He crossed the room and knelt beside the girl. He pulled a strand of red hair from her face and tucked it behind her ear. "And what of this one?"

Pierre-Jean shrugged. "She is unhurt—but maddened by the sea and sun. When she wakes, she sees phantoms. She raves of devils in the night and shouts orders as if she were a captain like you."

"Does she now?" Jeannot's eyebrows raised in surprise.

"She's quite impressive for a young woman."

The two men chuckled softly.

"She is quite pretty, I think," said Jeannot. He pulled another lock of hair from her cheek and arranged it gently.

"She will be herself in a day or two."

Jeannot nodded and touched her face with his knuckle before rising. "Send for me at once if she wakes."

"As you wish."

When Jeannot ascended to the deck, the crew hushed their mutterings. They exchanged guilty looks and turned back to their silent appraisal of the sea. Remy rolled his eyes at one of the men and walked to the rail. He certainly wasn't the best First Officer Jeannot had ever known, but he trusted his nerve in battle and the men liked him. Still, he would have to speak with him in private. Many captains would produce the flog for a thing as simple as the roll of an eye. Remy should consider himself lucky.

Jeannot took his place beside the helmsman and rested against the wheelhouse. Though there was wind enough at height to keep them moving ahead, the sea had turned into a glassy mirror. In such a crystalline sea it was easy to forget your intent and lapse into a glassy-eyed hypnosis. Jeannot shook his head clear and refocused his eyes on the surface of the water rather than the reflection it threw. No wonder the men were restless. They'd had their eyes on the water all day.

Murmurs from the forecastle drew his attention. A sailor pointed at the water and men shuffled forward. Jeannot resisted the urge to run and see for himself. Not a knightly thing to do. He waited as the crew gathered and leaned over the rail and talked among themselves. Remy jogged toward him with the news.

"A man, Captain!"

Then Jeannot did quicken. The men lowered a net to the water, and as Jeannot approached, two sailors climbed down to fish the man from the sea. When they came up, the crowd parted and the man was laid on the deck. He was naked to the waist, pale and blue-lipped.

"Retrieve the doctor," ordered Jeannot.

One of the sailors who had fished the man from the water looked up. "Too late for that, Captain."

Chapter Seventeen

FIN REMEMBERED A BLOSSOM of fiery light. And with the light, a sound like a thundercrack. After that—only a grey emptiness that carried and kept her. She lay motionless, wondering what the dreams had been about. They were full of shouting and fire, and they persisted into waking. So she lay still and stared at the ceiling of the cabin, waiting for them to drift into formlessness as dreams do.

No one ever entered her cabin without a knock for decency, so she was irritated when she heard the door swing open. Jack wouldn't disturb her unless it was important, so she held her tongue and sat up.

But the man entering the room wasn't Jack. As she struggled to understand, she realized that the cabin door wasn't hers—and neither was anything else around her. The man coming toward her was too tall for the room. He stooped slightly to protect his head from striking the ceiling timber. A black tabard bearing a white eight-pointed cross covered his chest. He stopped just inside the room and looked at her with his head tilted to the side. His face was vaguely familiar: deep-set eyes, a thin beard that contoured his face, giving it a depth that hinted at wisdom and experience beyond his obvious youth.

"I'm pleased you are awake," he said. His voice was pleasant and his words were given with a smile, but Fin jumped out of the cot and backed away.

"Who are you? Where am I?"

The man extended his open hands toward her, palms upward. "You are aboard the *Esprit de le Mer*. We took you from the water."

Fin's eyes shifted around the cabin, looking for an exit. The only door was behind the strange man in front of her. "Who the hell are you?"

The man lifted an eyebrow. "I am Jeannot Botolph of the Hospitalers, the Knights of Malta."

A faint memory came back to Fin: arms, pulling her up, carrying her. And his voice, *My name is Jeannot Botolph, and in the name of God, I have drawn you from the sea.* The memory frightened her. It felt like a dream that was too real. She put up her fists.

"Where's Jack?"

Jeannot pulled his hands back but kept them raised. His brow drew into a knot over his eyes as he considered her fists and the possibility that he might have to contend with them. "We drew you and two others from the sea." He motioned to the cot behind her. "This man. I do not know his name."

Fin shuffled to the side so she could keep Jeannot in sight while inspecting the man on the cot. As soon as she saw who it was, she cursed. Phineas Button. Damn the man. Where had he come from— and why? Again, a memory rose to the surface, faint and indistinct. Arms dragging her, throwing her, holding her afloat.

"What's he doing here?" Fin said. The way her words came out made her angry. She wanted to command an answer, but she heard tremors in her voice and knew it sounded frail instead.

"As I have told you. We drew him from the sea. You and he, together."

The images in her mind coalesced and took their places. Memories flooded back to her and she closed her eyes while they roared through her mind. When she recalled the memory of the *Fiddler's Green* blasted apart and raining into the sea, she opened her eyes and spoke. "My ship."

"We came upon the wreckage nearly a week ago. You are blessed, I think, that we have found you."

Fin lowered her fists and sank onto the cot. She put her face in her hands and wished she could go back to sleep and not dream. Her memory continued to rush back until it ended in the recollection of drifting, afloat on a wooden box. Fin's heart quickened. Was it gone at last?

"There was a case, a case for my fiddle—"

"It is there," said Jeannot. "You would not allow us to draw you from the water without it." He pointed to the floor beneath her cot. Fin pulled the case out and set it beside her. The leather binding was swollen and split. Water seeped from the joints. She flipped up the latches and opened it. The contents were secure. Betsy lay in her cradle and the fiddle beside. But the fiddle was ruined. The wood was swollen and waterlogged, and the finish was cracked and curling away from the wood. The belly had a hairline split that would widen as the wood dried; it would eventually sunder the entire instrument.

"Perhaps it can be mended," said Jeannot. Fin knew better. She clenched her jaw. As Fin closed the case and slid it back under the cot, Jeannot turned and opened the door. He ordered someone outside to bring food and water then drew a stool across the deck and sat upon it.

"What is your name?" he asked.

"What does it matter?"

Jeannot shifted uncomfortably on his seat. "I wish to help you. Perhaps if you told me your name, or where you have come from, I can send word to your family."

Despite her irritation at his questions and the confusion and anger she held inside, she laughed. It wasn't a joyful laughter; it was sad and uncomfortable, a laughter of spite. She pointed across the room at the man lying on the other cot. "There's my family," she said. The thought of it made her laugh until it began to look like crying. Then she quieted and dropped her face into her hands.

"Then you are blessed, indeed."

Fin looked up sharply. "I don't know who you are, but I assure you I am anything but blessed."

Jeannot didn't flinch or seem to take offense. He considered her gravely for some time before speaking again. "My parents were taken when I was a young boy. They left me in the care of my uncle and undertook a pilgrimage to the Holy City." Jeannot leaned forward on his stool and propped his elbows at his knees. "When two years had passed, a letter came to me. It bore the seal of the Grand Master of the Knights of Malta, and it told me that my parents' ship had been taken by pirates of the Barbary Coast." His voice came out of the deeps of him, and as he spoke, Fin was consoled, even though she didn't wish to be. His words siphoned the anger out of her and eased her mind. She kept silent.

"I made an oath to God," said Jeannot. "I would join the Knights and I would find my mother, my father. And I would free them." He became silent. He fell into his own thoughts and stroked his beard.

"And did you?" Fin asked.

Jeannot lowered his hand from his face. He met and held Fin's eyes. "I did not," he said. "And that is why I call you blessed."

In the silence of the room Fin heard her father's breath rasp in and out of his chest. She felt a sudden concern, a desire to go to him and touch him and care for him. But she didn't. She looked at Jeannot and then wrung her hands. "I'm Fin Button. I'm sorry I was rude to you."

Jeannot smiled and his smile tempted her own out of her. "In the name of the Knights Hospitaler of the Order of St. John, I welcome you to the *Esprit de la Mer*."

The door creaked open and a young sailor entered carrying a tray of biscuits and steaming tea. Jeannot took the tray from him and the sailor left without speaking. Jeannot placed the tray on the table beside the bed.

"Eat. Drink. And when you are ready, join me at the helm. Today we enter the City, and that is a wonder you should not miss."

Jeannot left Fin alone and she ate. The tea was too bitter for her liking, but she drank it all. When she finished, she crossed the room and sat on the cot beside her father. The wounds on his back were freshly bound and showed no signs of bleeding. Though his breath rattled in and out of him, he slept peacefully. Fin placed her hand on his arm and took the time to feel the warmth of it, the silkiness of the skin now hairless with age and loose over the flesh beneath. She squeezed his arm gently to feel the life in him, and it answered her with the throb of blood flow. Fin released him and left the cabin.

The *Esprit de la Mer* was smaller than the *Fiddler's Green*: a brigantine of some eighty feet, Fin estimated. The foremast was square-rigged as the *Fiddler's Green* had been, but the mainmast was rigged fore and aft with its massive mainsail raised by a gaff nearly parallel to the keelline. The sailors on deck stopped in their work and stared when they saw her. They chewed and spit, and those she came near bowed stiffly or nodded. None spoke. Ahead of the ship, the barren shoulder of an island heaved up out of the deep, and beyond the stony hills of its coast, spires and parapets jutted into the air.

"Do you see it?" shouted a voice from behind her. It was Jeannot. He stood next to the helmsman and beckoned to her.

Fin climbed the ladder to stand beside him and raised a hand to shield her eyes as she looked across the water.

"Valletta. Called the Proud City. Do you know of it?"

Fin said that she did not. She lowered her hand from her eyes and stepped between Jeannot and his view of the city. "You told me you drew two men from the water. Who was the other?"

Jeannot's face stiffened. "Come," he said.

Fin followed him through a hatchway and down a ladder into a dark room in the bowels of the ship. Jeannot plucked a lantern from the wall and knelt. He held the lantern over a blanketed form on the floor then reached out and withdrew the blanket. A hollow face stared up into the darkness beyond the light. Fin stared in horror. Before her lay the result of all her failures. The ultimate incrimination.

Fin pushed Jeannot to the side and fell to her knees beside Knut's body. She took his face in her hands and shook him. "No, no, no, no." Had he been lost at sea she could have lied to herself, told herself that he'd been rescued, told herself a thousand fictions to cover the guilt. But his cold body allowed no illusion. She tried to lift him into her arms but the rigor in his flesh held him stiff. Jeannot pulled her away but she shrugged him off. Knut was dead and beyond all help, beyond feeling, but Fin needed to keep her hands on him. She moved her fingers across his pale flesh, pressing and squeezing as if she might discover some lingering warmth to coax back to life. "No, no, no," she cried. Fin leaned forward. She pressed her forehead against Knut's and pulled his face against her own. She spoke into his mouth, forcing her words down into the depths of him. "No, Knut, no. Tommy, no, no."

Jeannot's hands wrapped around her shoulders and pulled her back. As her face drew away, her words became a groan. She strained toward Knut, holding onto him, trying to pull him to her, but Jeannot's hands wouldn't suffer resistance. When she let loose of Knut at last, she erupted. She kicked Jeannot and cursed him. She demanded that he unhand her, or fight her, or throw her back into the sea. But she couldn't provoke him. He held her fast until she spent herself and collapsed against him, at first wracked with tears, and then, finally, silent.

Jeannot lifted Fin into his arms and carried her upward. She lay numb. She didn't take hold of him to assist in his carrying of her. She merely lay, and if Jeannot had let her slip, she'd have fallen without raising a hand to protect herself. But his arms did not let her fall. He carried her through the darkness and the sweltering heat of the sub-decks, up, up, toward the sunlight and the cool breezes above. He bore her out, onto the deck, and he spoke into her ear.

"Behold, the City."

The *Esprit de la Mer*'s crew were in the lines and they called out to each other as the ship heaved to port and swung west for their final approach into the harbor. The Maltese headland was little more than a tumbled mounting of russet stone that climbed into a barren and dusty mainland. Truly, Malta was a rock stricken out of the sea. But out of the hard and uninhabitable promontory sprung the City. Massive bastions of stonework, centuries old, stretched into the harbor and loomed high as the ship drifted past. The City stepped out of the sea like a stairway of bronze, copper, and golden stone. Pillars and colonnades raised space out of the mountain. Paved streets ran the length of the harbor and switched back upon themselves, higher and higher, drawing up to a crest of domes set with pinnacles and spires. The sun drooped behind the mount in its setting and rimmed the utmost of these in shining light like great candles set against the darkening sky.

Fin saw all this merely because it poured through her eyes and filled the wasteland inside of her. She processed the scene as flatly as one surveying desolation.

Jeannot whispered into her ear. "We will bury your friend, Fin Button. We shall bury him among trees."

Fin heard his words but didn't speak. She closed her eyes. Jeannot carried her to the surgery and laid her upon her cot to sleep.

Chapter Eighteen

J EANNOT LED FIN ASHORE. A detail of sailors, under the
guidance of the ship's surgeon, Pierre-Jean, followed, carrying
Phineas Button between them on a pallet. The streets were thick
with people hurrying about their business, but Jeannot kept a quick
pace and the crowd parted before him. People scuttled out of his way
and looked on their humble procession with curiosity.

Jeannot led them up the winding streets, through the waterfront
and the market districts, until they arrived at a walled compound of
buildings hewn out of stone. Two men guarded the gate dressed, much
like Jeannot, in long red tailcoats over black tabards. They saluted and
swung the gate open.

"The auberge of the French knights," said Jeannot. They passed
under the arch of the gate into a cobblestone courtyard with a water-
less fountain at its center. Jeannot led them through a garden of marble
statuary and nodded toward the manor on the far side of the compound. Pillars lined the building's façade, and they were so thick Fin
didn't think she could wrap her arms around one. The stone blocks of
its walls were a mixture of creamy brown, vanilla, and egg white, and
its windows extended tall and slit-like from the foundation to the roof.
As they approached the manor, the great iron door whined on its hinges
and swung inward.

Jeannot's face twisted to one side and Fin thought he looked uncomfortable for the first time since she'd met him. They halted in front of the door, and an enormous man came out with his arms spread wide.

"Our dear Jeannot returns to us unharmed," he said. He let his arms fall to his sides limply.

The man was white-haired and fat, and his voice had a descending lilt of sarcasm in it. Jeannot didn't smile at his welcome; instead he stiffened and pulled his feet together then bowed his head. "Lennard," he said.

"And what have you brought me, Jeannot?" Lennard raised his eyebrows in expectation and looked suspiciously at Fin and then at the men behind her who bore Phineas Button between them.

"We came upon ruin left by pirates of the coast and have drawn two souls from the sea."

Lennard nodded impatiently and flapped his hand at Jeannot, urging him to get to the point. "And what else?"

"None else. We found a third but he was beyond help."

Lennard raised himself up and bristled. "A week at sea. A week of rations. A week of wages. I trust your ship at least is whole? Or must we repair it as well for the price of two slaves?"

Jeannot lowered his eyes and bowed his head. "The *Esprit de la Mer* is well-kept."

Lennard harrumphed and blew his breath out between his lips. "The grand master is waiting. I'm already late. We'll see what he thinks of you and your prizes, Jeannot." He waggled his hand at Jeannot in irritation then walked across the courtyard and out the gate, mumbling to himself all the way.

"Take the man with you, Pierre-Jean," said Jeannot. "Mademoiselle Button, if you will allow me, I will show you to your room."

"Who was that?" Fin asked.

"Lennard Guillot is the bailiff of the French *langue* of the Knights. There are eight *langues* in all, each with its own auberge."

Jeannot led her up the steps to the manor's high arched door and swept his arm forward to wait for her to enter. A long hall ran the length of the building, intersecting at the center with another hall running the width. At intervals, the tall, slitted windows threw sunlight to the floor and illuminated the space in sharp contrasts of light and shadow. Jeannot entered behind Fin and eased the door closed.

"This way," he said and went before her.

They walked in silence. The sound of their footfalls ran ahead of them like drumbeats echoing off the walls. At the extreme rear of the manor, Jeannot stopped and pushed open the door to a small room. Under other circumstances, Fin might have called it a cell.

"I can offer little," said Jeannot. "But it is freely given."

Fin entered and inspected the room. It was square but had a high ceiling; the illusion of space was a comfort. There was a bed against the far wall and a writing desk against another. A tiny window, high above, admitted a spear of light. Fin pushed the fiddle case under the bed and sat down. "Lennard called us slaves, but we weren't."

Jeannot pulled the chair from the writing desk and sat facing her. "When I pulled you aboard the *Esprit de la Mer*, you raved. The men called you sea-mad. They said it was an ill omen and begged me to throw you back to the sea. When you lay sick in our care, you cried out in your sleep. You called names, you swore, even gave orders and threats." Jeannot said this last with humor in his voice, and he tilted his head to catch Fin's eye and smile. "Pierre-Jean, the doctor, was quite unsettled, I think."

Fin fidgeted with her hands in her lap. "Pirates came on us at night. They set the ship on fire."

"What was the name of your ship?"

"The *Rattl*—the *Fiddler's Green*."

"And who was her captain?"

Fin drew in her breath and let it out slowly, anticipating Jeannot's disbelief. "I was."

Fin half-expected Jeannot to laugh at her, but he didn't. He leaned back in the chair and held her under the weight of his great consideration. Then he rose and removed himself to the door. When he spoke again, he was quick, distant, and formal.

"I shall ask Pierre-Jean to see to your needs and bring you fresh clothing. You are free to come and go as you will, but I must ask that until matters can be set in order you stay within the grounds of the auberge. I beg you to submit to Pierre-Jean and his inquiries. He is an able physician."

Jeannot left her alone, and she puzzled at his brusque exit. As Fin lay back on the bed and stretched her aching limbs she wondered what the doctor's inquiries might be. She felt well enough and thought she had made that plain to all by walking without aid and speaking civilly when spoken to. Then a sickening thought slithered through her. Jeannot thought she was still sea-mad, and in his mind, her claim to be captain had confirmed it.

When Pierre-Jean came, she complied with grace. She reasoned that protest was likely to prove his suspicions, so she submitted to his examination without contempt. He prodded her and pricked her and looked into her mouth and ears and he seemed to learn a great deal judging by the sound of his grunts and *hmmms* and the scribbling he did in his notebook. When he was finished, Fin asked him what he thought of her condition, and he scratched his head, wrote in his book, and proclaimed that she seemed the pinnacle of health. Fin heard a lack of conclusion in the tone of his answer though, as if he didn't quite believe what his examination had told him.

After he left, a servant rapped on her door and delivered a simple blue dress and fresh nether-linens. Fin thanked the man but asked him if there were any pants and shirts to be had instead. He nodded without speaking and returned with a pair of black canvas pants and a white shirt that buttoned up the front and had long ruffled sleeves. Fin smiled and thanked him.

WHEN MORNING CAME, JEANNOT presented himself at her door dressed in the habit of knighthood. His tabard was clean and crisp, and the white Maltese cross of the Order spread across his chest like a star. Beneath the tabard he wore a simple black woolen robe tied at the waist with a rope. He offered his hand to her and she took it. He said nothing of her trousers and shirt, or of the dress still folded neatly on the desk.

Jeannot led her out of the manor. The sky was unclouded, allowing the sun to paint the face of the city in a mottled earthen shimmer. A group of men met them in the courtyard, some of whom Fin recognized as sailors of the *Esprit de la Mer*. They flanked a tiny wooden cart and upon it Knut's body lay wrapped in white cloth. Fin pulled away from Jeannot's arm and approached the cart. She touched the burial wrappings around Knut's feet. He was so small. The wrappings bound his limbs so tightly and so close that he seemed scarcely like a man at all and more like a bundle of sticks, all bound in white linen. Had he really been so slight in life? Fin didn't think so. Life had filled him, made him more than the physical form of himself. When you saw him in life, you saw the secret thing that set him in motion. And now that the engine of his life was gone, all that was left was a pile of sticks wrapped white.

The cart lurched away. Jeannot took Fin by the arm and led her. Along the road, the crowds parted before them and many stopped to watch the cart and body draw past; old women crossed themselves and whispered blessings at the passage and children ceased in their play and stared. The procession wound through the streets, circling high into the stone-wrought city and over the crest of its upper reach until they came to a gate and passed through it into a different world. In all that Fin had seen of Malta, stone and sand had been the story of it. Seen from the sea, it was a barren heap of bedrock. From the city streets, it was a carved and constructed wonder, but yet a rock. Here, though, beyond the last gate, in the vaulted heights, a field of green spread out before her. Alabaster walls enclosed an expanse of a precious few acres, and within the walls the island's stone gave forth life. The enclosure was blanketed with shaggy, verdant grass that was thick underfoot and soft. Myriad flowers blinked and fluttered in the breeze, and strangest of all, the crown jewels of the garden were a circle of great, knotted olive trees sitting squat and ancient like the elders of some deathless arboreal tribe.

Fin stopped at the gateway, breathless at the unexpected beauty of it. Knut's body rolled ahead of her upon the cart and entered amongst the trees.

"We are the Knights Hospitaler," said Jeannot. "By ordinance of God we hold to the *corso*, sworn to protect all who go upon the sea and free those lost to slavery." His brow furrowed and his eyes saddened. "But our numbers are few and our resolve weak. I'm sorry we could not protect your friends." Jeannot stepped forward into the grass and then turned back and offered his hand to Fin. "It is said that whom the sea claims shall one day be given up to new creation. For your friend it will be so. Come."

Jeannot drew her forward into the garden. The cart, having gone before them, had reached the far side of the field and stopped beside a pile of dirt and stone. As they approached, the sailors (it took only two) lifted Knut's body and laid it in the open earth. Jeannot deferred to Fin, inquiring with his eyes whether she wished to speak.

Fin shuffled forward a step, not knowing what she ought to say or how. Knut's body was a finger trained upon her, pointing out of the earth, accusing its killer. And what could she say? How could she deny it? He was dead because of her. All of them were.

"Tommy Knuttle wasn't a hero or a patriot. He wasn't a husband or a father, or beloved of anyone. He was my friend and—" her chin stiffened and she could speak no more. She stepped backward and watched as the sailors filled the grave with earth.

Jeannot lifted a prayer, deep and even, driven out of him with confidence. "The Lord bless thee and keep thee. The Lord make his face to shine upon thee and show thee grace. The Lord lift up his countenance upon thee and give thee peace."

Fin watched in shame as the thrown earth obscured the last of Knut's frail form and she whispered one thing more. "And now I go alone."

Chapter Nineteen

A FTER THE BURIAL, FIN decided to leave Valletta. She tied her clothing into a bundle and slung it over her shoulder, leaving the dress she'd been given untouched on the desk. She traipsed out of the manor and set her bearings for the gate. The ragged fiddle case swung from her arm, leaden and heavy as an anchor.

As she crossed the courtyard, Pierre-Jean emerged and called out to her from the manor's doorstep. She didn't hear what he said and didn't care to. She intended to go, and she went. She had no idea where she was going nor how to get home, but going was necessary. She wouldn't sit and be inspected by doctors or thought mad or kept under lock and key.

The city erased her. It was a throng of men and women, some noble, some as vagrant as she, and Fin vanished among them. She wound through the streets, descending toward the sea, passing, in the city's highest levels, other great manors, "auberges" Jeannot had called them. Guards kept the gates of each, all wearing the same tabard that Jeannot wore, a white cross on a black field. But aside from the tabard, the knights of each *langue* dressed differently. Some wore hooded black robes beneath their cross, others red or white or indigo. A few shaded themselves under wide-brimmed hats pinned up above one ear and adorned with feathers.

As she continued her descent to the sea, Fin left the nobler heights behind and the city gave way to the homes of rich merchants. Long avenues climbed to ornamented and arched doors, and curtains of scarlet and lace bellied out of windows in the breeze. Servants draped in white linen attended callers with bows and practiced smiles, and here and there beggars slunk about the alleyways, foraging for cast-off food or stretching out their arms in search of alms.

The homes gave way to the market and merchant districts, where stalls and blankets upon the streets were covered with trinkets, luxuries, and necessities of every kind. She saw monkeys on leashes, birds like caged rainbows and other creatures whose names she didn't know. Curtains of exotic fruits and vegetables cascaded from every eave, and buzzing flies swirled between hocks and heads and the butchered meats of birds and goats and stranger things. Here the sounds and smells were greatest. It was the heart of Valleta. Here the city reveled in its chaos, spun in a whorl of acquisition and deliverance that swept Fin along with its strangeness.

When Fin emerged from the churning market, the world again seemed familiar to her. It was on the waterfront that she felt safe, felt at home. Among its warehouses and heavy-laden wagons and leather-skinned sailors she found the first sense of relief since coming to the city.

Yet, even in her comfort and familiarity, she was lost. She had no ship, no crew, no one to vouch for her skill or experience. She was a woman adrift, just as surely as she had been in the sea only days before. She wandered up the streets and back down—looking, listening, waiting for some opportunity to present itself and give her direction. The opportunity that came was not what she was hoping for.

What came, or rather who, was Jeannot. Either it was his height that drew her eyes or his manner. She spotted him hurrying in the crowd, his head and shoulders high above most others. But even in his hurry, his aspect was calm; his presence encouraged those around to move aside and give him leave. Where Fin had to bump and jostle and wend a shoddy path through the crowd, Jeannot moved fluidly, his confidence going before him, plowing a path of ease down the center of the street.

When Fin saw him, she tossed her shoulders in exasperation. He'd come to drag her back, and though she would resist, the kindness he'd shown her and the gentle humility in his eyes would make it difficult.

She set the fiddle case down and propped herself in the jamb of a warehouse door to wait. She didn't watch him come, preferring to let him think he'd found her of his own will.

Jeannot stopped before her and spoke plainly. "May I assist?" Before Fin could answer, he bent and took her fiddle case in his hand.

"Give me that!" Fin snatched it back. "I'm getting on that ship." Fin pointed down the pier vaguely indicating any number of vessels. "I'm leaving and—"

"And I will not stop you," said Jeannot.

"—you can't stop me."

Fin pushed past Jeannot and walked in the direction of the ships she'd pointed at. After a few steps, she glanced back to see if he was following. He wasn't. He was propped in the jamb of the door, just as she had been, watching her. Fin jerked her head back around, irritated that he'd seen her looking back. She wasn't sure, but she thought he might have been smiling.

As she neared the first ship's berth, she looked around for its crew. If she was lucky, she could sneak aboard and Jeannot would leave. If she was luckier, she'd even find a place to stow away.

There were two sailors at the forecastle polishing brass. They were busy at their work, so she dashed up the plank, hurried around the capstan, and with one look back at Jeannot, dropped into an aft hatch and held her breath to wait. No sound of footsteps running across the deck or shouts of alarm gave any reason for her to think she'd been seen. Fin wiped her face in relief. She sat down on her fiddle case and wondered what she ought to do. If someone spotted her and had to chase her off the ship, it would only reinforce Jeannot's opinion that she was mad.

She was in a narrow hall at the bottom of a companionway leading up to the main deck. The hall leading toward the amidships hold was unlit and dark. She'd have to wait for her eyes to adjust before she did much of anything. Then she heard a voice. It was far off, from the dockside, she thought. It was answered by another voice, much closer. She held still and tried to quiet her breathing so she could listen. The voice nearest called out again. It was close, on deck, not far from the companionway hatch.

"If I let a Frenchman aboard my ship, it'll take days to rid it of the stench."

The distant voice laughed. Fin heard and felt a man walking across the plank and boarding the ship.

"She looks fit as ever, Luther," said the man coming aboard. It was Jeannot. "No match for the *Esprit* in a fight, of course, but fit enough for a German. Then again, what did Germans ever know of the sea, eh?"

"And what do Frenchmen know of a fight?"

Jeannot chuckled. "And so it goes, my friend."

"I hear you've driven Lennard to drink."

"Greed drives Lennard. Where it takes him is no sin of mine."

"He will seize your ship if you drive him too far."

"And then you may see what the French know of fighting."

The man Jeannot called Luther grunted. "What brings you down the mountain, Jeannot?"

"Your new passenger."

Fin let out her breath and rolled her eyes. Rather than be ferreted out like a thief, she surrendered the game. "I am not mad," shouted Fin from below.

As she pushed the fiddle case up the ladder and climbed out after it, the two men stood with crossed arms and observed her appearance with interest.

"It seems you know more of my ship than I do, Jeannot."

"Luther, I give you Fin Button. I believe she seeks passage . . . home?" Jeannot inclined his head toward her.

"Does she now?" said Luther, and he too raised an eyebrow. He tilted his head and waited for Fin to speak.

Fin glared at them. Luther seemed genuinely boggled as he waited for explanation, but Jeannot's lips hinted at a smirk and set a fuse burning in Fin's chest.

Fin jabbed a finger at Jeannot. "I know what you think and you're wrong," she said. Then she drew herself up and addressed Luther. "I'm a sailor and I can work for my berth. I've sailed the Americas for three years." Both men peaked their eyebrows and nodded in unison. "Look," said Fin. She trotted across the deck, snatched the loose end of a line off the rail, and tied a bowline followed by a series of figure-eights, then stretched the line to the mainsheet, lashed them together with a sheet bend, and left it hanging. She narrowed her eyes at Luther and told him frankly that if he needed any more proof, she'd happily tie Jeannot up and hang him from a yardarm.

Both men's faces split into smiles and they laughed. Luther and Jeannot looked at one another as if they'd just discovered something they could scarcely believe and clapped one another on the shoulder. Despite the fuse Jeannot's grin had lit, Fin found herself struggling not to laugh herself.

"I believe it, Jeannot. I really do! Was it Button, did you say?"

Fin nodded, "It's Fin. All I need is passage home, and I'm willing and able to work for it."

"My dear girl, the *Donnerhünd* does not sail beyond Gibraltar. And though I have the highest admiration for your ability to tie knots and hang Frenchmen, I cannot allow a girl to my crew."

"Then I'll find another ship." Fin snatched her case off the deck and bounded across the plank.

Jeannot shrugged in mock exasperation. "My apologies, Luther."

"None needed, old friend."

Jeannot trotted down the plank and caught up to Fin. He walked beside her and pointed at the next ship along the quay. "Perhaps this ship? Her captain is a fine gentleman, and English," he said.

Fin ignored the ship, and Jeannot as well. She hurried on down the pier.

"Or this one perhaps? Another of the German *langue* but not so fine, I think, as Luther's *Donnerhünd*."

Fin stopped abruptly. She dropped the case to the ground and propped her fists on her hips. "Leave me alone."

Jeannot tightened his lips and creased his forehead.

"Can't you please just leave me alone," said Fin.

"To what end? You have no money, and no captain will have you among his crew. Will you deny the one who would help you? Have I done you aught but offer my good will?"

"I don't *want* your good will!" *Curse the man and his charity.* Why wouldn't he simply let her go? Fin jerked the case from the ground and started away but Jeannot took hold of her arm. Fin tried to shrug him off. When he held fast Fin dropped the case. She twisted violently out of his grip and threw her fist. She caught him in the eye. Her blow swept his head to the side, and Fin recoiled in regret. When he turned back to face her, she saw the skin under his eye was split and a rivulet of blood crawled down his cheek like a tear.

"I'm sorry. I didn't mean to— I don't know what—"

Jeannot reached out to her and took her hand in his. "Your anger is misplaced, but I accept it. Return with me to the auberge. Dine with me tonight, and in the morning, if you would still leave, I shall book you passage anywhere you wish to go."

Fin's gut advised her to refuse; it told her she didn't need his help or his money or anything else. She hadn't asked to be rescued or brought to Malta or chased through the streets. And yet as she opened her mouth to deliver her refusal, she stopped. All he had offered her was help, and she would be foolish to refuse food for another day and shelter and a safe bed, not even to mention his help in finding a ship home. She'd already struck him, should she insult him now as well?

Fin flushed with embarrassment and nodded. Jeannot bent down and took up the case then offered his arm. Fin suffered herself to be led back up through the city streets. They didn't speak as they walked, but the sight of a strangely dressed young woman escorted by a knight drew stares, as did the blood drying on Jeannot's cheek.

Chapter Twenty

J EANNOT LEFT FIN AT the manor to attend "the business of
the Knights," as he put it, and Fin, alone and restless, wandered
the halls in search of her father. She didn't dare open doors that
were closed, but she saw through those standing open that there were
other cell-like rooms, the same as her own. She found a separate wing
of stately suites filled with elegant furniture. In one she saw a brass
bathtub large enough to hold a half-dozen men. In another, a pair of
dogs, long-legged and slender; ropes of muscle rolled under their coats,
and they were adorned with golden collars and bracelets and leashed by
cords of knotted silk. Yet another room was a library filled with leather-
bound codices, maps, sea charts, and tattered scrolls.

At the end of the main hall, Fin found the manor's great room. A
group of gentlemen in black waistcoats sat in the sunlight beneath a
vast window in the western wall. They lounged on a curved velvet sofa,
stoking the bowls of their ivory pipes and conversing in solemn tones.
Occasionally, sharp bursts of laughter escaped their privacy and echoed
off the walls. At the other end of the room a fireplace wide enough
to encompass a half-dozen men abreast stretched across the wall. Its
mantel was pillared by marble columns, and atop it sat a collection of
squat, exotic urns and a shining astrolabe inlaid with gold and jewels.
A painting hung above. It was equal the massive width of the hearth

and depicted some great naval campaign of old, a hundred gallant ships embattled.

Fin strolled the length of the room and found that it also encompassed the dining area. A table of shimmering red wood as thick as her leg conscripted the center of the space. Each of its dozen legs swept to the floor and stood upon a foot carved in the shape of a lion's head. On the tabletop a plethora of strange fruits spilled from tangle-woven baskets, and dozens of silver candlesticks sat at intervals along the length.

She passed others in her explorations, mostly servants, but at times she recognized knights by the tabards they wore. Most were old men with graying hair, and though they all met her with smiles, they carried themselves with an aloofness that made her hesitant to speak or ask where she might find her father quartered. After wandering for the better part of the afternoon, she finally found him in a cell-like room on the far side of the manor. He was lying in his bed and Pierre-Jean sat next to him, examining the state of the wounds on his back. Phineas had his head turned toward the wall, and though he was conscious, he didn't react either to Fin or to the doctor's examinations.

"How is he?" she asked.

"He is healing well." Pierre-Jean scribbled in his journal then snapped it closed and tucked it into his coat. "He will not speak of it, nor speak at all for that matter, but I've seen the stripes of a slaver's whip before. The men we pull from their galleys, they are treated like animals. A man of his age, he is lucky to live."

Phineas Button listened dispassionately as Pierre-Jean spoke and didn't show any interest in correcting the doctor's guesses about his wounds.

"It wasn't slavers," said Fin.

Pierre-Jean looked at her uncertainly. "Well, whoever it was, he is safe from them now."

Fin stepped closer to the bed and touched her father lightly on the arm. He flinched away and Pierre-Jean observed their strange interaction clinically.

"To speed his recovery I have urged him out of bed, to walk, to build his strength, but he ignores me. I fear the worst of his wounds are beyond my reach." Pierre-Jean looked at Fin and tapped his forehead with a finger. Then he frowned and studied Phineas for a reaction. "Perhaps you can persuade him."

Fin stepped back as Pierre-Jean rose from the bedside. He collected his instruments and packed them in a satchel. "If you require my help, you will find a porter at the gate. He will send word to me at the hospital."

"Thank you." Fin smiled and Pierre-Jean left the room.

Fin stared at her father lying abed. She didn't know what she ought to say to him. She didn't expect he'd answer anyway. As she watched, he turned his head from the wall and looked at her. They stared at each other as if some silent debate hung between them, but when Fin opened her mouth to speak, Phineas casually shifted his eyes to the wall behind her and then rolled his head and turned away. Fin left the silence intact and retreated from the room. She could penetrate her father's mystery no further now than the day he'd first shuffled back into her life. She didn't know whether to pity him, revile him, or love him, so she tried her best to ignore him instead.

When Jeannot returned in the late afternoon, Fin was in the manor's library. She sat deep in the reaches of a leather chair with her legs tucked up beneath her and a book in her hands. The giant book dwarfed her, made her seem childlike and full of innocence. She was bent over the tome, studying it so intently that she didn't look up when Jeannot approached.

Jeannot cleared his throat. "Reading? Do you understand it?"

Fin let the book drop to her lap and fixed Jeannot with an insulted glare. "You don't think much of me, do you?"

Jeannot shifted uncomfortably, a rare thing, and Fin felt a twinge of satisfaction.

"And what should I think?"

Fin shook her head in irritation. "You should believe what I tell you."

Jeannot grimaced and studied the book in her lap.

"It's a history of the Knights," said Fin.

Jeannot slipped the book from her hands and perused the page she was reading. "Tripoli? The seat of the Knights, long, long ago. Chased out by the Turks, I'm afraid." The facing page was a map of the city and Jeannot ran his fingers across it with interest.

Fin pulled the book from his hands. "It says the Knights of Malta overtook Tripoli to keep it from the Barbary pirates. They built the keep and the harbor defenses and tunnels and even a cathedral."

Jeannot nodded as Fin spoke and then chuckled. "To keep it from pirates? And now they keep it from us."

Jeannot glanced around the library and noted several other knights taking leisure before the meal. Many of them looked at Fin and murmured, cupping their hands to hide the movement of their lips. Jeannot offered Fin his hand. "Will you walk with me?"

Fin put the book aside and stood without his assistance, knowing at once that she'd been needlessly rude. She tightened her lips and cursed her stubborn thoughtlessness then walked beside him in silence as they left the manor and strolled across the courtyard.

"What do you know of the Knights?" he asked.

Fin shrugged. "I thought knights were only in children's stories until a few days ago."

Jeannot smiled. "A man could do worse than to live in the stories of a child. There is, perhaps, no better remembrance."

"Until the child grows up and finds out the stories aren't true. You might be knights, but I don't see any shining armor," Fin said.

Jeannot stopped near the gate of the auberge and faced her. "Each time a story is told, the details and accuracies and facts are winnowed away until all that remains is the heart of the tale. If there is truth at the heart of it, a tale may live forever. As a knight, there is no dragon to slay, no maiden to rescue, and no miraculous grail to uncover. A knight seeks the truth beneath these things, seeks the heart. We call this the *corso*. The path set before us. The race we must run.

"You have seen the Maltese cross, yes?" Jeannot pointed to the cross on his tabard and then at the same symbol graven into the capstone of the gate. It was a squat, square cross that looked as if it were formed of four arrowheads with their points laid together; the outer arms of the cross forked, such that the whole emblem totaled eight outer points. Fin had seen it repeatedly since coming to Malta; it adorned each knight's tabard; it was engraved in their buttons and stitched into their clothing and etched into stones all across the city.

"Eight points of the cross." said Jeannot. "Eight precepts of the Knights. We are each bound by vow to these." Jeannot recited the precepts like an oath, and as he did so, he moved his finger clockwise over his chest touching each point of the cross. "Live in truth, have faith, repent of sin, give proof of humility, love justice, be merciful, be sincere, endure persecution. Each of these we swear before God."

"Tonight you will dine with the Knights. You think you are an outcast here, that you are unwanted, perhaps, or misjudged. But be vigilant in what you say and mark what you see."

Jeannot became quiet and studious of her, looking closely at the bones of her face, the sweep of her hair. He reached out as if to touch her but pulled away. Fin blushed under his consideration, suddenly aware of herself and anxious to speak.

"Do they know I'll be there?"

"I have told them. Lennard thinks you will make a fool of me, otherwise he would not permit it."

"Lennard doesn't like you?"

"These are troubled days for our order. Perhaps the last days. Few knights uphold their vows; they are filled with pride, and greed, and they thirst for power. Lennard does not like to be reminded of such things."

"Why are you telling me all this?"

"I would have you know my mind, and by knowing it, understand that I wish only to help you."

Fin felt her jaw tighten and had to force herself to relax. "I don't need your help."

"So you have said." Jeannot touched the welt under his eye. "But not all who need help cry out."

Jeannot escorted Fin back into the halls of the manor and to her room. When she was alone, Fin sat on the bed wondering what strange drama she had stumbled into. Jeannot's stubborn kindness and patience was as irritating to her as it was endearing. Each time her mind wandered toward accepting his friendship, though, she reminded herself that he thought she was either sea-mad or a liar, and that would settle the matter in her mind, though only for a time. She could come to no firm conclusion. He wouldn't settle where she wanted to put him. He stood where he stood and no place other. And this pompous Lennard thought she would make a fool of Jeannot, did he? It was a complicated challenge since part of her would love to do just that, but the better part of her would rather see Lennard himself made the fool.

Fin dragged the dress from the desk and held it out in front of her, measuring whether or not she thought it would fit. It was blue, the same loathsome shade as the dress Hilde had always made her wear as a girl, but this dress was a finer garment. It was meanly made of linen but ornamentally stitched, pleated in the skirt, and trimmed with lace at the sleeves and hem.

She put the dress on, impressed at how well it fit, and after a rowdy bout of scrubbing her face at the basin and a painful tussle between hair and brush, Fin stood in front of the mirror wishing Peter were around to see her now. In her own meager estimation she looked positively presentable. Even Hilde would have to look closely to find grounds for complaint. Fin grinned, thinking she quite liked what she saw, and was anxious to see Jeannot's look of surprise when she stepped into the hall. Then let this Lennard Guillot see who was made a fool.

Chapter Twenty-one

THE FRENCH *LANGUE* OF the Knights of Malta convened. On other evenings, each knight was free to dine when and where he wished, but by decree of Lennard Guillot, the mid-week meal was appointed. Each of the men arrived dressed in the black habit of the order, with mantles draped across their shoulders displaying the eight-pointed Maltese cross. Though some of the knights' habits were plain, many had jewels stitched into the fabric and braided tassels ornamented with gold and silver trailing from the sleeves. Upon some, their gems glittered thick and bright like stars on a black firmament, shimmering and roiling within each fold and flow of once-simple habits.

Lennard sat at the head of the table, and of all the Knights his habit was the most embellished. Every inch of hem was embroidered with lace and gemstones. A golden cross spread across his protuberant belly. His head was covered in a cap of white silk with flaps pinned up on four sides and folded together on the top. Each flap of the hat had a silver cross sewn upon it. He sat, fat and puffed up like a king. His fingers clattered with rings and he waited impatiently for the meal to commence.

When Fin entered the room, conversations hushed, and each knight at the table looked up or craned his neck around to look at her. She had never felt comfortable in a dress and the many eyes on her multiplied her unease. She nearly turned around and walked back to her room in embarrassment, but the sight of Jeannot reassured her. He stood beside an empty seat on the far side of the table dressed in his simple, unadorned habit and smiled. Fin walked across the room with her chin high, and one by one, the gathered knights pushed their chairs back and stood to bow. Fin blushed and nodded her head in acknowledgement, then sat.

Conversations resumed. The knights talked amongst themselves and occasionally called down the table to one another. Jeannot, however, kept silent. He poured a goblet of wine and offered it to Fin. She took it and sipped at it nervously, thankful to have something to do with her hands.

As the others conversed, Jeannot quietly told her the names and ranks of the men seated nearby. She could scarcely tell them apart; they dressed the same and each man's hair was either close-cut or shaved completely. For Fin, their chief defining feature was the state of their beards and mustaches; with beards, at least, there was a variety of colors, lengths, and styles. She remembered that the knight down the table with the waxed mustache that was preened out to fine, sharp points was Thibault; and she recalled that Benoit was the man whose beard was whittled down to a thin line along his jaw. But even these remembrances became muddy in minutes. There were simply too many new names and faces for her mind to account for in such a short time. There was one other familiar face at the table: Pierre-Jean, the physician. He sat half a dozen seats away and acknowledged her with a nod of his head and a curt smile.

Servants brought out dozens of baskets filled with steaming bread and set them along the table with pots of honey and butter. Knights plucked the loaves apart, dipping tufts of bread in the honeypots and stuffing their mouths, leaving glistening ropes of honey in their beards. Two more servants brought out a roasted pig on a silver platter. Four more pigs followed, each set end to end on the table so that no one was beyond reach of meat. The roasted pigs were surrounded with piles of potatoes, onions, carrots, and apples, and the knights took up knives and sawed off meat to fill their plates. Jeannot attended Fin's plate and then his own. The meat was soft and moist, better fare than Fin had ever eaten. She tore into it and tried to remember when she'd last had her fill of fresh food.

"She eats like a man, Jeannot," said the knight across the table.

Fin realized that she was eating too hastily and using her hands. Sister Hilde would have had sharp words for her. She was resolved that she wouldn't embarrass Jeannot, so she straightened her back, dropped the gristled meat from her hand, and took up her fork and knife.

"Maybe she's a sailor after all, eh?"

Fin opened her mouth to defend herself, but Jeannot cut her off. "A man of God should remember his manners, Henri."

The man grunted and stuffed his mouth with a potato. He stared at Fin while he chewed. "I hear you're a sailor. Captain even. That true?"

Jeannot drew his face tight and spoke harshly. "Henri!"

Every man at the table turned his attention their way. Fin opened her mouth to speak, but Jeannot touched her on the shoulder and interceded again. "Mademoiselle Button has suffered enough, she will not suffer your interrogations during dinner."

Henri dropped his meat to the plate and wiped his mouth with the sleeve of his habit. "Button? I've heard of a Button. The English knights tell of her. They say she was a pirate captain and the terror of the West until she was betrayed and sunk by her own countrymen."

Fin shrugged off Jeannot's hand and spoke. "In America some folks call her a patriot."

"Henri, enough," said Jeannot.

Henri ignored him and leaned closer. "Patriot or pirate? She's dead, no?"

The air between Fin and Henri crackled. Fin's face throbbed, hot and red.

Pierre-Jean spoke from down the table. "The girl was days adrift, Henri. You have seen the madness before. She is not herself."

Fin wanted to stand up and tell them all who she thought was mad, but she held her tongue. Jeannot's hand was on her shoulder again, urging her to silence. An outburst would only fuel their certainty.

Henri settled back in his chair and tore at his meat. "So, what do you intend to do with her, Jeannot?"

"I intend to see that the Order assists her in whatever way God wills."

The entire table rattled and shook as Lennard's jeweled fist came down on it. "And I suppose you've money of your own to lend her this assistance, do you?" The knights sitting between Jeannot and Lennard leaned back, clearing the air between the two of them. "The Order has paid for her to be pulled out of the water. The Order has paid wages for another of your wasted expeditions. And now the Order pays her way even here with food and shelter. I even hear the girl wishes to leave, yet you dissuade her. So tell me, Jeannot, how much more of this assistance should the Order pay for?"

"If she wishes passage home, it is our duty to provide it."

Lennard leaned back and laughed. "Duty? What do you know of it, Jeannot? What duty have you done?"

"I have done as knights do. Protect the weak, advocate for the poor, embolden the desperate—"

Lennard slammed his hand onto the table again, "Enough!"

Jeannot held his head straight and his stare steady. Lennard seethed; his chest heaved with anger. The knights between the two shifted uncomfortably as if preparing to jump clear if necessary.

"You are a ghost, Jeannot. A figure out of a song." Lennard chewed his words and spat them with vehemence. "Hold to your naïveté if you wish, but your charity will not be the ruin of our standing in the Order. You will sail tomorrow or you will be stripped of your ship and your habit. And this time do not return until your hold is filled, Jeannot. If you wish to offer this creature assistance, here is your chance, but it will be paid for by your own toil and not by my treasury."

Jeannot lowered his head. "As you wish."

The rest of the meal was an awkward silence punctuated by the ring and scrape of forks and knives. Men ate their fill and dispersed without speaking. When Fin pushed back from the table, Jeannot rose with her. Many of the knights stood in courtesy and offered their smiles and bows. Others ignored her or, worse, sat unmoving and made their offense with stares.

Jeannot escorted her through the halls of the manor and they spoke softly, hushing if anyone came too near.

"What did Lennard mean?" Fin asked.

"The Knights Hospitaler exist to protect. For a thousand years we have guarded the sea against pirates of the Barbary Coast. The *corso* calls us to free men taken in slavery, but our numbers are few and the Order is splintered by pettiness and politics. Each *langue* seeks standing above the others so that one of its knights might be named the next grand master and enrich them. Lennard cares nothing for our precepts or vows. He seeks only wealth and power. When we set out to sea, he commands that we fill our holds with spoil rather than men freed of bondage.

"Does the grand master know?" asked Fin.

Jeannot looked around nervously and lowered his voice. "The grand master is a good man, I think, and wearied by the bickering and pettiness of the bailiffs. But if I accuse Lennard openly, I am a traitor.

"So tomorrow I must sail against the Barbarie once more. Pray for me. Pray for the Knights. Our order is weak, and weaker each day. Should we disappear from the face of the sea, the Barbarie will prowl unhindered."

"All the knights aren't like Lennard, are they?"

"There are many good men. But few speak their minds or risk defiance. Lennard and the other bailiffs are powerful men. He wishes my death and hopes the voyage I undertake tomorrow will accomplish it. If not, he will send me again and again and no ship can withstand the Barbary Coast forever. I have been upon its reach three hundred days in the past year, and God has gone with me. The *Esprit de la Mer* has unfettered hundreds of slaves. But slaves do not enrich Lennard's treasury."

They arrived at Fin's door, and Fin turned to face Jeannot. "Let me come with you. I know you think I'm mad, but I can sail. And I can fight."

Jeannot smiled at her and touched the welt below his eye. "I do not doubt it. But I must refuse."

"Why? Because I'm a woman? I can fight, Jeannot, as well as any man, and I've lost my ship and my friends and you want me to sit here and wait. Could you do that? I need to do something, Jeannot, or else I really will go mad."

As she spoke, Jeannot's smile faded until he was somber. "I refuse because I fear for you. Though you are strong, you are filled with anger. You are reckless, and the fight you seek is vengeance." Fin tried to interrupt, but he held up his hand and pressed on. "I have seen men lost to the blindness of revenge and I would keep you from that. Learn to seek justice. Justice does not serve one's self, but others. Learn that, and then," Jeannot reached out and took her shoulders in his hands, "then you will be ready to fight." He squeezed her arms gently and his face softened. Though Fin wanted to protest again, she didn't. His manner calmed her and his hands were a warm comfort. He seemed about to say more, but his features hardened again and he withdrew a step as if embarrassed.

"*Adieu*, Fin Button. I hope to see you well if I return." Fin didn't want him to leave but he spun away. His habit ruffled and danced as he retreated down the hall. "Pierre-Jean!" he called out. "Assemble the crew!"

CHAPTER TWENTY-TWO

WHEN FIN AWOKE, BELLS were tolling in the distance and the whistles of the harbor were piping up into the city. She dressed, back to her usual pants and shirt, and ran out the gate to see off the *Esprit de la Mer*. But when she arrived at the waterfront, its berth was empty and there was no sign of its sails on the horizon. Fin meandered back up the street and wondered what to do. Though she could disappear into the city or stow away on a ship, she felt she owed it to Jeannot to wait. His kindness to her had sent him in harm's way. The least she could do was wait for his return.

"Still sneaking around my ship, I see."

Fin looked up. Luther stood at the rail of the *Donnerhünd*, smiling affably and tugging on his lapels. He was older than Jeannot. His hair had gone mostly grey, but his beard was still thick and black. He had a face of angles that didn't match, not ugly exactly, but peculiar. His nose cocked to the left, one eye was set too high, and when he spoke his mouth shied to the right and pushed his words out of the left. His voice had the hard cut of his native German but he carried English well.

"I came to see Jeannot."

"You missed him. Early tide. The *Esprit* left with it before dawn."

Fin frowned. She held her hand up over her eyes and scanned the horizon again.

"He'll be back soon enough. Perhaps two weeks. Maybe so long as a month." Luther swung his arm in the air, beckoning to her. "Come aboard the *Donnerhünd*. I have something to show you."

Fin, having nowhere else to go, trotted up the plank.

"Your fingers are no stranger to rope." Luther climbed down the ladder into the hold of the ship and Fin followed. The hatches were all open, and bright chunks of light tumbled in, illuminating the empty hold like a cathedral. Luther walked across the empty space and stopped before a heap of rope. He crossed his arms and stared at the pile with his mouth twisted and shook his head in disapproval. The pile was as high as Fin's waist. The ropes mingled together in a serpentine clutch of knots and tattered ends. Some were as thin as shoelace while others were stiff sheets thicker than Fin's wrist. The bulk of the great pile, though, was ordinary rope as used for lines and halyards in the rigging of the ship.

"Do you see?" said Luther.

Fin answered by continuing to stare at the rope.

"Pirates. Same as sunk your ship. They use chain shot. Two cannon-balls married together with links of chain."

"I know," said Fin. She'd seen it. It had torn the *Fiddler's Green* to shreds.

Luther looked at her as if he doubted the extent of her claim and continued. "They fire it from close range, and the chain slices through lines and sail," he made a whistling sound and a sharp cutting motion across the rope with the nail of his thumb, "like a knife. A lucky blow can topple a mast or bring a yardarm down on a man's head."

Luther raised his eyebrow at Fin as if to make sure she had a proper appreciation of the dangers of chain shot.

"I know," said Fin. She tried not to sound put off by his doubt, but she wished he'd get on with whatever it was he'd brought her into the hold to see.

"She knows, eh? Then you know this is the trouble it leaves." He picked up the tattered end of a rope and picked at it. "Ropes torn, split, cut to threads, useless. But the hemp that the rope makers use, where does it come from? Do you know?"

This time Fin didn't know. She told him so, and Luther raised his eyebrows in mock surprise. He seemed pleased to have discovered the end of her wit.

"America. And since the trouble began with England, hemp is rare. The price of new rope has tripled. And so, who do you think profits?"

Again, Fin didn't know. She shrugged.

"Those who can mend the rope, splice it." Luther tossed the rope back down onto the pile and turned to Fin. "So I wonder, after seeing your nimble fingers, if you can mend what the pirates have torn? I can pay you well."

"Your crew can't mend rope?"

"The *Donnerhünd* has had a difficult time. We lost four men on our last expedition. I prefer to allow my crew time to rest. They will do it, if you choose not to, but they have fat fingers, and they grumble. I only suggest. The choice is yours."

Fin jumped at the chance to do something useful. In truth, she'd have worked for free; the offer of a wage made the decision even simpler. Fin told him she was agreeable to the arrangement and Luther clapped her on the shoulder. He called out his first officer, a severe looking man named Johan, and instructed him to attain for Fin whatever she required. Johan nodded and, unexpectedly, Luther began to sing. He crooned out a German tune with his chin pulled back and his voice bellowing out of him bottomless and deep. Then he went ashore and strode down the pier singing and drawing stares. Johan watched his captain until he was out of sight. Then he turned to Fin and shrugged lazily. "He sings," he said as if he'd long ago grown tired of explaining Luther's behavior.

FIN ROSE EARLY EACH morning and enjoyed the daily stroll down to the waterfront. She spent the first day amused that Hilde's efforts to teach her a domestic craft had finally found a use. Splicing was not a far different discipline from sewing or crochet, and Fin's fingers found familiarity in it. She'd have spit at the thought of mending a dress, but mending something useful, like a rope, appealed to her. Luther paid her at the close of each day based on the gauge and length of the ropes she'd repaired, and he put many of them to immediate use re-rigging his battle-worn ship. At times, Fin went up on deck to help run the new lines, and Luther noted with interest her affinity for the terms and manner of ship work.

In her comings and goings from the French auberge, she came to recognize many of the knights. Though she never really spoke to them, she developed a friendly rapport in passing: exchanges of nods or smiles or rudimentary greetings. She suspected that Luther was passing around his good impression of her, because as the days went on, more of the knights offered her genuine respect rather than simple courtesy. Not all were so pleasant, though. Fin went to great lengths to avoid Lennard. On the few occasions that she passed him in the hall or on the street, he sneered at her or made pains to ignore her entirely.

Fin kept a leather coin purse in her fiddle case, and each evening when she returned to the auberge, the purse swelled a little fatter from the wages Luther had paid her. Fin wasn't clear on exactly how much the foreign currency was worth; the coins were a strange mix of copper, silver, and gold and they were imprinted with symbols and letters that Fin could neither read nor recognize. After a week of adding a few coins each day, the heft of the purse's weight began to impress her, and she wondered how long it would take to earn the price of a passage home.

During the second week of Jeannot's absence, Fin began to take Phineas Button with her to the *Donnerhünd*. She led him out of the auberge, and as they strolled through the streets, she pointed out sights she found beautiful or strange, but he kept his silence. If he turned to look, he only blinked and looked away moments later. The first day that she took him with her, he sat in the shadow of the hold and slept while she worked. The second day the same. By the third day, sleeping must have bored him, and he sat in quietude and watched. Though she merely tolerated him at first, in time she lost her need to be bothered by his distance. It wasn't something she hated or took offense to. It simply was. *He* simply was.

On the sixth day that her father was with her, Fin finished mending a rope and coiled the loose end on the deck. The other end was tangled in the heap, and she spent nearly an hour trying to wrestle it free. When she realized that she needed to pass the length of the mended rope underneath the heap, she turned to Phineas for help.

"Hey! Come help me out." Phineas looked up, but didn't rise. "Come here and hold this up so I can push the rope under."

Phineas blinked rapidly several times and chewed his beard. Fin decided he was going to ignore her, but he surprised her by rising and coming forward. He took the heap in his arms and heaved it up. Fin pushed the coil of rope underneath as far as she could. "Now I'll lift it and you pull the rope under on your side. Understand?"

Fin took the heap in her arms and lifted it. "Now, pull," she said.

Phineas jerked on the coiled rope and pulled it out. He backed away from the heap with the rope in his hands but a loop of it wrapped around Fin's foot and drew tight. Before she could say stop, he jerked the rope again and pulled her leg out from under her. Fin went down, landing with the heap of rope piled on top of her legs.

She cried out in surprise but she wasn't hurt. She was laughing. Phineas stooped over her and wrestled the heap of rope away. Fin propped up on her elbows and watched as he rolled the mass off of her. He traced the rope to her leg and unwound it.

"Thank you," she said.

Phineas wandered back to the dark corner of the hold and slid to the deck. It was barely a whisper, maybe a mumble, but Fin heard him say, "I'm sorry." He didn't speak or look at her again that day.

As they walked home, Fin detoured through the market and spent a few coins on a basket of nuts and dried berries. Phineas eyed them hungrily. She offered them, and he took two fistfuls without thanks. Fin told him to take as many as he liked, but she may as well have spoken to an animal for the acknowledgement she received. She wound her way through the market and he followed her, trailing a few steps behind, stopping when she stopped, keeping his eyes down. Fin wondered what he'd do if she ran. Would he run to keep up with her? Though she was tempted to find out, she was distracted from the thought by something she spotted lying on a merchant's blanket in the street. Among a scatter of earthenware, trinkets, broken furniture, and an assortment of bad paintings was a battered violin laying in a broken case. The lid was missing and the instrument was unstrung.

The merchant was crippled. His withered legs curled in front of him like desiccated wood, and he propped himself on his hands, leaning first one way and then another as if dancing to a music that only he could hear. His milky, blind eyes stared into the street, and when he sensed that Fin had stopped in front of his wares, he canted his head toward her.

Fin knelt down and asked if she could hold the violin. The man shifted his weight to his left hand and with his right felt along the blanket until his fingers touched the violin. He pushed it toward Fin.

"Is very good," he said to her. As she picked it up, he danced back and forth on his hands and nodded his head. The violin was different from hers. Hers was simple and functional, well made but plain; this one was the work of a true artisan. Its scroll was carved as a leaf and the pegs and tail were finely crafted in the shapes of a fleur-de-lis. But though it was finely made, it was poorly kept. It was covered in grimy deposits of use, thinner where the owner's fingers had touched it in the same places over the years. The finish was scraped and scratched, and in spots divots of wood had been chipped out of it by careless use. There was no way she could tell if it would still play if strung. In all probability, the tension of strings would shatter it.

"How much?" she asked but he answered in a language she didn't understand. She asked a man passing in the street to speak to the merchant for her, and after some confusion about currency and how much her coin was worth, she resigned herself to the fact that the violin was more expensive than she could afford. She thanked the merchant and laid the instrument back in its broken case.

That night she drew her own poorly kept case from under the bed and opened it. She picked up Betsy and turned the gun over in her hands. The water hadn't done damage of any real concern. A bit of oil to rub down its metal mechanics and it would be as ready as ever. The fiddle, though, was a ruin. As she feared, the crack in the belly had widened. The instrument was split down the middle and the strings hung limp. She gave one of the pegs a few turns, but the string wouldn't tighten; the pressure merely pulled the neck downward. She turned the fiddle over and saw a gap as wide as her finger between the neck and body where water had dissolved the joint and split the wood.

Fin removed the strings and bridge and laid them in the bottom of the case. Then she carried the rest of the instrument into the great hall where the fireplace was crackling. With one last appraisal of the broken fiddle and a swell of sadness, she laid it in the fire and watched it burn.

CHAPTER TWENTY-THREE

L UTHER'S HEAP OF ROPE was gone. Fin had repaired much
of it, and what remained she'd untangled and separated. But there
was still work to do. Now the bulkhead of the hold was lined with
some two-dozen coils of rope rather than the unwieldy chaos of the heap.
Somewhere above her, on the main deck of the *Donnerhünd*, Luther was
singing, a state that had become both familiar and welcome to her. She
had no idea what he was singing about, but the songs all had a distinct
flavor of patriotism and resolve, as of a man singing about pride in something greater than himself. Whether his pride was directed at a home-
land, a family, or a faith, Fin didn't know and didn't ask; he could have
been singing about wine and rabbits for all she knew. At times the crew
joined him, but generally he sang alone, and always loudly.

Fin had become so accustomed to Luther's serenades that the ship
felt lonely and unbearably quiet when he was away from it. Phineas
wouldn't speak, of course. He sat beside her, leaning against the bulkhead, staring into a dark corner or picking at the skin on his hands.
Some days, Fin talked to him. She even carried on entire one-sided
conversations to pass the time, to fill the quietness between them.

"When I get home I'll have to tell Carmaline I've been sewing. Well,
not sewing maybe, but near about. She'd love to know that. Do you
remember Carmaline? And Hilde?" She looked over at Phineas and

searched him for a reaction. He kept his head down and scratched at the deck with one finger. "Well, you must have met them when you— you know."

Fin finished with the rope she was mending and picked up the next. As her fingers teased the fibers apart, she felt a flood of words rising. Her instinct was to choke them out, push them down, but instead she let them come. They spilled out and didn't stop until they'd run dry. Though her story fell on deaf ears, she gave it to him. She told him what she remembered of her childhood and the sisters and the other orphans, even Peter. She spoke each memory out exactly as it came to her, an offering to accept or reject, given purely and without pretense. She was surprised to discover that she found joy in it. Even in her telling of Bartimaeus and Tan, she was strangely filled as she gave their stories away.

The rope in her hands was finished, two tattered ends spliced neatly into a single whole. She stood and coiled it then laid it along the wall with the others and plucked up the next in need of mending.

"Was never no good after Matilda-Mae gone."

Phineas wasn't looking at her. His head didn't come up, and Fin didn't risk speaking. She dropped down beside him and continued her work.

"Feared the pox would have me, same as it done them. Burnt the house. Burnt the field. Shot the horses, the cows, kilt the chickens and goats, even 'Tilda-Mae's dog. I kilt it all."

He was silent for a long time. Fin thought he must have said all he had to say. But then he did speak again, and Fin dropped the rope into her lap to study him as he talked.

"Aimed to kill my own self, too, and don't 'member much since. Ownt the bottle 'til the bottle ownt me. Years I reckon. All I know'd was my name. And the English come an beat me for it. Said I done things I didn't 'member. Sailorin' things." He tore a splinter out of the deck with his nail and snapped it in half. "Was you they wanted. Me they had. When they left me go, I hadn't nowhere else."

As he spoke, the blood drained out of Fin's face. They'd beaten him for want of her.

From above came the sound of Luther's return. He launched into a song and the intrusion was enough to sound the retreat for Phineas. He looked around, startled, then settled his stare into a corner and left it there. Fin wanted to pry him further or console him, but she knew by his manner that he was gone again, withdrawn to the inner fortress that warded him against himself or the world outside, she didn't know which. Fin reached out but saw him flinch from her. She pulled away and let him be.

When Fin finished her work, she led her father once more to the market. She sought out the blind, crippled merchant. He hadn't yet sold the fiddle. Fin sat down at the edge of the blanket and asked once more if she might hold it. The man said, as before, "Is very good," and nudged it toward her. Fin placed her hand in her pocket and pulled out the strings and bridge that she'd removed from her own fiddle. Carefully, she strung the instrument and nursed it into tune. With each turn of a peg, she feared the wooden hollow would collapse under the strain, but it held. After a few minutes she was able to pluck out a scale. The blind merchant attended all this activity by turning his ear down at each note, and he put himself in a frenzy of nodding as she brought the notes into their proper places. When she plucked the first full scale he said, "Is very good! Very good!"

"Yes," Fin said, smiling, "it is."

Then she took up the bow and began to play. The tone was warm and deep, storied with layers of age. The blind man slowed his nodding and shifting from hand to hand until he was still and cocked to one side, his mouth slack. Fin let herself fall away into the music. It carried her, assuaged wounds, bound things tattered and shivered, making them whole again, new again. And when she opened her eyes and lowered the bow, she saw a crowd had gathered. They looked at her as if they'd found a glimpse of something they'd looked for all their lives and never yet found. And then they offered her money. They threw it at her as if they could buy the thing inside her that they coveted. Though they knew they couldn't take it with them, they paid for what they'd been given.

Fin smiled and stood up to bow and thank them. Then she saw Phineas Button, still seated on the ground, gathering coins and stuffing them into his pockets. Fin wanted to believe he was doing it to help her, that when the crowd cleared he'd give her what he'd helped to gather, but she knew it wasn't the truth. He was taking it and would keep it unless she demanded it from him. She bent down and gathered up what remained and gave it to the blind man.

"Thank you," she said and placed the fiddle back in the case beside him. "May I come again tomorrow?"

The man nodded wildly. "Is very good."

As Fin walked out of the market, she looked back and realized Phineas wasn't with her. She retraced her steps and found him at the wine vendor handing over a fistful of coins for a bottle. Fin turned away and walked back to the auberge alone.

Each day after that, she returned to the market and sat at the blind man's crippled feet and played. Some days she recognized the people who gathered to listen. Often they came empty-handed, not having bought food or clothing or anything at all, and Fin wondered, had they come only to hear her? Whatever their reasons, they came. Again and again, they came. And they gave, much at first, then after a week, fewer and fewer coins, but each time she placed them firmly in the blind merchant's hands and he said, "Is very good."

One day, after she had given him her collection of coins, he held her by the arm and put her hand on the fiddle. He repeated what Fin now suspected was the only English he could speak. When he said it, his voice trembled and wavered with some emotion that Fin didn't understand. He pushed the fiddle toward her and said, "Is very good."

But Fin lifted the instrument and placed it back in its case. "I will come again tomorrow," she said. And she did. Every day.

A month and a day after the *Esprit de la Mer* departed, Fin spotted its sails entering the harbor. It was late in the afternoon; she'd finished mending Luther's ropes days before and lately had been coming each morning to assist with the repair of his ship. Luther professed his *Donnerhünd* would be fit as new within the week, and he was anxious to be at sea once more. When they spotted the *Esprit de la Mer* from the deck, Luther erupted into a spirited bout of singing. Johan explained that it was an old German hymn of homecoming.

Fin met the *Esprit de la Mer* at the dockside. Jeannot stood next to the helmsman and oversaw the mooring of the ship. He waved when he saw her but did not smile. He was haggard and dirty, and the crew looked equally weary. The ship itself had seen battle. The gunwales were dented and ravaged by cannon, and the rigging was tied together in places, stop-gap repairs awaiting a true refit. The sails, also, were torn and patched and in need of care.

When the ship was fast in her berth, Remy ordered the plank laid to the quay and Jeannot gave permission for his men to go ashore. Jeannot came across after his junior crewman.

"Welcome home," said Fin.

"I'm happy you are well," said Jeannot.

"What happened?"

Jeannot turned away and watched as Remy and another crewman lifted the hatches of the hold. They lowered down a ladder and men began to climb out. The men were gaunt and naked to the waist. Many were so skinny that their ribs protruded ladder-like under their skin and the tops of their hipbones arched out of their pants like shoulders. They were emaciated and skeletal, like dead men animated to life. The sight sickened Fin. She covered her mouth in horror. When the first of them stumbled ashore and approached her, she nearly gagged at the smell of human waste that accompanied them.

"Slaves. Taken from the galleys of the Barbarie. We engaged five ships. Two were sunk and all perished. From the other three, we have taken these. God be blessed."

"What about the cargo? Was there enough to make Lennard happy?"

Jeannot set his jaw and the authority in his voice was clean and sharp. "These alone are our cargo. What else we took, we pitched to the sea to make room for the last of them." One of the wraith-like slaves staggered and nearly fell. Jeannot steadied the man then called a crewman to assist him.

"What will Lennard do?"

"He will do what seems right in his own eyes. As for me and my ship, we will hold to the *corso*."

The remaining freed slaves crawled out of the hold and lurched ashore. At the last were two. One, a wreck of a man, his eyes sunken deep and ringed purple and grey. He hadn't the strength to stand alone, and the former slave beside him held him up. The man who helped him was thicker than the rest, as if he'd eaten better, worked less, or more probably, not been enslaved so long. The sturdier man caught Fin's eye and he gasped. He passed his fellow into Jeannot's arms and then fell at Fin's feet and wept.

"Fin! Fin, God bless ye! God bless, you're alive. Alive!"

Fin reached down and lifted his face toward her. Though thinner by far and wracked by misuse, there was, buried under the filth and running sores, a man she knew.

Chapter Twenty-four

Pierre-Jean ordered an entire wing of the hospital cleared to make room for the freed slaves. There were sixty-eight in all, many scarcely alive. The physicians of the Knights hovered over them. They ordered water and bread and wine be brought and proscribed how much should be allowed and to whom. The physicians inspected the men, and prodded them, and afterward huddled in small groups to argue best methods of care. They applied tinctures and poultices and salves of every kind, and here and there among the busyness lone knights and priests murmured prayers.

Fin sat next to Topper's bed and held his hand as he was tended. Though he was filthy and his face was covered in oozing scabs, he was every bit himself. Pierre-Jean approached him with a steaming bowl of liquid and a sponge, and Topper flinched toward Fin and protested.

"What's that?" said Topper. "I don't trust them doctors, Fin." He narrowed his eyes at Pierre-Jean and jabbed a finger at him. "Don't even try to stick me with nothing, or put nothing where it don't belong. You're worse than that Thigham, I wager."

"It is only water. To clean you—your wounds," said Pierre-Jean, inching closer.

When Topper heard the French accent he turned white. "A doctor *and* a Frenchman? God help us."

Pierre-Jean dipped the sponge in the steaming water and tried to wipe Topper's face with it. Topper batted his hand away.

"Git!"

Pierre-Jean's face hardened.

"Let me," said Fin.

Pierre-Jean handed her the bowl and sponge. "Gladly."

Topper settled back on his pillow. Then, as Pierre-Jean was turning away, Topper caught him by the wrist.

"Doc, I'm starvin'. Can you see they send some more o' that bread and wine?"

Pierre-Jean sighed and nodded.

"What about pastries? Ain't had a pastry in a terrible long time." said Topper.

Pierre-Jean jerked his wrist out of Topper's grip and walked away with a grunt. Topper settled back with a sigh of disappointment.

Fin soaked the sponge with water and squeezed it out then drew it across Topper's forehead, creating a clean streak as distinct as white paint on slate.

"Thought I was done for, Fin. Thought I'd die for sure chained up in that ship. The feller next to me keelt over dead the first day they had me chained to him, and I had to abide him like that 'til the fighting started and them accursed Frenchmen come and pulled us out. God bless 'em."

"What did they do to you?" asked Fin.

Topper groaned and pushed the sponge away. Fin merely switched from wiping his forehead to starting a new clean spot on his chest.

"Did you see anyone else? From the *'Snake?*"

Again, Topper knocked her hand away. Then he snapped upright in the bed and took hold of Fin by the shoulders.

"The rest of 'em, Fin. They're all there. All that's left leastways. Jack, oh God help him, Jack. They treat him terrible, Fin. They put him in a pen for sport 'cause they like to see him get riled and hop around on his good leg. Damn them rotted sonsabitches. I'll kill 'em Fin. We got to go. Thigham's there too, and Sam and Holler and that Tillum feller, and most of them green tars we took on." Topper worked himself into a frenzy. His breaths came quick and shallow, and he sweated and tried to stand up, but Fin eased him back into his bed.

"Lay down, Topper, before I have to lay you out with my fist."

Topper slammed his mouth shut and eyed Fin to see if she was serious. He decided he didn't want to find out and settled back onto the bed.

"We got to help 'em, Fin. We got to. Got 'em at a quarry all chained together. Swing hammers and picks in the sun all day. Lay in filth all the night long, and hungry. Powerful hungry, Fin."

"All right, Topper. All right. Just be easy."

Though his eyes were troubled and distant, Topper seemed to hear her. The desperation that seized him ebbed as he relaxed onto his pillow and slipped into sleep. The exertion and excitement were more than his sickened body could manage. Fin took advantage of his state to clean him—and his wounds. Beneath the dirt she discovered both of his eyes were blackened, not with grime, but with bruises. His lips were cracked by sun and swollen, and the skin on both cheeks was split in multiple places by what Fin recognized as knuckle marks. Under the dirt, his belly and ribs were a mottle of purple and brown bruises as well. There was a clear outline of a boot print in the center of his chest where he'd been stomped on or held underfoot. The sight of him lying injured, thinned, and helpless incensed Fin. Her skin prickled and crawled with anger.

"Don't worry, Topper. We'll get them."

Fin left Topper sleeping and walked among the others. They were each in far worse condition. Their stares were hollow and empty. As the physicians tended them, they didn't protest. They let themselves be lifted or turned or prodded without giving resistance. Their limbs flopped when shifted and lay akimbo where they fell. If anything human survived inside these men, it was well-hidden and fragile. In some it faded away entirely and was snuffed out as she watched. Priests were called more than once to administer last rites over the dying and dead. Fin watched as one man reached out with the last of his strength, too weak even to keep his hand from dangling claw-like at the end of his wrist. He willed the lifting of a solitary finger and touched the hem of the priest's robe. He stroked it down once and then up, an act that made Fin feel she'd stumbled upon a sacred intimacy. And then he died. It was as if he'd stored up all his hope of homecoming, and through years of enslavement he had spent it with great care, seeing that it need only carry him to this singular moment of ordination and then, spent entirely, he was free.

Fin moved among them, stepping lightly, taking her breath in long, slow draws for fear that any sudden move or stir of air might rustle and extinguish the broken spirits barely kindled around her. She stopped beside Pierre-Jean and watched as he cleaned the sores on a man's leg and bound it in clean linen dressings.

"Your friend will be well," he said when he finished.

"Thank you."

Pierre-Jean closed his eyes and bowed a slim inch at the waist. "You are welcome."

A door in the outer hall of the hospital banged against the wall as it was thrown open. The sounds of scuffling feet and alarmed voices followed, and a half-dozen men burst through the door to the infirmary wing, shattering the calm of the room. Lennard stormed through the group, pushing men aside and complaining.

"Out of my way."

He grumbled at first but shouted when he had to repeat himself. When he had a clear view of the room, he stopped and glared at it. "Where is Jeannot Botolph?!"

The physicians ceased their practice and the room became tense and expectant under the weight of his question. Knights and physicians cut their eyes around without turning their heads, wondering who would answer. Many eyes stopped on Pierre-Jean, judging him the proper candidate. Fin saw Pierre-Jean tense beside her and draw in his breath.

"I am here." Jeannot stepped through the door behind Lennard. He walked calmly among the beds, touching the rescued men each upon the shoulder or head, noting them. Lennard watched Jeannot's procession through the room. Everyone else watched Lennard.

"Who are these men, Jeannot?"

Jeannot did not look up but continued laying hands upon the withered flesh of men he'd brought back with him. "They are brothers in Christ, freed from bondage."

Lennard could find no purchase for his loathing of Jeannot in that, and so he fumed. He stepped to the nearest bed and glared down at the wreck of man lying in it. Lennard took the man's chin in his hand and jerked his head from side to side, inspecting him. He bent over and looked in the man's eyes, then sniffed of his stench.

"Dead men. You are gone a month and you return with dead men. I trust you profited enough from their ship to pay for their care?"

Lennard turned to set his face against Jeannot and wait for his answer.

"We jettisoned our cargo for the greater prize."

"So again, you have nothing."

"You would prefer that these men drown to fatten your vault?"

"*Damn* you, Jeannot!"

"You haven't the authority to damn me, Lennard."

Lennard began to laugh and Fin shuddered. It was a spiteful sound, full of malice and contempt.

"Very well. Pierre-Jean, see to these men. Treat them well. Spare no expense. The *Esprit de la Mer* will be sold at auction to pay for their convalescence. And you, Jeannot. You will learn something of authority."

Jeannot didn't betray himself to anger, though Fin was certain he must feel it. She knew very well the deep kinship a sailor felt for his ship, a kinship felt tenfold by a captain. What worse injury could a captain receive than to lose his ship, not in battle, or to the sea, but to avarice?

Lennard shook himself and straightened his clothes. As he walked out, the jingle of his finery was the only sound in the room.

Pierre-Jean hurried to Jeannot, and as they exited the wing together in solemn conversation, Fin could see something deep and wounded in Jeannot's face. Lennard's pronouncement upon his ship had put a crack in the edifice of his resolve. Fin could see it beneath his weariness, a thing like a fissure opened in the face of a mountain. When they were gone, Fin moved throughout the infirmary searching the face of each man, hoping to find another of her crew but recognizing none of them. But each time she looked into the harrowed eyes of an unfamiliar face, she felt the seed of something fierce and righteous growing in her chest. She'd led men across the ocean, far from their homes, and they were still out there, somewhere, and enslaved as these poor souls had been. And Jeannot was going to lose his ship for saving them. The idea of it stirred her, made her clench her fists; she heard the pounding of blood in her ears and felt a pressure in her chest that pulsed and throbbed and made her want to scream, or cry, or punch someone because she had no release for it.

That evening Fin went again to the market to sit at the blind man's feet and play. She poured out all her frustration in the music but few came to listen. The hour was late and the commerce of the market was nearly spent. When the notes were gone, only a single coin had been offered. Fin reached for the merchant's hand and placed the coin into it.

"I'm sorry, my friend, but this is all I have to give you."

The man smiled and shook his head. He pushed the fiddle into her hands as he had many times before, but this time, when Fin protested and tried to lay it down, he spoke in his own language. Whatever he said, he repeated it with urgency, and each time he said it he pushed the fiddle further into her hands and touched her face.

Finally, Fin accepted his gift. "Thank you," she said.

The blind man drew back and nodded. He frowned at her, but Fin sensed it wasn't an expression of sadness or disappointment. Rather, it was an indication of resolve, as if he'd set something right that had long been out of joint. Fin stood up and turned to leave, but said one thing more to him.

"I may not return tomorrow."

The man held himself still and turned his milk-flooded eyes on her. Fin felt something like vertigo and knew that, though blind, he was seeing. He wasn't looking at her or past her. He was looking *into* her. And what he saw, he judged.

"Is very good."

CHAPTER TWENTY-FIVE

WHEN FIN ARRIVED BACK at the auberge, the sun was down. Phineas slouched at the gate and cut his eyes away when he saw her. He swayed from side to side and smelled of his drink. Fin didn't bother speaking to him; he wouldn't reply. She walked past him and through the shadowed statuary to the manor. Inside, several knights were gathered by the fire and lounging, and as Fin walked to her cell, their conversations and quiet laughter babbled through halls.

Fin drew her fiddle case from underneath the bed and opened it. She removed the coin purse and weighed it in her hand. In the month of working for Luther, Fin had saved all her money against the hope of buying passage home and now the purse was so full that she could barely tie the neck of it. She stuffed the purse in her pocket and laid the new fiddle in the case beside Betsy. It didn't fit the cradle as well as the old one had. It was somewhat wider at the waist and shorter overall. But fit it did and filled the absence. She closed and latched the lid then hurried out of the manor with the case in hand.

Only a vague intention guided her. She saw the faint shapes and soft colors of a destination in her mind, little more than a course and direction, but it was enough. It was enough that she knew it was there and she felt it pulling her forward. Had anyone asked her where she went, she'd have had no answer to give other than to point to a place far ahead, and had anyone asked what she meant to do, she'd have calmly said, "I have to go."

Soft, orange light shimmered and blinked from the windows of the hospital. As she approached it in the darkness, her way was lit only by the emanations of its lamps from within. She didn't knock. She leaned her shoulder into the great iron door and it swung inward with a rasp. In the convalescent wing, candles winked in their sconces, and their tiny flames swaddled light across the faces of those in their beds like a sort of sacred bandage. Fin moved between them, lightly stepping. No one saw her enter nor stirred as she passed. She stopped in the center of the room and removed the fiddle from its case, then sat cross-legged on the floor between the bed rows.

She closed her eyes and began to weave a song. She abandoned the familiar melodies she'd played so many times before and went in search of something new, no longer wanting a song fed on pain or guilt. She needed one that could replace those wounds with strength, with resolve, with confidence. She needed a song that could not only assuage, but heal and build anew. The notes stumbled around the room, tripping over beds and empty stools and hollow men sleeping. They warbled and fell, haphazard, chaotic, settling without flight. Fin's forehead creased and she persisted. She let her fingers wander, reached out with her mind. She chased the fleeting song she'd glimpsed once before. In Madeira she'd felt a hint of it: something wild, untameable, a thing sprung whole and flawless from the instant of creation.

Men propped themselves on their elbows and looked around in confusion or alarm. They couldn't see Fin, seated on the floor, and the music, thin and lifeless though it was, seemed to come from nowhere and everywhere. Physicians came, too, searching for the source of the disturbance. An audience gathered upon her.

Fin ignored them and pressed on. She chased the song like a hound fast upon a scent. She pursued it through a forest primeval: a dark land planted with musical staves and rests and grown thick with briars of annotation. On she went and on still until she caught sight of the song ahead of her, fleeting and sly. "I see it," she said aloud, though she didn't mean to.

The physicians and nurses gathered around and shook their heads and pursed their lips. A mad woman, they thought. Pierre-Jean stepped in among them, calling for peace, and when he saw Fin, he reached out his arm intent to fetch her out of the music and send her home.

And then she caught the song. She fell upon it and music poured from the fiddle's hollow, bright and liquid like fire out of the heart of the earth. Pierre-Jean drew back and stood mesmerized. The room around Fin stirred as every ear bent to the ring of heartsong. It rushed through Fin and spread to the outermost and tiniest capillary reaches of her body. Her flesh sang. The hairs of her arms and neck roused and stood. She sped the bow across the strings. Her fingers danced on the fingerboard quick as fat raindrops. Every man in the room that night would later swear that there was a wind within it. They would tell their children and lovers that a hurricane had filled the room, toppled chairs, driven papers and sheets before it and blew not merely around them but through them, taking fears, grudges, malice, and contempt with it, sending them spiraling out into the night where they vanished among the stars like embers rising from a bonfire.

And though the spirited cry of the fiddle's song blew through others and around the room and everything in it, Fin sat at the heart of it. It poured into her. It found room in the closets and hollow places of her soul to settle and root. It planted seeds: courage, resolve, steadfastness. Fin gulped it in, seized it, held it fast. She needed it, had thirsted for it all her days. She saw the road ahead of her, and though she didn't understand it or comprehend her part in it, she knew that she needed the ancient and reckless power of a holy song to endure it. She didn't let the music loose. It buckled and swept and still she clung to it, defined it in notes and rhythm, channeled it like a river bound between mountain steeps. And a thing happened then so precious and strange that Fin would ever after remember it only in the formless manner of dreams. The song turned and spoke her name—her true name, intoned in a language of mysteries. Not her earthly name, but a secret *word*, defining her alone among all created things. The writhing song spoke it, and for the first time, she knew herself. She knew what it was to be separated out, held apart from every other breathing creature, and known. Though she'd never heard it before and wouldn't recall it after, every stitch of her soul shook in the passage of the *word*, shuddered in the wake of it, and mourned as the sound sped away. In an instant, it was over. The song ended with the dissonant pluck of a broken string.

Fin held statue-like. Her skin glistened with sweat and a tang in the air reminded her of the passing of thunderstorms. She lowered the fiddle and then, replacing it in its case, stood.

The people gathered didn't speak. Few saw her. They were lost, each in their own reveries, chasing the music still. Fin held up her purseful of coin, her savings against passage home, and placed it in Pierre-Jean's hands.

"For their care," she said. The money wouldn't go far. It wouldn't assuage Lennard's anger or satisfy his greed. But it was what she had, and she gave it.

Fin walked out of the hospital, picking her steps quietly around others where they stood. When she closed the door behind her, the convalescent hall was still as a painting. Men, both lying abed and standing, remained frozen, heads cocked to the side, eyes closed, or if open, seeing wonders in another world.

AGAIN, FIN WAS IN the manor's library when Jeannot found her. She sat alone, and notably so. The few other knights in the room clustered at the far end, away from her. As Jeannot approached, she didn't look up. She was huddled over a book and studying intently.

Jeannot sat on the edge of the hearthstone and faced her. "Luther speaks well of you."

"He better," Fin said without looking up. Jeannot chuckled.

"I had hoped to purchase your passage back to America, but it seems Lennard will prevent me. I will speak with Luther tomorrow. Perhaps he will help."

"I'm not going back to America," said Fin. The finality of the statement disturbed her, so she clarified. "Not yet."

"You are welcome to stay here. No one will turn you out until you are ready. Not even Lennard, I think."

"I'm not staying here, either."

Jeannot shifted nearer and frowned until she raised her eyes from the book. "Where will you go?"

Fin looked toward the other knights in the room. They were occupied with their own conversations, paying them no attention at all. Jeannot wore the effect of Lennard's offense as plainly as a scar running the length of his face. The impending loss of his ship hung over him and darkened him. "I'm going to the Barbary Coast," Fin said. She closed the book and laid it beside her then studied Jeannot's reaction; it was slight, thoughtful, a brief narrowing of one eye. "And you're coming with me."

Jeannot shook his head and leaned closer. "Your head is full of fantasies. You must see Pierre-Jean in the morning."

"I'm not crazy. Listen to me." Jeannot became momentarily restless with irritation or frustration, but he didn't call out or get up so Fin continued. "The man you brought back, his name's Flanders Topper. He was the helmsman on my ship and he can vouch for me and for everything I'm about to say."

Jeannot tightened his lips into a thin line of impatience and waited for her to continue.

"My name is Fin Button. I was the captain of the *Rattlesnake*. The English have a bounty on my head that'd make you rich if you wanted it."

"Is that so?"

"Listen! The Continental Congress, back in America, they hired us to come here. Have you heard of the Countess Caroline de Graff? She's French."

"I have."

"She's been kidnapped by Barbary pirates and I'm supposed to rescue her."

"This is nonsense. If the countess had been kidnapped, the Knights would know of it. And even if she was, why would the Americans ask you to recover her?"

"They need the French. They told me if we could get the countess home safe, the French navy might join the war."

Jeannot wrinkled his brow and rubbed his beard. "And you want me to help you?"

"No. Look. All I care about is my crew. Topper knows where they are. A quarry near Tripoli somewhere. I've got to save them, Jeannot. I can't leave them there and I need your help. I need a ship."

Jeannot laughed. "A ship? The *Esprit* has been taken from me. I have no ship." Jeannot tried to rise and walk away, but Fin grabbed him by the arm and hauled him back down.

"Isn't this what the Knights are all about? Protecting the sea, freeing slaves? The *corso* and all that? To hell with Lennard. We can sail with the tide before dawn and we'll be long gone before he's even done with breakfast."

Jeannot continued shaking his head. "This is madness. I will not steal a ship. Not even my own."

"So that's it? You just give up? Without a fight? Let him take the *Esprit*?"

Jeannot stood and shook Fin's hand off when she tried to stay him. "We have nothing more to discuss. I will fetch Pierre-Jean. I beg you to submit to his medicines." Jeannot turned to go.

"What if it was *your* friends out there? What if it was your parents?" Jeannot froze in the doorway and Fin knew she'd stung him. "I won't abandon my men to rot, Jeannot."

Though Jeannot wasn't facing her, Fin saw him bristle. The muscles of his back knotted and tensed under his coat. He inhaled a deep, ragged breath and walked from the room without another word.

Chapter Twenty-six

J EANNOT BOTOLPH WAS NOT a man easily unnerved. The walk from the auberge to the hospital should have calmed him, but it didn't. The quiet of the sleeping city and the lazy-eyed moon above only encouraged Fin's words to work on him, to burrow into his mind and gnaw. They chewed out memories and spat them back at him. He saw a man crawling out of the hold of his ship, bone-thin and sickly as all the others. But he knew this man. It was his father; his mouth yawned open and a voice stabbed through Jeannot's mind like an icicle. *Left us.* Jeannot shook his head to clear the vision and it scattered.

For the second time that night, a late visitor shouldered open the door of the hospital and entered its candled halls. Jeannot walked quickly. The heels of his boots knocked a rhythm out on the stone floor that quickened through the dim corridors and fell silent when he reached Pierre-Jean's door. Jeannot didn't knock, though he knew as soon as the door swung open that he should have. Fin's insistence had shaken him, and her childish accusation had nearly set his anger loose. The door swung open and Pierre-Jean stood before him.

"The girl is mad, Pierre. Can you do nothing for her?"

"Come inside."

Jeannot shuffled through the door, and Pierre-Jean offered him a chair. He sat. He ran his hands through his hair and rubbed his eyes. He hadn't slept well in days.

"I think she is not mad," said Pierre-Jean. "She was here tonight, do you know?"

"What do you mean?"

Pierre-Jean paced the room and recalled the fiddle song. "I was reading by the fire and I heard sounds in the infirmary. Sounds like the turning of an old wheel, or a door on a rusty hinge. I went to investigate and found her sitting on the floor playing a violin. I thought to stop her. She was disturbing the patients, and her playing grated the ear. But when I reached for her . . ."

"What?"

"It changed. It was as if . . . as if someone had reached into her and kindled a lantern. And the light of it spilled over me."

Jeannot looked sideways at Pierre-Jean as if he had heard him wrong. "Has she drawn you into her madness, old friend?"

"No, Jeannot. She is no madwoman. But neither, I think, is she any ordinary woman." Pierre-Jean stopped pacing and squared himself against Jeannot. "She is perhaps blessed. Touched."

Jeannot considered all this with a troubled brow. He put his face into his hands and sat huddled over. His father's icy voice shot through his mind again. *Left us.* Jeannot snapped his head up and looked around the room, but there was no one there other than Pierre-Jean.

"Her friend is still in your care?"

"He is."

"Take me to him."

"Jeannot, it is late. The man is—"

"Am I yet your captain?"

"You know you are."

"Then take me."

Pierre-Jean pulled a cloak over his nightclothes and lit a candle. He held the candle before him and led Jeannot into the convalescent ward. They picked their way quietly among the beds until Pierre-Jean stopped and held the candle near the face of the man lying in it.

"He is here."

Topper was snoring and his stomach rumbled nearly as loudly. Jeannot shook him by the shoulder until his eyes fluttered open.

"Strudel!" said Topper and looked around in confusion. When he'd worked out that his dream had been interrupted, he demanded he be let alone to go back and finish. "Leave off and let me sleep. Nearly had it in my mouth, I did! So warm, steamin' still, and flaky and sweet and honey-slathered and—"

"Tell me what you know of Fin Button," said Jeannot.

Topper sat up and looked at Jeannot like a proud man staring down an ignoramus. "What you want to know? And why? Don't know what you heard, but I don't know nothing."

"Was she your captain?"

Topper tried to work himself up into an admirable fit of indignation at the questioning, but Pierre-Jean quieted him.

"Be easy. We are friends. We mean neither her, nor you, any harm. Jeannot has been my captain for many years and he would not trouble you but for necessity."

Topper didn't seem entirely convinced, but he relaxed somewhat. "Aye, Fin's been captain of the *'Snake* since we headed out from Georgia. That's official-wise, mind ye. We called her captain since long before that even. Ain't you heard o' Captain Fin Button? Flame o' the West? Terror o' the British Trade?" Topper narrowed his eyes and looked for hints of recognition. He spotted none. "Don't they tell tales in taverns hearabout?"

Jeannot and Pierre-Jean looked at one another and shrugged.

"Perhaps you will enlighten us," said Jeannot.

Topper stretched a fat grin across his face and rubbed his palms together. "Why Captain Fin Button's the one what planted old Tiberius Creache six feet in the ground. She kilt the old devil himself in the church house and buried him 'neath it where he cain't never claw his way back up from the fires o' hell. I seen the fire leap from her eyes what kilt him even. I seen a passel o' British sailors run so fast to escape her fury that they run right across the sea itself, like Jesus done to the Galilee. When she's hungry, she calls for mackerel, and they jumps out the water and onto the deck. When she thirsts, she calls thunder, and the rain falls down and fills the water barrels full. She drives the sails of her ship by calling the wind with a fiddle tune. She's—"

Jeannot stopped him. "I think we take your meaning. But we're interested in less . . . ah . . . colorful information."

Topper frowned. "Well, shoot."

"How did a woman come to be captain of your ship?"

Topper shrugged, clearly disappointed by Jeannot's disinterest in his tall tales. Then he did his best to explain Fin's story plainly and factually. Jeannot and Pierre-Jean followed along with nods, smiles, and occasionally peaked eyebrows. Several times they had to remind Topper to tell the story without embellishment, and each time he wrinkled his face and complained.

". . . and that was the last time I seen her 'til you fellers snatched me back from them Barbary slavers." Topper spit in his hand and then wiped it on his shirt.

Jeannot and Pierre-Jean crossed their arms and took deep breaths and looked at each other, conversing with their eyes alone. Jeannot's eyes slipped past Pierre-Jean to a patient lying in a bed behind him. The man was sleeping peacefully despite the conversation taking place mere feet away. Then, emaciated and skeletal, he lifted his head and looked directly at Jeannot. His eyes were black and empty, and maggots squirmed at their corners. *Left us.* Jeannot blinked and the man was asleep once more. Jeannot took Topper's shoulder and looked sternly into his eyes.

"Tell me, do you know where your friends are enslaved?"

"Aye, it's a granite quarry. Terrible place. They took us to Tripoli first and then put us in a cage pulled by a couple of ox. Took us about two days I reckon 'til we got to the quarry. Nasty little place, all sand 'n rock. Nigh unbearable if it weren't for the wind off the sea."

"It was near the sea?"

"Aye, we could hear it off over the bluffs. The guards spent most their time fishing, I think, 'cause the only food we ever had was fish heads. Strange fish. Not like any I seen back home. None too tasty neither." Topper made a wretching sound.

"Thank you, friend," said Jeannot.

"Can I get back to my strudel now?" asked Topper.

Pierre-Jean nodded. "Sleep easy, and heal."

Topper laid back down on the bed and curled up under his blanket. He was smacking his lips as Jeannot and Pierre-Jean left the ward.

Jeannot didn't speak as he followed Pierre-Jean's candlelight through the halls. When they stepped back into the cell-like room, Jeannot sat. Pierre-Jean looked on him with concern.

"What is in your mind, Jeannot?"

"Why did you join the Knights, Pierre?"

Pierre-Jean shrugged his cloak off and hung it. "To study medicine. You know very well."

Jeannot squeezed his eyes closed and raked his fingers through his hair. "I do not know what to do, Pierre."

Pierre-Jean stared at him patiently.

"Do you remember why I came to the Knights?"

"Your parents."

"I didn't abandon them, did I? I've spent my life searching for slaves of the Barbary Coast. Defending Christians against captivity. Have I not done these things, Pierre?"

"You have."

"Then am I to stop because Lennard commands gold instead of men's lives?"

Pierre-Jean's eyes narrowed and his brow knotted with concern. He knelt down before Jeannot and looked up into his face. "What thing is in your mind, Jeannot?"

Jeannot sat up straight. "My sense tells me that I am a knight, sworn to God and bound to submit to the authority set over me. I may think Lennard a fool, but my station is to submit, not to defy."

Pierre-Jean nodded in agreement. "We all do as we must."

"And yet, a girl comes to me. And she would risk everything. And she asks for my help. Do you see, old friend? How is it that she stands where I would bend? Am I not the knight, and she the vagrant? A *girl*, Pierre. I, too, have seen the blessing within her. But I named it madness because I feared it. And because I covet it. You have heard how her man speaks of her. How is it the Knights are not spoken of with such reverence?" Jeannot jerked himself out of the chair and circled the tiny room with his hands at his head. "If Lennard takes the *Esprit*, how many who would be freed are lost?" Jeannot stopped and wheeled toward Pierre-Jean. His eyes were red and pleading for clarity. "What am I to do, old friend?"

"I cannot answer these things for you, Jeannot." Pierre-Jean curled his right hand into a fist and secured it over his heart. "But I will follow my captain, and I will not fear."

CHAPTER TWENTY-SEVEN

RESTFUL SLEEP WAS A luxury Fin had become a stranger to, but on her last night in the auberge it came easily. Her mind settled for the first time in as long as she could remember. She'd hoped to persuade Jeannot; his help would have been welcome. But even without him, she intended to leave. She didn't know how or with whom, but she meant to be gone all the same. She slept. And she didn't dream. The night passed; the world wheeled; constellations swept overhead. Fin floated at the crux, hovering over a vast stillness, bound in sleep until in the pre-dawn darkness, a voice stirred her.

"Wake."

Fin opened her eyes and looked up at Jeannot. He was bent over her, lit by a tremulous candleflame. The inconstant light rippled across his face, contouring it with a hundred subtle shadows and shivering highlights. The candle resolved to pinpricks of fire in his eyes, and for the first time, Fin felt he looked on her without doubt.

"Quietly. We must hurry."

Fin hadn't bothered to undress before falling asleep. She pulled on her boots, picked up the fiddle case, and was ready to leave.

Pierre-Jean was waiting outside the door. He bowed and smiled. Behind him, Phineas Button huddled against the wall. He glanced at Fin blankly then grunted and bowed his head.

"Where's Topper?" Fin asked.

Jeannot held one finger against his lips and spoke in a whisper. "Already aboard. Come."

They stepped through the streets, quick and silent, and descended to the harbor. When they reached the *Esprit de la Mer*, Remy was waiting at the rail. He rubbed his eyes and saluted as they boarded, then he withdrew the plank. Fin stood beside Jeannot at the helm as his crew eased the ship from the quay and maneuvered out of the harbor. They were in open sea and bearing south under an easterly wind by daybreak.

The rising sun revealed another ship. It followed the *Esprit de la Mer*, tack for tack, neither gaining nor falling behind. Fin assumed Lennard had discovered their crime and set out against them, but Jeannot explained otherwise. It was the *Donnerhünd*. Luther covered their departure and swore to drive off any ship in pursuit. Gladly, there was no need and the two ships sailed forth together, south, into the dark waters of the Barbary Coast.

Jeannot put his men to work at repairs. Their short time in port hadn't been sufficient to mend the damage the ship had taken. The crew groaned and mumbled but complied. The ship's carpenter, a man named Gautier, spent the morning on deck with a pair of sawhorses and an array of saws, shaves, and planes fashioning new planks and fixtures to replace what was broken. Remy ordered the rest of the crew to follow whatever orders Gautier gave and then stood nearby to make sure they did. Fin was anxious to help in some way and busied herself splicing rope until Jeannot sent word by way of Remy for her to join him in his cabin.

When she entered, Jeannot and Pierre-Jean rose from their seats at the table and bowed. Topper was lying in the captain's bed, propped into a near-sitting position by pillows. He looked like a man in perfect comfort except for the scowl on his face.

"I told 'em I'm good and fine, Fin. Make 'em let me out this confounded bed. I ain't got a straight answer out of nobody 'bout who they are nor where we is—but I'm right happy to see you're along, Fin. I'd near decided they was takin' me back to that blasted quarry."

Then Topper's eyes got big and he grinned, devilish and sly. "We're going to get our boys back, ain't we?" He looked at Jeannot, Fin, and Pierre-Jean in turn. "Ain't we?"

"We are," said Jeannot. "What do you remember of the quarry, the guards? We need to know their numbers. Can you remember the coast-line if you see it?

Topper scratched his balding head. "Yeah, I'd know it to see it. Bunch of crags and a cliff with a gouge out the center of it. Didn't get to see much afore they stuffed me down in the slave deck, but I seen what I could. I'll know it again."

"There is a dock?"

"Not that I seen. They anchored a ways out and ferried us. There's a little beach 'tween the rocks where to put ashore. No more'n a single boat at once, though. The place is smallish and likely watched."

Jeannot bent over the table in the center of the cabin and drew his finger across a map, following the coastline. "The Coast east of Tripoli is a bramble of sharp rock and cliff for a hundred miles. Are you certain?"

Topper blew out his breath, insulted at Jeannot's doubt. "I know what I seen. Look, they took us east for two days by wagon, can't have been more than forty, fifty mile. That's where they put us off at the damnable quarry. Then about a week ago a couple of the guards come through and picked out a few of us what they thought looked healthy and ferried us out to the ship. We walked down a little path between the cliffs and there was a boat waiting at the bottom. You want to find it? Let me out this confounded bed and I'll spot you from the tops. I can climb good as ever and got the eyes of an eagle. Ain't that right, *Captain* Button?"

Jeannot and Pierre-Jean turned to look at Fin.

"Let him up. If Topper says it, I believe it."

Topper smiled fatly and wrestled himself out of the bed.

"How many slaves are at the quarry?" asked Jeannot.

Topper massaged his belly and looked around for his boots. "A hundred if there's one. They work the poor bastards to death, and every few days they haul in a new load like they done me. Damn 'em to hell if they kilt Jack off. I'll eat their livers, I will."

"And how many guards?

"Couple dozen, I reckon. Each with muskets and them fancy Araby swords. They's a lazy lot, though, Fin. They ain't never do nothing but sit around all day to watch us work. Ain't but a handful of 'em got brains at all."

Jeannot studied the map. He repeatedly returned his finger to the same point along the coastline as Topper talked.

"We cannot possibly approach such a coast by night, even if you are able to spot it from well at sea. The rocks are too perilous." Jeannot straightened and turned away from the map. His face was grim. "We will be forced to approach by day. They will see us coming."

"Bah, we can take 'em," said Topper.

Jeannot shook his head. "I am not worried about us."

"Well then who—"

"They may kill the slaves."

No one replied. Fin's skin prickled.

"I have seen it before. When we assail their ships, if they see they are overwhelmed, they cut the throats of their slaves before they can be taken alive."

Topper exhaled and his breath whistled through his teeth.

"We will be upon the coast tomorrow evening," said Jeannot. "Until then, we rest, and pray we are not seen."

THAT NIGHT, FIN WANDERED the decks and put on a show of being dismayed when she overheard Topper, surrounded by half the crew, relating wild tales of Captain Button and her exploits. When she walked onto the gun deck and demanded Topper clam up, she was greeted by silence and the rustle of arms rising in salute. Topper chuckled and grinned and then made himself repentant and slunk out at her heel.

"You and your tales, Topper," said Fin in exasperation.

"Pah, let their imaginations run amok. Does 'em good."

Fin didn't protest. Unlike the fiction Armand had tried to force upon her, Topper's was harmless. Armand urged her toward something monstrous, and Fin was ashamed to admit he'd succeeded in some measure. But Topper's tales were different. They etched a picture of her in lines and shades of wonder rather than fear. Topper's fiction was a story that, however strange, she could live with, in part because no one would believe it, and in part because, secretly, everyone wanted to.

"Do you think Jack and the others are all right, Topper?"

Topper's grinning evaporated and he turned dire. "Don't know, Fin." He rubbed one hand over his head and patted his hair flat. "They throwed Jack in a pit. And then they throwed down a mad dog to watch 'em tussle."

Fin's lips twisted in disgust and she clenched her fists.

"Jack was still kicking when they hauled me out of there. Could hear him howling curses out of that hole. He cursed 'em day and night. Seen 'em throw dogs to him four times, and all's I could hear after was a growling fury while they tore at each other. I figured Jack was gone and done each time. But after the growl and yelp was over, his curse would raise again, each time louder and crueler than the last." Topper's eyes filled with tears and he looked away so Fin wouldn't see. "I know he's laying in there bit up and dying, Fin. Even Jack can't abide that. And they spit and pizzle down on him and laugh. Curse 'em all, Fin. When we get ashore I'm itchy to rip they eyes out, I am."

"What about the others?"

"Alive, mostly. Thigham, God bless him, looks after the lot. Even though he got no medicines or doctor's tools, they come to him at night with pains and wretchedness and he looks 'em over. He feels of their heads and touches their wounds and tells 'em they'll likely die come the mornin'. And they don't, of course. I think a man would keel over on the spot if Thigham ever told him he'd live. Bless that weasely feller; he gives 'em hope in his way and they sleep with smiles."

"Knut's dead," said Fin. "They pulled him out of the water."

Topper's face gathered up and wrinkled, and he looked down to hide it.

"We buried him way up on a mountain. It was a nice place, but I can't forget him laying up there all alone. Knut doesn't belong there. You know what I mean, Topper? He deserved better than what we all gave him and now he's alone on that rock and won't ever leave. And I did it, Topper. I killed him."

Topper shook his head.

"I did and there's no one can say I didn't. What was I thinking? That we could march right into that keep and come out clean? Well we sure didn't, did we? But we're going to make it all clean, Topper. We're going to get Jack out of there and we're going to get Thigham and Sam and Holler and Tillum and all the rest. And then—well, I don't know—but we're going to leave this place and get back where we belong. That's justice, right? To make things the way they're supposed to be? That's what we're going to do, Topper. Justice."

Topper didn't answer. He slouched toward the bulkhead and huddled against it. His shoulders heaved up and down, and Fin put her hand on his back.

"What if they kill 'em afore we get there, Fin? I don't think I could bear it."

"I got a plan, Topper. Don't worry."

JEANNOT'S PRAYERS WERE ANSWERED. The horizon remained clear of ships, and in the afternoon of the second day, the watch spotted the coast.

"East, Remy. Hold us along the coast and take her no closer." Jeannot extended his spyglass and surveyed the rocky shoreline, first west, toward Tripoli, then east. He snapped the glass shut. "Let us hope your man's eyes are better than mine," he said to Fin.

Jeannot handed the glass to Topper. Topper examined it as if he'd never seen such an instrument before, then he polished the lens off with his dirty sleeve and stretched it open. He held it to his right eye and winked the other closed, then swapped the glass to his left eye and squinted the right closed. Jeannot looked at him doubtfully.

"Ah, there it is," said Topper.

"The quarry?" asked Jeannot.

"The coast."

Jeannot shook his head and put his hand to his brow in irritation. Topper flipped the glass one way then the other and even aimed it up in the air for a moment. Fin decided she'd best captain him a bit.

"Topper! Quit foolin' unless you want a knuckle in your ear."

Topper jumped in mock fear. "Sorry, Captain. Ain't got to hold a glass in a long time." Then he got serious and scanned the coastline in earnest. Jeannot looked at Fin uneasily and Fin nodded to reassure him.

"Don't see nothing familiar," said Topper. "I'll shimmy up the mast and keep an eye peeled from there."

"Mind the glass, Mr. Topper," said Jeannot. "I haven't another."

Topper collapsed the glass and tucked it into his pocket. "I'll yell for wakin' hell when I spot it. Don't you worry, Captain." Then he trotted to the rail and hauled himself up the rope nimble as a man half his weight and age. Moments later he was sitting with his legs wrapped around the main yard. He leaned his back against the mast, fished the glass from his pocket and settled into a rhythm of swaying back and forth, east to west, scouring the rocks for the coastline he remembered.

Jeannot watched Topper with concern and Fin reassured him. "He'll find it," she said.

"Before sundown, I hope. If not, we must turn back north until morning. We cannot risk drifting near the coast in the night."

Fin nodded. "He'll find it."

Like Luther, Jeannot kept a massive tangle of frayed and damaged lines in the hold, awaiting repair. Fin went below and searched through the heap, pulling out rope and separating that which she judged neither too thick nor too thin. She needed something thick enough to wrap her hand around: something to give assurance of a steady grip, yet not so stiff that it wouldn't tie into a knot when needed. If the ends were frayed, she bound them. If the ropes were short, she spliced them together, piece by piece. Several sailors gathered around her throughout the day and watched in silence and puzzlement, but she continued her work undisturbed, and each in turn wandered away, leaving her alone mending tatters. In a matter of a few hours, she had four coils neatly situated on the deck, each at least eighty feet long. Then, down the length of each rope, she tied a single knot every three feet.

When Fin heard Topper hollering down that he "seen it," she carried the ropes up to the main deck and waited for Jeannot.

Chapter Twenty-eight

After Topper sighted the landing and convinced Jeannot of his certainty, the crew lowered the *Esprit de la Mer*'s two skiffs into the water. Fin passed down her mended and knotted ropes and climbed aboard with thirty other sailors, fifteen to each skiff, including Remy, Jeannot's first officer. Fin wished she knew the men with her. She'd feel more comfortable about her plan if she trusted and understood them. But Pierre-Jean judged Topper too ill to accompany her, and she refused to be burdened with Phineas. As she descended from the *Esprit de la Mer* into the skiff, Jeannot came to the rail.

"We will meet on the shore." He smiled with confidence.

Fin agreed. "On the shore."

She dropped into the skiff and settled herself on the thwart as the crew pushed away from the *Esprit de la Mer* with their oars. The sea was calm by Atlantic standards but the smallness of the vessel magnified the motion of even a light chop. Though Fin had been nearly two years at sea, she'd lived on the relative safety and solidity of the *Rattlesnake*'s expansive decks. Aside from ferrying to shore and affecting occasional repairs, she'd spent very little time in a rowing skiff. It was easy to become numb to the sea aboard a large ship, but on the skiff there was no escaping it; it was right before you, held away by a finger's width of wood. As the *Esprit de la Mer* shrank into the distance behind them, Fin remembered to fear the ocean.

Night came quickly. It slipped over them and took the last glimpse of the *Esprit de la Mer* with it. Fin's ears reached out for sound but all they caught was the rhythm of waves slapping at the hull and under that, the soft slip of the oars and the rush of the men's breath as they rowed. They drove through the dark, south. Fin crawled to the bow and looked forward, listening, holding her breath shallow and quiet, searching for any sign that they were nearing the rocks of the coast.

For hours, the crew rowed. At times, Fin spotted the faint silhouette of the other skiff twenty yards to port or heard the smack of water against its hull, but aside from those irregular reminders, she felt the night had swallowed them whole. The steersman kept his eye on the stars and his shoulder at the tiller, guiding them south, ever south.

Fin heard waves dashing on the rocks long before she saw them. A low, rolling rumble seeped in under the swish and smack of the water; it was so low at first that Fin thought she imagined it. But it grew until it couldn't be denied. The sound shook the nerves of the crew, a steely tension stretched through them. Somewhere ahead, the sea threw itself against the crags and rocks of the Barbary Coast. The men held their muscles taut. Cords stood out on their necks as they gritted their teeth and peeled their eyes in search of what they knew lay ahead.

It was the steersman that first noted the cliff. He lost the stars behind it as the horizon rose. Then, just visible in the starlight, Fin spotted a white trim of spray and foam where the sea hurled itself against the rocks. She held up her hand and pointed.

"There!" she said.

As the crew rowed the skiff closer, Fin picked up a thin coil of rope and draped it over her head and across one shoulder. She looked to the steersman and nodded. She was ready to climb.

Each successive wave swept them up and forward, closer and closer to the jagged rock. If they got too close, the tiny boat would be shattered. If not close enough, Fin wouldn't be able to reach the rock and pull herself onto it. When they were within a few yards, Fin perched along the starboard side, hands and one foot on the gunwale, ready to leap. The oarsmen fought against the waves to stay in position, first paddling one way, then the other as the water ran against the cliff and quickly back out. The steersman watched the waves as they came in, waiting for his moment of action. After every fifth or sixth wave there was a pause, and after every fifth or sixth series of such waves, an even greater pause. The steersman was counting. The timing needed to be perfect.

A wave passed and he called out, "Make ready!"

Another wave heaved under them and he repeated his warning. As soon as the wave swept them forward he cried, "Now!" and the oarsmen moved as one. The skiff surged toward the craggy face of the promontory and Fin leapt.

Her hands found an immediate hold, but her feet slipped on the wet stone. She kicked and scrambled, desperate to find solid footing. Just when she thought she had it, a wave slammed her against the cliff-face. The water surged up the rocks, nearly swallowing her. As the swell rushed back out to sea, it pulled and tugged at her, sucking her toward the open water. She clung tight to the stone and scrambled in a panic until she had a sure foothold then scampered upward, out of reach of the waves.

Fin turned her head to look back. The skiff was away and retreating to safety. If she fell, she'd drown in the darkness. But climbing was something she'd known her whole life and did well. Whether it was a bell tower, a tree, or a ship's rigging, she trusted her hands and feet to find a way up. She ignored the sea heaving beneath her and climbed. The jagged rock flensed the skin of her fingers. It didn't matter. She just had to get to the top. She inched upward by feel. A hand at a time. A foot at a time. As she climbed higher, the insistent clash of the sea against the rocks began to fade under the howl of wind. It cut along the cliff face in fat, blustery gusts that snatched at her and buffeted her against the rock. She didn't know how long or how high she'd climbed, but her strength was running out of her like sand through an hourglass. Eventually, she'd have nothing left and, empty, would fall. She kept her body pressed against the stone so the wind couldn't take hold and pull her with it. Her muscles burned. Each time she hoisted herself up another foot, a dozen grains of sand funneled away. Up, up. An inch. A foot. Her fingers and arms began to cramp and putting them in motion became an act of determination, of stubborn will. She envisioned Jack in his pit, torn and rent by dogs and she heaved herself upward. She remembered the sight of Barbary pirates loading their ships with her captive crewmen and higher she climbed. Tremors wracked the muscles in her legs. Another step. Higher. So high. How long before the hourglass ran empty? She couldn't hear the crash of the sea anymore. The shrieking wind raced across the rock face. Up. Up. *Don't look down. Look up. Look up.* She saw the sky widening above her. *Almost there.* She peeled her hands from the rock a finger at a time and climbed until, groaning, she heaved herself over the lip of the cliff and lay spread-eagled on the cold stone. Her limbs knotted and trembled with exhaustion.

She wanted to lie still and rest but she couldn't. The men below were waiting on her. Jack and the crew needed her. She gulped in air and the pain slowly pushed its way out of her. She raised her head to look around. To the east, the horizon was beginning to brighten. Dawn was coming and once it started, it would come quickly. There was little time to spare.

She unslung the thin rope from her shoulder then tied the end around a knob of rock and threw the length out over the sea. She crawled to the edge of the precipice and looked over. She could just make out the two skiffs below her. One kept some distance from the cliff; the other was nearer. They would be watching for the rope. She saw the nearest move closer to the cliff. She held the rope in one hand and waited, then felt vibration in the line and it jerked taut; they'd found it. A few minutes later there were three sharp tugs. Fin sat back, braced her feet on the rocks and pulled. The payload was heavy, but she hauled it up, hand over hand. When her arms tired, she leaned forward, took hold of the rope as far up as she could reach and then stretched out backward, pulling with her legs and back. Again, and again, and again she hauled, until the payload caught at the edge of the cliff top. She wrapped the loose end of the rope around a stone and reached over the edge. With one final heave she pulled up the four coils of rope she'd prepared on the ship. She unwound each, tied them fast to the crags of the cliff top and flung them down to the men waiting below in the skiffs.

Using the knotted ropes Fin had prepared, ten men from each boat scaled the cliff, making easy work of it, even in the darkness. After the last man clambered over the edge, they hauled guns and blades up from the boats. Fin was glad to have Betsy in her belt again, but she'd lost Tan's rapier along with her ship. The common cutlass Remy handed her was a crude substitute.

The party was armed and ready. The eastern rim of the world glowed in the preface of dawn. They looked to Fin. They knew what to do, she didn't need to give orders, but they deferred to her anyway. Had Jeannot instructed them to do so? It didn't matter. They had to get in position before Jeannot and Luther commenced their attack.

"Let's go," said Fin. She didn't wait to see if her order was obeyed. She crept west, toward the slave quarry.

The steersman had aimed well. They'd scaled the cliff less than a mile to the east of the quarry. In the light of the coming dawn, Fin spotted a narrow gorge running down between the rocks to the sea. The path was worn by foot traffic and marked at intervals by wooden posts stabbed into the rock and slouching at angles. At the top of the cliff on the west wall of the gorge, a tent quivered and flapped in the wind. A guard post. If there was any guard on duty, however, he slept or kept hidden. Fin urged the crew to keep low to the ground, and they slunk quietly and widely around the gorge.

Their first sight of the quarry wasn't the quarry itself but its small forest of hoists. It looked as if some monstrous insect had rolled onto its back and died, leaving only a clutch of legs struck upward, bent and jointed at inhuman angles. The quarry itself was a broad cauldron hewn out of the land. At either end, ramps cut down from the rim and wound toward the quarry floor. The belly and walls of the cauldron were an unnatural sight. The stone wasn't worn round as old desert stone nor chaotic and jagged like the sea-battered cliff; instead, it was cubic. Straight lines and hollows divided the rock where blocks had been cut out of it in perfect angles: here a rectangular void the size of a house, there a series of granite cubes stacked in perfect order, alien and strange. The entire cavity was filled with the shapes of construction where man had imposed a minor and unwelcome order on the subtler design of nature. Fin instructed the crewmen to spread themselves around the edge of the quarry and wait.

The eastern sky was bright, and the sun, yet hidden, set the clouds near the horizon ablush. The *Esprit de la Mer* was coming, and the *Donnerhünd* was fast at her heels. Jeannot and his men would be boarding the remaining skiffs and preparing to launch. Then, under cover of Luther's bombardment, Jeannot would lead them ashore. Fin and the men with her had only to prevent the slaughter of the slaves.

Movement in the cauldron caught Fin's eye. She dropped onto her belly and peered over the edge. Near the southern end there was a cluster of wooden structures built into the wall of the quarry. A man walked from the door of one of the buildings and relieved himself at a trench carved into the stone. Then, more movement. Light flickered in the window of one of the wooden huts. Two more men exited and walked to the trench. Fin heard wisps of conversation, a chuckle, a grunt. The men stretched and rubbed their faces and eyes then stumbled back to their huts. Moments later they re-emerged in full dress. They wore red and black robes, and each had a scimitar and a musket slung across his back. Fin counted four, then eight, then fourteen. Then she spotted another series of wooden shacks on the opposite end of the cauldron. Another twenty men were gathered there and spreading out around the quarry. They gathered in small groups, sitting on square stones or leaning against the sheer walls. They lit a fire and set a pot over it that steamed. They gathered around the fire and ate.

To Fin's right, one of the *Esprit de la Mer*'s men whistled to call her attention. He pointed to the tent above the gorge, the watch post. There was a guard standing beside it. He was shirtless and stood at the cliff's edge with his hand held above his eyes, looking eastward.

The crack of a whip made Fin turn back to the quarry. Somewhere below her a man was shouting, but not with the lilt of an alarm; it was a shout of command. The voice cried again and again. Each time louder, growing crueler with each repetition, and often punctuated by the sharp pop of a whip. The shouting was muffled, though. It sounded far away to Fin, farther than the distance of the quarry's far rim. She bent her head to one side and then another trying to pinpoint the sound. Other voices joined it, a murmuring. At the south end of the cauldron the stone descended to a small throat, a hole in the vertical cliff face, a cave. The entrance was gated by a latticework of wood that was propped open. It was the slave-pen. Each time she heard the whip crack, Fin gushed with anger. Her men were in there. And how many more? Out of the black eye of the cavern, a tormented wail arose. The whip drove it into a sob, then a muffled cry, then silence. Fin pulled Betsy out of her belt and caressed her. *Hold on, Jack. Just hold on. Jeannot and Luther are coming.*

From some pit down in the bowels of the quarry, a dog began to howl. It was a distant and lonely sound, an animal groan joined a note at a time by a miserable chorus of others. The baying echoed and resounded off the walls like horns. It throbbed and grew; it fed on itself; a bestial dirge, it rose out of the quarry and fled across the morning sea.

The guard atop the cliff began to shout. He ran into his tent and reappeared with a bell in his hand. He pointed to sea in the east and pulled on the clapper. The alarm rang out loud and crisp.

Dawn broke. The horizon unfurled in flame. The *Donnerhünd*'s sails gathered the light and the ship hovered over the still-darkened sea like a tongue of fire. And nearer the cliff, the *Espirt de la Mer* wheeled north, fleeing seaward while her skiffs approached the gorge. The guns of the *Donnerhünd* delivered a thunderbolt of cannon. One moment, the guard on the cliff was enlivened upon the rock, his bell raised high; an instant later he was gone. A fist of cannonshot caught the edge of the cliff, pulverizing stone and man alike, leaving nothing but a dust cloud and the dissipating ring of the bell.

In the cauldron of the quarry, the guards froze in shock and confusion. They each stood upright, faces turned to the north rim. The *Donnerhünd*'s guns struck again, raking the stone face of the cliff. The sailor to Fin's left sighted down the barrel of his musket, exhaled, and squeezed his trigger. A curling ring of smoke billowed outward, and across the cauldron a man crumpled and died. Then, all around the rim, the others fired. The guards below ran for cover, but the *Esprit de la Mer*'s twenty men had surrounded them and they pitched down a leaden hail of musketshot. Men ran and cowered and crawled into nooks and pulled themselves under wagons and threw themselves into their buildings. After two volleys, the quarry guards were emboldened. Some lieutenant among them shouted orders. Someone cracked a whip. Sharp voices barked forth. They leapt out of their cover and charged.

The sailors at the rim fired and fired again, but Fin had eyes only for the slave-pen. A guard stood at the entrance with his whip in his hand. He closed the latticed entrance and locked it. Slaves surged forward and pressed against the wooden gate. Arms protruded through it, groping and waving. The entire opening was clogged by a wall of faces pressed against each other, as if the gate withheld some strange subterranean creature of a thousand eyes and fleshy appendages. The guard turned and thrashed his whip, and the creature withdrew into the shadows.

Remy and his sailors charged around the rim toward the ramp and met the rush of guards with bayonets and swords. Fin ran the opposite direction, toward the southern ramp. Behind her the sounds of battle filled the air. The *Donnerhünd* hadn't fired again. That meant Jeannot was nearly ashore.

At the pen entrance, the slaves crowded forward once more and pressed against the wooden gate. The guard drew a pistol and fired into them. And again, the mass recoiled into the darkness. The unlucky recipient of the guard's musketball hung dead, his limbs caught and twisted in the lattice. Fin reached the slope of the ramp and sprinted down it into the quarry.

At the north rim, Remy and his men retreated to the mouth of the gorge. The guards pursued them, but when they descended into the narrow downward path they found Jeannot and his landing party ready. Two-dozen muskets exploded and the rout turned on itself. The guards fled back toward the safety of the quarry walls with Jeannot and fifty men at their heels.

The lone guard at the slave pen observed all this with rising apprehension, and the slaves he kept grew bolder. Rocks flew from the darkness of the cave and pelted the guard. He fired his pistol back at them. As he reloaded, the slaves ran forward and pressed against the gate yet again. They shouted and cried out and stretched their arms into the sunlight spilling over the rim of the quarry. The guard's eyes flitted from his pistol to the slaves and back again.

"Stop!" shouted Fin.

The man sneered at her. Fin pointed Besty at him, but the man only smiled. He stepped backward and positioned himself directly in front of the cave entrance so that a shot from Betsy was as likely to kill any number of slaves as it was to kill him. Cautiously, he continued to load his musket. Fin ordered him to stop again, but he ignored her, confident that Fin wouldn't risk a shot. Fin was certain he'd have no hesitation in shooting her as soon as his pistol was loaded. She rushed forward and punched him. The guard staggered backward into the reach of the arms outstretched through the gate. A brief look of horror crossed his face, and then they had him. He was pulled in every direction, choked, gouged, torn. What twist or break or stroke killed him, Fin couldn't say, but in moments the man was dead and dozens of arms were pulling at his clothes and dipping into his pockets. A hand drew out a key and passed it to another who passed it to another and so on until a hand took hold of it and slid it into the gate's lock. The key turned, the lock fell open, the gate swung wide.

Fin stumbled back as men shuffled out of the cave. They were chalk-white. The dust covering them cracked into pink lines at their joints and mouths. Their wide, wet eyes rolled and blinked in the morning light. Leg shackles fastened each slave to the man before him and behind. Metal cuffs chafed at their ankles. The skin was cut and blistered and blood-caked; it oozed in the dust and stood out boldly on their shock-white, chalky limbs.

A few yards from the cave entrance they sat down and waited as the key was passed from one man to the next and they freed themselves. They had eyes only for the key until the moment of its turning had come and gone. Once the shackles fell away, a few stood and walked aimlessly; one walked down the line touching each man and smiling, but most simply sat quiet and still. Strangely, though Fin felt she saw something heavy lift away from them, they were little different in their liberty than they'd been in their chains.

Fin knelt in front of one of the men and tried to look him in the eye. He sat with his legs crossed. Oozing sores and scars covered the raw flesh of his ankles. His hands lay limp in his lap, palms up. His fingers curled and twitched randomly. She couldn't be sure whether or not he saw her. He seemed to be looking at her, but he also seemed to look beyond her.

"We're going to get you home," Fin said to him.

The man didn't react, and Fin was reminded of her father and of Knut. Something fragile in the man's mind had broken loose, and whether in hope of life or death, had retreated.

"Captain?" A man sitting near the cave entrance leaned forward and squinted his eyes as he looked at her. She searched her memory for his face and name; he was familiar but the memory was faint.

"Cap'n Button! It's me. It's Billy Wright."

Fin remembered. He was one of her crew, young and green when he came aboard. And now, because he'd trusted her, he sat in chains, sickened, cut, bled, blistered. "We're getting out of here, sailor. Don't you worry."

"God bless ye, Cap'n! God bless ye!"

Fin's name began to spread; like the key, it was passed from man to man like something precious. Billy Wright whispered it to the man beside him. "Captain Button's come back!" he said, and that man sat a little straighter and bent his head to the next. They tendered it into one another's ears, and she heard her name catch and carry deeper into the cave where the murmurs rumbled lowly. "Captain Button's come fer us!"

"Huzzah!" "Flame of the West, kindled yet!" "The captain's come, d'ya hear? My captain's come!" The whispers rushed and grew and men came alive at the sound. Fin looked back at the man before her, who she'd thought lost within himself. His eyes focused and he saw her. His lips trembled and the chalk of his face broke into new lines when he smiled.

As the key passed down the line and deeper into the cave, more men emerged. They were in various states of health and dress, but Fin knew them immediately. She didn't recall all of their names, but they were the faces of her crew and they came out to her smiling. They wanted to touch her and embrace her, and she let them. Holler Engles came out and called, "Fin! By God!" And then Sam Catcher, and Pelly Quinn the cook, and Tillum, the carpenter who'd fashioned Jack a new leg. There were few of the old crew left, but she was glad to see them. They gathered around her and welcomed her like a lost family member.

Lucas Thigham stumbled out of the cave entrance and squinted. His spectacles were ruined, broken in half. Only one lens remained, scratched and nicked like the bottom of an old bottle. He held it up to his face like a monocle.

"Good morning, Dr. Thigham," said Fin. "I'm happy to find my crew unkilled."

Thigham frowned at her. "Not all of them."

Fin turned somber. She walked toward the doctor and past him into the cavern. The sunlight didn't reach far, but after her eyes adjusted she could make out even the dimmest corners. The ceiling of the chamber was low and uneven, requiring her to bend over as she walked further inside. The smell of death and waste was overwhelming. She pulled her shirt up over her nose and noted that Thigham and the rest used no such filter; they'd grown accustomed to the stench. Some thirty feet inside, the chamber split into two distinct rooms. Crowded together like cattle, a multitude of men sat in the leftmost chamber, patient in their chains as they awaited the key. The scant light caught in their eyes and threw flickers back at her from even the darkest corners. In the right-hand room, however, she saw only blackness.

"The house of the dead," said Thigham. He walked toward the chamber and she followed him. The smell of rotting flesh thickened. Fins eyes watered and burned with it.

Thigham stopped. "I tried to take care of them, Captain. Perhaps if I'd had my bag . . . or my books . . ."

The chamber was strewn with wrecked bodies. The nearest were the freshly dead and they looked scarcely different from the living, but the further back she looked, the worse the horror became. Beyond the recently dead, there lay bloated and misshapen forms; some had swollen and burst, and Fin saw the movement of insects and carrion crawling among them. Deeper in, what was left of the bodies was desiccated and leathery, and at the utmost wall only white bones remained. The dead were hundreds upon hundreds, one heaped upon the other in a union of atrocity. How many of these were her crew? Enslaved by her misbegotten leadership, they lay broken and rotting, far from home. Fin knotted up her fists to steady her hands.

Lucas Thigham lowered his makeshift monocle and hung his head.

"You did well, Lucas. Topper told me you took care of everyone."

As soon as the words escaped her mouth, she realized she hadn't seen Jack. Fin ran out of the cave. The quarry floor was covered in stepped stone and pits and small corridors where massive blocks of granite had been harvested.

"Jack," she called, but she hadn't hope that he'd hear. The prisoners at the cave were talking, chattering, some beginning to sing, and the barking and baying of dogs filled the cauldron with sound. Fin ran across the stone, jumping from one block to the next. Her heart skipped each time she spotted a pit and she raced to it. But each one she found was empty. Then it occurred to her: the dogs. She leapt onto the tallest stone she could reach and stood still. She cocked her ear toward the barking, and once she was sure of its direction, she bolted toward it.

On the west side of the cauldron she found a kennel of latticed wood. Inside it, dozens of mongrel dogs paced and snapped and barked. Beyond the kennel there was another pit. Fin rushed to the edge and stared into it.

The pit was a ragged rectangle cut out of the stone. It was about ten feet deep and a wooden ladder leaned against the wall at one end. At the opposite end, Jack was shackled like a beast. He had a metal collar around his neck. The back of the collar was affixed to a chain, and the chain affixed to the wall. From the front of the collar two more chains ran to his wrists and shackled them so that his arms could not hang straight or stretch to their full reach. He was kneeling on the floor of the pit, slouched to one side as he held himself up on the stump of his right leg. He hung forward, pulling the chain between the collar and the wall taut. Around him, the floor was strewn with the decaying corpses of dogs.

"You seen enough yet, Button? Quit gawking and get me out these blasted chains!"

Lucas Thigham ran up beside her and looked down at Jack. "Oh, dear," he said.

"Hold on, Jack. I'll find the keys," said Fin.

"You ain't got to find 'em. They're hanging right there." Jack lifted one hand as far as the chains would allow and pointed. The ring of keys hung from a nail on the ladder, plainly in front of him and as out of reach as a star. Fin and Lucas climbed down and fetched them.

When they had him loose, Jack collapsed onto the stone floor. He sighed deeply and lay with his arms and leg stretched wide. He was raw and blistered where the cuffs and collar had held him, and his hands and legs were badly cut up. He was covered in bite marks. Some were scabbed over, but others were swollen and oozing.

"Oh, dear. Oh, my!" said Thigham. As he bent over Jack's good leg and gently explored the wounds with his finger, he made a concerned clicking sound with his tongue.

Jack jerked his head up and snarled. "You even think about having that leg and you'll wish you was as lucky as them mutts."

Lucas looked around the pit and considered the dead dogs in alarm.

"This makes twice now you've hauled my arse out of a fix, Button. Let's don't have cause for a third. Don't know that I could weather it."

Fin smiled while Lucas paced to and fro beside them, clicking his tongue and muttering, "Oh my, oh dear."

Fin called Holler and Tillum to help Jack out of the pit, and as they rejoined the rest of the crew, Jeannot and his men descended the ramp at the north end of the quarry. Fin coaxed the miserable men around her to their feet and led them. They crowded around her as she went. Like a parade of beggars, they shuffled across the stone half-clothed, unconscious of their filth, and wide-eyed. In the slave pen, a man at a time, they shed their shackles, emerged, and joined the parade until the procession stretched the length of the quarry. Like some storied champion returned from exile, Fin walked at the head of them. Her face was set in an ageless cast, hard and doubtless. She radiated confidence and resolve that none behind her would disturb. Rather, they shied from it, they honored her, and they were careful in the sight of their captain.

Jeannot met Fin at the bottom of the northern ramp, and his men spread throughout the quarry to secure it. They gathered the wounded while Pierre-Jean and Lucas tended them.

"Are you well?" said Jeannot. He stepped nearer and touched her lightly on the shoulders and inspected her with concern.

Fin nodded. "I'm fine. But—" She frowned and turned to look at the wretched crowd behind her.

"Pierre-Jean will see to them. But we must be quick." Jeannot called forward one of his crew. "Take them to the boats." The man saluted and the crowd shuffled after him, up the ramp, over the rim, down toward the sea. Jeannot took Fin by the arm and led her away from the procession. "Have you counted them?"

Fin looked over her shoulder. A steady line of men still issued from the cave and joined the procession across the quarry, vanishing out of sight at the northern rim. "Topper said there were a hundred."

"More," said Jeannot. "Two hundred. Perhaps three."

Fin suspected he was right. Jeannot's face was troubled.

"What's wrong?"

"We are not safe." Jeannot scanned the rim of the quarry. "Who knows how long before we are discovered?"

"Then let's go. The quicker the better."

Jeannot shook his head. "Do you not understand?"

Fin looked back at him blankly.

"We haven't room for them."

Chapter Twenty-nine

A S THE MEN ABLE to walk crowded toward the sea, Fin and Jeannot moved among the sick and wounded. Some muttered thanks or blessings, others held silent or groaned in their infirmity. Pierre-Jean knelt over a man and reassured him then spoke to Jeannot.

"They are malnourished. Fever runs among them." He wiped the sweat from his brow and rubbed his eyes. "Most will live, I think. But Jeannot, we must get them to Valletta quickly. This requires the work of many physicians."

Remy shouted for Jeannot from the rim of the quarry; he waved his musket in the air and beckoned. Jeannot jogged up the ramp and Fin followed. At the top, Remy pointed down the slope of rock. Where the cliffs angled away from the sea they gave way to sand and grey-green bushes, and beyond, an expanse of flat dusty terrain that stretched flat and desolate to the horizon. At the base of the rock slope there was a round, fenced corral and six horses within it. The animals chewed lazily at whatever vegetation they could reach through the fence.

"Look there," said Remy. He pointed across the plain to the west. In the distance a cream-colored dust plume rose against the sky.

Jeannot's face tightened. "Are you sure?"

Remy spit in the sand and nodded. "Two of them. The tracks are fresh."

Jeannot turned and appraised the quarry below then scanned the sea to the north, calculating possibilities and dangers. "Any others?"

Remy grunted and shook his head. "All dead. Except these." He hooked his thumb toward the riders in the distance.

"Send word to the *Donnerhünd*. Ask Luther to meet us ashore. And have food brought for the men."

Remy grunted and lifted his hand in a lazy salute then trotted off toward the boat landing. Jeannot watched him go before speaking. "When Luther arrives, we must talk." Then, with worry in his eyes, he descended the ramp into the quarry.

Fin looked out at the pillar of cloud hanging over the desert. It moved west, toward Tripoli. The horses in the corral nickered and kicked at the dust.

JEANNOT HAD MEN CLEAR out the largest of the guards' buildings and bring food. Fin and Jeannot took seats at the table as Luther entered and closed the door behind him.

"The morning went well, my friend," said Luther.

Jeannot nodded thoughtfully as Luther dropped into a seat. Fin poured a cup of water and tore at a loaf of bread.

"So have you found your lost crew, Captain Button?" said Luther.

"What's left of them. And a few more besides."

"Remy spotted runners," said Jeannot. "Two. By horseback. They will make Tripoli by morning."

Luther grunted and nodded his head gravely. "And we haven't room to transport the men so quickly. What do you propose?"

"When they come we must be ready. I will leave twenty able men and the complete armory of the *Esprit*. Then I will sail for Valletta with as many wounded and sick as we can carry. I will return in three days' time with ships enough to transport the rest."

Fin sat forward and disagreed. "Why not Luther? If you go back, Lennard will arrest you."

"No, Luther must stay. The *Donnerhünd* is the better ship, and her crew is fresh. My crew is over a month at sea and weary."

"Why stay?" said Luther. "We sail together. We return together."

"When the Barbarie return, do you think they will come only by land? If we are to save these men, we must defend them from the sea as well. You will have to hold the landing. Or is the *Donnerhünd* not equal to it?"

The jibe wasn't lost on Luther and he laughed to himself. "She'll hold. It's you that I worry about, Jeannot. Fin is right. Lennard will not let you leave once he has you."

"He may not. But neither will he stand by while men are slaughtered, and your German brothers will come to your aid. I do not doubt it. Even if I cannot return, others will."

Luther leaned back in his chair, stroking his beard. He crossed his arms and held Fin in his consideration. "If I hold the seaward approach, it falls to you to hold the landward."

"My crew will fight. Don't worry about them. A night's rest, food and grog, they'll be all right." Fin took a deep breath. What she was about to say would be met with protest, but she needed to say it. She needed to hear her intent spoken aloud. "I'm not staying."

Jeannot and Luther passed a confused glance between them and straightened in their chairs.

"I'm going to Tripoli."

"She's sea-mad after all, Jeannot."

Jeannot contemplated her in silence. Fin stared back. The muscles of her jaw tightened as she readied herself for his rebuke.

"The countess?" he said.

"I brought eighty men across the sea, Jeannot. I told them we had a job to do and I promised them it would be worth their time, even their lives. And now their ship is sunk, they've been enslaved, beaten, God knows what else, and a hell of a lot of them are dead. So what am I supposed to do? Send them home where they'll be hung for pirates and mutineers because they believed the ridiculous stories about Captain Fin Button?"

Fin pushed away from the table and paced the room.

"I'm a day's ride from Tripoli. I can slip into the keep, get the countess, and be back in time to meet you. If I don't, it'll all be for nothing. The men rotting in that cave and dead in the sea will have died for nothing. I have to do this, Jeannot. I have to try."

A resounding silence filled the room and Fin crossed her arms. She waited to be ordered to stay and laid plans for her defiance. She conjured arguments and rebuttals and set her feet ready to run for the door if need arose. But Jeannot's face wasn't angry or doubtful. He stood and approached her. Fin flinched backward, but because he was calm and came to her in kindness, she stayed. He reached out to her and took her hands in his own.

"I have said it before," said Jeannot. "I saw it the day I drew you from the sea. You are blessed, Fin Button. There is a sacred fire in you, and I would not see it extinguished. Your cause and your heart are just. May God sweep your enemies before you."

Fin's breath caught in her throat and stuck there like a knot. Water swelled in her eyes and she very nearly kissed Jeannot. Had Luther not been watching, she might have. She suddenly wanted to feel what it was like to step forward and let him put his arms around her, but she didn't move. She wouldn't permit herself the freedom. Perhaps one day soon, when the countess was returned to France, when her crew was pardoned, when she was free to go home again, free to go to—Peter. Fin blushed and stepped away from Jeannot. How could she have forgotten Peter? The skin of her face burned and she couldn't bear to look at Jeannot. She turned away.

"Three days, Fin. You ride from danger into danger. We cannot wait for you."

Fin walked to the door and swung it open. Sunlight poured into the room. "You won't have to."

FIN CLIMBED THE RAMP out of the quarry and went looking for Jack. She made her way through the crowd of freed men to the boat landing where the sick and wounded were being ferried out to the *Esprit de la Mer*. To the great frustration of Remy and the other French sailors, Jack had appointed himself to oversee the operation. He set himself up on a rock overhanging the landing and directed the men below on whom to allow into each boat, and on what grounds, and how best to get them there. It seemed to Fin that much of his command went ignored, but the skiffs were loaded all the same and Jack seemed happy with the illusion.

A skiff out in the water waited for its turn to come ashore and take on passengers and one of the oarsmen stood up waving and calling out to Fin.

Fin waved back, "Hello, Topper."

He grinned and laughed and seemed in all ways pleased to have been recognized and acknowledged. Fin clambered up onto Jack's rock and sat down beside him. His wounds had been cleaned and bandaged, and aside from being thinner than Fin had ever seen him, he looked well considering what he'd been through.

"You in cahoots with another Frenchman?"

Fin laughed. "I suppose you could say that."

"Heard some of 'em talking German too."

"That's Luther's crew. From the *Donnerhünd.*" Fin pointed at the ship anchored in the distance. "Jeannot captains the *Esprit de la Mer.*"

Jack harrumphed.

"He saved me and my father after the *'Snake . . .*" Fin trailed off and bowed her head.

"I miss that old *Rattlesnake*, Button. Ain't decided yet if I oughtn't to box your ears for getting her sunk." Jack didn't look at her or laugh. A deep crease ran across his forehead. Fin didn't worry that he'd carry out such a threat, but she didn't doubt that part of him meant it.

"I'm going to make it up to you, Jack."

"And how's that?"

"They don't have room for everyone on the ships."

"Aye, wondered about that."

"And some of the guards got away. Gone to fetch help most likely. So Jeannot is sailing to Malta with as many men as he can while the *Donnerhünd* stays to defend the landing."

Jack nodded to himself quietly. He shouted an order to someone below then grumbled when he wasn't listened to. "How long 'til they get back with help?"

"Three days."

Jack harrumphed. "Better to die fighting than die in chains, I reckon."

"I ain't staying, Jack."

"What you mean, you ain't stayin'?"

"I'm going to Tripoli. Going to rescue that countess."

"We already been through this, Button. You still not wise? We'd need an army to get in there and out again."

"Or a map."

"Eh?"

Fin pulled a wrinkled piece of paper out of her pocket and unfolded it. It was a page torn out of a book. She spread it flat on the rock beside

Jack and tapped her finger on the map of Tripoli. "The keep was built by the Knights of Malta hundreds of years ago. And it's got secret passages going in and out of the keep—underground, in the sewers, in the catacombs. There's one goes from the old church to right underneath the tower of the keep. I can sneak in, Jack. And I can sneak out again. And I can make it back here in three days."

Jack was shaking his head. "You ain't gonna listen to me are you?"

"I can do this. I've got to try, Jack." At the landing below them, Topper's boat reached the shore. Topper clambered out, followed by Phineas Button and Sam Catcher. "I owe it to them, Jack. I owe them a pardon."

Topper and the others climbed up.

"You done it, Fin!" said Topper. He patted his belly and punched Phineas in the shoulder. "Ole Button done it! Ain't you proud?"

Phineas Button kept his head down and didn't speak.

Fin stood up. "Round up everyone we got left and arm them. There'll be fighting come morning. When I get back, we all go home together."

"When you get back? What—" Topper sputtered and looked at Jack for an explanation.

"See you don't get yourself caught, Button. I'm in no shape for rescuin'," said Jack.

Fin smiled at him and winked at Topper as she walked away. They called after her. They demanded to know where she was going, and when she'd be back, and what she meant to do. She ignored their questions. Jack would explain in his own time. As she mounted the top of the cliff and set off in the direction of the corral, Jack's voice thundered up the gorge.

"Give 'em hell, Button!"

She intended to.

Chapter Thirty

FIN HADN'T BEEN ON horseback in years and her body was quick to remind her of it. It took less than an hour of riding for her hips and tailbone to announce their complaints, but she had miles to go and refused to be hindered by a few aches and pains. To disguise herself, she'd taken the red robes and black headscarves from two of the dead quarry guards. She wore one robe herself and wrapped her head and face in the manner she'd seen men do in Tripoli. The other robe and scarf she wrapped in a bundle and took with her for the countess.

All she knew of the way ahead was that Tripoli was west. The road followed the coast, running flat and straight, mile after mile. The unchanging landscape wore on Fin's mind much like the riding wore on her bones. But the horse seemed to be a veteran of the journey, knowing the well-worn road out of habit and requiring little attention.

When the sun set, night came on moonless and impenetrable. It was so dark Fin feared the horse would walk right over a cliff and she wouldn't know there was trouble until she hit the water or the rocks below. She dismounted and led the horse off the road, fumbling in the rocky crags in search of someplace that would offer shelter, not from the weather, but from other travelers. The robe and headscarf wouldn't fool anyone if she had to speak.

When she found a small draw that hid her from the road, she hobbled the horse and tried to sleep. Every noise in the night startled her: a jackal baying in the distance, insects screeching like rusty hinges, rodents scurrying through the brush. It had been so long since she'd slept in the country that she'd nearly forgotten how much life went on in the dark. At sea there were night sounds, of course, like the creaking of the ship, the bluster of wind, the rattle of battens in a gale. But the sounds of the country were less predictable, less definable; they were the noises of living things diligent at work or play. Had she ever been used to such things? Surely she had, but they seemed foreign to her now, nearly as foreign as the remembrance of home, of Georgia, of Peter. Would she find, when she went home, that she couldn't sleep for the strangeness of it? Fin squirmed and wrestled herself on the rocky ground. Her thoughts made her uncomfortable.

THE *ESPRIT DE LA MER* sailed for Valletta. Jeannot took on over a hundred freed slaves, left twenty crewmen ashore, and kept thirty-seven aboard to sail her. The ship rode heavy in the water, every inch of cargo space packed with men.

Jeannot paced the quarterdeck until after midnight. Worry riddled his mind. The men on watch saw the twitch of unease in his shoulders and gave him a wide berth as he meandered from the starboard to port rail in silence. Lennard would have him arrested when he returned to Valletta. In all probability, the dockmaster had orders to arrest him on sight. The trouble plaguing Jeannot's mind wasn't worry for his own well-being, however; it was concern for those he'd left behind. If Lennard arrested him before he could send word to others, if he didn't get a chance to speak or entreat for help, no one would return to Luther's aid, or Fin's. And so his cares, like the ship, were heavy.

The wind favored them. It blew steadily and Jeannot put it to good use. The bulk of the ship's extra passengers had to cram together shoulder to shoulder throughout the lower decks, and Jeannot checked them often. They could scarcely move to relieve themselves or lay down to sleep, but their spirits were high. At times they sang, hymns usually. The deep voices of a hundred men seeped out of the holds like a distant muttering of thunder. It cast an eerie pall over the voyage, but it gave

Jeannot comfort. Singing was a sign of life, an indicator of hope; it carried them along as surely as the wind.

FIN AWOKE BEFORE DAWN and rode hard. Twice she passed caravans of merchants leading beasts piled high with furs and carpets and crates. By noon she could see Tripoli in the distance, shimmering in the heat like a city of phantoms. Roads from the south converged with hers, funneling their travelers toward the city, and Fin slowed her pace. Soon the landscape was populated with fields and pastures and shabby homes. Sheep and goats grazed in herds along the roadside, and the murmur of large numbers of people and animals replaced the relative quiet of the barren country.

When she was close enough to see the city walls, she dismounted and led the horse, keeping her head down and her face covered with her scarf. The travelers around her talked and laughed among themselves and tended their beasts. No one spoke to Fin or even looked at her. As she picked her way toward the eastern gate, a flurry of commotion erupted ahead. She stood on her toes to look for the source of the disturbance. At the gate, entire caravans and travelers on foot scurried aside and a group of armed horsemen burst out of the city. They yelled and beat their horses, driving them into a frenzied gallop. The riders wore the same red and black robes as Fin, and they charged east as the crowd scattered to the roadside. Fin tried to count them. There were thirty or forty at least. She had no doubt of their destination and hoped Jack and the others were ready.

As the parted crowds filed back onto the road and continued toward the gate, Fin climbed to the crest of the hillside and looked down into the harbor. It ran westward then curled north like a horn and was still but for two small ships easing their way eastward. They kept near the coast, as if to follow it rather than striking out to sea. There was no way to know whether or not they were heading for the quarry, but it was possible. Fin turned back down the hill and pulled the horse along behind her. She needed to find a place to hide until nightfall. Somewhere near the eastern gate.

As THE *ESPRIT DE LA MER* approached Malta that evening, Jeannot called seven trusted men to his quarters. He sat before them and arrayed on the table seven sealed envelopes.

"Gentlemen, it is likely that this is my last day as your captain." The crewmen stiffened. "The seven of you and myself will ferry ashore under cover of night. The *Esprit* will remain a'sea until morning. When we reach the shore, I shall deliver one last order. For each of you a letter, and on each letter a name. You will deliver them to the bailiffs of the other *langues* of the order. If you are questioned, you must deny me. Admit no knowledge of my whereabouts or the origin of the letter. Do you understand?"

Though there was confusion on their faces, they answered without hesitation. "*Oui, mon Capitaine.*"

Jeannot rose from the table and handed each man a letter. The crewmen studied the names and mouthed them quietly to themselves.

"Come, let us make ready. And may God be with us."

CHAPTER THIRTY-ONE

FIN TIED HER HORSE under the arm of a sycamore. The sun was down and torches lit the road leading toward the eastern gate. Two guards slouched at their posts and paid little attention to the comings and goings between them. Even so, Fin didn't want to approach alone. She waited until a group of travelers passed on foot and fell in behind them. She tightened the scarf across her face and kept as near the group as she dared. The walk was no more than yards but it felt like miles. For all her worry and stealth, though, the guards didn't even bother to look her way as she passed. Fin breathed easier and slowed her pace to separate herself from the group.

The skyline of the city was barely discernible. Torches and mounted oil lamps lit the main streets and dimmed the stars, turning the sky into a flat canvas of black. She'd memorized the map of the city and hoped to find her way by landmark, but in the darkness, the buildings she'd hoped to spot were all but invisible. She knew she needed to go north-west, though, and did her best to wend a path in that direction. There was little foot traffic and whenever she came upon others in the street, they looked at her. To Fin it seemed they looked too long and with too much interest, and her heartbeat skipped and pounded. She bowed her head and pushed on, relieved that they didn't speak to her.

As she slipped through the darkened city, she traced the likeness of Caroline de Graff in her mind. She recalled her face perfectly, framed in the open window of the keep as neatly as a portrait. Then a flicker of light high above the nearby rooftops caught Fin's attention. Over the city, as if magically suspended in the sky, a half-moon crescent shone like a head-cocked smile; it was under-lit by torchlight and hovered over a sharp minaret. It was the only mosque in the eastern city according to the map. She passed under an archway and across the courtyard of the windowless building. Two streets further north she found what she was looking for.

"REMY WILL SECURE THE *Esprit* at the quay in the morning. See that our passengers are taken to the hospital."

Pierre-Jean nodded. "*Comme vous le souhaitez, mon Captaine.*"

The sound of Pierre-Jean's French was refreshing, like cool water. It eased Jeannot's mind and he smiled. But he reminded himself that the time for ease was still far off. "English, Pierre. We are knights yet."

Pierre-Jean turned the corner of his mouth up slyly and nodded. "*Oui, mon Captaine.*"

Jeannot smiled then reached for Pierre-Jean's hand and shook it. "You are like a brother to me, Pierre-Jean Leroux. I hope to sail with you again tomorrow, but I do not think it will be."

"No man knows the mind of God, *mon ami.* It may yet be so."

Jeannot released his friend's hand and frowned. He was tired, very tired. An end would almost be welcome. But for Luther's sake and for the sake of the girl with the sacred fire, rest would have to wait. "Let us hope, *mon frere.*"

Without waiting for further words or well wishes, Jeannot departed. He called out his orders as he climbed onto the deck. His men watched him with buckled brows and sad eyes. They complied with his instructions in solemn resolve and lowered a skiff into the water. Seven sailors climbed aboard it. Each carried a letter in his pocket. Jeannot stood at the rail and looked around at his ship and his men. He nodded in satisfaction. The deck was scoured clean, the brass shined, the rigging tight, the men attentive. It was good.

"Remy!" he called.

Remy stepped from the helm and saluted.

"The *Esprit* is in your hands. Keep her well." Jeannot returned the salute and swung himself over the rail. He climbed down into the skiff and ordered it underway. Remy shouted orders for sails. The sailors in the skiff dipped the oars and heaved. As the *Esprit de la Mer* dwindled into the darkness, Jeannot turned away from his ship and set his face toward the Maltese shore.

THE ILL-KEPT CATHEDRAL LOOKED strange to Fin, out of place amid the smaller, more modestly constructed buildings. Tall, narrow windows segmented the length of it, and each corner and stone was carved with figures of robed men and angels and gargoyles. The carvings were chipped and ruined; their sculpted heads had been broken off and defaced, subjected to the methodical erasure of Turkish desecration after the Knights were driven out of Tripoli.

Fin circled to the front of the building. She looked around to be sure the streets were empty, then tiptoed up the steps and inspected the doors. They were broken and boarded up with planks crudely nailed across the opening. She grabbed a board with both hands and pulled. It didn't come off, but she felt it give. Fin put one foot on the doorframe and jerked the board again with both hands. It came loose with a crack, and Fin stumbled backward. She flattened herself in the shadow of the doorframe and scanned the street to see if anyone had heard the noise, then quietly lowered the board to the doorstep. The gap was just large enough for her to fit through.

Fin stuck her head between the boards. The inside of the cathedral was cloaked in darkness. There was no way she'd find a passage into the tunnel below without light. She pulled her head out and scanned the street again to make sure she was unobserved. There was no one nearby and no sound of footsteps. Fin darted to the nearest lamppost and lifted the oil lamp off its hook then sped back to the cathedral door and climbed inside. Rats scattered out of the light. The ceiling was lost in shadows, and Fin found that if she didn't keep near a wall she seemed to walk on a tiny island of stone illuminated in the darkness.

At the entrance to the nave, pews were thrown in a pile, splintered apart, and broken into pieces. Fin crept around the heap and on through the great open space toward the sanctuary. She passed other piles of wood and debris that rose out of the dark like small islands of refuse. At the sanctuary steps, the altar was sundered and lay on the floor in two great slabs. She walked on toward the sacristy at the rear of the building. It was a tiny room with a desk and wardrobe at one end and three doors along the back wall.

The first two doors opened on closets filled with shelves of moth-eaten priestly vestments left to ruin. The third was locked. Fin pulled on the door and jerked at it, but it wouldn't budge. She set the lamp on the floor and looked around the room for something she could use to pry the door open. There was little to choose from: broken pottery, an old candlestick, a couple of empty bottles. She tore a shelf out of one of the closets and tried to wedge it into the crack of the locked door, but it was too thick and wouldn't fit. Fin threw it across the sacristy in irritation. She went to the desk at the far end of the room and snapped off one of its legs. The brittle wood split along the grain so that one end tapered to a thin point. She jammed the pointed end between the door and the doorframe and tried to wrench the door open, but the wooden leg snapped before it had moved the door a finger's width. Fin cursed. She flung open the wardrobe looking for another tool. It was empty, but as she was about to slam it shut in frustration, she noticed something strange. The back of the wardrobe was made of a different kind of wood. It might have looked the same as the rest when it was new or freshly cleaned and polished, but time and neglect had faded it and revealed the difference. She knocked on the wood and moved her hand along its surface. At the edges, where it should have jointed to the rest of the wardrobe, there was a thin gap, and along the left edge there were hinges. She stepped up into the wardrobe, drew one foot back, and kicked. The back of the wardrobe cracked down the middle and flung open. Fin stumbled back and retrieved the lamp. She raised it in front of her and the light spilled into an ancient stone stair that spiraled down into the foundation of the cathedral.

She took a deep breath and climbed into the passage. The steps were coated in a soft, fine dust that billowed away from her footfalls in tiny clouds. The stair wound around and around, descending sharply with each revolution until it ended at the mouth of a narrow passageway. The lamp pushed light down the corridor, elongating it, ringing it in golden bands that knocked the shadows back into the corners. The air had a dry ashen smell that caught in Fin's nose and wouldn't leave. She tightened the scarf over her face and set off.

The centuries-old corridor bent sharply about thirty feet from the stair but was otherwise straight. On its walls she saw carvings of mysterious images that were as often monstrous as beautiful, and there was writing too, arcane letters from strange alphabets Fin had never seen. The stone and emptiness swallowed up her footsteps. Any sound she made was quickly snatched out of existence as if it offended the long-kept silence of the place.

A hundred feet further in, she caught the tang of water. At first it was so slight that she thought she was mistaken, but with each step the smell grew stronger. The corridor bent to the left and angled sharply downward. As the tunnel descended further and further toward sea level, the air grew dank and cool. Strange molds fuzzed the walls, and the floor was slick with a slimy film. As she crept on, the tunnel continued its downward slant until she was ankle-deep in water. It was thick and cold and smelled of decay. The light of the lantern ran along the water's surface and threw a dance of rippling reflections across the stone. The ceiling sloped steadily down until at the extent of the light, she could see that the tunnel was half submerged. Fin looked back, gauging the distance she'd come since the last bend; she felt she'd walked half a mile since she stepped through the back of the wardrobe. There couldn't be much farther to go or the tunnel would open onto the sea itself.

She removed her robe and bundled it up along with Betsy, her powder horn, and the robe she'd brought for the countess. She moved on, sloshing through the filthy water. Soon she was knee deep and shuffling forward a foot's length at a time. The walls were dripping with an oily black ichor, and when she steadied herself by putting a hand to the wall, the substance clung to her fingers and stank. Her foot slipped on the slimy rock floor and she landed on her rump with a splash. Although she managed to keep the lamp and bundle held high, she had a momentary fit of panic realizing that if she'd dropped the lamp into the water she'd be left in the utter blackness of the catacomb. She sat still and wet with the lamp held above her until the water calmed, and then she carefully climbed to her feet, planting each foothold firmly and deliberately. As she moved forward again, she went slowly, holding the lamp high before her.

Fin was waist-deep when she reached the next bend, and was afraid to look around the corner for fear she'd see the tunnel continue its descent and submerge completely. She held the lamp out and peeked around the bend, then let out a sigh of relief. As it had begun, the tunnel ended in a spiral stair leading up toward the surface. She climbed out of the water and ascended into the heart of the pasha's keep.

WHEN JEANNOT'S SKIFF REACHED the dockside in the hour before dawn, he watched his men labor in silence until it was secure. They worked without question or hesitation. Even in the night, their hands knew each rope and cleat of the boat. They simply reached into the darkness and took hold of what they knew was there as if sight was a secondary thing. Jeannot envied them.

"All secure," the sailor said. Jeannot stood up and climbed onto the dock. Above him, Valletta slept. The streetlamps had long burned out, and beneath the wind, an unsettling quietness hovered over the city. Any remnant of familiarity it held for Jeannot was gone. He felt like a stranger in his own house.

His sailors gathered around him and waited.

"Your letters," said Jeannot.

The seven men each pulled letters from their pockets and held them up.

"And you know where they are to be delivered?"

"*Oui, mon Capitaine,*" they said.

Jeannot shook his head at their French and they smiled. "Go then, and return here. The *Esprit* will dock at sunrise."

The men nodded and turned away. As they ran off down the quay, one paused and came back. "We will see you come the morning, *mon Capitaine.*"

"I fear you will not."

The man frowned then turned away and ran into the night. Jeannot watched them go until there was nothing more to see. The sound of their footfalls *tap-tap-tapped* on the city walls and across the rocks and black water of the harbor. Jeannot stood alone and tilted his head up toward the shadowy city looming over him. His eyes could make out nothing more than dark shapes against darker. He looked in the direction of the auberge and scanned the area; though he knew it was there, he couldn't see it. It didn't matter. That wasn't where he needed to go. As he walked down the dock, he tripped on a coil of rope and lurched forward with his hands out to catch himself. He didn't fall but muttered quietly as he regained his footing and straightened his coat. Then he took a deep breath and stumbled through the night toward the Cathedral of St. John, seat of Fra' Emmanuel, the Grand Master of the Knights of Malta.

Chapter Thirty-two

F IN CLIMBED TO THE top of the spiral stair. The corridor ended at a wooden door with a rusty iron ring hanging at its center. The lower half of the door was covered in mold and swollen with rot. Fin tapped the toe of her boot against it and pieces of decayed wood fell away in spongy clumps. She grabbed the iron ring and pulled. The door rattled in its frame but wouldn't open. She jerked several more times with the same result.

Fin set the lamp and bundle down on the step and toed at the rotten base of the door again. She kicked into it repeatedly, and in a few minutes had dug out a hole large enough to crawl through. She pushed the lantern ahead of her and entered the keep. When she stood up, she turned around, drew back the bolt on the door, and pushed it open.

Fin unrolled her robe and put it back on. She tucked the countess's robe into her own then repacked Betsy and picked up the lamp. If the map was correct, she was in the dungeon beneath the keep's tower. The room was cluttered with crates and barrels stacked one on top of another. A collection of paintings mounted in gilded frames leaned against a chest of drawers in the corner. Here and there, manacles hung from the walls. It may have been a dungeon once, but now it seemed to be no more than a storage space.

Fin wrapped her scarf over her mouth and nose and peeked through a thin horizontal inspection slot in the chamber door. The hall outside showed signs of disuse: undisturbed cobwebs stretched from wall to wall, and the floor was covered in dust. At the end of the hall she could see the faint flicker of lamplight. There was no sign of guards. Fin suspected there were few, if any, patrolling this deep inside the keep. She pulled the door open then snuffed out her lamp and used it to prop the door ajar so she could find it again. She tiptoed down the hall, ducking under the cobwebs, and came to an intersecting hallway. To her left, lighted lamps were set in sconces every twenty feet along the hall. On the right, there were only two lamps lit, and the hall continued into darkness.

She wondered which way she ought to go and decided to follow the lighted lamps to the left. At the end of the hall, she climbed a short stair into another hall that looked exactly the same except that all its lamps were lit. She followed it left again to another stair. On and on she wound her way up. She passed a window and smelled a fresh breeze. She stopped to look out and saw that the sky outside was lightening toward sunrise. Fin had hoped to arrive earlier, before the guards and other traffic of the keep awakened, but it was too late to think about it now. The courtyard was thirty or forty feet below her and the gatehouse was just visible to her right. She was higher than the level of the keep walls. Fin nodded to herself, she was certainly in the main tower. Somewhere above her she'd seen the countess's oval face and yellow hair at the window. She was close.

As Fin climbed higher into the keep, the bare stone became more ornate. Carvings and paintings covered the walls. Lush carpets blanketed the floors. Alcoves and corners were set with dainty tables and curios and other finery. She climbed two more stairs and stopped again at a window. She was on the opposite side of the keep from the countess's window.

Fin followed the hall around one corner and stopped at the next. She heard sound coming in at the windows: footsteps in the courtyard below, the grunting and whinnying of animals, and faintly, voices.

She peeked around the corner. The hall was empty. Halfway down the corridor there was a set of double doors flanked by golden candlesticks. The doors were ornately carved and inlaid with colored wood and gold.

A strange place to keep a prisoner, Fin thought. But she was sure the countess's window was in the room beyond the doors. As Fin approached, she wondered at the lack of guards. From what she could tell, they were only posted at the main entrances to the keep and tower. Why would they leave a valuable prisoner unguarded? And what if the door was locked or the countess was chained? The thought made Fin uncomfortable. There were too many things she hadn't considered.

Fin held her breath and stood in front of the door; an image of a crescent moon was carved into the surface of it. The moon was inlaid with mother of pearl, and it shimmered like a rainbow in the flickering light. Fin reached for the door handle. A sound from within stopped her. A murmur. A voice. Fin tilted her ear and listened. She heard the scrape of a stool or a chair on stone. And again, a voice. Voices. Soft, and no more than murmurs.

Fin's heart galloped in her chest. She withdrew Betsy from her belt and inspected the gun. She tightened the flint, repacked the barrel, and kneaded the handle in her sweaty hand. She held her breath and listened. The room was quiet. Fin pulled the door open and stepped inside.

JEANNOT SAT ON THE steps of the Cathedral of Saint John and watched the sun rise over the city. The bailiffs of the seven *langues* would arrive soon, all but Lennard, summoned to the audience hall of the grand master by seven letters. The letters were forgeries, of course, bearing the seal of a knight and not the grand master himself, but even though the bailiffs would almost certainly see through the lie, they would still speed to the grand master to report the crime. Lennard, no doubt, would embellish the offense and, added to the theft of the *Esprit de la Mer*, would call it treason. Jeannot expected to spend the rest of his days in a Maltese dungeon. But for the chance to confront the heads of the Order and press them to action, he would risk it. Fin Button risked death in Tripoli; at the very least a knight could risk his freedom.

Though the bailiffs were often blinded by greed and power, they were reasonable men, and each, in some measure, remembered their vows—each except Lennard Guillot. And Lennard would soon be in the harbor far below, where the *Esprit de la Mer* was creeping toward the dock. With luck, he'd been alerted and was already on his way there to arrest Jeannot. Lennard would be irate when he found another hold filled, not with plunder, but with freed slaves. Jeannot smiled to himself when he thought of it. He didn't take joy in his defiance of the Order, but it was difficult not to find amusement in Lennard's predictability.

A wave of sound swept through the morning air. The bells of the city began to ring. One or two at first, in the distance, then increasing by twos, by threes, by dozens—a processional knell that moved across the face of Valletta, growing and swelling until reaching its zenith in the towers of the great cathedral; out of the bronze hollows of its bells a toll rang sombrous, hallowed, and deep like the awakening groan of a titan, yawning and stretching the sleep from its arms. Valletta roused. Before the streets were fully lit, they buzzed with the passage of feet. The market opened. Voices arose. The city inhaled and lumbered to its work.

Rodolfo di Costa, bailiff of the *Langue* of Provence, arrived with two lesser knights at his heels. He walked up the steps, erect and proper. His habit swished and rippled through the crisp air. He was an Italian, from a wealthy family that some said traced their ancestry back to the Caesars. In Jeannot's experience, all Italians made that claim if you gave them the chance. Jeannot stood and tipped his hat as the bailiff passed, less for courtesy than to hide his face should the man recognize him. The bailiff smiled politely and tipped in return but didn't speak. He entered the cathedral, and Jeannot moved across the street to watch in secrecy for the arrival of the others.

The next to come was Giuseppe Grisafi, bailiff of the *Langue* of Italy, a large, red-faced man, alone and grumbling. Following after were Rafael Garcia de la Pena, Gregory Eddington, and Arnaud Pellitier, the bailiffs of the *Langues* of Aragon, England, and Auvergne. They arrived together, talking amongst themselves and laughing. The last were Ludwig von Gluck, the German, and a Spaniard, Osvaldo Torres, bailiff of the *Langue* of Castile and Leon. They sped briskly through the door, tense in their shoulders and urging men out of their way.

Jeannot followed. He kept ten paces behind and shadowed them through the hollow cathedral wings toward the audience hall of the grand master. Priests shuffled around the cavernous space lighting candles, and murmurs of prayer throbbed and bounced around the vaulted arches of the building.

The bailiffs filed into the audience hall and the door settled shut behind them. Jeannot stopped outside and waited. He listened through the door as they chattered amongst themselves. Some wondered at the reason for the summons and others doubted its authenticity. Jeannot heard the flap and rustle of paper. No doubt some of them had brought the letters with them and were shaking them in the air in confusion. Then the voices dropped away and Jeannot could hear nothing. He looked around to ensure that he was alone and then placed his left ear against the door. Jeannot held his breath. A single voice spoke.

"If you must bicker and argue, can you not wait until a decent hour?" It was Fra' Emmanuel, the grand master. He was a young man for his office, only fifty when elevated. The man he inherited the office from had been a lecher and a politician of the worst sort, and so Fra' Emmanuel was received with open-arms, beloved by the Knights and Maltese people alike. "Well, what catastrophe brings you all? I fear our dear Osvaldo has never seen such activity before breakfast. Have you Osvaldo?"

"No, Your Excellency."

Jeannot heard murmurs among the bailiffs as further confusion passed between them. That the grand master had not expected them confirmed their suspicions.

"Sir, it was your summons brought us."

"Nonsense. I was barely out of my own bed when Felipe informed me of Giuseppe's arrival."

"But, sir." Jeannot heard the rustle of paper as the speaker handed his letter to the grand master.

"We each received one—except, perhaps, Lennard. I've not seen him."

The grand master huffed. "A day in which Lennard is unseen is a blessed one."

"The letters are forgeries, sir." Arnaud Pellitier's voice. Jeannot had always considered him a perceptive man. It was no surprise that he'd spotted the ruse. "But whose, and why?"

"Whose, indeed," muttered Fra' Emmanuel.

Jeannot straightened away from the door and squeezed the handle. He filled his lungs and held his breath in his chest as long as he could. Then he pulled open the door and walked into the audience hall. The bailiffs were gathered at the far end of the room and the grand master held himself stiff in his seat. All eyes turned to Jeannot. He walked across the room, erect and confident, and knelt at the first step of the grand master's dais.

"It is my doing, Your Excellency."

To Jeannot's surprise, his admission was met with silence. He raised his head enough to see that the grand master was considering him with a puzzled look. To his right, Jeannot saw Ludwig von Gluck with his fists on his hips looking down at him slack-jawed and baffled. The silence grew and throbbed in his ears, and Jeannot was relieved when the grand master spoke.

"Arnaud, send for the guard."

Jeannot heard the click of Arnaud Pellitier's heels as he snapped them together followed by the brisk tap of his footsteps as he exited the hall. Arnaud would return with guards in moments and they would drag him away. Though Jeannot risked himself further by speaking without leave, he couldn't afford to remain silent. "Your Excellency, if you'll permit me a chance to explain."

Rodolfo di Costa stepped forward and raised his hand as if to slap Jeannot. "*Silencio!*"

Fra' Emmanuel waved his hand at Rodolfo to calm him, then he crouched forward in his seat to better inspect Jeannot. "What is your name?"

"Jeannot Botolph, Your Excellency, of the French."

"Ah, so it is. Your name is no stranger to this hall, Jeannot Botolph." The grand master straightened in his seat then sagged against the back of the chair. "Lennard Guillot speaks it like a curse. Stand up."

Jeannot stood and looked up briefly. Instead of anger, Jeannot saw a strange curiosity on the man's face, then he turned his eyes down out of respect.

"When the guards arrive, you will be arrested, Jeannot. You understand this. But you've caused yourself considerable grief to place yourself here, so I shall indulge an explanation. Spend your words wisely."

The bailiffs behind Jeannot erupted in a spasm of angry protest. Jeannot glanced up to ensure that he'd heard correctly, and the grand master nodded. He held one hand in the air to silence the bailiffs. "Speak, Jeannot."

"My ship stands at the quay heavy with men freed from a slave camp east of Tripoli. There are more than a hundred that still await rescue. I have come to entreat for them, though I forfeit my own freedom."

The bailiffs murmured to one another and the grand master considered Jeannot in silence. He held up one of the forged letters and rustled it in the air between them. "Then why this subtlety? There are proper ways to ask for help."

"Your Excellency, Lennard Guillot is against me. He forbids the pursuit of the *corso* and demands the capture of spoil rather than the freedom of Christian brothers. For the crime of freeing slaves, he has ordered my ship seized and seeks the ruin of my knighthood. Yet if I do not return, the brothers who await will perish. The Barbarie know of our trespass and surely they come in force." Jeannot turned to look at Ludwig von Gluck, the German bailiff. "Luther holds the seaward approach with the *Donnerhünd*. But I fear he cannot hold long. My men defend the landing ashore. They are few and weary. To win their lives will require the strength of knights. Strength such as of old, undivided by politics and greed, but firm, united under the cross and in pursuit of the *corso*. I beg you, Your Excellency, though I go to the lowest dungeon of Valletta, send them aid."

The doors swung open, and Arnaud marched in. He led four guards to the dais. Grand Master Fra' Emmanuel settled heavily into his chair and presided over his hall in silence. His brow was heavy and slung low over his eyes as he held Jeannot under the terrible weight of his stare. Jeannot felt he could see in the grand master's eyes the balancing of a great scale that tilted and swayed in the descent of his reckoning. After a time, the deliberation ended. The scale settled and those eyes, wizened but weary, turned to Arnaud and issued their silent judgment.

Arnaud pointed at Jeannot. "Arrest him."

CHAPTER THIRTY-THREE

FIN STEPPED INTO THE room with Betsy raised before her. The chamber was filled with color. Gossamer curtains dyed in shades of red and blue hung from the walls and swayed lazily in the morning breeze. The rough granite floor was covered in exotic carpets and barrel-like cushions. In the center of the room, a low, square table was piled with pomegranates, grapes, figs, and flat, round loaves of bread. An empty decanter lay on its side with a halo of orange liquid puddled around it. On the wall opposite the door, an arched window looked out over the courtyard. Fin eased her way across the room and peeked out, confirming that it was the same window she'd seen framing the countess's face over a month before.

There were two doorways leading from the main chamber, one on either side. Fin heard a voice come from one of the rooms. A girl's voice. High and lilting. Fin tiptoed toward the adjacent doorway and the soft voice called out again.

"Yusuf?"

Fin pulled aside the gossamer veil draped across the doorway and looked in. The room was a bedchamber. A lush pallet of silks and tasseled pillows was situated in the middle of the room. The sheets were strewn across it and splayed on the floor. Against the far wall, there was a redwood vanity table topped with a large oval mirror; the countess sat before the mirror, hairbrush in hand. She was frozen in mid-stroke with a lock of yellow hair stretched from her head to the brush. She was perfectly still with her back to Fin, looking at her in the reflection of the mirror.

"Who are you?" asked the countess.

Fin lowered Betsy and entered the room. "I'm here to rescue you."

The countess lowered her brush and turned toward Fin to look at her directly. Her face was lovely. A perfect white oval with thick lines drawn around her eyes in the manner of the local women. She was wearing a gown of scarlet gossamer and drew her tiny feet under the hem as she turned. The countess laughed to herself as if she were amused by a silly child. "Rescue? Me?" She laughed again and pulled the brush through her hair. "And what do you mean to rescue me from?"

Fin heard movement in the room on the opposite side of the main chamber and glanced back. "I'm here to take you home."

The countess jerked her head back in confusion and frowned. "My husband sent you?"

Fin nodded and walked toward the girl. "Something like that. Quickly, we have to go." Fin reached for her hand, but the countess stood up and backed away toward the wall.

When Fin took another step forward, the countess shouted. "Yusuf!"

Fin looked around in confusion and put her finger to her lips. "Sshhh!"

"Yusuf!" the countess shouted again and footsteps approached from the other room. Fin ran forward and clamped her hand over the countess's mouth. The girl struggled. Fin wrapped one arm around her shoulders and held her. A man stepped into the room and stopped abruptly when he saw Fin. It was impossible to tell his age. He could have been twenty or fifty; Fin had no idea. His skin was lustrous and the color of caramel. A fine black beard covered his lower face, jutting down over his chest, and his wet hair hung across his shoulders in ropes. He wore a pair of billowing yellow pantaloons and stood, shirtless, staring with his head tilted to one side and his lips parted as if he'd begun to speak but had forgotten his words. He lifted his hands toward Fin and showed her his empty palms.

"I beg you. Do not harm her."

Fin pointed Betsy at him.

"Who are you?"

The man frowned gently. "I am Pasha Yusuf Qaramanli."

Thick beads of sweat collected on Fin's forehead and crawled down into her eyes. She licked her lips and took a gulping breath. She felt like a player in a game whose rules had suddenly changed without warning or logic. The countess tried to squirm out of her arms and Fin tightened her grip.

The pasha took a step forward and Fin cocked back Betsy's hammer. He stopped and raised his hands higher. "Whatever you desire is yours," he said. The pasha nodded his head around the room as if pointing with his beard. "All the riches of my house. Take them and go." His eyes moved from Fin to the countess in her arms. "She is all that I treasure in the world. I beg you, do not harm her."

Fin tried to wrap her mind around what was happening. She spoke into the countess's ear and uncovered her mouth so she could speak. "What is your name?"

The girl took in a gasp of breath. "Caroline de Graff—" Fin clapped her hand back over her mouth. Though Fin still didn't understand what was going on, she was sure she had the person she'd come for. Fin pointed Betsy at the gossamer curtain hanging across the doorway. "Tear down that curtain," she ordered.

The pasha looked at it uncertainly and Fin ordered him again. "Tear it down!"

He took the curtain in both hands and jerked it sharply. It tore free of the rod above the door and he held it out toward Fin like a gift.

"Drop it. Turn around and get on your knees." The pasha complied. Fin let go of the countess and pushed her toward him. "Tie his hands."

The countess knelt down and pulled the thin material of the curtain into a cord. The pasha crossed his wrists in the small of his back and she wrapped the curtain around them and tied it.

"Tighter," Fin told her.

"If you want it tighter, do it yourself." The countess flashed a sneer at Fin.

Fin pushed the girl out of the way. "Move over there where I can see you." As the countess moved, Fin laid Betsy down and fastened the pasha's hands until she was satisfied. "Stand up." Fin pushed him to the pallet in the center of the room and ordered him to lie down then ripped another curtain from the wall and bound his feet.

"What is your name?" asked the pasha.

Fin ignored him.

"Whoever you are, you will not escape. Your name will be a curse on the lips of children. I will feed your bones to the dogs of my slaves. I will—"

"Shut up or I'll gag you," said Fin. As Fin stood up, the pasha opened his mouth to speak again and she kicked him in the ribs. He grunted and clenched his teeth. Fin grabbed the countess by the wrist and dragged her toward the door. The pasha stared after them, but when Fin looked back his anger was gone. She expected him to seethe with curses and threats but he didn't. All his attention was focused on the countess. His eyes were wide, deep, and black, and Fin thought she saw the quiver of emotion in his face. The countess tried to twist out of Fin's grip and run to him, but Fin jerked her back and held her. Fin stopped in the doorway and the girl craned her head around to look back.

"Yusuf?" Her voice was tender and soft as a kiss.

"Do not resist. Do as you are told. I will find you," he said.

The pasha lay on the pallet staring at them through the doorway and nothing could be clearer to Fin: he was in love with the countess, and she with him. He dared not even blink because he wanted to experience every last glimpse of the woman he loved and hold it dear when she was gone. Fin knew the look. It was the same she'd given Peter as he galloped away in Ebenezer. But this pasha was also the man who commanded pirates against the ships of the Mediterranean. It was his fault that her ship was sunk. His fault that so many of her crew had died. His fault that Knut was dead. It didn't matter that Fin had instigated the fight by sneaking into his keep with Armand. She needed a reason to believe he was incapable of love or kindness. He was a barbarian. A lord of pirates. As she pulled the countess from the room, she ignored the last whispered intimacies of the lovers as she parted them.

Fin fled down the halls and stairs of the keep with the countess in tow. The girl was in tears. She squealed and whimpered each time Fin jerked on her arm to keep her moving. As they descended toward the dungeons of the keep, the pasha's voice rose and filled the halls.

"I will find you!"

She should have gagged him. Fin quickened her pace to a run, dragging the countess along behind.

JEANNOT SHOOK THE GUARDS off when they seized him. He straightened his coat and walked toward the door with his head high and his shoulders square. The guards raised their eyebrows and Arnaud nodded, urging them after Jeannot. "Take him to the warden and have him wait in irons."

"That was most unusual," said Osvaldo. He harrumphed to himself and shook his head in disapproval. "The French, Your Excellency, one never can tell what they will do next."

"A disgrace to the knighthood." Rodolfo di Costa made a spitting motion. "In the old days a knight would never dare. Lennard will be glad to have this one out of the way, I think." The other bailiffs agreed and grumbled to one another.

When Jeannot reached the door of the hall, the guards held it open and he heard laughter behind him as the bailiffs scoffed at his audacity and mocked him. But over the babble of their ridicule, a command rang out and resounded through the hall.

"Hold."

The bailiffs quieted. They froze in mid-gesture, some with a hand in the air, some while fingering their beards, another while leaning in toward the man next to him. They each stopped and looked at Grand Master Fra' Emmanuel. An expression of descending sadness settled across his face and he shook his head from side to side in slow, ponderous movements.

"Jeannot Botolph. For the sake of the *corso*, he forfeits his ship and his mortal liberty." The bailiffs huddled at the foot of the dais and shifted their eyes, glancing at one another uneasily, unsure whether he was joining them in mockery or delivering a rebuke. The grand master tapped a ringed finger against his cheek. He gathered the entire assembly into his solemn consideration and his brow twisted and knotted upon itself as he weighed the matters troubling his mind. "He wagers his life against the lives of others. And when sent to judgment, he resolves himself to it with dignity. Even in subterfuge he demonstrates a manner becoming knighthood. Are these the actions of a criminal?" He swept his eyes from one bailiff to another, searching their faces and frowning at what he found there. "Humility, faith, justice, sincerity. Shall we deliver him to persecution for these? Rodolfo?" The grand master raised an eyebrow and let his stare linger until Rodolfo shied and bowed his head. "Ludwig, are you not concerned that your *Donnerhünd* is imperiled?"

Ludwig sputtered and looked from side to side. When he finally spoke, his tone was indignant. "I do not take the word of this man as honest report."

"If he lies, what does he gain by it?" The grand master looked around the room for an answer. "Have none of you heard? There may be a hundred slaves at the cusp of liberty? And the extent of your concern is to chuckle and mock the man who brings you the news. Do you not care that brothers of the order are in need?" No one answered. "Does no one here recognize the action and the presence of a Knight of St. John? I fear there is but one among us." He was looking at Jeannot, and one by one, the bailiffs turned to face him as well. Grand master Fra' Emmanuel placed his bejeweled hands on the arms of his chair and raised himself out of it. He straightened to his height and lifted his voice.

"Jeannot Botolph."

Jeannot dropped onto one knee and bowed his head. "Excellency?"

"Are you a knight of the Sovereign Order of St. John?"

"I am."

"And do you speak truth?"

"I do."

"Then rise," he said, "and lead."

The audience hall erupted in confused protest. The grand master sliced his open hand through the air to silence it. He lowered his chin and bent his stare over the heads of the bailiffs. His voice became solemn and graveled, as if it had lumbered from some distant region and traveled up like a wellspring through the bedrock of the island. "We are dwindled men indeed," he said. He pointed to the walls of the hall and the paintings hung there of sea battles and knights of legend. "How long since the Knights of St. John reminded the world that we were strong? A hundred years? Two hundred?"

The bailiffs shifted uncomfortably. They glanced at one another and stepped inches backward.

Fra' Emmanuel's shoulders sagged and his face elongated. He looked weary, sad, and older by years. "The world has moved beyond us, I fear. Soon it will no longer have need of knights and it will speak of us only in stories or songs, if ever at all. And so we go by degrees. We settle in our comforts and in our politics and petty wars, and in time none will remember that our tall ships once drove the Mediterranean before us. We have given up Jerusalem, forsaken the land of our first purpose. We have been cast out of Tripoli and we fled Cyprus. We were crushed at Rhodes and driven homeless to the sea to wander for seven years until, wrecked, we crawled to the barren shores of Malta. And here? Here we have lost far more than lands and deeds and titles. We have lost ourselves. We forget who we were, we forget who we were called out of the world to be. And if even we have forgotten, then who else will remember? The winds of history will scour us from the earth until our great city is barren once more as the rock out of which we raised her."

He motioned for Jeannot to come forward. The bailiffs parted and allowed him to pass.

"Today, Jeannot Botolph. Today you shall remind these corsairs of the Barbary Coast that there are knights yet among them. Let them receive the gifts of musket cock and cannonfire. The *corso* runs ahead. It is well lit and clear, and the ancient enemy is before us. Today will be a day of remembrance. Hammer the battle drum and aweigh the lazy anchor. The Knights of St. John will go to sea, and our sails shall cloud the horizon, terrible as a stormcoming. Go now, Sir Jeannot Botolph, return to your ship. All the strength of Valletta is yours, and should we Knights, in years to come, dwindle into memory, perhaps the world will recall that in the days of our demise we stood, hewing at the fetters of captive men. Go."

The grand master faced Arnaud and pointed to the door. "Bring Lennard Guillot to me that I may put my questions to him."

Chapter Thirty-four

F IN FLEW DOWN THE steps and through the halls of the keep while the countess in tow took every opportunity to stumble or slow their progress. Fin felt like she was dragging a stubborn child to church. The girl groaned and grumbled and twisted her wrist in Fin's hand, hoping to break loose of her. It occurred to Fin that her difficulty was a sample of the frustration Sister Hilde lived with every day of her life. Twice, the girl threw herself to the ground in a dramatic heap and claimed Fin had pulled her forward too quickly and caused her to stumble. Fin's patience quickly ran thin, and when they had gone down three levels, Fin began to doubt that she remembered the way back to the tunnel. She paused at an intersection of hallways, and the countess sagged to the floor and panted.

"Get up," Fin ordered her.

The countess heaved her breaths in and out of her lungs between sobs. Fin repeated her order, and the girl snapped her head up and shouted, "I can't!" She looked both fierce and ridiculous. She bared her teeth at Fin like a wild animal—a wild animal draped in a gossamer nightgown. The countess discovered a tear in the hem of the gown and mumbled something under her breath about Fin being made to pay for it.

From somewhere above them in the upper corridors of the keep a door slapped open and rattled on its hinges. The sound tumbled down to them, and they both looked up the steps, Fin with concern and the countess with satisfaction. The girl smiled. She knew it meant the guards were looking for her. Fin ground her teeth and jerked her by the arm, pulling her to her feet.

"Do you really think you can get away with this?" the countess said. She had a smug look on her face that made Fin want to slap her.

Fin bent over and snatched up the hem of the girl's gown.

"What are you doing?!"

Fin ripped the gown, leaving the countess's knees exposed, then pulled the remnant into a cord and snapped it tight between her hands. The countess gasped and tried to run. Fin was quick; she shot out one foot and knocked the countess's leg to the side. The girl tripped and fell with an unladylike grunt. Fin bent over her, and the girl rolled onto her back in tears. "What are you going to do with that?" she said, eyeing the twisted hem of her gown in Fin's hand.

"One way or the other, you're coming with me. If you can't come quiet and easy, I'm going to tie you like a hog and drag or carry you. And keep your eater shut, or I'll gag you too."

The girl quivered and wiped at her eyes.

"So, do you prefer to walk or be towed?" Fin said.

"What do you mean to do with me?"

"I'm not going to hurt you unless you make me, if that's what you're asking."

"Where are we going?"

"France."

"My husband sent you here, didn't he?"

Fin chewed her words and wondered how to answer. She was angry that she'd been treated like a puppet. Clearly the countess hadn't been captured by pirates; it looked to Fin like she'd run off with them of her own free will. But none of that changed what she had to do.

"I was told you were held captive by pirates, and I was sent to bring you home. Seems clear now that wasn't the whole truth, but I'm bringing you home all the same."

The countess spat in Fin's face. "You're a fool. I ran away because I was forced to marry a man I despise. Do you have any idea what it's like to live your entire life minded by others, by their rules and manners and intentions? To be forbidden to go to the man you love? Of course you don't. You're a mercenary pig. If you take me back I will be gone again in a month, and my Yusuf will hunt you like an animal. Let me go and I will persuade him to let you live."

Fin unwrapped the scarf from her neck and removed her hat. She let her hair spill down around her shoulders so that the countess could see she was a woman. The countess's eyes widened and her mouth fell open.

"You going to walk, or do you want I should tie you?"

The countess sneered. "I can walk."

Fin tried to pull her up by the arm but the countess twisted loose. "Don't touch me."

Another door banged open somewhere above them, closer this time. Fin pointed Betsy down the hall into the depths of the keep. "That way," she said and prodded the girl in the back.

They trotted down the halls, and soon the finery of the upper keep had gone. They were surrounded by bare stone and the dank odor of the keep's sublevels and dungeons. Fin was increasingly unsure of which way to go. She thought she remembered each turn and intersection, but her certainty fell further apart with each twist of the halls. They came to a crossway and the countess stopped. "Which way?" she said.

Fin didn't know. She looked into the hall ahead, then to the left and right. Not only did nothing look familiar, nothing looked different; the walls and floors were all the same with no indication of where the halls might lead. Fin saw the countess turn smug again as she realized that Fin was unsure of where she was.

The sound of doors opening and closing was now very close, and for the first time, Fin could hear footsteps and, occasionally, voices.

"That way," said Fin. She pointed Betsy to the right. The countess huffed as if amused and then trotted off. The hall turned left, then left again, and then the lamp-lit halls were behind them and they had to creep along in the darkness. The countess moved too slowly and Fin repeatedly jabbed her in the back with Betsy's muzzle. They had to be almost there. The way was so dark that they moved forward with one hand to the wall and slid their feet to ensure the floor didn't drop away down a stair. They rounded another bend to the left, and the hall came to a dead end with a closed wooden door on either side.

Fin cursed and yanked on the countess's arm to turn her around. They had to go back. The countess squealed and demanded to be let go. "Go back. Move," said Fin. But before they could backtrack to the previous bend in the corridor, Fin heard a set of footsteps coming. Fin wasn't sure how far away they were, but the last intersection was still far ahead and the footsteps were past it and coming closer. Fin cursed again and pulled the countess to a stop.

The girl complained about her treatment, but Fin dragged her back toward the dead end of the hall. The wooden door on the left was locked. Fin rammed her shoulder into it but it wouldn't open. She turned to the door on the right and yanked on the handle. It didn't budge, but when she threw her shoulder into it, it swung inward and Fin stumbled through the doorway pulling the countess behind. The stench of the room was so thick Fin felt it crawl across her skin. It was the smell of unwashed flesh and human waste. Fin retched and pushed the door closed behind her. The countess staggered against the wall and vomited into the corner.

"Quiet," Fin said. The countess wailed, and Fin clapped her hand across the girl's mouth. Fin bent her head down and whispered into her ear. "Either you stay quiet or I'll make sure every step from here to France is a lesson in unpleasantry and regret." The girl stopped wriggling under Fin's hand and calmed herself. "You understand?"

The girl nodded and hummed something that sounded affirmative. Fin removed her hand from her mouth and pressed Betsy's barrel into her ribs. In the hall, the footsteps *tap-tapped* closer. They stopped momentarily, and Fin saw light flicker through the crack at the bottom of the door. The steps came nearer still and stopped again. The light in the hall glimmered brighter. Someone was lighting the lamps. The guard was in the hall outside the door. Fin held her breath. She kept one hand hovering over the countess's mouth, ready to silence her if she decided to scream. The guard stopped and shuffled around outside the door. A jangle of keys on a ring. The scrape of metal on metal as a key slid into a lock. The clank and rattle of the key turning and tumblers falling into place. The door on the other side of the hall swung on its hinges and they heard the guard enter the opposite room.

As Fin listened to the sound of the room being inspected, she didn't have to guess where the guard would be coming next. She backed away from the door and dragged the countess with her. When she had a clear view of the door outlined by the faint shudder of lamplight from the hall, Fin raised Betsy and waited. Slowly, an inch at a time, she backed farther from the door, retreating into the deepest shadows of the room. The reek of the cell made her eyes water. Her feet knocked against things, things that crunched or scraped on the floor like dried sticks, and then against softer things, wet things, things that compressed and resisted when she nudged them away with her foot. Then something nudged back. Fin gasped and hopped to the side, away from whatever had moved. She looked down, blinking her eyes rapidly, trying to focus in the darkness. The footsteps outside were in the hall again, and the door across the hall slammed closed. Outside the door the keys jangled again on their ring. Fin looked around and saw two white orbs materialize out of the darkness. They began as slits, thin as splinters, but they spread and widened. Eyes staring back at her. They seemed lazy and indifferent at first, but as she locked her gaze with them she saw each white circle obscured in part along their lower curve. Fin had the unsettling feeling that they were smiling at her. A sickly sound rose up, something like a groan of laughter, and then a familiar voice.

"We meet again in darkness, eh *cherie*?"

Chains rattled and the countess was pulled out of Fin's grip. Before Fin could react, the girl screamed. The door to the room crashed open and shuddered against the wall. A guard hunched in the doorway, alert and wound tight like a spring. He held a scimitar in one hand and thrust a torch into the room with his other. It took him only a moment to scan the room and appraise what he saw, but Fin didn't give him time to act on it. Betsy roared to life. The crack of the shot in the small room drove a stab of pain into Fin's ears, and the flash illuminated the cell in a brief moment of clarity. The walls were lined with men hanging dead and dying in their manacles. They were cut and scarred and misshapen by abuse and torture. The floor was a wreck of bone, waste, and cadaverous ruin. The flash burned the images into her eyes and they floated ghost-like in her vision.

Fin picked up the guard's torch and scimitar. The crack of the gun blast resounded in her ears, and as she shook her head to clear the ringing it seemed to grow louder. Gradually, Fin realized that it wasn't the effect of the gunshot she was hearing—it was the screaming of the countess. Fin swung the torch into the shadows of the room. Armand Defain stared back at her. He was a remnant. The only recognizable thing about him was his eyes: terrible and white, they bulged and stared from a monstrous face. He was naked and emaciated. The hands and tools of a torturer had reshaped what was left of him. His body bled and seeped and shook. His wrists were bolted in manacles and chained to the wall. His arms were wrapped fast about the countess. He kneaded her throat with the stub of his hand, but it was nothing more than a paw with a single remaining finger, a thumb jutting off of it like the appendage of some stillborn abomination. All that remained of his other hand was a gnarl of tattered flesh.

His malicious whispers floated through the filth of the room. "Got your hands on the countess at last, eh *cherie*?"

"Let her go," said Fin. Armand dug his nubbed hands into the countess's flesh and whispered something that made the girl flinch and tremble. Fin grimaced in disgust. Armand was no longer merely twisted; he was wholly broken, either entirely mad or entirely evil. Fin didn't know which, but she was suddenly afraid, more afraid of him than of the guards who were pouring through the keep in search of the source of the gunshot. Fin raised the scimitar and repeated her order. "Let her go."

Armand lifted his head and let his grin slip. It was toothless now and scab-ridden, more disquieting than ever. "Leaving Armand again, eh? Take your pardon and leave him in the arms of the Barbarie?" Armand hissed at her through his gums and laughed. "I lusted after vengeance once, and you gave it to me. But now I have another wish, *cherie*. Grant it, and the girl is yours."

The tip of the scimitar wavered in the air. Fin shifted her feet and moved the blade an inch closer. "Let her go, Armand. Let's get out of here. Pardons for us all when we get to France."

Armand scraped his thumb into the countess's throat, depressing the skin as if he meant to dig a hole in it. The countess choked and cried. "You gave it to old Tiberius, didn't you?" A rivulet of blood ran down from a cut on his forehead and spilled into his left eye, spreading across it in a gory film. He blinked and squinted and fluttered his eye to see through it. "You even gave it to old Bart. Now give it to me, *cherie*."

"What are you talking about? Come on. I can get us out of here. All of us."

Armand snarled. He bared his gums and shook his head like an animal. He covered the countess's face with his fingerless hand and pawed at it. "Give it to me!" he shouted.

Fin turned her head toward the door; she could hear more footsteps coming. They were distant yet, but it was only a matter of time. She reached out and took the countess by the arm and tried to pull her away.

Armand snarled again and howled. He wrapped his arm around the girl's neck and began trying to wrench her face around. The girl kicked at him and gasped for breath, but he had her tight. He was trying to break her neck. He pawed at her face, pushing and pulling her head with his mutilated hands, fumbling at his murder like a savage.

"Stop it!" Fin yelled.

He flicked his eyes toward her and howled. "Give it to *me*!" He raved and gnashed his gums. Blood-spittle flew from his lips. And then amid his raving, as if some calmer thing existed at the center of his maddened howl, Fin saw that tears were streaming from his eyes. They ran down his face, and but for the violent shaking of his head might have washed him clean.

"*Give it to me!*"

Fin stepped forward and slid the tip of the scimitar between his ribs. Immediately, he loosed the countess. She fell and scrambled across the floor, collapsing in terror against the far wall. Armand's howl drained out of him and became a deep sigh. His lips spread apart, grinning, and he seized the scimitar blade between his wrecked hands. "*Merci*." He wrenched it from Fin's grip and pulled it into him, skewering himself as his face unfolded in a moan of ecstasy. He sank to his knees to die.

Fin grabbed the countess and pushed her out the door. "Move!" Fin ordered. The countess was terrorized beyond argument and ran. As they dashed around the corner, Fin heard the last of Armand's whispers uttered in the rattle of his decease: "*La mort, enfin!*"

THE DOORS OF THE Cathedral of St. John swung open, and Jeannot descended the steps. After him came the bailiffs of the other seven *langues*. They distanced themselves from Jeannot, considering him with sidelong glances as if he were something foreign, an agent of powers unknown. But although Jeannot baffled them, they acted on the decree of the grand master without hesitation. As soon as they were outside the cathedral, they called for runners and sent word through the city to every captain of the fleet.

Jeannot listened as they sent their orders, and he heard when they whispered his name to one another and muttered, grumbled, or wondered. But as they split, each to their own auberge, to ready themselves for sea, Jeannot quickened his steps toward the harbor. He could see the masts of the *Esprit de la Mer* and was anxious to return to her. As he wound through the city, a buzz of rumor grew. It began behind him and swelled to the east and west and then overtook him and sped down through the city as runners passed news that the fleet was being rallied and the Knights would sail in force.

Before he reached the quay, he passed the first of the freed slaves they'd brought back aboard the *Espirt de la Mer*. Led by physicians, they walked in a file toward the hospital. They stumbled along and flashed smiles at passers-by and stared at the wonder of the Proud City with wide child-like eyes that seemed too big for their bone-thin bodies.

When Jeannot neared the *Esprit de la Mer*'s berth, he clenched his teeth and felt the prickle of anger. His crew was knelt along the pierside in shackles. Lennard Guillot stood over Remy and slapped him. The blow wasn't serious. It was belittling. And it clearly hadn't been the first; a thin line of blood streamed from Remy's nostril into his mustache and was smeared across his cheek. Few things inspired anger in Jeannot; the mistreatment of his crew enraged him.

Lennard raised his hand to deliver another strike, and Jeannot caught him by the wrist. He dragged his bailiff away from Remy and shoved him. Lennard stumbled backward and fell to the ground.

"There he is!" shouted Lennard. "Arrest him." The guards watching the crew approached Jeannot, but he held up his hand, and they hesitated.

"I'm here by decree of the grand master."

The guards looked to Lennard for guidance. He wrestled himself up, grunting and straining against his obesity, then smacking at the dirt on his trousers. "He lies. Arrest him!"

Before the guards could obey, Arnaud arrived.

"Leave him be," said Arnaud. "Lennard, the grand master wishes to question you at once."

"What are you talking about? Arrest him. This man is a traitor!" Lennard fumed with anger.

Arnaud shook his head and frowned at both Jeannot and Lennard. "The grand master will explain, I'm sure." He nodded to the guards. "Escort him to the audience hall. Jeannot, my ships will be ready to sail at midday. I shall send my chief navigator to discuss the details of our departure."

Lennard flabbered his mouth open and closed. His meaty chins bounced and wobbled like fat, wet bladders, and he looked from Arnaud to Jeannot in disbelief until the guards took their places at his side. Arnaud ordered them away, and Lennard shuffled down the street between them.

Arnaud stepped toward Jeannot and offered his hand. "You walk a narrow path between fortune and foolishness, Jeannot."

Jeannot nodded. "I do not walk it lightly." He took Arnaud's hand and shook it. "But I am gladly a fool for the sake of my men and my friends."

Arnaud held Jeannot's hand and studied his face until he was satisfied. He clapped Jeannot on the shoulder and released him. "To sea, then. And God save us all."

Arnaud left and Jeannot turned to the men standing guard over his shackled crew.

"What are you waiting for?" he shouted. "Free them."

When the crew was loose, they gathered around their captain and chattered to one another, smiling and anxious for news. Remy pulled at his ear nervously. He still had a smudge of dried blood on his cheek.

"Nothing hurt but your pride, I hope," said Jeannot.

Remy grunted. "Taken worse from Sicilian whores."

Jeannot cringed then closed his eyes and shook his head. "Some things I'd rather not know, Remy."

Remy winked at the sailor next to him and chuckled. "To sea then, eh *Capitaine*?"

"*Oui*, to the sea."

"Other ships coming with us?"

Jeannot smiled. "They're all coming."

The crew tightened in around Jeannot and cheered and hugged one another. Remy ordered them back to the *Esprit de la Mer*, and they ran eagerly to their work.

Pierre-Jean escorted the last of the freed slaves ashore as Jeannot approached the plank. Pierre-Jean was haggard and exhausted, but his face lightened when he saw his captain. He ushered the sick man onto a wagon and ordered the driver to take them to the hospital.

"You look well for a man doomed to arrest," said Pierre-Jean.

Jeannot laughed.

"Have we aid then?"

"We have, old friend. The bailiffs are not all pleased, I think. But Fra' Emmanuel has spoken for us. His strength is ours. We leave with the fleet as soon as they can be rallied."

Pierre-Jean widened his eyes. "The fleet?"

Jeannot raised his eyebrows and nodded, "The fleet." Then he took Pierre-Jean by the shoulder. "You are weary, but we must be ready to sail by midday. Take what you require from the hospital. I fear we will need it when we return to the Coast."

Pierre-Jean ran down the pier and caught up with the wagon. He climbed into the seat beside the driver and they departed.

Jeannot spent the rest of the morning in congress with the other captains and navigators of the fleet. Though the Order commanded nearly a hundred ships in total, there were only forty-two able and in port. The rest were either at sea or under repair. Jeannot had hoped for three ships, perhaps four. Forty-two would be enough.

When midday came, it seemed the entire city of Valletta was at the waterfront to see the departure. People crowded the pierside streets and rooftops. They waved and pointed and held their children upon their shoulders. Pierre-Jean stood beside Jeannot at the helm and looked out across the city and the harbor. The air was filled with drums. "I have seen nothing like it in all of memory," he said. The *Esprit de la Mer* hove from the quay, and Jeannot Botolph led the Knights of St. John from the harbor. By ones and twos, the other ships wheeled to follow and the port emptied of its warships.

Jeannot paced the deck as they rounded the Maltese coast and turned south. The fleet came on behind him like a cloudbank. To his port side he recognized ships of the English *langue*: the sleek brigantine *Virago*, a smaller corvette named *Cormorant*, and others. To his starboard he spotted *Il Principe di Italia, Mare Ballerino, La Canzone di Guerra* and the rest of the Italian frigates painted in reds and greens. For a moment, Jeannot caught sight of the bailiff, Giuseppe Grisafi, on the deck of *Il Principe di Italia*. He was fat and orbular and dressed in a red coat ornamented with lace and a tasseled set of yellow epaulets. The feathers of his hat flapped in the wind. He wobbled across the deck and leaned at the helm as he patted his face with a handkerchief. Jeannot suspected he had not been to sea in a very long time.

When the fleet had made the southern turn and was set toward the Coast, Jeannot gave the deck over to Remy and retired. He hadn't slept for days. His eyelids were heavy as iron and his mind was clouded by exhaustion. He'd accomplished what he aimed to, and more. There was nothing left to do but hope that his crew and the *Donnerhünd* could hold out. His mind turned to Fin, blessed Fin, and though he couldn't imagine how she'd win an escape from Tripoli with the countess, he had to admit that in her wake the unlikely had lately veered toward commonplace. Jeannot smiled when he thought of her and he touched his cheek where once she'd struck him. He lifted her up in his prayers and hoped very much to see her again. Then he stumbled to his cabin and collapsed into sleep.

CHAPTER THIRTY-FIVE

FIN DIDN'T HAVE ANY more trouble with the countess not wanting to move. Instead, she couldn't seem to get her to stop. The girl's encounter with Armand had terrified her, and she fled blindly in any direction Fin pointed her. Several times Fin had to catch her and yank her back when she careered past a turn Fin wanted to take. Luckily there were few passages to choose from. They'd found one other dead end, but after that, Fin was certain they were going in the right direction. She was also aware that once the guards got this far down, that would work to their advantage as well as hers.

They sped around a corner, and Fin spotted the door she'd left propped open. Fin pushed the countess inside then grabbed the oil lamp and darted back up the hallway to light it with one of the other lamps lining the walls. When she returned, the countess was huddled against the doorframe. She turned her head away when Fin looked at her. In the short space of time since Fin had met her, she'd gone from a creamy-skinned lady dressed in finery to a rapidly unraveling girl. Her hair was a serpentine mess that hung across her face in scraps and tatters, and she was filthy from her falls, covered in smudges of dirt. Her tears left white streaks in the grime on her face, making her an almost comical sight.

"This way," said Fin. She tugged on the countess's sleeve and guided her down into the tunnel. Fin rummaged around the room and picked out four crates. The largest, she pushed across the floor and arranged in front of the tunnel entrance. She stacked the others on top of it, leaving a gap wide enough for her to climb through. With one look back at the door and the sounds of the search coming nearer, Fin squeezed between the crates and the doorframe then closed up the gap to conceal their escape.

The countess had gone down the steps far enough to find they ended in water. She cowered against the wall at the last dry step and looked at Fin in terror.

"Let's go," said Fin.

The countess closed her eyes and shook her head. Fin grabbed her by the shoulder and pushed her forward. When the girl's feet hit the water she whimpered and began to cry. Fin pushed her again, and the girl let out a moan as she stumbled in chest deep. Before stepping into the water herself, Fin pulled out the second guards' robe and then removed her own. She wrapped them up with Besty and waded in behind the countess with the lamp and bundle held high.

"It gets shallower. Come on."

The girl's eyes flitted up the steps, hoping to see a rescuer appear, but from the sounds Fin heard when she sealed up the exit, she estimated they still had several minutes before the guards were even close. Fin slid around the countess and led her, pulling on the sleeve of her gown as the girl whimpered and sobbed. Fin knew exactly where she was going now and sped through the tunnel as fast as the countess would allow. They emerged from the slimy water and trotted through the remainder of the tunnel at a high clip. They came to the end and climbed through the wardrobe into the chancel. Morning sprung through the cracked windows and hurled bright spears of light through the dust-filled air. Fin resumed her disguise, putting the robe back on and covering her face with the black scarf. She handed the second robe to the countess. "Put this on."

The countess took the bundle and unrolled it. She turned up her nose and considered the garment with disgust, but when she caught Fin's impatient look, she slipped it on.

"Cover your head." Fin handed her a scarf and veil and reloaded Betsy while the countess did as she was told. When she was done, Fin arranged the veil across the girl's face and ensured that none of her golden hair was visible.

"This way."

Fin led her to the cathedral door and peeked out. From behind the slats barring the door, Fin could see only a single man, walking lazily away to the north.

Fin tucked her own hair up and clapped the hat onto her head.

"Now listen. When I tell you, the both of us are going to climb out quick and walk direct for the west gate."

The fear that Armand had struck into the girl had begun to wear thin; her lip was curled into a sneer. "You will never get out of the city alive."

Fin raised her eyebrows and shook Betsy in front of the countess's face. "You'd best hope I do. I hear a peep out of your mouth and old Betsy here will be the end of you. Understand?"

The countess looked at Betsy with suspicion and didn't answer.

"Sure wish you'd a been kidnapped," muttered Fin. "We're going to walk quiet-like right through town as if you were any poor woman going her way. Me and Betsy'll be right at your heels. Give me your hand."

"Why?" snapped the countess.

Fin snatched her hand from her side and pulled the torn hem of the gown out of her belt. She tied it around the girl's wrist and then tied the other end around her own.

Fin bent down and picked up the oil lamp. "You ready?" she asked.

The countess gave her a dirty look and took a step toward the door. Fin hurled the lamp into the nave of the cathedral. It arced through the air like a flaming pinwheel and shattered on the stone floor. Oil splashed across the desiccated pews, and fire raced across the wood with a *whumpping* noise, not unlike the pop of a sail.

"Go!" ordered Fin.

They climbed through the slats of the door and hurried down the steps. The street was empty. Fin directed them east and tugged on the cord between them to slow the countess to a casual walk. Fin kept close at her side to conceal the bond and held Betsy inside her robe with her free hand. In the distance, alarm bells rang in the keep. It would only be a matter of time before the keep guards discovered that she'd escaped, and when they did, they were sure to send word to close the city gates.

A block east of the cathedral, the streets were busier. Several times Fin spotted armed men hustling toward the keep in answer to the alarm. The countess leaned toward them as they passed, and Fin thought for a moment that she would cry out. She jammed Betsy's barrel into the girl's ribs and whispered in her ear. "Walk." The girl jerked away from her and hissed, but she did as she was told.

As they neared the gate, Fin heard shouting behind her. Crowds of people pointed up at the sky. Fin turned and saw a billow of black smoke rising from the old cathedral. The traffic in the street shifted as people turned to run in the direction of the fire. Fin prodded the countess in the shoulder and they quickened their pace.

At the gate there were half a dozen guards milling around, but their attention was divided between the fire and the alarm bells from the keep. When people approached from outside the city, the guards waved them through with impatience, scarcely taking their eyes off the fists of smoke punching skyward from the cathedral. Fin took full advantage of the confusion. She tightened her hand on the countess's upper arm and goaded her forward. They hurried through the gates, and the guards gave them no notice at all. Once through, Fin began to run. She tugged the countess along behind her. The girl saw her last chance for rescue slipping away and cried out for help, but her voice was lost in the clamor of people shouting and rushing toward the fire.

The horse waited lazily, still tied to the sycamore where she'd left it.

"Up!" Fin ordered. The girl balked and Fin ordered her again. "Up! Or I'll tie you and throw you across like a sack."

"I'm wearing a dress!" The girl shook the skirts of her robe and stamped her feet.

"You're going to wear a bloody lip if you don't get in that saddle."

The girl huffed and mumbled all the way up and sat with her skirt pulled up to her thighs. It was as indecent a thing as Fin had ever seen, and she tried meagerly to suppress a chuckle. She climbed into the saddle behind the countess, wrapped her arms around her, and grabbed the reins. When she dug her heels into the horse's flanks, the horse complained and stepped sideways then lurched into a trot. The countess shrieked and yelled. She called out in the strange language of the city. Fin looked around and saw the heads turned their way. She kicked her heels into the horse again and the horse quickened into a canter. The countess left off her cries for help and wrapped her hands around the horn of the saddle tight enough to whiten her knuckles.

As they sped away from the city, Fin felt her muscles unclench and realized she'd been as taut as a fiddle string since she entered the city hours before. Now that she was in the open again and aimed toward the countryside, she gave herself permission to relax. To the north, the morning light washed across the Mediterranean, cutting through the grey water like a vein of gold. The sight of it renewed Fin and let her breathe easier. Then she spotted a dark shape on the otherwise unblemished surface of water. A small ship intruded upon the vista like a cockroach across a wall. The ship was bound for the Tripolitan harbor. It listed to starboard and its sails were shredded, flapping loose in the wind. Fin recognized the vessel. She'd seen it and another like it departing eastward as she approached the city the day before. The damaged and tattered sails were Luther's work. Fin was sure of it. She kicked the horse again and snapped at the reins.

By midday they had left the city and its traffic behind. The countess hung limp before Fin and made no effort to hold herself in the saddle. Fin had to constantly steady the girl between her arms to keep her from falling off. She took time to stop at creek beds to water the horse in whatever muddy puddles it could find but the country quickly turned barren and dry. It rolled and stretched eastward like an earthen blanket settled meanly over the crust of the earth. Here and there stubborn tufts of green sprouted among the bleakness of the land, but they seemed less an affirmation of life than an exception to the sovereignty of death. They rode on. The sun stabbed down, searing the countess's delicate skin and turning it first pink then deep red. The girl slept at times and pitched from side to side in Fin's arms. When awake, she sobbed quietly and often threw her head back to scream until her voice cracked and broke. Fin allowed it; she made no protest against her cries. There were none to hear her in the wilderness. Fin had done her share of screaming in the past. She wouldn't deny the girl her own.

In the afternoon they came upon a draw in the land and Fin saw at its lowest extent a smatter of green brush. She hied the horse from the road and walked it down through the rocks. There were signs of a watercourse but it had long been dry. At the utmost of the draw, however, the dirt was moist and sucked at the horse's hooves. Fin jumped down, caught the countess, and lowered her to the ground. Fin dug in the soft, wet earth with her hands, scraping out handfuls of dirt and piling them aside. When she'd dug a few inches deep, water seeped through the ground and filled the hole. Fin bent over and put her lips to the water as if kissing it and sucked the water up. It was gritty on her teeth and foul, but the coolness of it made her sit back and sigh deeply. Water refilled the hole, and she drank again while the countess pulled off her robe and mumbled over the state of her torn and soiled gown. When Fin motioned for the countess come and drink, the girl ran. She scampered up the rocks and sprinted across the dusty landscape in a burst of speed that quite impressed Fin. Fin didn't bother to give chase. She waited patiently while the horse sucked up its fill of water then she eased her way into the saddle and walked the animal up the rocks and out of the draw. The countess had made it about three hundred feet. She was a tiny, heaving lump on the brown expanse. The sun caught in the last bit of color left in her gown and brightened it like a flower. Fin guided the horse toward her. The girl's shoulders were wracked by sobs. As Fin came up behind her, she saw that the brief run across the sun-blasted sand had blistered the soles of the girl's feet.

Fin hopped down from the horse. She bent and took hold of the girl under the arms and knees. Fin groaned and strained but managed to pick the girl up and carry her to the horse.

"Get on," Fin told her. The girl obeyed, and Fin pushed her up, allowing her to climb without putting her blistered feet to the hot earth. Then she clambered up behind her and set them back toward the road.

"Why are you doing this?" the countess mumbled.

Fin didn't know what the use of giving an answer would be. It certainly wasn't going to give the poor girl any comfort. But answer she did, and more to remind herself than to assuage the countess.

"If I take you back to France, I can go home," she said.

"I hate you."

"I know you do."

Fin dug in her heels, and across the blighted land they rode.

CHAPTER THIRTY-SIX

A GLOWERING RED SUN DROOPED below the horizon.
Evening set. Fin hobbled the horse and left the countess sitting in
a cleft of stone with her knees drawn to her chest. The girl shivered
and shook and stared blankly, not answering any of Fin's interrogations
about her health or state of mind—that, in itself, a kind of answer.

Fin climbed the rocks and sat atop a bluff that overlooked the sea.
She drew her own legs up and stretched the pain of the day's ride from
her muscles. She couldn't afford to stop for the night, but she needed rest,
as did the horse. And she worried about the countess. The poor girl was
addled, badly shaken. Embers of fear and helplessness sputtered in Fin's
chest; she had been the victim of such a crime once and knew well the
hateful thing Caroline de Graff was nurturing in her heart. Fin winced
and creased her face. She hadn't bargained for kidnapping. She'd imagined her return as the celebrated rescuer. Instead, it seemed she would
once more be the seed of scandal and infamy. She wondered, though,
who had known. Was it possible that the French had lied to Captain
Bettany and the American Congress? Or had everyone known? Everyone
but her. Fin Button, fool of nations. It didn't matter. Her aim was the
pardon of her men. Her aim was home. More than ever she was weary of
running, weary of being chased. She closed her eyes and tried to picture

Peter, but she found that she couldn't anymore. She could recall the feel of his hands, the smell of him, even the outline of his individual features, but she couldn't picture his face in her mind. He lay apart like a shattered glass, each shard reflecting a piece but never a whole. Fin squeezed her eyes tighter and gritted her teeth and tried to order the fragments together, but the harder she tried the finer they splintered and broke. Fin laid her face on her arms thinking she'd cry, but no tears came. Behind her, the sobs of the countess eddied across the rocks. Fin stared at the ground between her feet and wondered at what a cruel and hardened thing she'd become.

The ringing of a bell stirred her out of the reverie. It clanged faint and windborne from a point far west. She looked toward the sound. The red dome of the sun lingered, setting high clouds in blazes. Again, she heard the faint chime of the bell and narrowed her eyes. Far to the west—sails. She saw only a few at first, but as she looked, her eyes picked out more and more, a half dozen, then ten, then two dozen, then more than she could count. Sails of the Barbarie. They crept small at the horizon line, wisps of candleflame against darkening the sky. The battered ship she'd seen earlier must have taken word of the *Donnerhünd's* presence. It had stirred Tripoli and roused the swarm. Further south, a milky column of dust hung at the horizon of the western desert, no more than a thin finger in the distance. Riders.

Fin descended the rocks and found the countess curled on a flat stone. Fin pulled her up and helped her onto the horse. The girl didn't speak or resist. She let herself be moved, pliable as a doll. Fin mounted behind her and set the horse at a walk. The night gathered before them. The road ran ahead like a ribbon undulating across a shamble of hill and rock. Fin settled into the saddle and let the horse pick its own way.

Through the night they rode on. Fin nodded in and out of sleep. At times she awoke to the lunatic yap of jackals flitting between the rocks as the horse stepped sidewise and rolled its eye in fear. Once she started awake to a sound like the low roll of drums, and to the south she saw an endless congregation of antelope that moved across the nighted plain, raising a cloud of dust behind them that swallowed the stars and turned the moon rusty brown as a scrape of ruined iron. Near dawn, in that darkest hour, she raised her head again and saw to the north the passage of sails. They hovered across the deep like a parade of phantom cavaliers tilted upon hellish steeds. They passed in waves, ranks upon ranks of ghostly warlords bent toward the coming dawn as if to impale the sun itself and set it atop a spike in the blackened sky.

Like a celestial herald, the sun hearkened the rise of gunfire. It came in light pops and snaps of musket at first but built to a crescendo of roaring cannon. The sound rasped across the landscape from points remote and unseen. Fin shook herself and rose up stiff in the saddle. She craned her head high to see across the rocky land toward the distant battle flashing. The terrain rose sharply before her, mounting up in steps and rocky steeps toward a higher plateau. Fin saw cottony wisps of smoke bellying over the ridgeline and caught the faint tang of powder on the wind. The quarry was ahead. The riders behind had ridden through the night and harder than Fin. The dust cloud of their pursuit roiled and billowed no more than ten miles to the west.

The countess awoke.

"We're almost there," said Fin.

The countess kept her silence but looked around, scanning the landscape in a slow sweep from left to right. When she'd appraised the scene, she asked, "Where?" but Fin didn't answer.

Fin kicked her heels and urged the horse forward. The beast was nearly ruined. Its head hung low, and when it quickened at Fin's command, its steps were leaden and sorrowful. Fin dismounted and led the horse afoot as they climbed the narrow steeps. Upon crossing the lip of the plateau, the land around became familiar. Men of the Barbary Coast lined the rim of the quarry and fired across the gulf of it. Fin counted eight as they raised their arms to pack their guns and then laid prone to aim and fire. Beyond them, from over the cliffs, came a continual thundering of cannon. Fin pulled the horse to a halt. "Get down," she said.

The countess crawled off the horse and wobbled on her legs as she straightened her robes. She glared at Fin but turned her eyes down quickly when Fin looked back. Fin slapped the horse on the flank, and it lumbered off toward the corral.

"Follow me," said Fin. She started toward the corral, moving quickly and bent at the waist. She circled toward the rocks to conceal her approach from the men at the rim of the quarry. The countess came after, erect and looking back at intervals as if she expected the arrival of a rescue at any instant. Fin doubled back to fetch her. She took the girl by the sleeve and dragged her to the crags beside the corral. Fin stuck her head around the rock and looked up at the rim of the quarry. The men continued their fusillade and occasionally a musket ball from the far side cracked the air above them. Between the pop of musket and the rumble of cannonfire, Fin also heard a steady chant of mockery and taunts launched from the eastern side of the quarry. "If you're aiming at them rocks, you're a hell of a shot!" said one. And another: "'At's a good shot for a blind woman!" Fin was sure one of the voices was Topper's.

Fin spotted movement to the south. Along the crags below the rim, a train of a dozen men in red and black robes picked their way toward the southern reach of the quarry, a position from which they could flank Topper and the others.

Fin pulled her head back. The countess sat against a rock with her head leaned back and her eyes closed. "Get up. Give me your hands." Fin repeated her instruction and the girl complied lazily. With the cord of cloth torn from the hem of the gown, Fin bound the girl's hands behind her back then pulled her to the edge of the corral and tied the cord to the fencepost. The countess tugged at her bonds and demanded to be loosed, but Fin ignored her. She removed her own robes and threw them on the ground, glad to be rid of the disguise. Several of the horses stamping in the corral had scimitars sheathed and hung at the saddle. Fin hopped the fence and retrieved one then rejoined the countess at her post.

"If you don't want to get hurt, I advise you keep down and out of sight." The countess heard, but the baffled look on her face told Fin she didn't understand. She didn't need to understand. Fin didn't elaborate. "I'll be back. Just you keep down." Fin knelt and tore a strip of cloth from her robe and frowned at the girl. "Sorry, but I've got to do this." Before the countess could realize what the apology was for, Fin pressed the strip over her mouth and gagged her.

Fin took Betsy in one hand and the scimitar in the other and crept along the fence to the gate of the corral. With Betsy's muzzle, she lifted the keeper off the gatepost and let the gate swing out. The horses milled around and considered the open way before them, but sensing some ruse, they only snorted and stamped nervously. Musket fire popped at the quarry rim and the horses shuffled. They threw their heads and nickered at the air. Fin crept back to the countess's post at the end of the corral then leaned over the fence and, using the flat of the scimitar, slapped the hind of the nearest horse. The beast whinnied and started and ran out the open gate. The others shuffled around then followed.

Four men dropped their guns and ran toward the corral, shouting and waving their hands in the air as they chased after their mounts. The horses circled and weaved across the sand and paid no mind to the men running after them. While the four men chased the horses, Fin watched the others. Each man fired his shot and then spent a leisurely minute reloading his musket before firing again. Fin waited until three of the men fired in rapid succession, nearly in unison, and as they rolled onto their elbows to reload, she charged. They saw her at once but seemed hypnotized by the strange sight of Fin, wiry, ragged, and sunburnt, sprinting and huffing toward them. One of the men looked at the man next to him and laughed. She was nearly upon them by the time the humor and unlikelihood of the spectacle wore off. Fin put Betsy before her and fired. The man nearest flopped to the ground dead. She completed her charge and dove into the next man as he rose, knocking him over the lip of the quarry to land broken on the rocks below. The third man finished packing his musket and almost had time to put it to his shoulder before Fin jammed the point of the scimitar through his chest. He wheezed and ground his teeth then slumped to the side. Fin took a breath and sagged with relief.

But there had been a fourth man. She turned in time to see the spout of fire erupt from his musket. The ball sizzled forth like a meteor and slid across her face, searing a line into her skin that extended back from the cheekbone under her right eye. The fiery ball moved on and took with it the uppermost of her ear, leaving behind a trail of cauterized flesh forever burned across her face like a strip of dried leather. The man dropped the musket from his shoulder. He lifted his head and squinted at the billow of gunsmoke before him. Like a star emerging from a wrack of cloud, the point of Fin's scimitar pierced the haze. Fin followed after and drove the blade home.

The men running after the horses left off their chase and turned back. They pointed at her and shouted as they ran. One waved a scimitar in the air, the others came on empty-handed and seething. One at a time, Fin picked up their muskets, finished loading, and took aim. Each shot missed, but the runners turned away. They collected them each a horse and departed westward toward the approaching riders. Fin stood from the last shot and let the musket clatter to the ground. At the corral, the countess pulled and twisted at her bonds and shouted after the men as they fled.

Fin felt blood roll down her neck, and she touched her cheek with the tips of her fingers. The flesh was crinkled and moist. She ran a finger across the top of her ear and jerked it away. It didn't hurt, but the alien feel of the now reduced shape of the ear startled her. She lifted the collar of her shirt and wiped the blood from her neck. Across the cauldron of the quarry, a dozen heads and shoulders rose up and stared. They looked like small forest animals frozen in alarm with their paws drawn and ears tuned. Fin raised the scimitar over her head and waved it back and forth. One of the heads shifted and dipped, and then the man stood up and waved back. It was Topper. Fin saw the bottom of his face split open as he began to laugh. He danced and tugged at the shoulder of the man next to him.

"Topper," Fin called. He waved again but kept up his dancing. She called again and he stopped and cupped his hand to his ear. Fin pointed toward the south end of the quarry where the rest of the Barbary men were trying to flank him. Topper looked once and shrugged and cupped his hand back to his ear. Fin pointed again; she picked up a musket and put it to her shoulder, pointing it south. Topper considered this for a moment then turned to the men with him and pointed in the direction Fin had indicated. They ran off with their weapons and Fin nodded.

Fin retrieved the countess and removed her gag. The girl followed behind her alternately skittish and indignant as she was led through the quarry. The floor of the path was littered with the dead; they all wore the red and black robes of the pasha's men. It appeared the Barbarie had tried to assault Topper's position directly, and judging by the body count had been stopped hard and cold. Fin doubted the men had even expected a fight. They were surely surprised when they found themselves at the bottom of the quarry caught in a hail of fire and lead. As Fin led the countess up the far side of the quarry toward the landing path, pops of gunfire erupted southward where Topper's men engaged the flanking force.

Topper ran down the path to meet her, his belly abounce and protruding pale and hairy from under his tattered shirt. "Fin, you missed it!" he said. "We walloped 'em sound!"

"Good to see you, Topper."

Topper studied the girl behind Fin and widened his eyes. "That the countess?" He dropped to one knee, covered his heart with one hand, and swept the other out to his side. "It's an honor, ma'am. Never met me a countess before, but we'll have you home lickety-split, don't you worry."

The countess wrinkled her nose and frowned at him with disgust. Topper noted that her hands were tied and he scratched his head.

"She ain't kidnapped," said Fin. "She's ran away."

Topper rubbed at his nose and looked the girl over with grim curiosity. "Huh."

"There's riders coming in, lots of them. Where's Jack?"

Chapter Thirty-seven

A THUNDERCLAP OF CANNON SPLIT the air. "Follow me," Topper shouted, and he led Fin toward the path to the landing. Where the path wound down through the rock, the entire way was crowded with men. They were packed together, all standing and pressed toward the water. Grey-brown heads knocked around and undulated as the men furthest back craned from side to side to see further down the path. One face turned toward them. It was Phineas Button. He saw Fin and she waved to him but he only stared at her blankly and then turned away. Topper led her up onto the cliff face overlooking the Barbary Coast. At the cliff's edge, Jack sat with his sole knee propped up and leaned his bear-like frame in the hollow of a boulder. He cradled a musket in the crook of one arm and held the other over his eyes as he surveyed the sea below.

The first thing Fin recognized was Luther's ship, the *Donnerhünd*. Half a mile distant, it beat a course windward in retreat. A plume of smoke rose from her amidships and trailed through the air behind. She had but a single remaining mast, and every sail save one blew torn in the wind, tattered into flapping pennants as the ship fled northeast. Behind the *Donnerhünd*, less than a half-mile off her transom, the swarm of Tripoli raced in pursuit. They were a chaotic wrack of shallow-bellied xebecs and pirate galleys oared Homeric like vessels sailed out of an elder and more savage age. With cannons bursting, on they came. Oars beat the sea, tall tri-angled sails towered skyward like pointed teeth, guns barked and flashed and spent a vomit of iron upon Luther and his flight. Their cannonshot dappled a frothy circumference around the *Donnerhünd*. Splashes peppered the water and white stripes speared across the surface as missiles skipped and rolled over the sea. Often came the sharp crack and crunch of a ball punching through the deck.

"Look there," said Topper, pointing. "Off yonder."

Topper's indication led Fin's eye past Luther's harried retreat toward a sight greater still. Beyond the *Donnerhünd*, the sea stretched out blue and calm for some two miles or three, and past this middle stillness there approached a force that was, in living memory, unreckonable upon the Barbary coast. The fleet of the Knights of Malta, war-wakened and favored by winds of the north, drove forth in vast array upon the blue-green face of the deep. The sea broke before them, parting in runnels of foam and spraying fountain-like into the air. On the passage south, others had joined the forty-two that departed Valletta; now they numbered better than sixty ships of war. Acres of sail sprung over the waves: white, square, full-bellied, and taut with spritely zephyrs. Maltese crosses on great black ensigns trailed each mizzenmast, flapping wild and ridden high. The wind drove them on, hurling all their tons of cannon, sheet, and timber through the sea, and they seemed weightless as if borne aloft upon the air itself. At the foremost of their line, the *Esprit de la Mer* stretched ahead, pulling the plane of their approach into a sharp point that drew the other ships along behind.

"Handy, these friends of yours, Button." A fat smile lurked under Jack's beard. "Get our countess?"

Fin tugged the girl forward and told her to sit. "Complicated," said Fin. "But I got her."

Jack dropped his hand from over his eyes and shifted around to look at the countess. She leaned against his rock and glared at him. "Don't look so happy to be saved, does she?"

"She's ran away," said Fin. "Not like we thought."

Jack huffed. "Were you followed?"

Fin nodded and looked west. "Don't know how many, but there's no few and they'll be here soon."

"Topper," said Jack, "get them boys ready."

A sputter of cannonfire cut through the air and they all hushed.

The Maltese fleet parted and enveloped the battered *Donnerhünd* as it approached. The Barbary swarm came on, and the Knights slowed their line and hove their ships around broadside to the onrushing horde. They formed an *L*-shaped line that extended south toward the cliffs and west, casting the entire snarl of Barbary sail under the shadow of a thousand guns. The charge of the Barbary ships slackened not at all; they drove on, direct into the crook of the knight's formation without tactic or command. Pirates lined the gunwales of their ships; they beat their scimitars against the rails and howled. Then the frigates of the Maltese line put forth the first volley of an iron deluge. The eruption began at the center of the formation's south-reaching arm and radiated outward in a wave of fire. A wall of searing metal shot toward the Barbary line so thick and coordinate that it was visible to the eye like a deathly grey membrane rushing across the sea. The barrage struck the ships at the center of the Barbary line and they faltered. Masts fell. Sails split. Screams hovered in the air. The Barbarie came on. Another volley leapt from the knight's line and the formation's western arm unleashed its enfilade of cannon. Fearless or maddened, still the Barbarie charged. The boldest drove past the Maltese frigates into the heart of the fleet where the smaller, faster corvettes and brigantines of the knights fell upon them. Ships tacked and hauled over, grappled to one another and sent boarders into melee. Cannonfire sputtered everywhere, raising dozens of clouds that puffed over the surface of the sea and swirled like infant tornados. And still the frigates loosed their hail of iron, no longer in unison but now each cannoneer picking his target and firing precise. In the tops of the Knights' ships, Fin spotted sharpshooters. They lashed themselves to the utmost masts and took aim with patience, spending each shot with bloody thrift.

Three fat-bellied transports broke from the Maltese ranks and approached the cliffs. Each transport launched a skiff, and when the men at the landing saw this they sent up a cheer.

Fin handed the countess's leash to Jack and ran back toward the quarry's rim. Topper, Tillum, Sam Catcher, and the crew left behind by the *Esprit de la Mer* lay along the edge of the cauldron and trained their muskets on the far side. The dust cloud that had followed Fin from Tripoli obscured the western sky beyond the quarry. The riders had arrived. Fin scooped up a spare musket. She laid down beside Topper and took aim.

"How many you reckon?" said Topper.

"A lot."

"Just pick 'em off when they come. Can't but a handful at a time make it down the ramp and back up on this side. We kilt them fellers so easy yesterday that I nearabout felt sorry for 'em."

"What about those?" Fin pointed toward the south end of the quarry where they'd tried to flank him.

"Whooped 'em," said Topper. He dug something out of his ear and flicked it over the rim into the quarry below. "Them boys is still down yonder to hold 'em off if this bunch tries the same thing. If the fight turns sour, fall back into the gorge and pray."

"If we back into that gorge, they'll fire down on us from the bluffs, you know?"

"I know it. That's what the prayin's for."

Fin looked back uncomfortably at the gorge running down to the water. Jack hobbled off the top of the bluff, tugging at the countess's leash, and herded her down into the gorge where the first skiff had landed and was taking on passengers.

"Here they come," said Topper.

On the far side of the quarry, the first man appeared. He was dressed in red robes and a black headdress like the others. He walked calmly to the top of the ramp and looked down at the bodies strewn below him. A musket fired. The man flopped to the ground dead and slid several feet down the ramp before coming to rest with one arm twisted under him. Somewhere to Fin's right, the musketeer who had shot him hooted in victory.

"Well, that's one," said Topper.

Then there was motion on the opposite rim. All along the western edge the line at the top of the quarry rippled as men crawled and inched their way up and jutted their musket barrels out over the cauldron. They kept low to the ground, and none presented enough of a head or shoulder to shoot at. Their musket barrels settled and reached out like the hundred legs of some terrible insect. A voice called out a command. Muskets shifted and aimed and sent fine dust drifting down from the ledge like grey snow. A strange command again and fire answered it. Fin pressed herself to the ground and put her hands over her head. Musket balls whizzed all around, and splinters of stone pelted her. When she looked across the cauldron, she saw muskets swinging and arms withdrawing their ramrods to reload. Then there was a shout, and men poured over the lip of the ramp and charged down into the quarry. The men around her fired on them. The front rank of Barbary men sagged and crashed to the ground like a breaking wave, and those behind trampled over them and came on. Fin took aim and fired, but in the chaos had no idea if her shot struck. The musketeers on the opposite rim fired again. To her left and right she heard men scream and curse, and when she looked up again, the men in the quarry had gained fifty feet and charged on.

Fin crabbed her way back from the ledge as musket balls ricocheted off the rocks and crags then crawled down into the gorge. At the water-front, men were clambering into a skiff and Jack barked and ordered them to it. There were another fifty men awaiting transport.

Fin looked out over the procession of skiffs coming ashore and returning to sea laden with men. Two Barbary ships had broken off from the main flotilla and were sailing toward the transports. To the east, the *Esprit de la Mer* looked like a child's toy among the larger frigates. Fin could see Jeannot at the helm. He pointed toward the Barbary ships intercepting the transports, and the helmsman spun the wheel. The *Esprit de la Mer* leaned away from the wind and her crew trimmed in the sails. As she came near the shore, Jeannot ordered the wind spilled. The ship hove to and turned its broadside to the pirates' approach. Cannonfire blew from her starboard guns. While the last of the slaves were ferried out, Jeannot held the *Esprit de la Mer* like a pro-tective shield. A constant barrage of fire flew from her, raking any ship that came near.

Once all the men were aboard, the last of the transports hauled up its skiff and set sail. They bore away behind the main line of the knights and north, toward Malta. As they went, Jeannot launched the skiffs of the *Esprit de la Mer* to fetch back his own crew from the shore.

"Let's get us off this rock," said Jack.

Fin could scarcely think of anything she'd rather do. She ran back up the gorge and dropped to her belly to crawl up next to Topper. The men below in the quarry had given up their advance and they huddled behind stone blocks on the cauldron floor, peeking out at intervals to spend their shots.

"It's time, Topper!"

Topper aimed his musket and fired. He looked at Fin and wiped his hand across his face. "Soon as we fall back they'll be up out of there and on us."

"Then be quick."

Topper sent a runner south to call back the men guarding the flank then put two fingers in his mouth and whistled. When the men turned to look, he waved them toward the gorge. They fired off their final shots then backed down from the ledge and ran. Topper spit in his hand, rolled over and fired his musket then retreated himself, loading a new shot as he went.

At the water's edge, there was a skiff waiting and another behind it ready to come ashore. The crewmen Jeannot had left insisted that Fin and the countess go first. Her crew piled in after: Jack, Phineas, Topper, Tillum, Thigham, Pelly, Sam, and a handful of others. As the skiff pushed away from shore, the first of the Barbary pirates appeared on the bluffs above and at the head of the gorge. Jeannot's crewmen shouldered their muskets and drove the first wave back. Fin and the men in her boat aimed and fired. One of the men atop the bluff fell forward and plunged to the water. Shots smacked against the skiff's hull and into the water all around. Fin sank into the bottom of the boat and reloaded, peeking up over the gunwale to aim and fire. The second skiff landed. It took on the last of Jeannot's crew and pushed off. Fin and her men covered their launch with musketfire. Cannonshot whizzed and howled overhead and splashed into the sea. The air itself seemed to tremble.

When the skiff was a hundred yards offshore, Fin saw a single rider walk his horse up the bluff and sit there still, silhouetted against the sky. It was the pasha himself. His men scurried on the cliff top, and he sat his horse and held calm and resigned among them, looking out over the sea, powerless. The countess saw him too, and her eyes would not turn away. She called his name but it was lost in the din of cannonfire and she wept.

When they reached the *Espirit de la Mer*, Jeannot met them, offering his hand at the rail and inspecting every man for injury as he came aboard. When Fin and the countess climbed up, Jeannot removed his hat, swept his hands out and bent low. "Mademoiselle de Graff."

The countess loosed a litany of harsh words in French and punctuated her outburst with a spitting sound.

Jeannot straightened and lifted one eyebrow at Fin. He called one of his men and ordered him to show the countess to a cabin. The girl raised her chin and looked at the man with disgust before following. Jeannot watched until they descended through the companionway then took appraisal of Fin. "You are well?"

Fin nodded, but before she could speak, a sailor called out from the transom. "Skiff secure, Captain. All hands aboard."

Jeannot touched her shoulder and tightened his lips as if to apologize for the interruption. "Your safety is a great blessing to me." Then he clasped his hands behind his back and walked across the deck with his head held high and confident. "Bear us around and beat north!" The helmsman repeated the order and spun the wheel. The yards creaked, the rigging groaned, and the ship hove into the wind. "Signal the fleet," ordered Jeannot, "Let them know we have success." A sailor at the transom ran a green flag up the mizzen.

The *Esprit de la Mer* sailed northward. All sense of the Knights' formation was broken; the two fleets ran among one another in chaos. Ships were everywhere; in every direction a new battle raged. Ship against ship, they pounded one another with iron. Boarders ran across decks, their scimitars and sabers ringing. Cannonballs and chain shot screamed through the air. Immense sounds. The *carrack, carrack, carrack* of grapeshot against gunwales. The wooden moan of masts falling like high mountain timber. The *thunk* and whine of hulls slamming and sliding against one another. A strange chorus hovered under the tympanic thunder of the battle, sounds of men in agony or bloodlust or murderous joy. Their cries underslung the seething cataract of war like a blasphemous chant of worshippers calling upon some Philistine god. To the starboard, a Barbary galleon toppled and lay on its side as men scrambled out and across its hull like ants. The water around it came alive with the frantic weltering of arms and the kicking of legs as men flailed at the sea. Ahead of the *Esprit de la Mer*, a small pirate sloop drew alongside a ship of the line with intent to send boarders, but the frigate's guns blew across its deck, pulverizing the anxious grapplers, leaving only a fine red mist that washed through the air and settled into the sea like crimson rain. Smoke. Gun smoke was everywhere. With every blast of cannon, the cloud of it thickened until it seemed the *Esprit de la Mer* had passed into a netherworld where horrors loomed. A Barbary xebec careened out of the grey smoke, engulfed in flame, a monstrous djinn sprung of some vulcanic sultanate, a fiery dromond spat from hell, her sailors burned and scampered like daemonic forms trailing black smoke and dying in a hiss of steam as they leapt into the sea. As quickly as it had appeared, the flameborne ship passed away, vanishing wholly into the swirling cloudbank.

As the *Esprit de la Mer* passed other ships of the fleet, men saw the green flag raised at her mizzen and they cheered, "Huzzah, Huzzah!" But Jeannot guided them through a cataclysmic sea. The crew knelt at the rails, horror-stricken yet bold. They trained their guns on the enemy and fired and fired and fired again. When boarders came they were met with shouts and outrage. Blades fell in gleaming arcs, whistling. The deck writhed and crawled with men embattled. They locked themselves in a terrible embrace to tear at flesh with bare hands and teeth and to stomp bone to splinters underfoot. Fin loosed Betsy's roar again and again until her ears were numb from the crackle of the gun. The world became a muffled drone of distant wailing and thunder.

In the gun-spat fog they came upon the *Donnerhünd*. Even broken and battered down as it was, Luther had positioned his ship between two behemoth frigates, and his cannons flared and spewed as he stood at the rail singing. He turned at the passing of the *Esprit de la Mer* and raised a fist in the air. He held his chin down and opened his mouth wide and bellowed out some folkloric song of storied German warfare and pounded his fist against his heart. Jeannot raised two fingers to his temple in salute and smiled. When the *Donnerhünd's* guns blew again, Luther turned back to face the enemy. He held his arms out wide in front of him as if welcoming an old friend into his embrace. The Barbary pirates came on, and Luther greeted them each with song and fire until Fin lost sight of him in the smoke. Then, as if emerging from a dream, the air cleared and the sea was empty and blue ahead. Jeannot ordered all sails set and guided them away north, leaving the battle shrinking behind and grumbling like a distant storm.

A sort of weary joy covered the faces of the crew. They slumped along the rails and curled into the nooks and corners of the ship to truly rest for the first time in days. Few spoke, and many stared southward, dazed, looking toward the muttering battle and the hellish land they'd so shortly been delivered from. Fin walked among them. She smiled at each man and touched him upon the shoulder or the face. They each turned to her as she came and muttered thanks or blessings or simple hallos. In her wake, she left eddies and swirls of whisper. She heard her name breathed out like a prayer or an invocation. She felt foolish and entirely unworthy of such awe, but she wouldn't deny it to them. *Let them tell their stories*, she thought, *they've earned them*. Even her father, lurking in the shadows of the forecastle, met her eyes. Fin dared to imagine that she saw his face lighten and warm beneath his beard. She inquired after his health, but he put his hands in his hair like a man presented with great difficulty and turned away. Fin reached out to him, but he refused to look at her again or speak.

In the hold she came upon Lucas Thigham. He was bent over a sailor, cleaning his wound with a wad of bandage. The sailor, a Frenchman, one of Jeannot's crew, held his jaw clenched and kept his head turned to the wall as the doctor worked.

"How is he?" asked Fin.

Thigham didn't look up. He pulled the wound apart with his fingers and dabbed the bandage into the split flesh. "I'm afraid he will surely . . ." Thigham blinked rapidly and then looked up at Fin. "I think that he will live." He blinked again and pushed his broken spectacle up on the bridge of his nose. "I think so, Captain."

Fin patted the leg of the young man and returned to the deck where Jeannot leaned wearily near the helm.

"Are your men well?" he said as Fin approached.

"They're tired." Fin wiped her eyes and massaged the muscles at the back of her neck with her hand. "And sick for home."

"May they rest well. We sail for Le Havre-de-Grâce. A journey of four days, perhaps five. To deliver the countess." Jeannot turned Fin's face to the side with his thumb and inspected the burn on her cheek. He traced the line of it back to her bloody ear and gently wrapped the tangle of her hair behind it. "You are hurt. You should see Pierre-Jean, and rest."

"I'm fine." Fin pulled away and tugged her hair over the wound.

Jeannot shook his head and pulled her back toward him. "You are fierce. But even winds and furies must rest."

Fin rubbed her eyes again and then stepped up to Jeannot and wrapped her arms around him. She held on and laid her head against his chest. When she felt his own arms enveloping her and the pressure of his hand on the back of her head, she let out a long, deep sigh: a sound of relief, of long-awaited ease.

"Thank you, Jeannot."

Jeannot's chest swelled under her cheek and he spoke softly.

"*Sois en paix, et repose-toi.*"

They stood at the helm, weary and embraced, and no sailor or man on deck took undue notice—none pointed, nor laughed, nor even whispered. Fin and Jeannot held to one another as surely as a sail lashed to its yard and mast; they were as unseen and as wholly alone as ever two were upon a ship in that age. At length, Jeannot heard the deepening of Fin's breath and he pressed his lips into her tangled hair. She was fast asleep.

PART III

THOSE WHO SEE IT HOME

Chapter Thirty-eight

J EANNOT SET A TABLE in the center of his cabin and drew chairs around it to accommodate those summoned to meet. Fine moldings trimmed the white walls, and rosettes overlooked the room like tiny, ornamented suns. Crisp morning light streamed through three great windows in the aft bulkhead.

Fin and Jack dropped into their chairs, and Jeannot remained standing, waiting on the countess also to take her seat. The girl had cleaned herself and tied her hair back, but her face was immobile, a dead and emotionless thing. She lowered herself into her seat with a kind of determined dignity that had the effect of an insult. When she had arranged herself and the filthy remains of her skirt over her legs, she folded her hands in her lap. Jeannot sat.

The countess gazed blankly at the table before her while the others shifted in their seats and considered one another in uneasy silence.

"I think it best that we discuss the situation before we reach Le Havre." As Jeannot spoke, he angled his eyes toward the countess. "Mademoiselle de Graffe?"

The girl blinked and shifted her eyes from side to side but didn't look up.

"Mademoiselle, I hope that by talking together we may become civil."

The countess drew in a sharp breath and spat it out. "Civil? You are barbarians." She sneered at Fin.

Jeannot sighed and slid his hands across the table before him as if smoothing down a wrinkle. "While I have had a full account of your travel from Tripoli and understand your distaste, I assure you that we are, none of us, barbarians. My name is Jeannot Botolph, of the Knights of Malta." Jeannot smiled weakly and motioned to Jack. "This is Jack Wagon, formerly First Mate of the American ship, *Fiddler's Green*." Jack made a guttural noise and narrowed one eye, and Jeannot turned toward Fin. "You know Fin Button, of course, formerly captain of the *Fiddler's Green*."

The countess kept her head down but scowled at each of them from beneath her wrinkled brow.

Fin leaned forward and cleared her throat. "I was told pirates kidnapped you. The American Congress hired us to fetch you back. We never had any intent to take you where you didn't want to go. We only thought you wanted to go home to France all along." The countess made an unladylike snorting sound in her nose. "Problem is, whether you want to go or not, we got to take you because if we get you back then maybe the French navy will help with the Revolution. That's why I took you. I'm near as unhappy about it as you are."

They all sat in silence looking at the countess, and the countess only looked into her own lap. When it became obvious that the girl didn't intend to speak, Fin stood up and dragged her chair across the floor. She set it next to the countess and sat down beside her.

"I don't know how things are in France, and I don't know anything about kings and their counts and countesses, but I do know something about running away. I was nineteen. I didn't like rules. Didn't care to do like someone else told me. Didn't like much of anything except a boy named Peter LaMee." Fin's voice caught in her throat and she paused to gather herself before continuing. "We might be different in as many ways as you can count, but I reckon we might be somewhat the same too."

The countess shifted uncomfortably then straightened in her chair and looked at Jeannot.

"Please ask this . . . *person*"—she said the word with contempt—"to move away from me."

Fin and Jeannot exchanged a quick glance, and Fin dragged her chair back around the table. When she had reseated herself next to Jack, the countess shifted her chair in Jeannot's direction and spoke.

"My marriage to the count, Martin de Graff, was arranged when I was fourteen years old. I did not love him then, nor do I now. He is a tiresome man. Boorish and simple. And older than me by ten years. A year ago he permitted me to embark with my mother on a pilgrimage to Jerusalem, and there I met Yusuf, the Tripolitan Pasha, a beautiful man, and kind to me. When we left Jerusalem, I told Yusuf the name of our ship and the route of our return. He said he would come for me. I spent every moment of the voyage waiting for him. In the night of the fifth day his men found us. They harmed neither the ship nor anyone aboard and they took me to Tripoli. Yusuf received me like a queen and I have been there ever since. I love him. And he loves me."

As the countess spoke, Fin's face turned cold and her chest tightened as if beneath an ever-increasing weight. The thought of what she'd done to the countess horrified her.

Jack tapped his fingers on the table and looked at Fin. "Then there never was no ransom at all."

The countess blushed and cut her eyes at Jack. "The ransom was my idea. Yusuf was against it, but I convinced him that my husband would pay any price for my return. We did not think he would involve King Louis. We only intended to take my husband's money."

"So they didn't lie to us," said Fin.

Jeannot scratched his beard. He leaned back and crossed his arms. "It seems you've put us in a very bad spot, Mademoiselle. Yourself, not the least. What would you have us do now?"

The countess blushed again and lowered her eyes to her lap sheepishly. "I would return to Tripoli."

Jeannot sat forward and glowered at her. "Men have died. You think you can return to your lover as if it were all no more than inconvenience? I think you are a fool. The pasha is a tyrant, a man of deception, vice, and violence. Are you so certain the ransom was not his ruse? You have been no more than his puppet. How long before he tires of you and finds another plaything?"

The countess clenched her jaw and remained silent. Jeannot sat back again and looked at Fin.

"She is your charge. Her fate is in your hands. We will be in Le Havre in three days. Do with the girl as you will."

THE *ESPRIT DE LA MER* sailed unhindered through the Strait of Gibraltar and followed the coast northeast toward Le Havre. The weather was light and calm, and what was left of Fin's crew spent the days in lazy relaxation. With each hour of sleep they became more vital, and with each meal, grew thicker, stronger, as if they sailed back through time and their bodies reconstituted into forms forgotten in the abuse of slavery.

Phineas Button once more became Fin's shadow. He lurked wherever she went. At meals, he sat nearby; at work, he hovered just out of reach; at night, he slunk in shadows and settled and watched over her sleep. He looked at her when he thought she didn't see, but whenever Fin turned her head to meet his stare he looked away. He often muttered to himself, and Fin awoke once in the night to find him writhing near her hammock. He was caught in a nightmare, and he pulled his hair and clawed his flesh and cried. Fin went to him and woke him. He leapt and sat upright in the darkness, shivering. His eyes focused on Fin before him, and he took her face in his hands, touching her slightly with only the tips of his fingers and the balls of his thumbs. They sat in the dark, each looking at the other as if into some twisted mirror. Fin reached out to touch him. She stretched her hands toward him slowly, as if daring to touch something feral and untamed. In all the time it took her to reach him, he sat motionless with his hands cupped at her face. His eyes were pulled wide in the dark and his mouth hung open. But when Fin's fingertips touched the naked flesh of his chest, he recoiled. He put his hands in his hair and pulled at it. He slammed his eyes shut and rolled to the wall and coughed and sobbed and yanked at his hair, and nothing Fin could say or do would console him. When at last he spent himself and softened back into sleep, Fin crawled into her hammock and lay awake in worry.

The next day he didn't shadow her. She went looking and found him in the hold clutched to an empty rum bottle. He was sauced in drink. His head rolled from side to side, and he had on him a stupid, toothless smile that looked to Fin sadder than all the frowning she'd ever seen. He'd urinated on himself and sat in it. Fin tried to help him up, but he slumped over and pushed her away.

The night before their arrival in Le Havre-de-Grâce, Fin awakened as someone shook her gently. Her father was sprawled drunken and unconscious on the deck beside her, and the countess knelt in the darkness at her elbow. The girl wrapped her tiny, white hands around Fin's forearm and squeezed gently.

"What will you do?" she asked.

The question confused Fin. She squinted her eyes and pulled her arm free. "What are you talking about?"

"I am prepared to beg," said the countess. She bent her head down and lowered herself completely onto her knees. "Let me go free." She looked up, and in the darkness Fin could see the glimmer of tears in her eyes. "I beg you. Do not deliver me to my husband. Set me free. Tell me what you desire. Yusuf will give it. I beg you." The girl took hold of Fin's arm again and kneaded it in her grip; each time she squeezed she sobbed, "I beg you."

Fin was overcome with a mix of empathy and disgust. She rolled out of her hammock and pulled the girl to her feet. The countess wrapped her arms around Fin's waist and sobbed into her neck, repeating her beggary. Fin led her back to her cabin and laid her in the bed where the girl tried to stifle her sobs and reclaim her dignity. As Fin left the room, the countess whispered, "What will become of me?"

Fin whispered back, "I don't know."

LE HAVRE-DE-GRÂCE LAY CORNERED by the Atlantic and the river Seine. A humble city, low and flat, and unremarkable save for its cathedral; its minaret overlooked the port like an artificial moon scaffolded into the sky.

The *Esprit de la Mer* slipped toward the wharf in the late morning, and by noon was tied and secure. Jeannot gave leave for his crew to go ashore, and Fin did the same for her own crew at Jack's suggestion. Of late, it had been a relief to her to be rid of the farce of captaincy, but Jack insisted that she maintain the position and appearance, at least until they were home. Fin sighed and complained, but she accepted his guidance.

As the crews went ashore, Fin stood at the plank and watched them go. Topper could hardly contain his excitement as he approached her. "I hear French pastries calling me name, Fin. Oh, I hear 'em singing and humming and anxious to be ate." He rubbed his hands together and smacked his lips.

"Bring me back a strudel if you find one," Fin told him.

He tapped his temple with one finger and smiled. "Aye-aye, Captain." He bounced across the plank and strutted down the pier with his nose high in the air as if he'd find the nearest bakery by scent alone.

Jack dragged a chair from below and set himself up on deck to be measured by Tillum for the fitting of a proper new leg. Tillum squatted next to him and wrapped a length of rope around Jack's stump at various points. He'd mark the string and then hold it up to his measuring stick and scrawl down his findings on a plank of wood that apparently served as his journal of design.

The countess emerged from her cabin with a bearing of imposed dignity that quite exceeded her clothing. She'd refused all offers of men's clothing and as such had nothing at all to wear save the torn and filthy gown she'd worn when Fin abducted her. She looked like a street urchin in possession of a misplaced air of nobility. When she approached the plank, Fin stepped in front of her and shook her head. The girl opened her mouth to protest and Jeannot intervened.

"Mademoiselle, I fear we must ask you to remain aboard for the time being. I'm sure you understand." Jeannot's tone was conciliatory and far gentler than Fin could have managed. Despite his manners, though, the countess took it badly.

"You cannot keep me here," she said through clenched teeth. "I will not be a prisoner in my own country."

"Mademoiselle. Please. You must understand." Jeannot extended his hand to indicate the direction back to her cabin then called two crewmen to him. "Would you escort Mademoiselle de Graff back to her quarters, gentlemen?"

The countess huffed and spun and stomped back to her cabin without waiting for her escorts.

Jeannot frowned and then spoke to Fin. "She is a child in chase of womanhood and thinks her pasha can give it to her. I think I shall purchase her some proper clothing. She may be petulant and foolish, but she is a lady. She deserves her dignity." Fin rolled her eyes but admitted that he was right. "If you require assistance, call upon Remy or Pierre-Jean."

When the *Fiddler's Green* sank, so had the instructions for delivering the countess. Fin remembered only that she was to contact Monsieur Terrasson at Le Bureau du Maire. She'd need a translator.

Fin found Pierre-Jean in the surgery debating medicine with Lucas Thigham. They had books spread before them on the table and were in a fury of pointing and flipping pages and conferring upon similarities and contradictions. Pierre-Jean graciously agreed to accompany Fin ashore to translate and assured Lucas that their discussion would resume at the earliest opportunity. Lucas nodded happily and squared his single spectacle over his right eye.

Once ashore, Pierre-Jean quickly learned the location of Le Bureau du Maire from a boy hawking newspapers. The office was a half-mile from the waterfront situated at the town centre along an avenue of meagerly ornamented stone buildings that rose four stories over the street. The inside of the office was hot and stuffy, and a sweaty porter stood at the door sweeping air through the room with a fan made of bird feathers. The rest of the room was empty save a desk set in the center and a row of chairs lining the back wall. Pierre-Jean spoke to the porter, and the porter pulled a tasseled bell from his coat and rang it. A moment later, a fat man wearing an ill-fitting wig wobbled into the room. His face was powdered white and his cheeks were rouged like a porcelain doll. He stuffed one hand into his coat pocket and greeted Pierre-Jean formally. They exchanged pleasantries, and then Pierre-Jean bent to Fin's ear and translated.

"This is monsieur Etienne Terrasson, aide to the mayor. What would you have me say?"

Fin looked at the powdered fat man as he bent toward her in anticipation. "Tell him that the Americans have a delivery for Mr. Franklin."

Pierre-Jean straightened and relayed the message. Monsieur Terrasson's smile faded from his face and he looked at Fin very seriously. "*La comtesse?*"

"*Oui, monsieur,*" said Pierre-Jean.

Monsieur Terrasson hurried around the desk and arranged himself in the chair behind it. He snatched a quill and inkwell from the drawer and slapped a paper on the desktop and began to write. As he wrote, he looked up at intervals and spoke to Pierre-Jean. Then he signed the paper and folded it. He retrieved a stick of wax from his drawer and, tilting a candle over the letter, melted the wax until a red puddle the size of a coin had collected. He pressed his ring into the wax and spoke again to Pierre-Jean. Then he stood and looked at Fin once more and bowed.

"What did he say?"

"He sends word to Paris. He says to expect reply within the week."

"Is that it?" said Fin.

Monsieur Terrasson flapped the letter in the air and shouted at the porter. The boy took the letter and ran out of the room.

"It seems so," said Pierre-Jean. "*Merci*."

The fat man bowed lowly and left the room shouting after the porter.

BACK ON THE SHIP, Pierre-Jean begged his leave and returned to his discussions with Lucas. Fin kicked her heels around the deck fighting off memories of days past when the leisure of port had been a happy thing. Without the company of Knut or Tan, she scarcely cared to go ashore at all and dreaded the thought of a full week awaiting news of what to do with the countess. She hadn't written Peter in ages, not knowing what to say, but now she felt she could put it off no longer. She pulled an empty crate out of the hold to use as a desk and sat on the quarterdeck to write. She tried to put into words all that had happened but found the task too momentous to boil down to a simple letter, so she merely rambled, often scratching words out or scrapping the letter entirely to begin anew. Hours later, when Jeannot returned with two wrapped packets under his arm, she'd written little of any coherence. Jeannot greeted her and went directly below to deliver the new clothing he'd bought for the countess.

When he returned, he still had one packet under his arm. He approached Fin and stood behind her, looking down at her shoddy penwork.

"Any news? What will become of her?"

"They sent word to Paris. Said it will be a week."

"She will at least be decently clothed as she waits. Tomorrow I shall find her a brush and powder and whatever else a woman of her dignity requires."

Fin rolled her eyes. "Is 'dignity' what you call it?"

Jeannot offered her his hand. Fin took it and pulled herself up from the deck. She was barefoot and her pants and shirt were stained with everything from blood to oakum to lampblack. She stretched her shirt out between her hands and considered its mottle of stains. "I'm not dignified?" she asked.

When Fin looked up, Jeannot had an eyebrow cocked high and one side of his mouth was curled in amusement. "Where you are concerned, much requires redefinition." He pulled the wrapped package from under his arm and laid it in Fin's hands. "Something for you, if your dignity will suffer it."

Fin tore open the package and pulled out a silky green dress. Its sleeves and neck were festooned with lace, and the bodice and skirts were stitched with a swirling motif of leaves. Below the neckline an embroidered white swan spread its wings across the chest. It was the finest garment Fin had ever touched, and she held it by her fingertips and away from herself so that she wouldn't soil it.

"Would you delight me with your company tonight?" asked Jeannot. "Though Le Havre-de-Grâce is no Paris, there is much to see. Musicians, jugglers, the city lights reflected in the river. I am told there may even be a dance."

Fin squinted at the dress and then up at Jeannot as he stood expectant, leaning slightly forward with his hands held behind his back. His eyes traced the lines of her face until she blushed and looked down. She held the dress out and shook her head.

"Thank you, Jeannot, but I can't."

Hesitantly, he put out his hands and took the dress. "I ask only to walk with you, Fin. Nothing more."

Fin looked away and walked across the deck to sit on the rail. "I'm going home, Jeannot. As soon as this business with the countess is done, I'm going. I thought I wanted all this. I always did. Maybe sometimes I still do. But there's someone waiting on me, and what I want more than anything is to go back to him. We've got a house outside of Savannah. It's small and it's meager but it's ours and I've never slept a night in it. I want to go back. I want it so bad that I see it when I close my eyes. I see the house, I see the field, green and flowered, I see the mossy oaks and the skinny pines and the pecans and the palmetto fans and the carpet of needles and leaves between them all, but I can't see Peter anymore. I can't see *him*. No matter how hard I try, his face won't come to me. How could I have forgotten him, Jeannot? How could that happen?" Fin clutched the rail with her hands and held herself steady and tight. Her eyes burned and blurred and she squeezed them shut. "Why can't I see him? He told me he'd wait. He told me so many times, so many times and I never listened. I just couldn't be—*still*. And now I've left him back there and can't even remember. He's the only person that I— the only person that ever—what kind of person am I, Jeannot? What will he say when he knows all the terrible things I've done? How can I ever hide it from him? I've killed people, and I've hated people, and I've liked it! And I whipped my own *father*! And I kidnapped that poor girl and all she wanted was to—how can he ever forgive me, Jeannot? Why would he ever want to?" Fin put her face in her hands and tears wracked her. "Why can't I see him? Why can't I see his face?"

Jeannot dropped the dress and knelt. He pulled her hands from her face and held them firmly until she looked at him.

"I do not know this boy, Fin. Perhaps I don't even know you. But I tell you truly that you are blessed." Fin twisted her wrists in Jeannot's grip and shook her head, but he held her. "Hear me. I know you are blessed because your men whisper your name and hide it in their hearts. You are blessed because the passion within you compels others to action. You are blessed because you choose to speak and to act when others hide themselves in silence. You are blessed because men once were chained and now walk free. I know your blessing because you have made of me more than ever I was before." Fin shuddered and sobbed and tried again to wrench her arms away but Jeannot kept her and his voice was steady. "And you will return to this boy, to Peter, and he will smile at your coming and your days together will be filled with joy and with peace. These times of war and ruin will pass, and by love, you will be renewed and all terrible things shall be undone. Do you hear me, Fin Button?" Jeannot pushed the hair from her face and though shaking yet, Fin nodded. "In the name of God I drew you from the water, and in his name shall you be delivered home."

Jeannot took her face in his hands and thumbed away her tears. From out of the shadows of his deep brow he beheld her and smiled.

Fin didn't try to speak. She let Jeannot gather her up. She twisted her hands into his coat, and she pulled herself close to him as he carried her to her cabin. Fin watched his face, watched the stiff cords of his neck, saw the ripple of his jaw as he turned and ducked and carried her effortlessly down the companionway, and when the time came she found she didn't want to be lowered or let go or left alone. But Jeannot set her upon her feet and she kept these things to herself.

"I'm all right," Fin assured him. She sniffed and smiled at Jeannot pitifully. "Thank you for the dress. I'm sorry if I was rude."

Jeannot smiled. "We will walk together some other day."

Fin agreed, delivering a series of anxious nods. She wiped her eyes and laughed to disguise her embarrassment. Jeannot bowed and touched a knuckle to Fin's face then withdrew. When Fin awoke in the morning, a small package had been placed atop her fiddle case. It was the dress, folded neatly and bound into a bundle with a cord of hemp.

Chapter Thirty-nine

F IVE DAYS LATER A carriage clattered down the pier. Its driver hauled it to a stop at the *Esprit de la Mer*'s plank. He slouched, dropped the reins, and beat his fist on the carriage rooftop. A young boy dressed like a miniature gentleman climbed out and looked around. He wore a yellow coat complete with epaulets, a powdered wig that fit too loosely, and shoes with enormous brass buckles. The boy opened his mouth and gaped at the ship in front of him and then tilted his head back to trace the line of the mast into the sky. When his neck reached the limit of its motion, the wig fell off and dropped to the ground in a puff of powder. The driver beat his crop on the seat and shouted at the boy.

"Enjolras! *Vite vite! Dépêche-toi!*"

The tiny gentleman, surely no more than ten years old, stuffed his wig back onto his head, ran up the plank, and jumped onto the deck of the *Esprit de la Mer*. Remy stood in front of the boy, barring any further advance, and crossed his arms.

The boy looked around nervously and said, "*Il y a un invité qui souhaite s'entretenir avec le capitaine.*"

"The captain, eh?" Remy turned his head and ordered a crewman to notify Jeannot, then he growled at the boy and stomped as if scaring off a stray dog. The boy yelped and ran back to the carriage. Remy chuckled in satisfaction.

Jeannot emerged from his cabin, and when he saw the carriage, he sent for Fin. They walked down to the pier together, and as they approached the carriage the boy gentleman beat his tiny fist on the door. An elderly man clambered out, dropping a selection of mumblings about joints and age in the process. He was dressed in a dark grey frock that he appeared to have worn since he was a thinner man, and as he turned to greet Jeannot the tiny boy-gentleman scrambled into the carriage and out of sight. The old man dragged off his tricorne hat, revealing a great dome of a head, wholly bald on top but wreathed above the ears with long grey hair that hung around his shoulders. He was unbearded, and a pair of spectacles perched on the tip of his nose.

"Captain?" he said, extending his hand.

Jeannot shook the man's hand and bowed. "Captain Jeannot Botolph, of the Knights of Malta."

The old man's eyebrows arched up and he studied Jeannot with curiosity. "The Knights. Of course! One hears the strangest news of them these days." He looked from Fin to Jeannot and back again. "Business of yours, no doubt." The man considered them each with some seriousness and then waved his hand in the air. "It is no matter. In all likelihood, it's better that I don't know the details. How rude I am, talking on and on without even the courtesy of introduction. It's the age, I tell you. I often fear I've forgotten more than I ever knew in the first place. What does that leave me with, eh? Little enough, you can be sure. Benjamin Franklin is my name, and you must be the fabled Captain Button." He smiled at Fin and studied her with enormous curiosity. "I declare there is no shortage of strangeness in the world these days. I've printed you in my gazette, did you know?"

"Read it myself, yes sir."

He fanned his hands out in front of him like a magician announcing a trick. "War Woman!" he said and winked. "Came up with that one myself. What did you think? No offense meant, you understand."

Fin smirked and glanced at Jeannot, who had taken a step back to watch the two of them. "It's better than what the Tories called me," she said.

Mr. Franklin stiffened and blew out his breath. "And no worse than what they call me either, let me tell you. But we'll lick them, Captain

Button. Never you fear. The French are on the verge of committing their navy to the war. Very soon. Very soon now. I understand you have a certain Countess de Graff in your company?"

"We've got her, but she's not so happy about it."

"Not happy about it? Does she prefer the company of pirates?"

"You might put it like that," Fin said. "She wasn't as kidnapped as everyone thought. Says she's in love with the pasha. Met him in Jerusalem and arranged to run off with him."

Mr. Franklin frowned and looked at Jeannot, who nodded to confirm Fin's story.

"I had to tie her and drag her away screaming. Like I said, she's not so happy to be back in France."

"I see, I see," Mr. Franklin said. He frowned and arranged his spectacles and looked over her shoulder at the ship behind.

Fin stepped forward and touched him on the arm so that he'd look at her again. "Bringing her here had best do some good, sir. I don't think I can live with what we done to her otherwise."

Mr. Franklin nodded his head solemnly. "The countess has a reputation for—unpredictability. She was wedded to the count for political gain and has never been agreeable to it. But these things are delicate matters. The way of the world, I'm afraid. Begging your pardon, Captain Botolph, but the French court can be rather ruthless in its politics. And no matter what girlish fantasy the young countess has of the pasha, her husband, even if only in name, cannot be thought to have abandoned her to pirates. The girl's family has clamored for King Louis to take action on her behalf nearly every day since her disappearance, and I fear it's begun to be a source of some embarrassment. Her return will be very well looked upon. May I see the girl?"

"Of course," said Jeannot. He shouted an order to Remy, and moments later Remy led the countess onto the deck and guided her down the plank. She wore the dress Jeannot bought for her. It was white and elegant and she held herself like a lady, seeming to glide toward them, and though she was the least in stature, she carried herself as if she looked down upon them all.

Mr. Franklin swiped one hand out to his side and bowed at her approach. "Countess," he said. "You look lovely, as ever."

The countess curled her lip into a sneer and looked over his shoulder as if he were beneath her notice.

"Your family anxiously awaits news of your return."

Again, the countess ignored him. With a haughty sniff, she stepped past them and climbed into the carriage without speaking.

Mr. Franklin frowned and wiped his forehead with his handkerchief. "She seems well cared for. I thank you both. And you, Captain Button, your help in the matter shall be held in the deepest appreciation. When I told the Congress that I knew of the person for the job, I was not mistaken." His eye twinkled and he grinned at Fin. "And I shall be overjoyed to point that out to Mr. Paine when next we speak. He holds me in continual contempt if you can believe it." Mr. Franklin looked at the carriage behind him and saw the countess sitting at the window with her face drawn into a smoldering scowl. He cupped one hand at his mouth and leaned toward Fin. "I fear it will be an awkward and unpleasant ride back to Paris." Then he jerked up straight as if he had just remembered something important and walked to the front of the carriage. "What do you make it to be, Claude?"

The driver shrugged and said, *"Deux cent cinquante?"*

Mr. Franklin bent over and stared at a metallic device fixed to the front axle of the carriage. It was a slender black box with three white dials on it. Franklin moved his finger from one dial to the next, inspecting each and mumbling to himself. When he completed his investigation of the box, he stood up and proclaimed, "It is two-hundred and twenty-seven. Didn't I tell you, Claude? Had we taken the southern road at Louviers, I'm certain we'd have cut thirty kilometres. We'll test it on the return." He bent over and turned the dials on the device until he was satisfied then returned to Fin, smiling with delight.

"It's an odometer, you see? It measures each turn of the wheel so that once you've arrived at your destination you can determine exactly the distance traveled. Very useful. Made it myself, did you know?"

"What's a kilometre?" asked Fin.

"Ah, a wonderful system of measurement. Much more orderly and logical than speaking in miles and gallons and pounds. All that will be gone in a year's time. It's the metric system for the Americans. I'm convinced of it. Kilometres for miles, hectares for acres—you'll see. In a hundred years no one will ever recall what a 'mile' was nor why we ever used such a confounding and ridiculous system." Franklin sighed and patted his belly and nodded to himself as if he were settling grave matters in his mind. After a moment he blinked and remembered the business at hand. "Very well. Very well, indeed. If there's nothing else to discuss—"

"There were to be pardons for my crew."

"Ah!" Franklin struck one finger into the air and tapped his cheek then pulled a battered leather wallet of documents from his coat and flipped it open. He pushed his spectacles up the bridge of his nose and inspected the papers, thumbing through each one and wetting his finger on his tongue at intervals, nodding and humming to himself as he flipped down each corner. "Yes. Yes. Yes. Everything is in order. A letter of congressional pardon for each man of your crew—and for one extraordinary woman." He flicked his eyes up and looked at her over his lenses, smiling. "And I shall send word of your success through my own personal courier. The Congress will be most pleased, I'm sure. I hope you will continue your harassment of our British friends, but may I suggest an end to your days of mutiny?" He slapped the wallet closed and offered it to Fin.

"Thank you, sir."

Mr. Franklin picked his spectacles off and extended his hand to Fin. She shook it, and then he bent at the waist and lifted her fingers to his lips and kissed her lightly upon the knuckles.

"You have my most humble thanks, Captain Button. It has been a pleasure. Godspeed. And *vive le Révolution*." He winked again and bowed to Jeannot then clambered into the carriage and knocked upon the wall to signal the driver.

Before the carriage lurched away, Fin ran to the window. The countess sat inside, opposite Franklin, with her hands folded and her lips pursed tightly. She glared at Fin when her face appeared, and they stared at one another as if exchanging some silent dialogue that neither was willing to speak aloud. Mr. Franklin leaned forward and lowered his spectacles. "Is everything all right, Captain Button?"

Fin looked on the countess with pity. "I'm sorry," she said.

The countess's stare hardened. She bristled. Her breath deepened and her lips trembled with anger. Fin felt the heat of the countess's hatred. She wished she could reach into the girl and salve it, but she couldn't. Fin had kindled it herself, and now it burned beyond her control. Mr. Franklin beat on the carriage wall and the driver snapped the reins. Fin stepped away. The carriage clattered down the pier and off into the city, toward Paris.

As Fin watched the carriage go, she held the wallet of precious documents to her chest and then lifted it to her nose. The leather was soft and floppy with age, scored with creases and nicks and stained dark by the frequent rub of fingertips. It had a musty scent that mingled with the lingering fragrance of oils used in its original tanning. It smelled like a thing embalmed, a rag of skin by secret craft made immune to the withery of decay, flesh itself repurposed.

Fin walked back to Jeannot.

"Would you ask Remy to gather my crew?" she said. "I'd like to talk to them."

CHAPTER FORTY

OF THE EIGHTY MEN that departed Charleston aboard the *Rattlesnake*, less than twenty remained. They gathered on the main deck of the *Esprit de la Mer*, and Fin stood at the helm and looked over them. At first glance, they were a sight to pity. No face was without a scar or a peeling scab, not even Fin's. Their cheeks were hollow, their beards thin. They were bent with infirmities, twisted by abuse, purpled with bruise, and winnowed down to clattering bones. But their eyes, their eyes were fierce. Their pupils radiated color, and they held their heads high and unbowed. They'd among them seen wonders and horrors both, and they breathed yet to think on them and carry forth their hard-bought memories like badges to confound lesser men. They collected around them a silence that no man deigned to sully, and they stood in their rags, resplendent.

Jack leaned his bulk against the mainmast and towered over the rest. Tillum had completed his new mechanical leg and had improved greatly upon the design of the first. It was of a subtler devising, and Jack was no longer heralded by the creak of its hinge nor bound to quiet it with oil. The new leg fit naturally into his trousers, and to see him now, leaned-to and scowling, none would suspect at all that his great corpus was lessened by a limb. Jack's eyes skipped across the heads of the crew, anxious to spot any hint of an unruly act, but they found none and his scowl deepened as though he mistrusted the information his own sight relayed him.

Fin pulled the leather wallet from beneath her arm and flipped it open. She read the name written on the first letter of pardon and mouthed it quietly to herself, then spoke. "Flanders Topper, come on up."

Topper stuffed the pastry he'd been nibbling at into his pocket then licked his fingers, wiped them on his shirt, and climbed up the ladder to stand next to Fin.

Fin began to read. "Now therefore, I, John Hancock, President of the Congress, by the power confessed upon me by delegates of the American states assembled, have granted, and by these presents do grant, a full, free, and absolute pardon unto Flanders Topper for all offenses against the United States of America which he, Flanders Topper, has committed or may have committed or taken part in.

"In witness whereof, I have hereto set my hand this twelfth day of May in the year of our Lord seventeen and seventy-seven."

Fin pulled the document from the stack and held it out for Topper to see. He stared at it dumbfounded and then licked each of his fingers thoroughly once more and scrubbed them on his shirt. He reached out and took the pardon by the edges and held it delicately so as not to soil it by any errant drop of honey. A fat grin spread across his face. "I'll be damned," he whispered.

Fin read each name, and each came forward. Those they'd taken aboard in Charleston didn't bear the guilt of mutiny against Creache, but Fin noted in the manner of their reactions that even those innocent of that crime held other untold offenses in their hearts. The sea has ever been the refuge of outcast men, and seeing them each approach, each heavy in debts both civil and moral, Fin felt she took part in some sacred and holy rite. Breathlessly, they took their pardons from her hands, and like men shed of chains, they went away buoyant.

Name after name she called them out, and a man at a time, they came. And if none answered her call, they bowed their heads and nodded and murmured prayers for the lost of their company who would not return.

John Cornelius Tillum. Tillum had himself been a prisoner of the *HMS Justice* before escaping with Fin and her crew, and when she began to read his pardon, he crumpled to his knees and pressed his forehead to the deck and wept. When she offered him the document, he stood up and kissed it dearly.

Samuel Freeman Catcher. Sam had been with her since the beginning, since Creache. He stood before her and erected himself taller with each word she read until it seemed to Fin that he'd keep on growing and crack free of himself, sloughing off the old for something new and unseen in the world. He took his pardon and folded it and slipped it into his coat over his heart. "Hell of a thing, Captain Button," he said, then he smiled and shook Fin's hand vigorously and ran back to the crew hooting in celebration.

The last she called was the greatest of them. He'd watered the seed of mutiny against Creache and plucked it once the fruit was heavy, and though he was the best of them and in all likelihood the most honest, his flesh told a ragged story. John Amos Wagon. Bereft of a leg, and his arms now a waxy gnarl of scar left by the teeth of dogs set against him, he came forward. The crew parted, sliding to the right and to the left, affording him an aisle between them. He'd not mastered the new leg yet but each step seemed more certain than the last. He climbed up the ladder and took his place before Fin with a grunt. As she read his pardon, he tapped his foot impatiently and glared at the crew. He muttered and groaned while she read as if disagreeing with points of phrase, and when she was finished, he said, "You done yet?" He swiped the paper from Fin's hands and stuffed it in his shirt pocket. He picked out a crewman whom he judged to be looking at him too closely, and he shouted, "Quit off your gawking!" Then he clambered down and resumed his place at the mast.

Fin folded the wallet and tucked it under her arm, then shrugged at the crew. "I don't know about the rest of you, but I'm ready to go home."

The congregation began to whistle and shout, and singing followed. Fin sent for meat and wine. She went to her quarters and returned with her fiddle and bow and played for the crew, and they danced and cheered and held her aloft on their shoulders. Topper went among the Frenchmen of the *Esprit de la Mer* winding yarns of the great and terrible deeds of Captain Button and her ragamuffin crew.

They celebrated until the sun slipped away, and darkness drew many of the men to the city to further their carousing. Fin, Jack, and Topper dragged chairs up from the quarters below, and they sat in a row at the starboard rail with their feet up, wine flagons close at hand, a lantern set at their feet, and starlight on their faces. Phineas Button sprawled drunken nearby, not in celebration, but at the urging of whatever demons hounded him. Stowed away as he was and no known member of the crew at their departure, no pardon with his name had been delivered.

Fin flipped through the remaining papers. There were more than fifty of them. More than fifty lost. More than fifty never to return.

"When we're back, we ought to send the pardons to their families," said Topper. Jack agreed with a grunt.

"If we can find them," said Fin. She pulled one document from the stack and held it apart. "Thomas Knuttle."

They sat quietly in the wake of Knut's name, each with a mournful face.

"Don't seem right, do it?" said Topper.

"It ain't right," replied Fin. "Not at all."

Jack guzzled his wine and wiped at his beard. "Mayhap it's right and we can't see it. He wouldn't have lasted a day of the slave pit. They'd have made sport of him and laughed and sent him out of this world in ways best not to think on. Maybe sometime mercy's not a pardon. Maybe sometime it's the short straw and the quick exit."

Topper scratched his bald head and hummed in thought. "Still don't seem right," he proclaimed when he'd hummed enough.

Jack dropped his flagon to the deck and it rolled away clattering. "Yeah, well, what seems ain't always what is."

Fin kept her silence. She folded Knut's pardon neatly and slipped it away into her shirt. She pulled another sheet of paper from the wallet and read the name upon it.

"Armand Defain."

None spoke. Fin plucked the lantern from the deck and raised the glass. She dipped Armand's pardon into the flame, then set the lantern down and held the paper aloft. The fire sawed and swelled across the document, pushing before it a black line of char followed by a smoldering rim of ember that fluttered into the wind and away. The three of them watched it reduced by the flame until only a corner remained, and Fin flung this to the sea.

"I saw him in Tripoli," she said. "He was chained to a dungeon wall, and they'd cut on him. Worse, even, than he was before."

Topper and Jack both turned their heads to look at her, and Topper said, "Didn't leave him there did you?"

Fin took a long draw off her cup of wine and wiped the back of her hand across her mouth. "He didn't want to leave. He'd gone lunatic. He wanted to die."

"Well, what happened?" asked Topper.

Fin set her cup on the deck and stared over the rail at the last ember of Armand's pardon sailing away. "I gave him what he wanted."

Topper sat back and hummed to himself again then said, "Huh. That don't seem right."

Jack took a deep breath and grumbled.

Fin retired to her quarters and pulled her own pardon from the stack. She opened the fiddle case and slipped the document into the lining where Bartimaeus had hidden his map. The wine had lightened her head, and when she crawled into her hammock the cabin around her seemed to move as if the ship were far out at sea. She closed her eyes and thought of going home. If the French joined the war as Mr. Franklin said they would, the British would be chased out in a matter of weeks. That would be the real pardon, and until then there could be no real homecoming. But she was anxious for it. Anxious for the sandy banks of the Carolinas, the long Floridian beaches, the waters of the Chesapeake thick with fishermen, and the hundred inlets and estuaries of the whole American coast where the winds, currents, language, and faces all reflected back at her a long-missed familiarity. Her mind circled Georgia, circled Ebenezer. It called up images and memories and things nearly home but never that final destination itself, as if it existed at the center of her mind, shining like a sun too radiant. She knew there was a face at the center of that radiance. A face too bright. A face she sought and longed for but could no longer bear the light of. She drifted into sleep, circling, circling, circling.

THE NEXT DAY, FIN set her mind about the business of passage to America. She and the crew had between them almost no money, only what they'd scavenged from the dead at the quarry, and it seemed to Fin that the best course was to secure each of her men work aboard ships bound westward. She confronted Jeannot with this plan of action, intent on gaining his aid, and he listened patiently and nodded and agreed, but Fin sensed in his manner some hesitation.

"Should you or any man of yours wish it," said Jeannot, "I can provide a recommendation and any aid necessary. But I have, perhaps, a more accommodating solution."

Fin narrowed her eyes at him. "What sort of solution?"

"It would be unwise to return to Malta so soon, I think. The grand master showed me grace in my offense, but Lennard Guillot has been publicly humiliated. Though I doubt he would raise his hand against me directly, he is a politician, and politicians have subtler means of retribution. Therefore, I've written to the grand master, requesting permission to sail with the French navy if they—when they—depart for America. You and your crew would be welcome guests aboard the *Esprit de la Mer*."

Fin shook her head. "But it could be months before that happens."

"Or it could be a matter of weeks." Jeannot studied Fin's face and his features saddened. "I only offer. If you—or your men—wish to find your own way, I will assist however I can."

Jeannot walked away, thoughtful and silent.

Fin presented Jeannot's offer to the crew, but in the days following, they began to break company. Various sailors took work on the docks or claimed to have found true love in the arms of a French mistress and departed in that pursuit, or they took contracts aboard ships bound home or elsewhere, and when two weeks had passed, only a handful remained. Even Topper came to Fin, sad and furtive, and wringing his hat.

"Fin," he said, "there's a bakeress down the lane yonder. Sweet as honey she is, and without a husband nor any man at all to see after her. Y'ought to come down, Fin. Come down to the bakery. She makes a strudel that's nearabout as fine a thing as ever I did taste." Topper looked at his feet and kneaded his hat and let a frown hang down his face. "Think I might just stay 'round here, Fin. Always wanted me own bakery, you know. Never hardly dreamt of nothing else. I'm sorry, Fin. Feel like I ought'n to stick, but I can't help thinking that if I don't see to this, I might not get another chance." He looked up at her and squinted. "Know what I mean, Fin? Ain't sore are you?"

"Topper, I could hardly be happier."

Topper stopped wringing his hat and let his frown straighten out. "Really, Fin? Hellfire, I was sure you'd be sore."

They grinned at each other like fools, and Fin hugged him. "I'll miss you, Topper."

"Shoot, Fin, you come visit. Free pastries any time for Cap'n Button.

It's been fine, Fin. A fine long sail and like'n the kind a man don't soon forget neither. One for telling little ones when they ask about their fat old Papa and his days on the sea. And you can bet I'll tell 'em, Fin. They'll know their Papa steered the helm of the old *Rattlesnake*. They'll know he heard the fiddle sing and the cannons clap. They'll know I seen the days when Cap'n Fin Button set British seas aflame and sailed the *Fiddler's Green* clear to Tripoli. I'll story 'em, Fin. I'll story 'em clean. I'll tell 'em how we sailed with them knights and seen the fleet of the Barbarie ride cross the sea like devils out the sulfur regions. I'll tell how they come and how we sent 'em the iron of a thousand cannon. They'll hear on how you called thunder and lightning itself to sail against 'em and shiver 'em back to the fiery realm. I'll tell 'em about the time you—"

Fin smiled and laughed each time he refused to leave his tales at an end, and she pushed him gently away. As Topper wound his way down the crowded pier, he grabbed passers-by and bothered them with his storying. They pulled away and swatted him off, but by the time he reached the street corner and turned into the city, he'd gathered a train of dirty children and they chased after him as if hungry for his words and he dropped them like breadcrumbs. Topper sauntered into his new life of bakery, and Fin raised him a smile of well-wishing and felt something akin to the pride of a mother seeing her child gone forth into the wider world beyond.

Two weeks after Benjamin Franklin collected the Countess de Graff, word spread through Europe that the French navy was to join the war and sail to America. And Fin, anxious to be home, agreed to stay with Jeannot and sail on the *Esprit de la Mer*. But the fleet didn't embark that week or the week after and the waiting didn't suit her. She was restless. Each day she asked Jeannot if there were orders for departure and each day he frowned and shook his head. Day after day, Fin griped and complained over the slovenly pace of the navy's embarkation.

Of Fin's crew, all that remained were Jack, Lucas Thigham, and Phineas Button. The rest had scattered to their various interests, and though Fin was relieved to be divested of her captian-ish façade, she felt a measure of true sadness in the breaking of their long company.

Phineas seemed determined to find his end in a bottle and nothing Fin said or did would sway him from it. He wandered the streets of Le Havre vagrant and drunken and often the sailors of the *Esprit de la Mer* found him passed out in a gutter and carried him back to the ship.

Once, a messenger came from a nearby tavern requesting that someone come and collect him, and dutifully, Fin did. He exasperated her but she couldn't bring herself to abandon him. So she looked after him, fetched him in his drunkenness, tended him in his sickness, and hoped that someday he'd come to himself again and finally *see* her.

In April of 1778, Fin's wait came to an end. The *Esprit de la Mer* set sail from Le Havre-de-Grâce as member of a fleet of more than a hundred ships. To Fin it looked like the city itself had broken loose of the coast and gone afloat. They struck out across the Atlantic and Fin climbed the mast, light and filled with gladness. She stood high in the tops looking west, toward home.

CHAPTER FORTY-ONE

THOUGH JACK WAS A guest aboard the *Esprit de la Mer*, he was no mere passenger. Without someone to growl at or kick, he was more irritable than ever. He shuffled around the deck and mourned his lack of a crew. He watched the French sailors at their work and mumbled about how he thought they were a lazy lot, and he complained to anyone in earshot of all the ways he saw that they ought to sail the ship better. Remy petitioned to have him removed or quieted, but Jeannot had other ideas. He put him to work. Remy turned red as a beet when he heard this suggestion, thinking his own authority as First Officer was put in doubt, but after a few days Remy and Jack managed to devise between themselves a relationship that suited them both. Jack took over the stomping, barking, and kicking aspects of the First Officer's post, and Remy happily oversaw the more civil duties of maintaining watches, receiving Jeannot's orders, and settling disputes. Though Jack's gruffness and irritability were none lessened by the new arrangement, Fin, knowing him well, saw in his swagger that he was content to have an outlet again for his particular talents.

The closer they drew to America, the more Fin worried about her father. He still lurked wherever she went, but he had changed. Instead of disappearing into the shadows or huddling in corners as he always had, he seemed agitated now. At times he paced the deck, mumbling to himself like a mad prophet. At other times he stood at the rail looking west, and he pulled his hair and moaned at the wind. Nightmares troubled his sleep, and Fin often woke to find him standing across the room, looking at her, and clawing at his chest or his face. Any time he found the means to do so, whether by beggary, ration, or barter, he lost himself in drink and wallowed in drunken stupor.

Fin didn't fear him. If he'd meant to hurt her, he could have done so a thousand times. But he was a mystery she couldn't unravel. And the closer they got to home, the worse his condition got. He talked to himself constantly, indistinct mutterings that Fin couldn't decipher. If she tried to speak to him, he withdrew, quieted, and turned his head away until she left.

At the end of the fourth week at sea, Fin caught the first sight of the coast and ran to her quarters to pack. She threw open her fiddle case. Betsy lay inside, long silent and finally seeming to disappear into the shadow of the fiddle. She'd kept the green dress Jeannot had given her, and though she doubted she'd ever wear it, she treasured the gift and tucked it neatly into the case.

The fleet anchored off the Delaware coast to await orders. Courier ships dispatched to Philadelphia, and Fin waited patiently as they spent days and then weeks without direction. Meanwhile, ships, a handful at a time, shuttled into the Philadelphia harbor to resupply and grant their crews shore leave.

In June, the *Esprit de la Mer* was finally ordered to harbor. Fin wanted to dash ashore and run free as soon as the ship was tied at the wharf, but she didn't. She assisted the crew in loading stores and making repairs. She was patient, but she was distracted, having eyes only for the southern horizon. When evening came, her bones were sore from the work and she retired to her cabin. She washed and, as she was settling down for the night, noted that Phineas Button was conspicuously absent. Fin roamed the decks, looking through the holds and asking after him, but he was nowhere to be found. Several sailors told her they'd seen him stumble ashore but no one had seen him since. And that was it. He was gone. Fin wasn't surprised. She found it fitting that he'd walked out of her life as mysteriously as he'd come into it. But part of her suffered a breaking, and she wept when finally she settled down to sleep.

Work resumed the next morning, but by noon the bulk of it was finished and Jeannot began granting the crew leave to go ashore. Fin was anxious and left the ship at the first opportunity. Her business was to find news of the south. She wandered the city, listening to people as they spoke to one another and paying special attention to boys on street corners hawking the day's news and selling papers. But until she sauntered into an establishment heralded as CRIEVE'S PUBLIC HOUSE she hadn't heard anything at all specific to Georgia.

Fin gathered a seat among a number of men who each sat with elbows propped and a stein of beer at hand. They turned to look at her as she took her place, but they judged her of no account and returned to their own discourse without greeting. The men spoke privately among themselves, and Fin did her best to lean in and listen discreetly. One of the men had a thin face made to look thinner by his mustache, which was waxed and drawn to a sharp point on either side; he saw Fin's interest in their conversation and held up one hand to quiet his partners.

Though he looked like an Englishman, he had a thick Irish accent. "Something we can help you with, lass?"

"Just come from France," Fin said. "Hoping to hear news of Georgia."

"Unless you've got Tory blood in your veins, you'd best keep wide 'o Georgia, lassie. The English got themselves dug into Savannah, and none goes in or out saving the English says it's so."

Fin's face prickled with dread, and she broke into a sweat.

"You don't look so good," said one of the men, a Bostoner by the accent. Fin felt sick and small and the men could see it. "Best run back to your ma. Waterfront's no place for a girl."

Fin bristled at his dismissive tone. She scowled and cracked her knuckles and the men laughed.

"Watch yourself, Munroe. Might be Fin Button back from the grave. She's got red hair like the devil herself."

"What do you mean by that?" Fin asked.

"Take no offense, lass. Naught but old sailors' tales. Used to hear tell of a red-haired lassie like yourself that run British in circles. Folk told she captained a ship-o-the-line, said she could call the wind with her fiddle and all other manner of fool's talk."

"Why'd you say she was back from the grave?"

"If you believe them sort of tales, then they say the Continental navy sunk her ship and all aboard was lost. Captain Button's not been seen in nearly a year." The Irishman leaned in and studied her, scratching his chin in mock interest. "Lessin', of course, you're her." His partners burst into laughter.

Fin nodded slowly. She'd forgotten that Captain Bettany had reported her dead. The British weren't looking for her anymore.

"Shame she's dead," said Fin. Her color returned and she felt very much alive and well.

Fin spent the rest of the day roaming the city. She had no motive and no destination, she was merely happy to walk free with no need to look over her shoulder for soldiers—not British soldiers, since they thought she was dead, and not Continentals since the pardon had cleared her name. She wandered the streets and alleyways and markets and smiled at passers-by and whiled away her time until evening.

When she returned to the *Esprit de la Mer*, she found Jeannot in his cabin conversing with Jack and Remy. She strutted across the room with a silly smile on her face and said not a word as she dropped into a chair and threw her feet up onto the table. Jeannot and the others cut off their conversation. Jack stared at Fin like she'd grown another head.

"What's got into you, Button? You ain't smiled like that since—hell, you ain't never smiled like that."

Fin swung her feet down and jumped up, spreading her arms out like a preacher addressing the lost. "Gentlemen, I am going home."

"Well, good riddance," said Jack. "Don't think I could abide this prancing around for more'n a Yankee minute." Remy and Jack looked at one another and laughed.

"Is it safe?" said Jeannot.

"They can't kill me if I'm already dead, right?"

Jeannot and Jack looked at one another.

"What are you on about, Button?"

"When we left for Tripoli, Captain Bettany reported he'd sunk us. Everybody here thinks we're dead. They got no reason to look for me any more. Captain Fin Button? Terror of the British trade? Dead. Me? I'm going home." Fin laughed and hopped around the table to hug Jack. Jack rolled his eyes and tried to shrug her off.

"A letter came for you today," said Jeannot. He leaned forward and slid an envelope across the table.

Fin stepped away from Jack and stared at it. "A letter?"

Jeannot nodded. "Delivered by messenger, not by post."

Fin picked it up. It didn't make sense. No one knew she was here. Fin looked around at Jeannot and then at Jack; both of them stared back expressionless. She tore open the envelope and pulled out the folded letter. It was a shabbily written message and a hand-drawn map.

Daughter,

Someone for you to meet. Will you come?

Phineas Button

The map indicated a farmhouse a few miles southwest of Philadelphia and was clearly drawn by a different hand than the message.

Fin stared at the paper. The skin of her face tingled with excitement. Was one of her sisters alive? Maybe an aunt or uncle? If nothing else it was a sign that her father hadn't run off and left her. Was it possible that his drunkenness was merely a symptom of homesickness—now cured? She'd never known him to write anything. Surely this was progress.

Fin read the message aloud. She looked up at Jack with amazement but his face gave her pause. His forehead was knotted and his mouth was drawn with concern.

"What's wrong?" asked Fin.

He exchanged a worried look with Jeannot.

"It don't feel right, that's what," said Jack.

"What do you mean by that?"

"I mean there's something squirrely about it. He might be your father but I never knowed him to do more than slink, steal, and drink."

Fin gaped at him. "Is it so hard to believe that he wants me to meet someone? It must be my family!"

Jack scratched his beard and shrugged. "Don't know. Just feels wrong is all."

Jeannot cleared his throat. "Perhaps it is as you say. But if you go, be cautious. I do not trust him either."

Fin bristled. "He's my father! He saved my life when the *Rattlesnake* sank. Why would he want to hurt me?"

Jeannot nodded and tried to smile. "Of course, you are right. When will you go?"

FIN WALKED TO HER cabin in a daze. A thousand possibilities ran through her mind and excited her. She hadn't expected Phineas Button when he walked back into her life on the *Rattlesnake*; he'd come out of nowhere. But now she had the pleasure of anticipation and mystery. Who did he want her to meet? She desperately wanted it to be her mother, but he'd told her she was dead. Or was that only a part of his madness? Could she be alive?

Fin didn't waste any time. She had to leave immediately. She washed her face and brushed her hair. She even considered putting on the dress Jeannot had given her but decided against it. Whomever Phineas wanted her to meet, she would be herself. No disguise. No lies.

Jeannot knocked on the doorframe and stepped into her cabin.

"Do I look all right?" Fin asked. She smoothed her shirt and rolled up her sleeves.

Jeannot smiled at her and nodded patiently then took a deep breath and measured his words with tender concern. "Allow me to accompany you."

Fin stopped and frowned at him. She ground her teeth and shook her head. "I'll be fine. It's not far outside of the city."

"There are reports of British soldiers in the countryside. It is not safe."

"I survived Tripoli. I can manage Pennsylvania."

Jeannot took her by the arm. "I do not doubt you. But please, if you will not allow me to come with you, at least arm yourself. The roads are not safe. It would ease my mind."

Fin sighed and pulled her arm free. "All right!" she said. Her tone was sharper than she meant it to be. She lowered her voice. "All right. I'll take Betsy. I'll be fine, Jeannot. I don't need looking after."

CHAPTER FORTY-TWO

F IN PAID THE DOCKMASTER for use of a horse and departed well before sunset. She had to stop often to ask for directions, and by the time she left the city, twilight was upon her. The farmhouse indicated on the map lay only a few short miles ahead and though she was anxious, she resisted the urge to goad the horse and hurry. Along the way, she passed other homesteads and smiled at the life evident upon them. Planted flowers at the doorstep. Animals at pasture, lowing and snorting. A stand of golden-tasseled corn. Two young boys wrestling in the grass. Each in its way put her in mind of her own homestead that, far away south, lay waiting. She wondered what Peter had done with it in the years since she left. Had he painted it? Built a barn? Fenced the yard? Was there a chicken coop or a flowerbed? But inevitably, her mind was drawn from those wanderings toward her rendezvous with Phineas Button and the possibilities his message implied. The closer she came to her destination, the more her stomach fluttered and heaved.

Fin followed the road around its subtle bends and across its dips and gullies until she crested a hill and looked down into a shallow vale. At the bottom of the hill a wooden bridge humped across a dry creek bed. A farmhouse sat atop the hill on the far side, staring at her out of its dark windows. Its yard was overgrown. The wind batted a loosened shutter against the window frame. *Clack-rattle-clack.* A rusted plow leaned on the gatepost like a lazy farmhand. Neglect hung over the place, a pall of abandonment. Fin frowned and her gut tightened. She kicked the horse and walked it down the hill. The bridge's joints complained when the horse crossed it, and in the farmhouse, a window came alight like the opening of an eye. Fin continued up the hill. She pulled the horse to a stop at the gate and looked around. Beyond the house, the countryside became a dense wood and she could see no other homes. Even the road itself twisted out of sight in a stand of trees half a mile off. She pulled the map from her pocket and strained her eyes to see it in the twilight. She confirmed her location and stuffed it back into her pocket. *This is it.* Another light flickered on in the house. *Clack-rattle-clack.*

Fin dismounted and tied the horse to the gatepost. She looked around nervously and settled Betsy in her belt. She felt ill at ease but couldn't pinpoint the source of the feeling. By the look of the house, whoever lived there was either unable to keep it well, or unwilling— perhaps too old? Fin had hoped to find herself walking up to a house filled with light and noise and children, but she chided herself for her disappointment. She should be grateful. The door of the house opened and Phineas Button shuffled out. Fin lifted her head and smiled. He waved and she waved back. Then he turned abruptly as if called and slunk back into the house leaving the door ajar.

Fin took a deep breath. Her stomach did a somersault and her hands trembled. She told her legs to walk but couldn't seem to make them listen. *Clack-rattle-clack.* She couldn't move. Across the vale another rider walked his horse over the hill and eased down toward the old bridge. The sight of him spurred her into motion. The last thing she wanted was to have to speak to a stranger on the road. She pushed open the gate and walked up the path to the house.

The front steps sagged and creaked under her feet. She pushed open the door and stepped into the quiet house. No one greeted her. The place had the smell of dust and old hay. A coat and hat hung beside the door. Somewhere a floorboard creaked. Down the hall, lamplight shimmered through an open door and she went to it.

Inside the lighted room, Phineas Button sat slumped at a dining table with his head down and his hands in his hair. Slowly and repeatedly he raised his head an inch and thumped it on the tabletop. He was either humming to himself quietly or moaning. An overturned bottle rocked back and forth with each vibration of the table. Fin sat beside him. When he tried to pound his head again, she took him by the shoulder and held him back.

"I'm here," she said. "I came."

Phineas sat up. He let out a long alcoholic breath and looked toward Fin but not at her. He chewed at his lips and mumbled and pulled on his beard and opened his mouth as if he wanted to speak. But he didn't. A floorboard creaked in the adjoining room. Phineas looked down.

A man stepped into the doorway and smiled at her. He was dressed like a gentleman and wore his hair in neat curls. He scratched his head and said, "You Fin Button, then?" He glanced down at Phineas. "This her?"

Fin studied the man's face but saw nothing familiar in it. She started to stand and greet him, but he put out his hand and shook his head.

"Don't stand on my account." He walked around the table and sat beside her. He put one hand on the back of her chair.

"I'm Fin," she said. "My father asked me to come."

The man chuckled and nodded. He leaned closer and slid his arm around her shoulders. Fin shirked away briefly but didn't want to be rude, so she smiled.

"Well, don't you worry now. We know all about you, Fin. Phineas here told us. Did he tell you he'd been writing us letters? Oh, yes. Letters from Malta! Letters from France! Been all over haven't you now? What's that you got there?" He looked down at Betsy tucked into her belt.

Fin shrugged and pulled the gun out. "It was a gift from an old friend. Just brought it to keep safe on the road."

"No need for that now, then, is there?" He slipped Betsy away from her and laid it on the table then patted it and kept it under his hand.

"I'm sorry to be rude," said Fin. "But what's your name?"

"There's someone itchy to meet you, Fin Button. Someone been looking for you a very long time."

Fin's heart leapt. The floorboards outside the room creaked again. She threw a hopeful glance at Phineas but he stared down into his lap. The man beside her got up and stepped to the back of her chair as someone darkened the doorway. Fin held her breath. A man entered and there was something vaguely familiar in his movement and gait. He approached the table opposite Fin and turned toward her. His lips curled up. But it was his eyes that gave him away. The man behind her threw a rope over her shoulders and cinched her tight to the chair. Fin was too shocked to move. Across the table the soldier sat down. An old scar ran across his face from temple to temple. One milk-white eye stared blindly, the other rolled and bulged in its lidless socket. Fin shuddered and came alive. She bucked in her seat and snatched at the air but she couldn't reach Betsy. The man behind her tossed another coil of rope around her and tied her fast. The soldier laughed and watched. Memories almost forgotten flashed through Fin's mind. She recalled screams and Bartimaeus's knife as it cut through the fire-lit night. When the soldier spoke, his voice came at her sharp and cruel as a blade.

"Knew you wasn't dead."

The soldier reached across the table and picked up Betsy. He ran his hands across the barrel and admired the workmanship.

"Got to admit, I didn't think he'd do it. Took him what? A year almost? But he surely done it, ain't he, lassie? Brought you back alive and still kicking. Brought his little girl in like a pig to market." Phineas shifted in his chair and muttered to himself. Fin shook her head. She didn't want to hear it, couldn't stand to know it. Her mind raced. Had he really saved her life only to sell it? "Want to know how much you went for? Oh, it weren't a lot. Not much at all. Expect he'll drink it gone in a year or two, saving he lives that long."

Fin strained at the ropes and shook her head. She wanted to shake loose of his words, to clean them out of her head. "No," she moaned. "No!" She screamed. "*No!*" Her face shot red and she shook and shook, enraged. The soldier laughed. He tilted his head back and his laughter poured out of him in heaves.

"What's it feel like?" He leaned forward and looked into her eyes, studying her. "What's it like to know your own daddy give you over to be hanged?"

Fin snarled at him. Anger rushed through her. Her skin itched with it. "You son of a bitch, I'm going to—"

"Going to *what*?" He pounded his hand down on the table. Betsy bounced and clattered. "Blind me other eye? Stick a knife in me chest? No, lassie, let me tell you what *I'm* going to do!" He stood up and threw the table aside. He sneered at her and bared his teeth. His lidless eye bulged and swam in a pool of red flesh. "*Let me tell you all the terrible things I'm about to do, lassie.*" Fin kicked at the floor and pushed her chair backward, away from him, but the man behind stopped her. He clamped his hands down on her shoulders and held her fast. The soldier threw back his head and let great peals of laughter out. He stood over Fin and gloated. Then he drew back his hand and slapped her. Fin's head whipped to the side and she was left staring at Phineas Button. He sat. His hands in his lap, he sat. And he stared at the floor. The soldier pulled a long knife from his belt and then—

There was a clap of thunder. The room went eerily silent. The soldier tottered. A bloody fountain sprang from his chest. He blinked his lidless eye then toppled backward. He hit the floor, kicked once, and died. Jeannot rushed through the door. He cast his smoking pistol aside and tackled the other man. Fin pulled and strained to break free of the chair, but she couldn't. All she could do was listen as Jeannot struggled and fought behind her. Groans. Deep breaths. The smack of fists. Then silence.

The ropes slackened. Fin pulled herself out of the chair. The man who had tied her lay motionless on the floor and Jeannot stood over him. Fin panted and cried and sank to her knees. Jeannot tried to take her in his arms but she pushed him away. She reached across the floor and grabbed Betsy then got up and crossed the room. She stood over Phineas Button. He sat in his chair nodding to himself and muttering under his breath. He hadn't moved from his seat in all that had happened.

"Get up."

Phineas ignored her. He looked around the room and then at the floor.

"*Get up!*"

When he didn't move, Fin took him by the collar and hauled him to his feet.

"*Look at me!*"

Phineas tried to look down but Fin grabbed his chin and forced him to face her. She cocked Betsy's hammer and pressed the muzzle against his heart.

"Why?" she whispered. She kicked the chair away and drove him backward against the wall. "Tell me why." His eyes steadied and for a brief moment, he saw her. "Why don't you *want me?*" Her finger trembled at Betsy's trigger.

And then he was gone again. He looked away. His muscles went limp and he sagged so that Fin was forced to let him slip to the floor. He sat against the wall and stared into whatever nothingness he saw before him. Everything about him disgusted her. His stink filled her nose. Lice scurried through his filthy tangle of hair. Sores puckered at the corners of his mouth. His clothes were torn and unwashed. The room around him seemed to droop and drain of life. And what was she to do? Put him out of his apathy? Pull the trigger and be rid of him at last? Though some old voice inside of her wanted that very thing, Fin chose against it; she set Betsy's hammer down with her thumb and put the gun away. Instead, she gave him what *she* so desperately wanted. She gave him what he was never willing to give her. Fin knelt beside him and pulled Phineas Button into her embrace. She held him. So tightly, she held him. She laid her face against his and pressed her flesh against his own. She gave him all the tenderness she could muster. Though he wouldn't take it or offer it back, she gave. She squeezed it into him and held it there. She accepted him. She loved him in his wretchedness, kissed his ragged cheek, and called him *father*.

Then she stood and said goodbye.

THAT NIGHT, AS FIN and Jeannot rode back to the city, she took in the full measure of her father's betrayal. The English knew. They knew she was alive. And they knew she'd returned to American waters. She couldn't go home.

In all the ride back, neither she nor Jeannot spoke. But Jeannot's silent presence was a comfort, and though she never said so, Fin placed great value in it.

Chapter Forty-three

FIN THOUGHT THE WAR would end in weeks. It didn't. From Newport in the far north to St. Augustine in the south, it dragged on. And it took Fin wherever it went. The *Esprit de la Mer* became as feared on the American seaboard as the *Rattlesnake* had been in years past. They hounded the British anywhere they found them. And rumor of Captain Button followed; it swelled and grew. It ran among the crews of British ships like a scathefire. Back from the dead, they said. A devil. Sailed from the lower regions, from the far beyond. And Fin would not say otherwise. She was quiet in those days and not given much to joy. War was her vocation and her only care, and its end her deepest hope. She often tried writing to Peter, but she could never settle on the right words and convinced herself each time that the war would soon be over and she'd be home again and have no need of letters.

In October of 1779 the French fleet laid Savannah under siege, and Fin, so close to Ebenezer, was eager and restless. But when the British at last drove them off and kept the city, Fin turned dark and unapproachable. To have come so close only to be driven away—she feared her heart had finally been broken one too many times and nothing could console her. The war dragged on.

Three long years passed. In time, Fin's knowledge and experience at sea were such that she could have captained a ship of the fleet as well as any man. And though she had many opportunities to leave, she kept aboard the *Esprit de la Mer* and learned to be among the crew like family. Jack was there, of course, and Lucas Thigham, and in time there were others close to her as well: Davey Walker, Atticus Will, John Obadiah, and even Old Thurston and his wife Belinda-Lee (though their stories are not a part of this telling). Greater than the others, though, was Jeannot. And while she held him away and kept herself apart, he became her dearest companion. Most often, their association was one of silence, but that is a thing of uncommon worth when partaken of in the ease of another. Often Jeannot asked her to walk with him at night but always she refused. "Peter," she'd say, "Peter's waiting," and she'd go alone onto the deck to fiddle in the dark and stare at the southern horizon.

But the war did end. It ground to a halt, died a miserable death, and like a dream, was gone. The British left Savannah in the summer of 1782, and when Fin heard the news, she did a rare thing—she smiled. Jeannot saw it and he cherished the sight; its appearance had become like a precious gem to him. And so for Savannah they sailed, and Fin, as she so often did, hoisted herself into the ropes and climbed. Hand over hand, she pulled herself up, up, until she stood on the highest yardarm and watched the coast sweeping past.

THE *ESPRIT DE LA MER* docked in the Savannah harbor on August 2, 1782. After nearly seven years of war, Fin Button had returned. The crew met her on deck. Some bowed to her as she passed; some saluted; others stepped out and shook her hand. They honored her. Many had known her since the days of Tripoli and all that high adventure. Others only knew her in the years after and honored the stories and yarns they'd heard. But all knew her for what she truly was: a sailor, one among them, an old salt, a patriot of the revolution, a friend, and these things needed no embellishment by barroom tale.

When she'd passed the crew, Jack Wagon heaved himself into her path. His beard was grey and his hair thin, but his chest was thick as a wine barrel. Fin jumped up and wrapped her arms around his neck.

"Damn it, Button. I ain't fit for huggin'." She laughed and he pulled her up and squeezed her like a toy. When he set her down he said, "Take it easy on folks. Keep them fists in your pockets." Jack's mouth broke into a giant smile and she walked to the plank.

Jeannot was there. With one finger he wrapped a lock of Fin's hair behind her ear and then ran his thumb across her scarred cheek. Fin blushed and pushed his hand away.

"The *Esprit de la Mer* will be empty without you, Fin Button."

Fin shifted nervously and took his hands in her own. "The *Esprit de la Mer* is a fine ship, Jeannot. But she doesn't need me. It's time for me to go."

Jeannot raised her hand and held her fingers to his lips. He drew in a deep breath and held it long. Then he nodded and stepped back. "She will remember you. You will always be welcome on her decks."

Fin went ashore. She took with her a fiddle, a gun, a green dress, and a pardon—all packed up in the case she'd carried to sea years before. She didn't look back. She bought a horse and rode for Ebenezer.

Chapter Forty-four

IN LATE AFTERNOON, FIN pulled her horse to a halt. She patted the animal's withers and sat. The air smelled of childhood. Pine. Moist earth. Dried leaves. A hint of honeysuckle. An old moss-bearded pecan tree stood beside the road and stretched its weary arms out above her. In the brush a possum scurried away and palmetto fans rattled and swayed in its wake. Ahead of her, the road ran off toward Ebenezer, and to her left, under boughs of gnarled and ancient oak, a narrow wagon trail cut through the trees toward an open field.

As Fin sat at the cusp, she felt, for a moment, as if perhaps she'd stay there, stay in the mystery of it, balanced at the threshold, never crossing. Or she could turn and leave and always keep the memory to cherish, making an ideal of it rather than a reality. But even as she thought these things, she knew the truth. She would go. Like a stone set in motion and tumbling down a hillside, she couldn't stop now. And so she went.

Fin goaded the horse and walked it off the road, down the trail, beneath the trees of her youth. The trail ran ahead like a tunnel, sun-dappled and elongate, and at its distant end: light. It was a blinding radiance at first, but as she closed upon it, the brightness dispersed and the wood opened onto the field. *Shiloh*, Peter had named it. The house sat tiny and humble, so much smaller than she remembered. The sun had faded its wood to ashy grey and the porch had a hint of sag in its boards. The field around was little more than a shaggy yard, again so much less than her memory had made of it. She walked the horse to the house and dismounted. She was strangely calm.

The door opened and a young man walked onto the porch. He kicked his boot heels then held up a hand and waved. "Can I help ya?" The man tilted his head and leaned forward, studying her with intense curiosity. "Fin? Fin Button? Is that you?"

The door opened behind him and a young woman came out. She wore a dingy blue dress that was patched many times over and stained brown around the hem. A white bonnet covered her head and loops of blonde hair had fallen out and dangled lightly at her jaw. The woman stepped off the porch and looked at Fin. She put her hand to her mouth and inhaled sharply.

"Land o' Goshen."

Fin stared at the woman blankly, then looked up again at the man on the porch.

"Don't you remember me, Fin? It's Delly. Delly Martin—well, Delly Sheffield now. You remember Owen don't you? Come down here, Owen."

The man stepped off the porch and stood next to Delly. He put his arm around her waist and smiled. *Owen Sheffield. Could it really be?* He was a man yet scarcely more than a boy. His clothes swallowed him. He'd be seventeen, Fin thought. And Delly had grown into a beautiful woman. Delly *Sheffield* now, she'd said.

"Well, I swear." Owen shook his head. "We thought you was dead, Fin."

Delly jabbed him in the ribs with her elbow and whispered out of the side of her mouth. "Don't be rude."

Fin tried to speak but found she couldn't stammer out so much as a word. Her eyes watered. She put her head down and squeezed her eyes shut then took a deep breath and let it out slowly. She clenched her teeth until she was sure she was ready, and then she raised her head and spoke. "Where—where's Peter?"

Delly's eyes widened and then her whole face drew tight and mournful. She leaned against Owen and squeezed his arm. They looked at one another and then at Fin. It was Owen that spoke. "He's gone, Fin."

"Gone?"

Owen nodded and then frowned and looked at the ground between them.

Fin's face drained. "Gone how?" she asked.

Delly let go of Owen's arm. She stepped forward and took Fin's hand. "You'd best see."

Fin followed Delly. They walked past the house, across the yard, and into the edge of the wood. Delly stopped in a small clearing amid a stand of cypress and held her hands to her mouth. Fin's eyes were clear. She stared at the forest floor and knew. It seemed to her now that she'd always known. Before her, planted in the rich soil, was a cross, and upon it a name: Peter LaMee. As she looked down, she knew with a strange certainty that her grief had begun years ago and coming home was the end of it somehow. Though there were tremors in her hands and her breath came in stilted gasps, her eyes remained clear.

But next to Peter's grave was a second memorial, and when Fin saw this she had no defense against it. It was another planted cross and this writ meanly upon it: Phinea Button, Lost at Sea. It was the sight of this grave, and not of Peter's, that dealt the hammer stroke to Fin's calm. It sundered her like the shattering of glass. And not because she'd lost Peter and all the dreams of her youth had come to nothing. It was because she'd put upon Peter the grief of her death. The thought of it wracked her. That innocent Peter had waited and waited and been so kind and so good and so, so patient and then had come into the grief of thinking her lost and dead, it ran her aground; she foundered and broke.

Delly laid a hand on Fin's shoulder and cried. "He thought you'd died, Fin. It was news all over. The whole town came out. There was a service and everything." Delly leaned against her and wrapped her arms around Fin's shoulders. "Then soldiers came. And they shot him, Fin. They said they'd burn the house if he didn't come down and let them have it. Peter sat on the porch, and he told them no, and they shot him for it." Delly squeezed Fin tight and brushed her hair out of her face. "Hilde took care of him but the wound wouldn't heal. I'm so sorry."

Fin collapsed into the fallen leaves and wept. Delly held her a while, abiding with her in mourning, but when the sun went down she stood and walked to the house. Fin stayed. She crawled across the leaves and laid her head at the foot of Peter's cross. She sought his face in her memory, hoping to catch a glimpse of his smile, or the shade of his simple eyes, but the images eluded her until finally she ceased and, shivering, lay broken. She opened herself and let her long-withheld grief come upon her and do its work at last. It came like spring rain, washing through her, swirling, churning in gullies and crystal pools, streaming across her soul in thick, plentiful sheets. It cleansed her, and more, it nurtured inside her a fertile soil that, in time, would seed again and bear fruit as yet undreamed. She cried a long time before settling into the peacefulness that follows in the wake of tears. The moon rose full in a clear sky, turning the night into a thing luminous and shimmering. Fin closed her eyes and slept a sound and dreamless sleep.

Chapter Forty-five

F IN STIRRED IN THE early light and arose. She tended the ground around the burial plot, pulling weeds up by the roots, clearing the soil of dried leaves and sticks, leaving the area fresh and clean. When Peter's grave was in order she did the same to her own and pondered the strangeness of it. Though she considered scouring her name from the cross or ripping it out of the ground and hurling it into the woods, she left it. It seemed right to her that it should stand and keep with Peter and testify to the passage of things gone by.

When Fin was satisfied with the state of the gravesite, she walked through the woods, across the road, and down to the river. She stepped neatly out of her clothes and hung them across a cypress log and waded into the Savannah to wash. The lap of cold water on her skin gave her a shudder. She went in slowly at first, inches at a time. The morning sun lay golden upon the surface. Gentle waves washed sunlight toward her in sparkles. It seemed she'd strayed into a river of halcyon light and the sun himself had come down to splash his morning upon her. She dove, plunging fully beneath the surface and came up again in tears. Rivulets ran from her face, and the sun ignited them each, transforming them, even amid her sorrow, into gilded runnels set with a diamond shine. In the midst of that sun-limned font, her memories of Peter returned. They leapt afresh in her mind and made her smile; the images solidified like painted icons and she hid each one away in her heart and cherished it there. She laughed and remembered and swam and played until by action of innocence and joy she was scoured white once more and wholly clean.

When she came up from the river it was morning yet, and Delly would not suffer Fin to depart without breakfast. She dragged her into the house by the sleeve and sat her in a chair and cooked a meal of eggs and cornbread. "I'm afraid it won't measure up to what you and Brother Bartimaeus used to manage, but it keeps us kicking," she said.

"Delly's a fine cook. Don't mind that nonsense," said Owen.

Fin thanked them both and ate.

"Thought I'd go into town and see Hilde," she said.

"Oh, you should, Fin. She'd like that. She's not like she was, you know. Carmaline passed on three years back and she's been tame as a kitten ever since. Go see her, Fin, won't you?"

Delly spooned another egg onto Fin's plate and then sat down next to her husband and picked at a thread hanging from his collar. Fin watched them with satisfaction and wonder. It seemed impossible that the children she remembered had grown into the man and woman before her. She thought about how strange it was that the house she'd so long thought of as hers was now theirs and decided it was entirely right that it should be so.

Fin left them waving from the porch and rode into the ruin of Ebenezer. The British had razed the town. All that was left of Thom Hickory's house were three charred posts sticking out of the ground in a field of ash. Not a habitable home remained. Every one was burned, gutted, lying in shambles. But above the ashen ruin of the town, above the tall pines, Fin saw a white glimmer and walked her horse toward it. It was the swan mounted atop the chapel's tower.

The roof of the orphan house had caved in and one of its walls had toppled, scattering bricks across the courtyard. The windows of the dining hall were broken and the door hung loose upon a single hinge. But the chapel stood. A fortress among ruins, it stood. Fin dismounted and entered. It stank of manure, and piles of hay cluttered every corner. Flies buzzed, swirling in black clouds. The floor was caked with mud and covered with hoof prints, and there was an ill-made patch over the hole that Creache had torn up. Most of the organ's pipes were missing, and those that remained hung out of their housings and leaned over the sanctuary as if they might fall at the least provocation. As Fin surveyed the pitiable state of the sanctuary, a solemn expression descended upon her face and resolved in the set of her jaw. She felt the onset of a purpose years in the making, as if some great clock had been wound in another age and its hands, moving steadily through years of revolution, had struck now upon their mark and set loose the chime of an appointed hour.

Fin walked out of the ruined chapel and went to the headmistress's chambers. It hadn't been burned, but the windows were smashed and the doors were torn off. As she approached, she heard a soft swishing sound from inside it. Again and again. *Swish. Swish.* Fin stepped into the doorway. The room had been stripped of its furnishings. All that remained was a rocking chair beside the hearth. A neatly made pallet of blankets lay by the wall and Hilde was sweeping the floor with a straw broom. Her years had gnarled her such that she could no longer stand upright. *Swish. Swish.* She swept, bent over like a hunchback.

"Sister Hilde?"

With some effort, Hilde shuffled around to face Fin and look up at her. Hilde's nose no longer stuck out on her face like a spike; instead, it hooked, curled down like a broken finger.

"Sister Hilde, it's me. It's Fin."

Hilde's eyes narrowed and her head wavered back and forth in uncertainty. Though time had worn her down, it hadn't siphoned away any of her old intensity; rather, it had leavened it with a measure of kind thoughtfulness that Fin had never before known her to show. Her look was as sharp and piercing as ever, and it saw to the quick. Hilde reached for Fin's hand and took hold of it. She felt and pinched and squeezed first her hand and then her arm and worked her way up until she held Fin's face. "Oh, my dear girl," she said. Her voice was thin and trembled lightly without a note of shrewdness. "Do you see what they've done? Do you see?"

"I see."

She pulled on Fin's arm. Fin bent down and Hilde ran her fingers across the scar on Fin's cheek and then across the top of her misshapen ear. "Oh, what have they done to you, my Phinea?"

Fin smiled at her. "It's all right, Sister Hilde. It's all right. Come and sit down. I want to tell you what I'm going to do."

THAT NIGHT, WHEN THE moon was high and bright, Fin stood in the courtyard of what had once been the Ebenezer orphanage. She closed her eyes and sank into the well of memory. She remembered the town as it had been in her youth. And, eyes closed, she walked. Remembrance guided her until she stood once more in the place that she, only she in all the world, knew how to find. And she began to dig. The moon and stars wheeled overhead and shone down, watching, until in the deepest hours of the night, Fin pulled a battered sea chest from the ground. The mud-caked vessel lay in the moonlight and glistened like an earthen cocoon, swollen and ripe. Age had weakened the lock and a single kick broke it open. Fin threw off the lid and—

Gold. A king's wealth of it. In coin. In jewelry. In goblet and dish. It gleamed in the falling starlight. Fin smiled and cried for joy. She remembered Bartimaeus and his creaky laugh and laughed, herself, to recall it. But she wasn't finished. She dragged the chest aside and went to her horse. She untied her fiddle case and opened it, and out of it she took the old thunder gun. Betsy. She flung it into the hole without ceremony or regret or the shed of any tear. And there she buried it.

FIN DIDN'T KEEP THE gold, not an ounce. She gave it to Ebenezer, entrusting it to the old town mayor, Mr. Bolzius. In the year that followed, the town inched back from the brink of ruin. Foundations were laid, sturdy homes were built, crops were planted anew. Children returned to the streets and laughter to the air. Fin laid a new floor in the chapel where Creache had ripped it up. She painted its walls and fashioned new doors and replaced broken windows, and in time the organ also was restored and there was music again.

Fin stayed with Hilde, looking after her and assisting her, and eventually they shared laughter together, a thing unknown between them in more years than either could remember, and often this laughter ended with happy tears, a long embrace, and soft whispers of apology.

But though Fin found happiness in the rebuilding of Ebenezer and steady fellowship among its people, she was often distracted. While chopping wood, or mending a roof, or helping Hilde cook, she'd find herself standing still with her head cocked to one side, listening intently to some far-off sound. She heard it only faintly at first, a call toward something other. But the longer she stayed in Ebenezer the more insistently it beckoned. She knew what it was; she'd heard it all her life. So she climbed to the bell tower in the evenings and let her eyes drift east where, out beyond the pine forests and Georgia hills, the sea was calling to her. She answered with a smile and lifted her face into the breeze.

But Fin stayed in Ebenezer for another season and her presence was a comfort to Hilde, who had lost all the orphans to sickness, adulthood, and war. Fin lent her labor to the restoration of the town and gave her whole self to the work until she felt they needed her no longer. And then, amid the murmur of Ebenezer's life, amid the smell of hearth fires lit, amid the lowing of animals, amid the clatter of wagons returning home and the distant singing of a mother to her children, Fin sat in the evening twilight and wrote a letter. The whole of it was this:

Jeannot,

Will you walk with me?

Fin sent the letter and tarried another week before saying goodbye. She left Hilde in Delly's able care, put Ebenezer behind her, and traveled alone to Savannah. There she rented a room near the waterfront and in the early morning took from her fiddle case a fine dress, never yet worn. It was sewn of green silk and stitched with leaves, and across its bodice the wings of a swan outspread. She slipped it on, smiling, and found it was tailored to a perfect fit. Then, so gracefully dressed, she went out and stood by the sea to await the coming of the *Esprit de la Mer*.

The End

MUCH THAT HAPPENED AFTER can only be guessed at or surmised, but Fin Button and Jeannot Botolph found this much to be true: that in all the vastness of the world, the deepest adventure is not of war or mortal danger, but of heart, of soul, of the infinite discovery of a beloved other. In this they were both suited and well satisfied. Carried together by the *Esprit de la Mer*, they traveled afar to strange lands and stranger seas and were given to know many things both hidden and wondrous.

Fin Button's reputation and legend grew until she passed out of the memory of any individual mind and became known only in the second-hand. When Napoleon warred on Europe, some said his navy was captained by *The Flame*, and people wondered. When the pasha of Tripoli declared war on the new United States, marines stormed his keep and ended the Barbary threat forever, and rumor held that a woman led them forth. Wherever sailors met and sparked a tale, Fin Button was a part of the telling. And though some of what was told may have been fact, it is certain that in time she belonged wholly to the bosom of legend, for even as late as the American Civil War, wretches in sea-side taverns and 'round ember-smoldering fires spoke rumor of a flame-haired woman fiddling in woodland vales and setting captives free; people whispered her name, they nodded their heads, and they wondered.

The truth, however, is that Fin had long-since passed this world. Where and when and how no longer matter, nor ever did. What matters is that she slipped beyond these hinterlands and awakened in the light of the risen sun. She walked that day upon a field of green and saw in the distance a house handsomely prepared. Her shoulders rose and her senses woke as they had not since she and Bartimaeus stole mornings along the Savannah River in a world gone by. Wind blew soft and tickled her face and she smiled. The green of the world was alive and something more than any color she'd known, as if she once again knew life for what it was and not what she'd come to believe it to be. She drew a deep breath and filled her lungs with honey-sweet air and began to run. She could think of no other response to such revelation, to such life, but to run. Hands out, head back, a laugh on her lips, running, running, drawing ever closer to that distant home. She could almost see faces there, familiar shapes nearly forgotten. She heard laughter and voices calling. *Come*, they cried. *Come, oh fiddler, come.*

Here I raise mine Ebenezer;
hither by thy help I'm come;
and I hope, by thy good pleasure,
safely to arrive at home.

The Jerusalem Lutheran Church in New Ebenezer is
the oldest public building in the state of Georgia.

The fingerprints of its builders are
still visible, imprinted
on its bricks.

The book you hold in your hands exists, not because I wrote it, but because the following people believed in the value of its creation.

The Patrons of Fiddler's Green

Aaron Roughton
Abby Orchard
Adam Isaacs
Alyssa Ramsey
Amy Riley (she's friendly)
Andrew Scott
Ann Gehin
Arthur and Janis Peterson
Ashley Elizabeth Graham
Ashley and Ben Barber
Brenda Lewis Graham
Breann Stephens
Barbara Lane
Ben Yancer
Benjamin Ward
Bob Soulliere
Brenda Arbogast
Chad and Brittany Kalas
Chris Hokanson
Chris Robbins
Chris Whitler
Collin Foster
Connor Luedtke
Cory Martin
Curt McLey
Dale and Christina Googer
Dan Kulp
Daniel Foster
Daniel Hennigan
Dave and Heidi Chupp
David Elkins

David King
David Smithey
David Van Buskirk
Dieta Duncan
Duane Kelley
Eric West
Eden Goodwin
Giff Reed
Glenn Johnson
Greg Fisher
Greg Schambach
Hannah Holman
Hannah Nielsen
Hannah Solbach
Hunter Chorey
J. J. Mahoney
Jackie Wilson
Jaclyn Lewis
Jake Willems
Jared Radosevich
Jason Neufeld
Jeannette McIntyre
Jennifer Edwards
Jessie Rae Elders
Jodi Kiffmeyer
Johnny and Jenni Simmons
Jon, Anne, and Aidan Swanner
Jon Dostert
Jonathan Hurshman
Jonathan Jimison
Jonathan Yoder

Josh Bishop

Joshua Dean

Joshua Kemper

Judson Neer

Justin Orton(ian)

Kaitlin Hensal

Karen Merry

"Sweet Potato" Kate Hinson

Katherine Kamin

Katherine Santora

Keith Schambach

Kelli Rowley

Kelsey Hill

Kim Kuzmkowski

Kirk Plattner

Kristen Sharpley

Kurt Walker

Laura Cole

Laura Preston

The Ling Family

Lucy Bruno

Logan Heinrich

Lori McCurry

Luis Hidalgo

Malia Mondy

Margaret Hinson

Mary Newcomb

Matt and Kristyn Zion

Matt Losey

Matt McBrien

Matt Schwenk

Melanie McGuire

"The Scientist" Michelle Becker

Mike and Heather Ramsay

Miranda Waldner

Nan Doster

Nathan Bubna

Nathan Green

Owen Beatty

Olga Petrovna Saxno

Paula Shaw (see you at Hutchmoot!)

Peter Brunone

Peter Gaultney

Rachel Dahl

Rochelle Jameson

Rebecca Hurshman

Sarah Noe

Sarah Winfrey

Scott Rinehart

S. D. "The Wrestler" Smith

Shauna "Ruthie" Peterson

Sondra Lantzer

Stephanie Berry

Stephen Lamb

Steve Byrd

Steve Fronk

Steven Miller

Susan Duncan

Tenika Dye

Thomas Bingaman

Toni "The Sailor" Whitney

Vanessa Hodgson

Veronica Cross

Virginia Berlin

Muchas gracias to Luis Hidalgo for his help with my Spanish.
And *merci beaucoup* to Michelle Becker for her help with my French.

Special thanks to Andrew Peterson, Jason Gray, Eric Peters,
Jennifer Trafton, Kate Etue, and Evie Coates for helping me shape
and fine-tune Fin's story. I owe you all my deepest thanks.

An extra spoonful of thanks to Evie Coates
for her beautiful artwork.

A Brief Guide to Terms of Nautical and General Significance

-A-

ABOARD: on or in a seagoing vessel

ADRIFT: afloat, unattached to either shore or seabed, and uncontrolled, therefore going wherever the wind and current command

AFT: toward the stern of the vessel

AGROUND: resting on or touching the ground or sea bottom

AHEAD: forward of the bow of the vessel

ALL HANDS: the entire population of a ship's crew

ALOFT: above the vessel's uppermost solid structure; in the rigging of a sailing ship

ALONGSIDE: parallel to a ship or pier

AMIDSHIPS: the middle portion of a ship

ASHORE: on the beach, shore, or land

ASTERN: toward the rear or transom of the ship

AUBERGE: a manor housing one of the *langues* of the Knights of Malta

AWASH: dangerously low in the sea, such that water is constantly washing across the deck

AWEIGH: an anchor is said to be "aweigh" when it is raised to the point of breaking contact with the seabed.

AYE, AYE: reply to an order indicating, firstly, that it is heard and, secondly, that it is understood and will be carried out

-B-

BARBARIE: a native of the Barbary Coast

BARBARY: region of northern Africa on the Mediterranean coast between Egypt and Gibraltar

BARBICAN: the defensive structure protecting the gate of a castle or keep

BEFORE THE MAST: often used to indicate the area in the forecastle of the ship where sailors of the lowliest rank lived. Once promoted, sailors moved amidships (hence midshipmen), and when granted officer standing, moved once more to the rear nearest the quarterdeck.

BERTH (as mooring): a location in port or upon the quay used specifically for mooring vessels while not at sea.

BERTH (as sleeping): a space used as sleeping accommodation aboard a ship

BILGE: compartment at the bottom of the hull of a ship where water collects so that it may be pumped out of the vessel

BOWSPRIT: a spar projecting from the bow used as an anchor for the forestay and other rigging

BRIGANTINE: a two-masted sailing vessel square-rigged on the foremast and fore-and-aft rigged on the mainmast

BULKHEAD: a load-bearing wall within the hull of a ship

-C-

CAPSTAN: a waist-high cylindrical device operated by a number of hands each of whom, working in concert, inserts a capstan bar into a hole in the capstan and walks in a circle. Used to wind in anchors or other heavy objects.

CAT O' NINE TAILS: a short nine-tailed whip used to flog sailors in disciplinary measure

CLEW: the lower corners of square sails or the corner of a triangular sail at the end of the boom

COMPANIONWAY: a raised hatchway in the ship's deck, with a ladder leading below

CORSO: literally: "course"; term for the mandate of the Knights of Malta by which they protected the shipping routes of the Mediterranean Sea

CORVETTE: a small, highly maneuverable warship

CROW'S NEST: a masthead constructed with sides and sometimes a roof to shelter lookouts from the weather

-D-

DAVY JONES' LOCKER: a sailor's idiom denoting the bottom of the sea

DROMOND: a medieval galley-style warship propelled by both sails and oars

DJINN: a genie; a supernatural being from a parallel plane of existence

-F-

FIRST MATE: the second in command of a ship

FORECASTLE: a partial deck above the upper deck and at the head of the vessel; traditionally the sailors' living quarters. Often contracted and pronounced "fo'csle".

-G-

GALLEY: the kitchen of the ship. Also a type of large medieval ship propelled by both oars and sails.

GANGPLANK: a movable bridge used in boarding or leaving a ship

GUNWALE: upper edge of the hull

-H-

HAMMOCK: canvas sheets, slung from the deckhead, in which seamen sleep

HELMSMAN: person who steers a ship

HOLD: the lower part of the interior of a ship's hull, considered as storage space for cargo

-L-

LADDER: aboard a ship, all "stairs" are called ladders. Most "stairs" on a ship are narrow and near vertical, hence the name.

LANGUE: a division of the Knights of Malta. The order was divided into eight *langues* or "tongues" based based on native language of its knights.

LETTER OF MARQUE: a warrant granted to a privateer condoning specific acts of piracy, usually against a foreign power during time of war

LINE: the correct nautical term for the "ropes" used on a sailing vessel. A line will always have a more specific name describing its function, such as "mizzen topsail halyard".

LUFF: the forward edge of a sail

-M-

MAINMAST: the tallest mast of a sailing ship

MAN-OF-WAR: a warship

MARINES: soldiers afloat

MIZZENMAST: the third mast of a ship, or mast aft of the mainmast

-P-

POOP DECK: a high deck on the aft superstructure of a ship

PRESS GANG: personnel from a ship, usually of the Royal Navy, that would force men into maritime service against their will

PORT: refers to the left-hand side of a vessel as perceived by a person on board and facing the bow

PRIVATEER: privately-owned ship authorized by means of a Letter of Marque to conduct hostilities against an enemy

-R-

REEF: to reduce the area of sail exposed to the wind in order to guard against the effects of strong wind or to slow the vessel

RIGGING: the collective system of masts and lines on a sailing vessel

-S-

SCIMITAR: a curved sabre originated in the middle east

SCUTTLE: to cut a hole in an object or vessel, especially in order to sink a vessel deliberately

SCUTTLEBUTT: slang term used by sailors to mean gossip or rumor

SEXTANT: navigational instrument used to measure a ship's latitude and longitude

STANCHION: a timber fitted between the frame heads of the hull

STARBOARD: refers to the right-hand side of a vessel as perceived by a person on board and facing the bow

STERN: the rear of a ship

-T-

TACKING: zig-zagging so as to sail directly toward the wind

TOPSAIL: the second sail on a mast (counting from the bottom)

TOPSIDES: the part of the hull between the waterline and the deck

-U-

UNDERWAY: a vessel that is moving under control

-W-

WATCH: a period of time during which a part of the crew is on duty. Changes of watch are marked by strokes on the ship's bell.

-X-

XEBEC: a three-masted sailing ship favored by pirates of the Barbary Coast

-Y-

YARD: the entire spar upon which a sail is set

RABBIT ROOM
— P R E S S —
Nashville, Tennesee

www.RabbitRoom.com

CPSIA information can be obtained
at www.ICGtesting.com
Printed in the USA
LVHW052103260220
648276LV00004B/111

9 780982 621417